Praise for

MURIELLA PENT

"The heart of the novel beats in time with D.H. Lawrence and Henry Miller and all the writers before and after them who, when you sweat their books down to the essentials, say simply that sex is an artery of life. Ignore it at your peril. . . . *Muriella Pent* plays out on a bigger canvas than Smith has worked on before. It's the work of a good novelist who wants to be a better novelist. And has become one. There's a gifted and sensually alert writer at the wheel here."

—*National Post*

"Smith . . . widen[s] his focus beyond the hepped-up youth culture he celebrated and satirized in his earlier work. The scenes of Muriella alone in her mansion stricken by sudden bouts of grief are elegant and moving, providing a touching counterpoint to Marcus' own sense of personal desolation."

—*Toronto Star*

"We care about Marcus [Royston] and Muriella [Pent]; their vulnerabilities and the risks they take win our sympathies. We sense that Smith has invested a great deal in his two age-ing protagonists and the investment pays off. These are two of the strongest characters in recent Canadian fiction . . . serving to confirm *Muriella Pent* as Smith's finest achievement to date. . . . We need writers like Smith to remind us of the grim truth of this strange country. . . . It's a funny, poignant, ambitious, and highly entertaining book and [Smith's] boldest work yet."   —*Books in Canada*

"Smith has been getting progressively better throughout the decade he's been putting Toronto on paper. . . . He is a talent."   —*eye* (Toronto)

"Smith [has] a keen eye for the nuances of class and colour. . . . With his latest novel, *Muriella Pent*, Smith broadens his scope, marching with boldness and humour into the mine-filled topic of race. . . . Apart from comedy and brave insights, Smith writes some of the most luminous prose in Canadian fiction. This is partly due to his literary intelligence, how broadly and deeply he has read. He mines and refines the best of what has come before on the way to making it his own. Also, Smith is entirely credible when writing female characters. In his joyful, delicate portraits of Muriella's flower garden, in his velvety depictions of the tapestries within her home, in his sensitivity to her feminine engagement with colour and light, one catches quiet echoes of Katherine Mansfield and Virginia Woolf. Smith's style alone would make *Muriella Pent* a delicious read, even if he had nothing whatever to tell us about race and life and art."　　　　　　　　　　　　　—*The Gazette* (Montreal)

"While the urban spectacle still provides fodder for Smith's carnivorous wit, he also descends into the loss, loneliness and sadness beneath the metropolitan sheen of his characters' lives. In doing so, Smith emerges with a melancholy that marks a deepening of his art. . . . This is also Smith's most sensual novel. It is much like a luscious oil painting, filled with a deep, rich use of colour and sophisticated interplay between light and dark."　　—*Echo Weekly* (Kitchener)

"*Muriella Pent* is a smart, sexy, satisfying read."
　　　　　　　　　　　　　—*The Chronicle-Herald* (Halifax)

"Smith is very good. His touch with dialogue is among the best in CanLit. . . . This is a valuable addition to the Canadian canon, rivaling the early work of another skilled satirist of the urbane and urban, Mordecai Richler. There is a roaring party scene that matches those described by Evelyn Waugh." —*Ottawa Citizen*

"Readers looking to spice up their book club will have plenty to talk about with Russell Smith's latest, *Muriella Pent*. . . . Irresistibly poignant." —*Flare*

"Read any page of *Muriella Pent* at random and it will become immediately obvious that you're in the presence of a talented writer." —*The Record* (Kitchener-Waterloo)

"*Muriella Pent* is a scrumptious confection and a hilarious satire." —*The Sun Times* (Owen Sound)

"[Smith] is a clear-eyed social and cultural observer. . . . *Muriella Pent* . . . [is] a social satire of surprising nuance and maturity. . . . Smith's rich use of language . . . can turn on a dime from lush and expansive to curt and cutting." —*Quill & Quire*

M.P.

MURIELLA

ALSO BY RUSSELL SMITH

Noise
How Insensitive
Young Men
The Princess and the Whiskheads

A Novel ~

PENT

R<small>USSELL</small> S<small>MITH</small>

A<small>NCHOR</small> C<small>ANADA</small>

Library and Archives Canada Cataloguing in Publication

Smith, Russell, 1963–
Muriella Pent : a novel / Russell Smith.

ISBN 0-385-25979-4

I. Title.

PS8587.M58397M87 2005   C813'.54   C2004-906480-0

Cover image:
John, Augustus Edwin (British, 1878–1961), *The Marchesa Casati*
(date unknown), oil on canvas, 96.5 x 68.6 cm, Art Gallery of Ontario, Toronto.
Purchase, 1934. Photo by AGO/Carlo Catenazzi
Cover design: CS Richardson
Printed and bound in Canada

Lines from "The Sunlight on the Garden" by Louis MacNeice, first published in *The Earth
Compels* (1938), collected in *Selected Poems* (Faber and Faber, 1998), Michael Longly, ed.

Lines from "Hotels" by Guillaume Apollinaire, from *Alcools* (Gallimard, 1920).

Excerpts from *Les Fleurs du Mal* by Charles Baudelaire, first published 1857
(Librairie Générale Française, 1972), translations by the author.

This book is a work of fiction. Names, places, characters, and incidents
are products of the author's imagination or are used fictitiously. Any resemblance
to actual events or persons, living or dead, is strictly coincidental.

Published in Canada by Anchor Canada,
a division of Random House of Canada Limited

Visit Random House of Canada Limited's website: www.randomhouse.ca

TRANS   10   9   8   7   6   5   4   3   2   1

For Jowita Bydlowska

MURIELLA PENT

The flotsam of bottletops, glass shards, paper strands like seaweed
washed up on the curb, the receding waves of visitors flash
as whitecaps in the sun. And when the tide goes out
it leaves the concrete dusty. We scavenge what we can,
boys in ragged khaki shorts, looking out to sea.

This is a tide that burns and leaves
the taste of money in the mouth
and bananas in the sand.

A girl sits in shadow, sullen as heat. Her skin
is velvet dust. And although her mouth is tightly shut,
I know it hides a cave of wet, with hidden glints
of metal, flashing like traps. I know her salt already.

I will turn into an arrogant god, metamorphosed
into shepherd, warrior, whatever shape
is primed for rape
by respected purveyors of myth.

I will pay and take her. I will carry her away.
For Jupiter she would kick, shrink from the scratch
of feather and beak (how oily that down, up close!).
For Apollo she would shiver and freeze with fear,
wooden in retreat. For me she is merely cold, silent as a bruise.

A ground that many have trod becomes compact and hard.

We have known so many visitors here,
we exchange the roles of conqueror and slave
like blocks slid around a grimy board,
in the cafés of the port. It is my turn now.

MARCUS ROYSTON
(from "Island Eclogues XII")

MESSAGE FROM THE CHAIR

It's almost impossible for me to imagine that a full year has passed since last year's spectacular and highly successful Trillium Ball. I can still remember the highlights of that night—the fabulous music from the Caramba Tango Ensemble, the stunning performance of an excerpt from the new ballet *Rodeo* by members of the National Ballet, the hilarious auctioneering style of our resident comedian, Marv Dunleavy (who also moonlights as the President of Dunleavy Goldfarb Investments). In that one night we raised, thanks to the generous donations of all of our corporate sponsors,* as well as by our generous Members, in excess of $300,000 for the Princess Alexandra Hospital Redevelopment Fund. Well, we have had no time for those memories to fade before getting right back into the swing of the preparations for this year's Ball, and what a preparation it has been! I am pleased to announce that this year's Ball is on an even grander scale than ever before, and promises to be even more dazzling and entertaining than last year's—if that's possible! We are proud to announce the participation, this year, of the Fur Board of Canada, who have donated seventeen luxurious coats for our silent auction, and the generous donations of six of the city's top chefs (including Damian Buhr of Coterie, Kenneth Woo of Pearl, Bodo Kraftmeyer of Elements, and Ritchie LeBlanc, ex of Mirage) for our Trade Routes Food Stations, plus the usual fun-filled costume parade and steel-drumming by the Caribbean Cultural Society. I have nothing but awe and admiration for my fellow board members, and my vice-chairs Sandy Dunleavy, Gaye Northwood, and Sonia Gjurdeff, who have donated more of their time in putting this massive project together—along with the usual time-consuming obligations of family and demanding husbands!—than I would have thought humanly possible. I have had the honour of working with a board composed of the most dedicated and hard-working volunteers I have ever had the privilege to meet, and so it is with many thanks that I invite you to enjoy the fruits of their labours. This year's proceeds will go the newly launched Lupus Research Centre of the Princess Alexandra Hospital, and it is an honour for all of us to be associated with this much-needed initiative. And finally I offer my thanks especially to those without whom none of this would occur: the generous patrons who have bought tables. Now sit back and enjoy a well-deserved evening of entertainment, and above all, have fun!

Muriella Pent
Chair, Organizing Committee

*a full list of corporate sponsors will be found on pages 3–5

Photo by Andy Nottingham, styling by Nadir Group. Mrs. Pent's wardrobe courtesy of the St. Regis Room at the Bay.

A CHECKERBOARD OF YELLOW LIGHT ON the carpet. Her head is on its side. She can feel the pile making an imprint on her cheek: gentle bristles. She can't at first make out why the light is so perfectly divided in squares. The windowpanes, their leaded squares. There is dust hanging in the shafts like a kind of mist. It is hardly moving, just hanging. From outside, the sound of a lawnmower, incongruous so late in the year. She stretches her hand out and strokes the pile. Her fingertips feel sensitive, as if she can distinguish the floral patterns on the rug by caressing it.

With her nose this close to the rug, she can for the first time discern its dusty smell. It is a bit barnyardy. The rug is wool, and very old, dyed, by no doubt dirty hands, with vegetable extracts. She imagines that it has been carried by a camel at one time. Perhaps this is what camels smelled like.

A sweet smell too, like burning sugar. Spilled brandy, soaked into the rug beside her. It is a little dizzying. It is like something rotten. And there is brandy on her chest: her nipples burn a little where he has dripped the brandy on them, then rubbed it in. Then he filled his mouth with brandy and sucked her nipple into it. "Oh," she says, as if hurt. It is almost the same feeling: her chest has filled with air. She expels it. "Goodness." She shivers, rolls over onto him, runs her hand over his chest and soft belly. It is flat, but soft. There is roughness only in the very centre of his chest,

~ 3 ~

a sparse patch like dying grass, a memory of fur. Even this stubble is soft.

He is breathing steadily, not asleep. His eyes half open. She strokes his nipple, which makes him sigh. He smells damp. His skin is salt. She thinks she probably smells stronger than he does. She can smell herself. It is not just perspiration. She has not ever smelled herself like this, or at least can't remember it.

Her belly is sticky. That is him. She is curious to smell it, but does not want to touch her finger to her nose in front of him. Not that he would be shocked (he seems shocked by nothing), but it would be admitting a naivety.

Her eyes travel the room. She begins to take in minor damage. A smashed vase, thankfully only glass, on the hardwood beside the writing desk, a great lake of water, also soaking into the rug. Yellow lily petals floating in it, soggy stems everywhere. His trousers, twisted inside out, a dam at the hardwood's edge. An anemone of wet silk: her panties.

Perhaps the fetid water is contributing to the vegetal atmosphere. Red rose petals float too: where did they knock them from? A dark ceramic vase on the mantelpiece stands intact. It is patterned with apples and grapes, and sprouts drooping roses. Her head brushed against it as he pushed her up against the stone, her head stretched back, his lips on her neck, under the portrait of Arthur. She must have been spraying rose petals about with her hair. She reaches a hand behind her head and extracts a few more.

That's where they started, and then she doesn't remember hitting the glass vase on the writing desk. She remembers slipping in the water in her bare feet, though, as he pulled on her skirt, and him catching her, his hand tight in the small of her back.

Then sitting on the leather sofa, his face between her legs. Then together on the sofa.

Then, she supposes, they slipped off, lapping at each other, down here on the furry carpet, in the fruity smell of evaporating alcohol. She wants to rub her hair in the wet patch, scent herself with it.

She looks over at the leather sofa to see if they left a smear. But she looks the wrong way at first, over towards the bookcases. She is looking from an unfamiliar angle. It is as if she is looking at this room for the first time.

She drapes some more of her hair over his chest. She wants him to say something.

"That vase," she says. "On the mantelpiece."

He says nothing.

"It's lucky we didn't knock that over. It's an antique."

"Yes." His voice is distant.

She doesn't want him to fall asleep. "It's colonial era. New England. It's a Moorcroft. It was Arthur's mother's. It's apparently quite valuable."

His eyes are closed. "I don't think so," he says in a low voice.

"Oh, it's valuable all right. Arthur wouldn't have—"

"I'm sure it's valuable. I don't think it's American. Moorcroft was an English firm."

She is silent for a moment. "Oh. I thought it was American."

A square of sun on his skin makes it shiny, almost yellow. Her mouth feels dry. It is the brandy.

It makes her sad that he knows more about Arthur's mother's vase than she does. Not sad: small. She should have known about it. It makes her chilled that she doesn't. If he knows more about even that than she knows, then what does she know? What does she know?

"Stoke on Trent, I think," he says in his sleepy voice. "England somewhere." It is strange to hear him say England. With a stressed, flat *a*. *Eng-lant*. "Did we knock over the brandy?"

"Just one glass. The bottle is behind you."

"Would you like some more?"

"No, thank you. I'm not used to drinking brandy in the afternoons."

He gives a deep laugh, but makes no obvious joke on what else she isn't used to doing in the afternoons, for which she is for some reason grateful. "Have some brandy," he says, "for your own comfort and safety."

This is the kind of thing, she now knows, he says as a joke. He has been saying that comfort-and-safety bit for a few days. It is something he heard on a plane. She still does not understand it, but at least she understands it is a joke now.

"I would love another drop." He slides his glass along the floor towards her, but makes no move to rise. She understands that he wants her to find the brandy bottle.

She has found it and poured him a drink and is down beside him again before it occurs to her to ask him to get his own drink. It would never occur to either of them, she realizes. Not at this stage, for her. Not ever, for him.

He balances the snifter on his chest. The alcohol fumes sting her eyes.

She says, "We should get up."

"Ah," he says. "Parking is never free."

This is another thing he has been saying.

"What colour," she says, her nose against his shoulder, "would you say your skin is?" As she says this she realizes she would not have asked him this before, when they were clothed; it is not something he invites discussion of, although all his writing seems to be about it and everyone seems to expect him to talk about it all the time. He doesn't seem to care.

He is silent for so long she is worried she has offended him.

But he is considering. "Greenish," he says.

"*No*. Yellowish, perhaps."

He laughs again. "All right."

"This is what I find so strange. It's beige, with some brown and some yellow. I would say coffee, but it's more yellow. It's not black at all."

He laughs like an explosion, like a sneeze or a shout. "Yes," he says, when he has stopped laughing, "this has been remarked on. Where I come from." He continues to laugh.

She slides his snifter over his smooth chest and takes an awkward sip. It tastes of headache. Still she can't get up: she feels as still as she does after a massage, her limbs full of sleep. She slides his hand down his belly, into the fuzz of his groin. She stretches her fingers through the tight curls. She feels a pulse at the seam of his thigh and hip. It is so light and fluttering and close to the skin she wants to kiss it. She lets her hand lie there instead, on the pulse under the skin.

"'The sunlight on the garden,'" he says in a slow voice, "'hardens and grows cold.'"

She feels the heat of light on a bar across her calf and says, "I'm still hot. Are you cold?"

He sighs.

"Oh," she says. "Is it a poem?"

"'The sunlight on the garden. Hardens and grows cold. We cannot beg for pardon.'"

She is silent for a moment. "Is that yours?"

He sighs again. "No, my dear. No, it is not."

"Sorry. I'm glad, because it's not a nice thing to say."

"Ah."

"I'm warm, not cold, and we don't need to beg for pardon."

"It doesn't just refer to us," he says softly.

"Who wrote it?"

"An Irishman. Called Louis MacNeice. They know a lot about gardens." He takes another dribbly sip. "'The sunlight on the garden. Hardens and grows cold. We cannot beg for pardon.' I think. No. 'We cannot cage the minute.'"

"That's nice. We cannot cage the minute."

"Yes. It is very nice."

There is long stillness then, in which she watches the lacework of shadow, from the ivy, now leafless, shift in the squares of light on the patterned rug. There is some kind of white creeper hanging over the back of the telephone chair. She squints at it and makes it out to be her bra. She says, "Tell me one of yours."

"Mine are not as good."

"They're beautiful."

He says, "I read a great deal of that Irishman once."

"Tell me one of yours."

He puffs out his cheeks. He recites:

The tessellation of F's on poetry books,
lined like ripples in sand

(Faber and Faber and Faber forever—
they are the Bibles of the young, on dusty islands anyway)
the furry wallpaper of a child's mind,
like the carpeting of coloured distant rooms,
bright as petals crammed in heaps,
whose imprint takes the empty shape of words.

She spreads her fingers out on the swirl of red wool beside his head. She says, "That's lovely."

He says nothing.

She says, "What's tessellation?"

"Tessellation. When things, shapes, join together. In a repeated pattern."

"I love it when you speak. I love your voice."

He sighs again. She seems to be making him sad. She knows it is best not to use the word love at all, or men tend to get sad. She will try not to.

She remembers something and feels a tongue of heat in her belly. She can feel her face flushing.

She thinks about it a long time and then whispers to his ear, "I liked that thing you . . ."

She stops. She tries again, "I liked what you said to me."

"Hmm?" He is lifting his head on a bent neck to gulp at the brandy on his chest. There is a shiny dribble of it at the corner of his lips.

"What you said about a part of my body."

"What did I say?"

"You know what you said."

"Can you not say it?"

"No, I can't."

"It was a rude thing."

"Yes." She wraps a leg over his. She slides her thigh up and down his. She wants to straddle him again. Has she already done this? "Say it again."

"I forget. You'll have to remind me."

"No. You say it."

He says, "You'll have to remind me."

"I can't say it."

"You can't say the word pussy."

"No."

"You like that word?"

"It's awful. Usually."

"You don't think I should use that word."

"No."

"No one has used that word to you before?"

"No."

"What did I say about it?"

She squeals. "You say it." She is laughing. Then her head jerks towards the window and she shrieks. "Oh God." She sits up, grabs the cushion that is next to her. She holds it to her chest. There is a hat at the window, bright red. A canvas tennis hat. And then a face, looking in, blinking.

She screams, or at least she thinks she did. (He tells her later it is more like a bark.) And the hat disappears.

He has stood up. He stands there, droopy, his hands on his hips, standing naked in the checkerboard of yellow light that is now almost horizontal. "Who the hell be that?" he thunders.

She crouches over her little cushion as if she could hide her whole body behind it. "It was David. My neighbour. Oh Christ."

"What the hell he be doing over here?" His accent has suddenly changed. But now he is smiling.

"Oh Christ. Oh shit. He's been threatening."

"Threatenin' to do what?" He stands tall and naked and slim over her.

"Oh fuck. He was going to clip my rosebushes. He said he would have to do them himself if I didn't."

He laughs. She begins to laugh too.

"Well he got an eyeful," he says. He roars.

"Yes. He's seen all he wanted to, now."

"His worst fears come true." Laughing, he picks up his trousers, brushes at them. He looks around for the rest.

She stops laughing. It is funny, but she feels a hollowness. There might be consequences. Everything is going a little too fast.

He is pulling on his shirt, his socks.

"Don't get dressed."

"Have to piss." He stalks out, humming.

"Stay a minute," she calls out.

He doesn't answer. She hears him in the downstairs toilet, a loud stream. He is pissing with the door wide open, singing something in dialect. She knows he will go downstairs again quickly. He probably wants to be outside on such a day.

She gathers another cushion and sits cross-legged, holding two cushions against her breasts. She shivers a little; she feels sick. She looks around the wrecked room, the twisted clothing. Her panties in the water bear a honey stain, upwards. The fallen books, the water, the smashed glass. The leaded windows open. There are wet marks on the sofa. It doesn't look the same. It doesn't look like her room any more. She doesn't know which sofa the cushions came from, which shelves the books belong to. It has cracked somehow, shifted in its frame.

THE DEPUTY MINISTER SENT FOR MARCUS
Royston in the late afternoon.

Marcus was in the bar at Joyce's Hotel with the chairman
of the Dunstanton school board and the white marketing
woman from Petron. The meeting was supposed to be
about sponsoring an exchange of teachers with Texas, but
they were waiting for the marketing woman to stop com-
plaining about the beaches. She was very much looking
forward, she said, to the changes the new government
would bring, as she was sure it would, to things like the
beaches. Where she was, she said, and she didn't know if
this was typical of the whole island, you understand, but she
could only talk about where her hotel was, the beach was
dirty, really quite noticeably dirty, and she didn't feel comfortable when there were so many people—she hesitated
before saying people, as if she wanted to say something else
and changed her mind—who seemed to be just camped
there, cooking and everything, and the young men would-
n't leave her alone. They were friendly, very friendly, but
they were very persistent. She laughed tightly and sipped
her club soda.

She had asked for a grapefruit juice but Joyce didn't
stock grapefruit juice. She had commented lightly on how
it was funny, you had to admit, that grapefruit juice was so
hard to come by in a country that produced so much tropical fruit, she meant how hard could it be to jog half a mile

up the mountain and bring back some actual grapefruits, and she laughed again.

There had been a short silence and then the chairman of the Dunstanton school board, whose name was Desmond DuPré, and who had actually been at prep school with Marcus, said gently but without a smile that there were no grapefruits grown on St. Andrew's, whose principal and indeed only export was bananas. This had encouraged the monologue about the beaches.

They were all wondering when she was going to reveal to them the extent of the subsidy Petron was prepared to grant, which apparently had been decided that morning and was the point of the meeting. Marcus thought she had probably been briefed before leaving on the necessity of long small-talk before business in the Caribbean; *they don't like to work too hard*, she would have been told. She seemed nervous now: she wiped at her lip with the back of her hand. She wore khaki trousers and a linen tank top that exposed her red shoulders. Her face shone. Marcus had forgotten that Joyce's bar was not air-conditioned and that she would not be prepared for that.

Her hair was short and wiry and her arms were rather thick, and mottled now with heat, but there was just the hint of cleavage at the neck of her top, just the shadow of a cleft, and a heft to the sway of her breasts, definite movement as she leant towards the peanuts at the bar. She wore no ring. She would be staying at the Continental or at Williams' Tourist; only the Continental had a bar, which would be where Marcus would suggest they meet, after dinner. He pictured her thick thighs beneath the khaki, the damp concrete air of a room at the Continental. The smell of towels.

But only briefly, in fact only idly, for he was more interested in providing some proof to his new masters that he had
some productive role in the island's well-being—or economy, he should say, he should start talking like that now, it was
what everyone wanted. When he was first deputy minister, in
1980, in the heady days of the Freedom party, you would have
been sneered at for talking of economies all the time. One
spoke of . . . what did one speak of? Identity. And identities.
Culture. All the time. And production, productivity—they
had nationalized almost everything, so productivity was the
economy, it was all you had to worry about, or so it seemed—
and it was unproductive, really unproductive, to reminisce
like that, so Marcus tried to concentrate. He said, "So. Have
you any news for us. From Houston."

"Well," she said, "we talked about the numbers on
Tuesday, and I have to say head office is, really, I should
say, encouraged by the recent change of direction you've
had here, and we, the thinking is that we're going to be able
to move forward together here, because we're more or less
on the same wavelength now. Now their only concerns are
really concerns about optics, for the moment." She leaned
forward and Marcus glimpsed a strand of plain white cotton, without any lace. He sighed.

"Optics," said Desmond.

"Perceptions. There are some perceptions we want to
address head on."

But Marcus didn't hear the rest of this most important
answer, because he had seen the tall silhouette of Fenna St.
George, the deputy minister's assistant, at the door of the
bar. She was standing there watching him and she didn't
smile when she saw him. She stood still.

It was as if the day had gone silent around him. He watched her come through the dim air towards him as if she were not walking but sliding, hovering. Her face was somber.

Desmond was also not listening to the Petron woman. He looked first at Fenna's long face, her formal dress. Marcus knew that Desmond knew that she had come straight from the ministry and that any one of the young messengers could have been sent if the message were not grave and final, or indeed that Fenna could simply have called the bar at Joyce's to ask to speak to Marcus Royston, since everyone knew he was there every afternoon. Then Desmond looked immediately at his friend, who had sat back in his chair with a little smile on his face and his eyes slits to watch Fenna weaving through the tables.

Marcus nodded at Fenna and smiled. The Petron woman noticed that no one was listening to her and stopped talking. Everyone looked at Fenna. Fenna said softly, "Marcus, the deputy minister wants to see you."

Marcus nodded and rose slowly.

"We'll see you back here in a few minutes then," said Desmond tightly.

Marcus was looking out over the patio, whose tables and chairs were empty in the burning poisonous sun. Across the Promenade was a parking lot, and then the water. A white cruise ship like an office block was moored the length of the Promenade, blocking any glimpse of sea. The passengers were disembarking, buzzing into bright knots in the parking lot, little congregations of hats, then flowing into the street and moving towards the marketplace in dribbles. He could hear their laughter from half a block away. "Goodbye, Desmond," he said.

"In a few minutes, then," said Desmond.

Marcus smiled. "Perhaps not."

Desmond turned to the white woman. "Marcus will be back."

"See you in a minute, then," she said gaily.

"Desmond will be your liaison," said Marcus. "All right, Fenna."

He left his brandy unfinished.

They walked in silence past the cathedral, the crowds of lazy men in Alexis Square, and up the hill towards Government House. Jackie Mornay called to him from his taxi. He said hello to fat Patrick as he passed his restaurant. Maria the German lawyer waved to him from her car. Two young teachers called to him from the open window of the Spice House Café and he waved and nodded. Even tourists looked at him as he walked very slowly along the Promenade in his grey English suit and tie, bestowing greetings as an important man would, with tall Fenna and her straightened hair and her dark skirt and jacket at his side.

He was pleased that Fenna was seeing this effect, when he walked down the Promenade. People knew who he was. He knew this would make her feel even worse, and he took a bitter pleasure in it. She said nothing, walking slightly behind him, seeing the preachers and the beggars look up and nod as he passed.

There was a scattering of nutmeg, big as golf balls, on the shady road up the hill.

He had not acknowledged the girls sitting under the awning at the dank and unnamed café before the roundabout, but he looked quickly back at them to see the one called Jannette smiling quickly at him, behind Fenna's back. And the rastaman in the shadows by the bar, nodding briefly, his gold tooth a glint.

"Les Chutes was thirty-seven not out before lunch" was the first thing he said when he was shown into Michael Morris's office. He stayed standing, his hands in his pockets. "What do you make of that?"

Morris was standing with his hand extended, a big smile. He hesitated a moment, as if to answer would be to fall into a trap. "I am not surprised," he said finally. "Longue Anse is not so strong. Without their fast bowler, the priest, what was his—"

"Father Simeon."

"Ah yes. Father Simeon. The flying father."

"The jumping Jesuit," said Marcus. He turned to the little bookshelf, cocked his head to read the spines. He whistled a little.

Michael Morris dropped his hand, which Marcus had not touched. He closed his jaw. "Well, Marcus," he said, "you dropped in for a chat about cricket."

"I want to see the minister."

Morris exhaled at length. "It's me you should speak to. You know that."

"I want to see the minister."

Morris sat behind his desk. "You don't want to speak to your old friend?"

Marcus stayed standing. Fenna had closed the door behind him. "My old friend is not the one making the decisions."

"How do you even know what the decision is? How do

you know I don't want to talk to you about a dinner party on Friday night?"

Marcus looked at him with no expression.

"Please sit down."

Marcus hesitated, then suddenly felt listless. He sat, he told himself, out of fatigue, not because he wanted to listen to what Michael Morris had to say. There was a blind over the window so he couldn't look out of it. The office was air-conditioned; why did they need a blind?

"Marcus, this is very difficult for me, as I'm sure you understand."

Marcus stared at the blind.

"But you understand that a lot will be changing around here. We're taking a very new direction, and it's my job to. To."

"Yes. What is your job, Michael?"

"To implement a lot of those changes."

"And I am one of them."

"Marcus, your role was an important one in the Freedom-party years. At a time when independence from everyone, in every regard, was, was more, was more how shall I say, emotionally important, to all of us, than economically productive. That's all well and good, we needed a vision at that time, we needed an artistic image, we all benefited from that. And you have had some very productive years with the ministry, on board with us." Morris dug a hand into his pocket and pulled out a handkerchief. He wiped his face. It was as cool as evening in the office. "And now we're putting together a new team."

Marcus wondered where Morris had picked up this talk of teams and being on board. Probably from the Petron people.

"I feel with the change of direction, it is no longer . . . appropriate for you to be with, to be on board as education consultant. It is simply no longer appropriate. We are making a lot of changes around here, Marcus, you're not the only one."

Marcus stood and waved his hand at Morris as if silencing him. He went to the blind and snapped it up. A blanket of heat fell on his face. There was a square of light on the linoleum. "What I want to know," said Marcus, squinting, "is not what you are told to say, Michael, but what you want to say. We have known each other for almost forty years. We all know what is happening here. I am out of favour. We no longer need poets of the colonial era representing our . . . whatever I represent. What I want to know is—"

"Your work is still very much admired, Marcus. Don't talk this way."

"No," said Marcus gently, "it isn't." He turned to Michael Morris. "All I want to know, Michael, is where this is coming from. Is it coming from you or above you? I want to know where you yourself stand or I want to see the minister."

Michael leaned back in his chair. "What I want to say, Marcus, is that I'm very sorry."

"Then why do you give me the speech in American about the boats?"

"I—boats? What boats?"

"You talk about being on board."

"Ah."

"As if we were all on some kind of ship."

Michael Morris laughed. "Yes. Well, I—"

"You'll be talking about addressing optics next."

"Optics?"

"Never mind. Do you agree with all this, Michael? Do you want to throw me out?"

"The decision is the minister's, Marcus. You know that."

Marcus stared Michael Morris in the eyes. Morris looked away.

"But he has my support, Marcus. He has my support on this one."

"Thank you." Marcus stood up.

"Sit down."

"No, thank you."

"Marcus, the climate is not what it once was. We cannot afford to keep paying you a salary for just being a famous poet."

"You should know, and perhaps the minister himself would like to know, that we have arranged for an exchange of teachers between the Dunstanton school board and a school board in a place called Fort Worth in Texas. It will probably be largely paid for by Petron. I was negotiating it when you sent for me."

"I'm well aware of what you were—"

"It works largely in our favour, as we have no teachers to speak of, as you know, since we have shut down the teachers' training school. We are going to get a herd of American teachers and send a hundred high school graduates of ours to get an education in America. I thought I was learning to live by the new rules, Michael. I was trying to cheat them too."

"Well, talk like that won't—"

"What am I supposed to do now, Michael?"

Morris closed his mouth with a snap. "You used to be so idealistic, Marcus."

"So did we all. So did you."

"*I* still am." Morris said this with a quick heat. Then he put his fingertips together and breathed deeply. "We all believed that we could run a socialist paradise here, Marcus. So did I. But you know what has happened. You know that we no longer have any markets to speak of in Cuba—"

Marcus waved his hands vaguely. "I know all this. I know." This was exhausting.

"Or in the East. And the more development we do in conjunction with the Americans the more money there is for—you know all this, I know—for everything. And you know this too. The difference between us is that I believe we are doing the right thing for the people of this country."

"Oh for God's sake," said Marcus listlessly. He didn't know why he couldn't stand talk like this any more.

"And you no longer believe in anything."

Marcus looked at the square of light on the floor. It was so bright it made the linoleum almost colourless. He wondered how far it had moved since he had been standing there.

"I would have thought," said Morris more gently, "that a man of your experience would welcome a change. Change is good for all of us, Marcus. I'm sure you have a new book you're working on."

"I haven't written a book since nineteen eighty-two."

Morris paused. "That was the one got nominated?"

"It was nominated for a prize, yes." He nodded slowly. For half a second he closed his eyes. "And it won the prize."

"The Commonwealth prize?" A frown crossed Morris's face.

"The Commonwealth Writers Prize, yes. And I know. We don't like to talk too much bout the Commonwealth round ere." Marcus gave his last phrase a twist of local accent. He smiled.

Morris smiled back. He raised his hands, palms up. He returned Marcus's accent with accent. "It be North America we focused on now, Marcus."

Marcus gave a short laugh. "That book, Michael, do you remember that book?"

"That won the prize? Certainly. It was a great success for—"

"For the island, yes, a great public relations success. I'm sure it did something for the tourism."

"It certainly did. Now I'm sure you welcome the chance to—"

"Do you remember what that book was about?"

Morris opened his mouth and closed it again. "I forget the title just now."

"Yes, everybody does. It was called *The Rapture*. It was one long poem."

"One long poem." Morris nodded vigorously. "I remember that."

"It was about Daphne and Apollo." Marcus smiled. He too held out his hands. "Nobody remembers that."

"I thought it was about the island."

"Yes, it was," Marcus said softly. "It was that too." He turned towards the door. "I don't think I have any more poems in me, Michael. You know that."

"It's not just your work, Marcus."

Marcus stopped with his hand on the door.

"It's also about the problems at St. Hilda's."

Marcus dropped his hand. He looked long and hard at the linoleum. It was textured like shallow waves, as if the rubber or plastic laminate that made it up (what was linoleum made of, anyway?) had simply been poured on the floor, rippled across the room, and hardened in those swells. There was grime accumulating in the cracks between squares. Some of the squares were broken too. The linoleum was lime green. Marcus felt cold. His fingers tingled. "That was," he said with effort, "that was almost a year ago."

"We know they dropped the charges. I know it was nothing in the first place. One silly girl. And luckily it hasn't come up in Parliament. But it doesn't look good, Marcus. It's not good for the new image. We have to be squeaky clean now."

Marcus walked through the reception area without saying goodbye to Fenna.

The squat office block the Ministry of Education shared with the Ministry of Natural Resources and the law firm of Deesarap and Pajmin and the Katmandu Bicycle Shop was next to Government House. Marcus weaved through the tourists who were mounting the hill. They were perspiring and silent. They did not look at him.

Near the roundabout he stood still. But only for a second. He turned towards the unnamed café. He had to duck his head as he entered the darkness. There was a television playing the cricket game. He shook the hand of the man with the gold tooth and the dreads. "Jannette," called the man.

II

THE HEAT WAS TROPICAL.

The boundary between shade and light at the door of the shed was like a pane of glass. Muriella stood in the darkness of the shed and looked out at the garden. She wore her canvas hat and canvas trousers and rubber shoes, and clutched in one hand her canvas gloves, in the other her trowel. She stepped out of the rubber clogs, which were ugly. Her daughter-in-law, who lived in Edmonton, had given them to her, she suspected, precisely for that reason. She wiggled her toes on the concrete. She breathed the smell of rotting grass, rotting something, the cool air. From where she stood she was invisible; anyone in the house, or the garden itself, would see the open door of the shed as a rectangle of sheer darkness, even if she was just inside, standing still. A person would go blind on stepping inside from such a pure light, he would squint and call her name—"Muriella?"— holding his hands out before him, blinking away the buzzing circles on his retinas, the imprint of suns. And she would back away, further into the shed, saying nothing.

She was not expecting anyone to come looking for her. She was alone in the house, these days. But she enjoyed the feeling of invisibility, standing as still as she could in the silence of the shed.

The air shimmered over the black earth of the new bed. A butterfly bleached of all colour went silently hysterical in the nicotiana.

The fountain, she saw, had stopped running again.

She took a deep breath. David Rodney was in his garden. She could see his canvas hat flashing behind the hedge, among the tropical roses. His were so bright and velvet and dark inside the furled petals as to be unseemly.

As soon as she stepped into the light and heat he would smell her presence somehow, although she had camouflaged herself in khaki and grey, he would come rushing at her sad bare arms like a dog who has seen a ball. He would dart for her. She would see his canvas hat bobbing slowly. Then he would get aggressive about her peonies. His face like a cliff.

Muriella stepped into the heat. The air steamed. She began the long walk back up the pitched lawn to the house. She would start with the roses on the trellis, as that's what David Rodney would want to see her fix first. She didn't really know what she was supposed to do with them.

There used to be gardeners, a whole succession of them, with international names: Horst, Jacek, Anton, something French, and that punky couple with piercings—she came on the girl working topless one weekday afternoon, singing to herself like a child playing in mud. She had not told Arthur.

Muriella could still afford gardeners if she wanted them, but there were good reasons for her to take up gardening. People talked about it with such satisfaction. They talked about the exercise. And she kept thinking about the topless girl, the shine on her gliding ribs, the joy of it. Were it not for David Rodney's cap, she would consider doing it herself. She could do whatever she wanted now.

She scanned the top floor of her house, its falsely half-timbered facade, half obscured with (real) ivy, all the leaded windowpanes open, looking for once as it was supposed to look, which was quaintly English and rural and vaguely medieval.

She reached the house and found one of the outdoor taps and a watering can. There was also a hose coiled somewhere, but it could have been around the side. She began filling the watering can, which was an undemanding and yet satisfying task. The water sprayed cool on her hand.

There was a whining in the air; perhaps one of the Huntley teenagers with a radio? She stood straight and listened. It was singing, a thin voice.

A door thudded on the air, distant. She knew which door it was, for the Park was constructed like a bowl, with the swan pond at its centre, banked with tangled bush and weeping willows (more images, she supposed, of England, where she had never been), and sounds echoed across it. If people had been playing tennis, as they seemed to do less and less often, you could have heard the wooden tocking as if it was next door, and it was down beside the pond. But the tennis court was silent today.

The door that had shut was the Cuthbertsons', right across the bowl. A year before, that sound would have occasioned her to scuttle inside, to avoid pleasant conversation with Eric Cuthbertson the lawyer, during his divorce, and now it made her stand up in curiosity. She couldn't see the house, though, through the trees, thick as a curtain. Perhaps one day they would part and reveal a scene in progress in each illuminated window. But it was very difficult to see inside the houses in the Park. Muriella had been living there for thirteen years and had not seen inside many of them. Still she had a feeling that her own house, at the top of the slope surrounding the pond, was more visible than others, that if the bowl was an amphiteatre then its focal stage was her garden. Not that anyone seemed to be watching her today.

That singing again.

She kneeled to peer through the boxwood. David Rodney was bent over his massive roses, chanting: "*Blow the wind southerly, southerly, southerly.*" His voice was raspy, frail.

Muriella snorted.

David Rodney's house was also a Nathaniel Stilwoode, vast and blocky, with long sloping roofs, a good hectare of shingling, the real thing. They had this between them. They did not share a taste in ancestral folk music.

She heard the gurgling of her can overflowing and scuttled to it. As soon as she turned she knew she had been scented; the singing stopped. She heard him shuffling the ten yards to her hedge.

"Muriella." It was like an order. "Lovely day."

"Hello, David. How are you?"

He was breathing noticeably as he stopped at the hedge, his eyes wide under his floppy hat. "Holding out. Holding out. Lovely day."

"A little too hot for me."

"Love it hot. Be nice at the cottage, this weekend."

Muriella smiled, hauling up her watering can. David Rodney's cottage was an estate with four boathouses and a music room. "Why don't you go up today?"

"Oh." He frowned. "Only go up on weekends. Kids there, all the grandchildren. No one there in the . . . weekdays."

There was a silence as they waited for a sadness to pass over them both like a momentary indigestion.

"Well," she said, when it had passed.

"Yup. Be nice up there."

"I'm doing the roses today," she said.

David Rodney crept closer, thrust his head above the prickly green. "You want to wrap up that peony, after it's bloomed. Before the winter comes."

"I know. Thank you."

"I'm surprised it survived, last year, exposed. I couldn't believe it."

"Well, it did."

"I wouldn't chance it again."

"No. I'll take your advice this time. But it's still July, isn't it?"

"For now," he said. "It'll be over before you know it." He began to hum his blow-the-wind song to himself. It was the only song he ever hummed. Then he said, "Thank God this Campbell is finally doing something about the assessments."

Muriella flashed her eyes around her suffering beds. She was not aware of having planted anything called an assessment. "Who is Campbell?"

"The mayor. The new mayor."

"Oh yes."

"He's finally doing something about the real estate value assessments. All that nonsense about reassessing everything for contemporary market prices. It would have put us all—it would certainly have, I can tell you, it would have caused some problems for all of us. Some real hardship. It would have put us in the poorhouse."

"Oh good," said Muriella. She gripped her watering can.

"He's not bad, this chap. I say thank God he's done something about the beggars on the streets, too. It was the services downtown they were coming for, that's what no one understood. They were coming from everywhere to live on the rest of us. Three square meals a day, never have to lift a finger. It was a big hotel for them, a big spa. You cut the services, they stay where they are. They stay put. Already the streets are looking cleaner."

Muriella watered the dying roses. She felt his eyes on their tangled dessication. She turned to catch his frowning face, parched. She wanted to lift the can over his head and water him.

"Are you doing all right," she said suddenly, "in the big house? Is it okay, during the week, when there's . . ."

He glanced away. "Oh, I'm fine. I'm fine. Don't worry about me. There's good days and there's bad days. But I'm used to it now. It's been three years now." He hesitated. "I've been meaning to ask you the same thing." His face was turning red and he was staring down at the end of her garden.

"I'm all right, David," she said. "Thank you."

He nodded. "Good then. Good."

"I'm keeping busy with all my . . . all my activities. I have my book club, my arts work."

"Fundraising and that?" He was nodding vigorously.

"Well, I'm still very much involved in the arts."

"Oh yes. Fundraising," said David Rodney weakly.

"Well, that too. Mostly committee work. At the City Arts Board, and the union."

"Union?" David Rodney's forehead was lined as tartan.

Muriella glanced around quickly, as if to make sure she was not being observed talking to such a man as David Rodney by any of her colleagues on the City Arts Board Action Council

(Literature Committee). She stiffened a little at the thought of what Jasminka Sthenos-Jones would do to David Rodney if she met him. "The Writers Union of Canada."

"Ah yes. Well," he said, sighing as if in resignation, "you wrote a book once, didn't you?"

"Yes. I'm writing another."

"Well *that's* good. Now that's excellent. You want to have some activity that you can really get into, really plunge into, really occupy your mind, now that you don't . . ." He trailed off.

"Now that Arthur's gone. Yes."

There was a long silence as they both looked up at the unblemished sky, blue as a paint chip.

"Arthur," said David Rodney finally, "was a good man." She did not answer this.

"He left you well provided for, at least." Rodney nodded at the wandering walls of ivy, the pretentious little turret on the south wing, the merry little leaded windows, open as if singing.

"Oh, it's a lovely house." Muriella began pulling out dead rose stalks. They caught and tangled in the live ones, crackling like fire. Dry thorns sprayed.

"A book. Yup." He looked at his watch. Muriella could not imagine why. "That will be really . . . that's a good idea. I've always had half a mind to write a book myself. Now that I'm not quite so busy. Never had a second to think, before."

"A memoir, David?"

"Well, more like financial advice." He thrust a rocky hand at her rosebush. "You want to be deadheading those a little more often. And you should have pruned them a lot more, but it's too late now. Back in the—"

"Oh, I know. I know." She permitted herself just enough firmness to shut him up without making him huffy. She wondered what he was doing alone in the massive dark house all week. She said, "Of course I'm still dealing with all the paperwork of the estate. The insurance policies, things like that."

"You need any help, you know I have a lot of old friends from Bay Street who can—"

"Thank you, David. I have Arthur's lawyers."

"Right."

Muriella stretched. She had watered and straightened the roses. "I'm off down to the other end now," she said gaily.

"Right. See you tonight, I hope."

"Tonight?"

"At the residents' association meeting."

"Ah yes. I'm not sure if I—"

"Very important meeting tonight. Very important. We have to get this goldfish decision worked out once and for all. We have to fix up that pond. The water's stagnant, it's all choked up with algae and silt and what have you, the swans—"

"It's not really my, my area of expertise, David."

"It's *everyone's* concern, Muriella." He slapped the back on one hand on the other palm. "If we all don't make it our business, it all goes to, it all goes to—all of us, now. We have to get those goldfish out of there."

"Well, if they've been in there for fifty years, or more, as I understand—"

"They have *not*." David Rodney's breathing had accelerated again. He had his hands on his hips. "And I don't care what Frank Daurio and Ralph Poziarski and their whole, their whole gang has got going. I don't like their whole . . ." He snatched at his hat and snapped it against his wrist. His hair was white bristles. "Their whole *tendency*. I've been living in the Park for thirty-five years now, Muriella, my father bought this—"

Muriella began walking, limping with her full watering can. "I'll try and make it, David. I might have a—"

"And he was the one," he shouted after her, "who had that very pond *filled*."

She waved, kneeling by the empty bed. "Kiss my ass," she said lightly, smiling and waving.

"What was that?" David Rodney was cupping his hand to his ear, his eyes tightly closed, as if by eliminating all other sensory perception he could hear better.

"Gobo—booboy," she murmured, nodding. "Boobah wampum. Ah-hmmm." She turned back to the baking bed. A hot fecal smell.

She had a paper bag full of bulbs in the shed, but she was going to wait until he disappeared before finding it because she had no idea if she was supposed to plant them now or how in fact she was to do it, and he would be sure to notice.

But here he was shuffling down the long slope on the other side of the hedge. His hat hovered. "Muriella," he called. "I just hope I can count on your support."

She stood and dusted her knees. She shouted across the garden, "It's not really my biggest concern, David."

"No," said David Rodney, so low she almost couldn't catch it. "It wasn't your husband's concern either. And that's partly why we're in the—" But he was actually limping away again. He was talking to himself.

A few minutes later she heard his whine from half an acre away. "*Blow the wind southerly, SOUtherly, SOUtherly, blow the wind southerly . . .*"

"*Blow me now patiently, patiently, patiently,*" sang Muriella to herself. She dug her hands into the hot earth and played with it. "*You are a bumberly, prickerly, buggerly, you are a pimple-y sill-y old man.*"

Drops of sweat slid down her sides. She was wearing no bra. David Rodney did not know that.

It was with a certain relief that she heard the phone ringing from one of the open windows. She scrambled around the house, down the sooty path to the side door, kicking off her rubber clogs. She grabbed it in the kitchen, found her son on the line, told him to wait, ran into the library, trailing dirt from her bare feet on the red Shirazes, picked up the phone there, told him to wait again, ran into the kitchen to hang up the phone there, then walked, glistening with exertion, back into the library, where she sank into a leather sofa and said, "Yes, lovey."

"Just checking. How you're doing and all."

"Very well, thanks. How are the kids?"

"Great. Just great. Off at camp at the moment. Great for Deborah. She needed a rest."

"Yes. Good." There was a silence during which they both strove to avoid discussing Deborah's sensitivities.

"And you?" said her son, over some kind of radio in the background. An Edmonton radio, Muriella could not help thinking. "How are you keeping busy?"

This line of questioning irritated Muriella, for it indicated that her son thought of her life as a series of hobbies which had no purpose other than to keep her distracted until she died. "Oh," she said, "I'm seeing very many people. I'm quite busy. Don't worry about me."

"Well, that's great. That's great. What kind of—"

"I'm thinking of going back to school."

"Really? That's a great idea. A terrific idea. Night school sort of thing?"

Muriella laughed a little. "No, Johnny, real school. Real school for grown-ups. I'm thinking of finishing my master's."

"Oh," he said. "Right. I forgot about that, I forgot you did that. It was just after I left home, I think. Really? You want to go back into that? Full-time?"

"Yes, full-time." But as she said it, she wasn't sure. She would have to start again, from the beginning. Courses on Chaucer and Spenser. Or perhaps they didn't even teach that any more?

"Well, that's great, but, ah, a little ambitious, maybe."

The irritation caught her in the throat again. She stared up at the portrait of Arthur over the fireplace. It had been painted in the offices of McMaster Life. He was holding on to a desk with one hand, his glasses in the other. The desk, the walls, and his suit were all the same shade of grey. She said, "I only quit, lovey, because you and Janie and Daddy made fun of it all the time. You don't think I'm at all capable of—oh, lovey, hang on a minute, I have another—hang on. Hang on." She stared at the receiver, momentarily unable to remember where the little button was that you pushed to link to the waiting call. There was a button that said "flash" and a button that said "channel." She could still hear John's radio, his impatient breathing. She pushed "channel." "Hello?"

There was crackling, and then John's voice came fuzzy again. "It's me, Mom. Push the flash button."

"Hello?"

"Hello, Mrs. Pent? It's Julia Sternberg."

"Oh Julia! Julia! Wait! Wait one minute!" She pressed the button again. "John? It's Marjorie Sternberg's daughter. I've been waiting for her call."

"Who is Marjorie Sternberg?"

"Oh, lovey, you know Marjorie, from Côte St. Luc, Julia is the beautiful one, she's so lovely, you'd love her. I've been wanting to see her, we're becoming so close, she's my new best friend."

"Marjorie or her daughter."

"Julia. That's why I have to—"

"You're best friends with her *daughter*? Isn't she nineteen or something?"

"Something like that. She's on the other line, so I have to *go* now, all right? And we can't chat on Thursday because I have a meeting in the afternoon."

"A meeting?"

"Yes, a meeting. I am capable of more than shopping. I have told you about the arts council twice already."

"Arts council." His voice was already fading back to Edmonton; she could picture him looking at his watch.

"My arts council. The Arts Action Council."

"Oh. Right. Great then. So you're sure you're okay."

"Perfectly."

"I'll call soon."

She hung up and punched the button, saying *Edmonton* through clenched teeth.

"Sorry?"

"Hello. Nothing. I was on the other—Julia! How nice of you to call!"

"Oh. Well." Julia Sternberg giggled down the line. "I wanted to."

"Well, that's very sweet of your mother, to ask you to call me."

"Well. I wanted to."

"That's very sweet of you then."

There was a silence.

"How have you been?" said Julia Sternberg.

There was something just faintly nurse-like enough in her brisk tone to make Muriella say, "Oh, sitting up, taking a little soup."

"What?" said Julia meekly. "Have you been sick?"

"No. Never mind. It was a silly joke. I'm fine. I'm very well." Muriella swung her bare legs up onto the sofa. She left a smudge of mud on the arm. The leather was cool on her skin. She looked up at Arthur, put a hand on one breast, and said, "How are you? You're at university now, right?"

There was a little pause before she said, "Yes. I'm at the University of Toronto. I'm studying English."

"English! Excellent. That's really excellent. That really is."

Julia laughed for real now. "Oh, my mother doesn't think so."

"No," said Muriella. "But she wouldn't, would she?"

Julia stopped laughing.

"My son wouldn't like it either. My son doesn't like the fact that I wrote a book."

"You wrote a book?"

"A few years ago, yes. A book for teenagers."

"Wow. I didn't know that."

"No. Nobody does. It was about a girl and a horse." Muriella snorted a little. "One of those books." She hesitated, then said, "For girls who grow up to be dykes."

"Sorry?"

Muriella shrieked. "I'm sorry. I don't know what's making me crazy." She wiggled her muddy toes on the leather sofa.

"Oh."

"My son lives in Edmonton." Muriella found this funny. Julia apparently did not. "Oh?"

Muriella sighed. "What are you reading right now?"

"In school, you mean?"

"Or for yourself. Yes. In school."

"Oh. Well, I have a lot of courses. We're reading a lot of . . . we're reading a lot of Derrida right now."

"Oh yes," said Muriella. She could see David Rodney's hat bobbing outside the library window, over the hedge. "I did a master's degree myself once." Muriella did not know why she had felt the need to say this, but there it was. Julia did not answer this. Perhaps she found it boring as well. But wasn't English Julia's subject? "I mean I almost did, I didn't finish it. At U of T. I did the first year and then I had trouble with the thesis."

"What did you study?" Julia's voice was faint.

"Oh English, of course, English. Like you."

Silence.

"I was going," said Muriella quickly, "I was planning to do a thesis on Browning. The professors were very rude, at that time, about women like me, married women doing it part-time. They made it difficult for me."

"I bet," said Julia.

Muriella tried a new tack. "We'll have to have you in my book club."

"Oh."

"I know a lot, well, quite a few writers. I'm on the City Arts Board Action Council. On the Literature Committee. You might be interested in . . . well, I don't know. You might be interested. We do a lot of important work."

"Yes." Julia's voice was faint. "Why I was, the reason I was calling, was to ask if—I enjoyed talking to you so much the last time I was there—I wonder if you would like to have tea with me. Some time."

"Of course. I would love to. Would you like to come over here?"

"Sure."

"Would you like to come this afternoon?"

"This afternoon? Oh. No, I don't think I . . . I don't think I could."

Muriella's phone beeped again. "I have to take another call, sweetie. Can you come on Wednesday?"

"Ah."

The phone beeped again. "I really have to go, lovey. Is Wednesday all right?"

"Yes. Yes. Wednesday is fine. At what—"

"I'll call you tomorrow. Bye-bye lovey, and thank you so much for calling. Say hello to your mother for me. All right. Bye-bye." She squelched Julia with a button. She wasn't sure if it was the right one. "Hello?"

"Hello, Muriella?"

This was Brian, the young man from the literature committee. He treated her the same as all the others did. He was polite enough, certainly, stiffly so, but she couldn't help feeling he was rolling his eyes as he spoke to her. He repeated the date and place of the meeting twice, the second time slowly. Once she had not been told of a meeting at all, but had raised such a fuss afterwards that they now told her two and three times. And still she was always the last to know.

"Jasminka wanted you to know particularly," Brian was saying, "that we would have no time to discuss the poetry proposals at this meeting. It's just about the voice appropriation resolution and the Developing Regions Exchange, this one. We won't have time to get into the poetry."

The poetry grants had been steadily delayed for six months, and everyone knew that it was because she had for some reason been interested in them. At one time she had thought it might be interesting to learn something about contemporary poetry. She had thought that her half a master's degree in Romanticism would make her views on poetry respected.

She hadn't realized that all the poetry applications would be quite so white. And an interest in poetry of the nineteenth century, her boastful admission that she had once had such a thing, made her more suspect than respected. Now she was on the wrong side of something she had tried, it must be admitted, rather feverishly to stay on the right side of, and it would take some major gesture on her part to prove her commitment again.

There was, she had to concede, so much she still had to learn. They had every right to condescend to her, as they knew so much more about the Issues than she did. She was still learning what the Issues were. And she was determined not to make a fool of herself again. She would keep her mouth shut about poetry and painting, and listen. She went to every community theatre performance she could, unless they were under bridges or in abandoned subway stations, as they so often were—she could claim, if queried on this selectiveness, the frailty of age, although the truth was she had no appropriate footwear, unless she appeared in her green plastic gardening clogs—and she was reading, rather slowly, the works of Ignatius Barnabas, the local writer who had so far benefited from more Action Council grants than anyone else, and she was learning a great deal from it. She had had no idea that life in her very own city could be so miserable, and it had certainly changed her ideas about how art could be a force for social good.

"Okay Muriella?" said Brian Sillwell so sharply she sat up straight.

"All right, Brian. Thank you." She hung up the phone and stood up. She looked out the window on the garden and said, "And you are younger than my youngest, my daughter, who, you may be interested to know, married a urologist." She trailed off, feeling guilty. It was good work that the committee was doing. And Brian had as hard a time of it as she did.

She realized, in a flash of self-pity, what a liability she would be to Brian if Jasminka and Iris Warshavsky and Deepak and Ignatius and the rest of them were to see him as linked to her in any way. She didn't blame Brian.

David Rodney's hat fluttered up above the hedge and dipped again, fragile.

He was only ten yards away, and her window was open. If he stretched his head over the hedge he might make her out, in the darkness of her leathery library, staring at him.

Standing in the centre of the room, her toes on the furry pile of a red carpet, she lifted her blouse. She felt the cool air on her bare breasts. She wiggled them at David Rodney. "*Bugger me fuckerly*," she sang. She tried to match the tune he was singing. "*Bugger me fuckerly, fuckerly, fuckerly, bugger me fuckerly, fuck-me-so-hard.*"

She took off her blouse entirely and walked to the window. David Rodney was trundling away from her, up the long path to his house. The shadows were long on the garden. Her poppies were deepening in the glow. There was a slight breeze. Muriella stood in the open window and felt her nipples harden. Anyone could see her standing there. But there was no one anywhere she could see.

She turned back inside and picked up her blouse. She looked up at Arthur's portrait. He was looking through her.

She looked at her watch. No one was coming to tea today. She had nothing until Julia on Wednesday. And then committee meeting on Thursday. That was something.

III

"Elizabeth," he called.

The rattling stopped. Silence.

"Elizabeth." He was sharp.

From the passageway came an echo of voice. But she wasn't answering him, she was singing. A thin wail of kitchen song.

He knew the song was a rebuke for being rebuked. It would end. He waited.

Silence.

Then a massive rattle, an avalanche of crockery, subsiding into aftershocks of glass detonations, a trail of cracking crystal.

Marcus Royston laughed. "Then spoke the thunder," he said aloud. He held both hands above his head. "Da." He put down his hands and sat still.

His window looked onto the harbour. Hot haze, and clouds as well. The sun seemed to have stopped moving. The long wooden freighter, a thin lozenge at this distance, which he had watched all morning being loaded with sooty beams that looked to be used or ancient railway sleepers, had also stopped moving in the middle of the bay. The sails were furled. All activity on board had ceased. But then he couldn't imagine they actually used the sails anyway.

He glanced at his watch without moving his hand. Two o'clock. *"Elizabeth."*

All this was about the radio, he knew. She was furious when he chose to work in the afternoons, when he was normally at Desi's, having coffee (with discreet brandy) with Richard and Jean-Claude. But the new deputy minister would be there now, and Marcus didn't want to see him. And besides, it was time to get stuck back into work now. The time for brandies with the Martiniquais or the Petron safety experts was over.

But this was her radio time: there was a patois evangelist. There was lots of singing along to be done. She was refraining from switching on the radio, in respect for his "work," and wanted him to know it. So she was ostentatiously simulating noiselessness.

He knew she had heard him. If he called her name one more time, she would answer. But he had made his point.

He had nothing to ask her anyway.

A fly settled on the sticky rim of his glass, and Marcus Royston did not attempt to dislodge it, although he could have lifted his long finger, looped around the same rim, to convincingly signify ownership. He did not want to take that step, as his relation to this drink was not something he wanted to classify so strictly, not something he wanted to face head-on.

He let a drop of sweat trickle on his temple without wiping it.

He tried to delay his next sip. The sweet and bitter rum punch colonized every surface inside his mouth. The thing to do would be to have water as well, at one's side, and sip the two intermittently. It would both delay and decloy the process. He took another sip.

The clouds over the harbour always seemed to hold rain, but never rained. They too seemed immobile in the haze, like solid objects embedded in jelly. A particularly Caribbean jelly: sweet and yellow-grey. And hot.

Even a kind of silence had been accumulating imperceptibly over the previous hour, unbelievably, given that he lived just above the market square, in a pink house on a narrow street cut into the rock of the hill, could even look down into the market if he chose, which he didn't. (If he were to look down, he would have seen the rows of tin roofs of stalls, the bright rows of T-shirts for tourists, the piles of coconut and corn and their attendant old ladies in turbans, squatting on the concrete, with their machetes flat on the ground. Ready to cut.) For now there was no whining moped or hysterical klaxon from the street, just the passing thrum of reggae from the minicabs, throbbing and fading as they careered around the stone and brick and stucco houses that overhung and obstructed any attempt at an actual street, a noise that was actually unnoticeable because it was more like a natural sound, the sound of the air.

He took another sip and brushed at his temple with sticky fingers. In St. Andrew's, rum punch is made with heavy doses of nutmeg syrup, which is bitter and stings. There were easier drinks to consume consecutively, less sticky, less laborious to concoct. But he had Elizabeth to do that (Elizabeth whom he heard now recommencing an informative clatter, gently and insistently, reminding him about her suffering). And besides, this was the drink he had grown up with, he was a St. Andrean at least in this one strangely sentimental respect, and he would stick with it.

Perhaps he shouldn't stick with it so closely. Only two o'clock and already his third. He had been good, since his newfound freedom, at not letting it begin any earlier than lunch; starting before eleven, say, would be fatal. But he had made up for that success by increasing his consumption after lunch, which was just as bad.

He ratcheted the paper in his typewriter, on which he had typed,

> *In the afternoons the battlements are thinned in haze*
> *from campfires and dingy stalls*
> *where smoke-skinned boys beneath the walls*
> *sell meat on sticks against the blaze*
> *of setting sun. Atop the towers glint the tips*
> *of metal, sullen as the soldiers' eyes*

Only the last two lines were today's work, and they were distinctly inferior. The a-b-b-a business was proving impossible to maintain. And the rhythm was all goofy. But he could picture the city: the dusty scattering of encampments outside the main gate, between the impassive fortifications and the first lines of the besieging army which were just out of range of bows and catapults, the vendors and whores who were left alone, trailing behind the invaders like streaks of grease or worse, excrement, the cloud of commerce which provided this ragged link between the city and the massed armour just over the nearest dunes. They were tolerated and ignored, as one ignores a smell. Occasionally they would get too close and the Trojan sentries would fire off a volley of arrows at a trail of creaking caravans, just to see the lines breaking up and whirling, dissipating like smoke, and then regrouping farther away. It was rather like brushing off flies.

No one here recalls the prize.
A roaring dream of vanished ships.

He wanted to make the market stalls like the ones outside his house, with sheet-metal roofs and a smell of curry. The whole idea, which was as fluid as a dream, was to make Troy modern Africa, which he had, admittedly, only ever seen briefly, in a surreal trip to Senegal five years ago on official business. And he wasn't sure if it was the inhabitants of the walled city who were African or just the stragglers outside.

But really, what he was more interested in, he had to admit, was those walls: how massive they must have been! Dusty, pocked with battle. Even crumbled and patched in parts. Nothing but scrub and sand, endlessly trampled and bloody, stained with burnt patches and scored with the ditches of latrines, for miles around. The air that always smells of fire and sewage. He could see the orange sunset, the smoky desert sky, and the last rays of sun on the battlements, where you could not make out faces, but the sudden glint of metal, the surly reminder of weaponry, as the tips of lances shifted uneasily on the ramparts. A gleam like jewellery under folds of clothing. The promise of battle.

Over the horizon, out of sight of the sentries, would be the heart of the Greek camp, with orderly rows of tents, and the palatial marquees of the aristoi, the fluttering standards of the hoplites. The hoplite tents he would make bright blue, he would put blue plumes in their helmets. There would be batmen polishing shields, brass shields, and tall leather boots, around the campfires. And when the hoplites strode through the tent city, taller and heavier and older than the bedraggled conscript army, soldiers would scuttle out of their way. The hoplites were hard; their faces were scarred.

Marcus scribbled *hard/scarred* on a square of paper.

The hoplites were the core of the army that had conquered six or seven people of varying skin colours. They were the tip of the wedge, the salient—there was some military term for this kind of unit Marcus couldn't remember. He would have to find it. Something that meant penetrating arm or finger, something with a hard sound. He would have to find it. The hoplites would have conquered here, he thought dully. They would have killed me or enslaved me. He was filled with sadness and awe of the hoplite units, an awe that for Marcus always turned into a kind of love. He could not help but look at things objectively. Who would not want to be a hoplite?

He closed his eyes and he saw the women hidden in the dank tents of the encampments, the women brought skinny and toothless from Asia and Africa, lying wrapped in skins and old cloths in the dank heat of the tents. Their salty bodies, their barely formed breasts.

Marcus shifted in his chair. His groin was tight. This was troubling. For some of them must have been children, surely. It was unpleasant to react in this way. But there he was again, in that stifling, furry space, unwrapping the sooty robe from a quivering slave girl's legs.

He opened his eyes. This was all becoming a little too clichéd, like a historical romance novel.

He stretched his legs. He wanted to walk. He pictured the perfumed girls standing in a row under the awning of Fitzroy's café, just past the market, in Petit Havre. They wouldn't be there this early.

Dusty lips, he typed.

Which was useless.

Smoke-skinned was good, anyway.

He took another fiery sip of punch.

With all this fire imagery, why not skip ahead a bit and do something on the sacking of the city, the collapse, the holocaust: fire, confusion, smoke, the evacuation, and the young Aeneas rescuing the old man, his father, Anchises (this would have to be looked up, the names were confusing), fleeing the burning ruins with Anchises over his shoulder like a sack of old potatoes.

He was always thinking of destruction now. And he realized with a certain coldness that he was thinking of himself, of course, as Aeneas the rescuer, pious and athletic Aeneas, son of Aphrodite herself, and the old man as his own father, whereas his age was now closer to that of the old man, the helpless bundle on the hero's back. He did not think he could imagine playing that role. And it would be ridiculous to imagine himself, now fifty-four, as the heroic son of Aphrodite.

And his own father had not needed rescuing from anything, except a life of well-meaning uselessness and genteel poverty as a Methodist minister in a rural parish. And a sudden heart attack in the garden, beside the chicken coop. Marcus had not rescued him from that.

This was the kind of disheartening thought that was preventing the writing of anything these days.

Furthermore, another Trojan poem was exactly what the people at the ministry didn't want. They didn't want Troy or Persephone or Daphne resisting the colonizing white phallus. They didn't want this kind of melancholy any more, not here, not in the offices of his American publisher, not even in the dank little British offices in Russell Square, not even among the bearded Swedish prize-givers or the clean-shaven young academics with nose rings in the United States or even among the cultural committees of the ministry, who had turned on him as one, suddenly—he couldn't stop thinking about it now, though he wanted not to, he was gone in an eruption of prickly hurt—turned on him, snarled, bitten him, and thrown him out.

With surprise and embarrassment he felt his throat closing, his eyes filling with tears.

Which was just the moment that Elizabeth entered behind him. Her feet slipslopped on the bare floor. He did not turn.

She stopped. He could feel her staring at the back of his head. He held himself absolutely still, blinking. He could not trust his voice.

She took a long time before saying, "Look at yourself." Her voice had a biblical quaver. "You look at yourself, Marcus Royston."

She shuffled to him, her feet like mops on the ends of her thick legs. She slid the glass of punch off the table.

He put his head in his hands and sobbed.

She stood and watched him for a moment, as if hesitating. "You had better get out of the house," she said. Then she shuffled away.

IV

"HOPLITES ARE OFFICER CLASS. YOU don't train them through the barracks, you train them at the academy. You have to build an academy. How big are his fortifications?"

"Medium walls. With ballista towers. They're practically impregnable."

"Do you have heavy catapults?"

"Just regular. I can't develop heavy catapults. For some reason, he has them and I don't. It's not giving me the option."

"You have to research siegecraft. It's in the marketplace options. First stone mining, then you upgrade to siegecraft."

"Shit. I should have done that—"

"You have to get on that. Get on it. That's the first thing you do—get siegecraft. But listen, get your academy going and train hoplites. Then research aristocracy, through the government centre, and then you can upgrade the hoplites to phalanx units. It costs a ton, in food and gold. It costs like fuckbunches. But the phalanxes are fucking brutal. You can take on like elephant archers, anything with a bunch of phalanxes. They have like a hundred and twenty hit points, twenty attack points, which you can add to if you research, I forget what it is, I think it's called metallurgy. They're fucking brutal. They're elite units."

"Phalanx," said Jason deeply. "Cool."

"They're super cool." Brian was walking rapidly up and down the little corridor that ran the length of the basement, with the phone wedged into his shoulder, so that he could pound the air in front of him with his fists. He wore his glasses and his at-home sweater and the ridiculous moose-fur slippers that his uncle had given him. His bedroom smelled gamey now, of moosehide, from the slippers, and he liked it. He had to bow his head each time he passed under the hot-air duct. "Research metallurgy and you get extra attack points. What culture are you playing?"

"Ah. Phoenician."

"Oooh. That's shitty for a land war. You should be playing on sea for Phoenicians. Who are you playing?"

"Yeah, but I get faster production on war elephants. Hittites. The computer's Hittite."

"Oh, man, you are so screwed. You are totally screwed. You will never, ever beat Hittites with Phoenicians."

"Okay, now you're depressing me. Let's stop—"

"Hittites have double catapult hit points. You can never crash those damn things. They'll kill you."

"We have to stop talking about this now," said Jason. "We're being too geeky."

"Tell me about it. I played this game for three weeks over Christmas. Every day. Three weeks non-stop. It was like crack."

"What are you doing now?"

Brian stooped to walk into the kitchen-living room. He put his head into the window casement and looked at the asphalt of the driveway. The landlord's car was gone. "What am I doing now today or what am I doing now in my life?"

"Now in your life. Now that school's over."

"I'm . . . I'm not sure. Nothing right now. I'm teaching ESL part-time. I'm starting my master's in the fall."

"Me too. But you're staying here, right?"

"Yeah." There was a silence. Brian stood on his toes to rest his chin on the windowsill. "I might not do it."

"What, you might go somewhere else?"

"No. I might not go back to school."

"Right."

"No, really."

"Right. What else would you do?"

"I don't know. Work in a bookstore or something. Maybe meet a girl once in a while. Seriously. I might not."

"Don't tell me. You're writing some . . ."

"Yes."

"Some work of Literature."

"Yup."

"Oh, don't. Please."

Brian said nothing.

"Well," said Jason, "it's been nice, but I think I have to scream now."

Brian said nothing.

"You're insane."

"I don't even know yet."

"What is it? A novel."

"Of course."

"A bloody novel. The great Canadian novel."

Brian snorted. "No."

"What then?"

"I don't know. I haven't started it yet. Great Russian novel would be more like it."

"Okay. You're crazy. Brian, I really would suggest you try that after you—"

"Okay. Whatever. I don't want to talk about it right now."

"Are you tossing your head?" said Jason.

"What?"

"I don't want to talk about it, she snapped, and she tossed her head. Tossed her fiery red mane. Is that the kind of thing you're thinking? I don't want to talk about it, said the countess, and she *stormed* out of the room."

Brian made the sort of whinny that embarrassed him when he was with girls. It meant he had found something very amusing. He controlled himself. "I have to go to this meeting."

"What meeting?"

"I'm on the City Arts Board. The literature committee. Except it's called the Action Council."

"I thought they cut all that. The city. This Campbell. Didn't he—"

"They're probably about to," said Brian. "They've cut everything else. I don't think they'd dare cut this, though. It's one of the few multicultural—"

"You know," said Jason, "I think you—I think there's a part of you that wants to be like a missionary or something. You want to help the poor, you want to live in a *more authentic* place, you—"

"Yes, yes I do want to live in a more authentic place." Brian put both palms flat on the ceiling.

"Putting aside for a moment that jejune conception—"

"*Jejune!*" whinnied Brian.

"—and restraining myself from excoriating the notion that where you live is somehow inauthentic because it doesn't happen to be involved in a war or a riot or I don't know, an Ebola outbreak, that where you live is somehow not real, as if you yourself are not real—"

"This basement doesn't seem real," said Brian.

"I will limit myself to criticism of your altruistic tendencies. You want to make up for your bourgeois heritage. You want to make reparations."

"First of all, I'm no bourgeois, I'm from Barrie, which is hardly either a capital of power or genteel whatever, and second, no. That's not it."

"You want to make agitprop theatre in the streets like Brecht and, and who was it, the painter—"

"Rodchenko. I'd rather be Rodchenko. No, I just feel that—"

"You want to be *engagé* like the Surrealists, you want literature in the service of the revolution. You're going to write a manifesto."

"I don't think it's so ridiculous," said Brian. "Besides, I have nowhere else to . . . to do something with my stupid education."

This silenced Jason for a second.

"I'm actually interested in writing," said Brian, "and it always frustrated me that we never did anything local or even very contemporary at school and I want to make all that feel real somehow."

"There's the idea of the real again. You really think that what isn't—"

"I really think there's some kind of writing outside the academy, and yes I do think it's more real. Let me tell you, this arts council thing is real, all right." He was thinking of Jasminka, in her towering turban. Her stentorian breathing. "It's as real as it gets. There are some people we're funding who are really dealing with issues, with real issues, like how do you live if you've got no money kind of issues, not just I want to re-evaluate conventions of communication kind of issues. I'm sick of that."

"No you're not. I bet you're not. You're still part of *Haʒe*, right, you're on the board?"

"Yeah. Look, anyway, I don't want to argue about it because—"

"Well you can't get any less real than *Haʒe*. You can't get any less real than the subversion or transgression of linguistic systems through the anti-linear language whatever you publish in that thing. You love it."

"It's a collective," Brian whined. "I'm only part of a collective. I'm trying to change all that, but I don't make all the decisions myself. Look, I have to go, really, I really really have to go now. Let me know if you're going to the Culture Corner reading on Tuesday."

"Who is it?"

"It's those guys from Possible Press. They put out *Coelacanth Apartments*. They should have Leanne Grissom there—"

"Weeping, as usual. Christ, those guys are assholes."

"Yes. Are you going?"

"Oh yeah. I'll be there."

Brian had to rush to get himself out of the apartment. He wore khaki shorts and a white short-sleeved shirt for the Action Council meeting. It was best not to be too conspicuous. He waited for the College streetcar and sweated. All the passing girls had bare legs. He clenched his jaw and thought of the hoplites in their phalanxes. He would be calm and quiet and strong.

He would write a novel of conquest and devastation.

V

The Scent of Lace

A novel by Muriella Pent

CHAPTER ONE: ARRIVAL

The rain pelted down on the bedraggled families as they waddled down the gangplank, clutching the bags that contained all they had left in the world. They were herded by men in uniforms into a vast hangar or warehouse with the words "Pier 21" painted in white paint in vast letters across one side. The words meant nothing, of course, to Natalya and her family; the only English she knew was "please" and "thank you" and "I am married," which she still could not say without provoking giggles from the swarthy deckhands on the ship these past three weeks of travel.

Natalya clutched the baby, Moishe, and tried to cover its bare head from the rain with her own tattered scarf, and looked around for her other daughter, Julia, who strode ahead, her little legs bent under the weight of an enormous bundle: all the clothes they had. Ivan, her husband, had pushed to the front of the crowd, squeezing into the warehouse—always trying to get them a better deal, she thought. She panicked a little, seeing Julia disappearing into the sea of old wool overcoats, but she had to smile to

~ 56 ~

herself too: the girl was braver than she was, always eager to taste a new experience.

Natalya herself felt nothing but fatigue and a vague dread. They were all exhausted after the draining, uncomfortable weeks on the boat, the endless nausea, the stinking toilets, the smell of unwashed humanity sleeping together in the rows of bunks in steerage, the constant worry about adequate food for the baby, about the unwanted attentions of the crew. (Ivan had stayed oblivious to this— consciously or unconsciously, she didn't know.) And now here they were in another cold country, a country with no history and no luxury, just this assembly of squat port buildings hunkered around this giant wharf, and railway lines and a towering grain elevator, and grey skies and grey seas and shouting brutal men in uniform, and her people reduced to this, to this sodden mass, pushing and pleading to be first in line. Who knew what awaited them inside this building that smelled of hay and sewage? How long would they have to wait here? Natalya knew that they would have to be examined and then quarantined, like so much cattle. And after that . . . all she knew was that Ivan had some plan of crossing the country in a train, that he had plans for setting up his tailor shop in a city many days away, as far away from the sea as Minsk had been.

They were now inside the shed, and she called in a high voice for her family. Little Julia came running towards her on the stick legs. "What have you done with our belongings?" cried Natalya in a panic.

"Papa has them," said the girl. "Don't worry, Mummy, it's safe here, we've arrived." And she put her small hand in her mother's.

Natalya felt a tear welling in her eye and wiped it with a corner of the tattered scarf, which had once been bright with embroidered threads. The scarf was the last keepsake which her own mother had given her as they left her in the village with the others who were too old or sick to make the journey to the New World. The babushka was all right, she knew; cared for by a whole village of relatives, but still she could not stop from shaking with grief as she looked around her at the misery of her surroundings. Nobody, she felt sure, would embroider scarves as beautiful as this in this barbarous land.

And yet at least there were no pogroms here, either; no daily fear of the distant thunder of horses' hooves, the Cossacks with their (get details of uniforms).

Little did Natalya know that this huddled mass of seasick tradesmen would be the first wave of immigrants in a great city, a city that would house the most vibrant communities of

*Lupus committee 7 pm

Ideas for novels:
—massacre of Iroquois by smallpox
—Riel Rebellion
—Dieppe raid
—Vimy Ridge (maybe parallels between?)
—Canadian participation in bombing of Hamburg and Dresden
—computer crime using Internet

VI

THE PREVIOUS SPRING, MURIELLA HAD gone to consult with the writer-in-residence at the Metro Reference Library and shown him a few pages of the immigrant novel. He was just a young man who had published a novel about rock-and-roll bands. They met in a small room without a window and a fluorescent light that buzzed. He had sideburns and some kind of Hawaiian shirt that was too tight and had long sleeves. Muriella had worn her most casual trousers and a cotton sweater and still she felt as if she looked like someone who owned a golf course. The writer-in-residence said that he wasn't that interested in immigrants, to tell the truth, because everyone was an immigrant, really.

He told her that she should try writing something about her own experience. She said that her experience was of being an immigrant. He looked surprised and said maybe she should write about that, about her past, and she said her past was really not dissimilar to that of the family she was describing, and he looked at his watch, so she told him that she was not actually an immigrant herself but her parents were, from Greece, and that her father had owned a furniture store in Montreal, where she had grown up, with quite a lot of money really (although she didn't tell him that), but in a quarter called Côte St. Luc, often called Côte St. Jew, where she did not feel at home because she attended a blocky Orthodox cathedral downtown and attended a great many Greek weddings, which were even more tumultuous and cathartic than the Jewish ones, although not quite so costly.

He smiled a little at this, so she told him that she was, as a child, often mistaken for a Jew, which was fine, since all her friends had been Jewish, until she went to McGill and met Arthur.

But by this point the writer-in-residence was looking at his watch a lot and so Muriella stopped talking. He said that she needed more of a story than that, and that maybe she should move away from autobiography, as he had a problem with a lot of confessional writing.

Muriella thought of this as she dressed for tea with Julia Sternberg. She was holding a grey sweatsuit in her hand, which she dropped onto the floor of her dressing room and just left there. She stepped on it as she walked into the closet again.

There had been no possibility of confessional writing or any other kind of writing in the eight or ten or maybe even twelve months after Arthur's death. She remembered that time not as dark but as blinding white, like overexposed film: every day had been flooded by dazzling pain like a desert light. She still found the daylight too extreme: it exposed every sharp edge around every useless and use-lessly beautiful rooftop or unpruned hedge or steaming highway or abandoned car wheel (those images were what were left of that time); she was still wearing sunglasses much more than she had, before.

No reason to try to write about that, even now, even now that the white light had faded to this constant late-August glow—loneliness was like a light that shone from inside things, made them at once more poignant and more opaque.

She could remember those hysterical weddings of her childhood, though. She wondered if that would count as confessional writing. She wondered what writing wasn't confessional.

Why then, there, standing in the closet looking at her skeletal legs in the full-length mirror would she have a searing image of Arthur? But there it was: at a dinner party, about three years before, before he was ill, someone had mentioned a building downtown and he suddenly grew talkative (which had generally not been the case at dinner parties, or at any kind of parties, or at all), speaking in a quiet and measured voice and looking up over the flowers, about the first offices he had worked in at McMaster Life, in the original Commerce building, the old stone one with the step-backs and the Deco ornaments, which had still been one of the tallest in the city, then, when he was a young man in the fifties, and how there had been a lounge, a corner office which was a sort of lounge, and the senior partners would ask the younger men in after work (people didn't work as long hours then, and there was more drinking) and they would drink Scotch and watch the sun set on the other buildings, and how beautiful it was, and simpler (by which he probably meant, Muriella now realized, that there were no women), and when he thought about it now (he concluded with sudden firmness) he realized that those had been the happiest days of his life.

This was stomach-upsetting. Muriella wrenched out three pairs of trousers and left them in a pile for Salvation Army donation. The story had been sad at the time, too, but for different reasons.

It wasn't that she missed her previous life, really, even the galas and the performances, which had often been embarrassing, as Arthur was not afraid to sleep and to be seen sleeping, particularly at the symphony (he said it was the only place where he didn't feel he had to be doing something, so he didn't mind paying a hundred and twenty bucks a ticket to sleep there without the sense of guilt that simply going to bed at eight o'clock would have given him; it was refreshing and he was supporting a good cause, or something, while doing it). There had always been the question of his age, his asking her without even asking her to be quieter, calmer—but also that sense of exclusion always there, of seeing something different in, say, views of the highway overpasses on the way in from Muskoka, from what he would see, or indeed what anybody—Olivia Daurio and Shirley Melnyk or any of her neighbours—would see, and from what he would see, that she had always felt she had to keep quiet about. (Except on the few Park occasions when she had met Gaye Northwood, who was so much wealthier than any of the others that she was different: she was so much more elegant and calm and travelled to London rather than Bel Air, you could say anything to her. Although, sadly, Muriella had never found anything to say to her, in the moment.)

Arthur would have been happiest, she thought, in a small town in Scotland.

Perhaps some people had lives that one could write about, but she wasn't one of them.

And why had clothing become so problematic?

She hesitated between khaki trousers and some tighter and warmer but more elegant patterned paisley ones in a sort of corduroy with cigarette legs. But these would necessitate some kind of heel, which would separate her even further from Julia Sternberg. Muriella knew that one couldn't dress down enough for the young: they would always look better in something cheaper, and if one tried to dress as sloppily one would look lumpy, and if one dressed to flatter oneself one would look old. Julia Sternberg would probably be in some variant on a survival suit made for desert warfare, some kind of full-body decontamination suit, or maybe just a set of creosote-soaked rags, it was impossible to tell. Or maybe, in this heat, it would be the opposite: some kind of bikini top made of kitchen cling wrap and jeans around mid-thigh, with her underwear showing, or perhaps no underwear at all. This thought made her uncomfortable in a way she could not pinpoint. The image of the crease between thigh and abdomen, the flat bottom of the belly.

Nakedness was not frightening, not even self-conscious-making, to the girls that she saw strolling on the shopping streets, their bellies swelling over the curves of their groins and the promise of pubic hair—perhaps Julia would be swanning around her deliberately impractical and romantically dilapidated dwelling (for they had agreed, at the last minute, to meet there, in the rented house in the Junction, for a thrill) in a thong and body paint. Not that Muriella would be shocked: she just didn't want to be reminded of the perfection of anyone's body, any man's or woman's body.

Muriella herself was wearing a short silk robe that was quite lovely but was in itself evidence of a cultural gulf that she feared neither she nor Julia Sternberg could cross.

Why Julia Sternberg's approval was so important to her she did not know. Everyone's was, at the moment.

And something was changing: she was aware, as she had always been aware, that she was not as clever as everyone else was, but she was not being reminded of it so often, without Arthur, and with John in Edmonton and Janie in Vancouver. And it was coming out, slowly and thrillingly, in her book club, which was the only place where she really spoke, was allowed to speak a great deal, that she was one of the few people with any ideas at all, and that because of her degree and her master's degree (which everyone knew she didn't really have) people actually listened to her and wanted to hear what she had to say; it was the only area in her life to date where these things had had any currency at all. Not only was she listened to: she was discovering a certain superiority of tone she could use to withering effect. She could lay down a judgement and it would lie there, intimidating, in the cakes and the coffee cups, and it would slyly (she noticed, if no one else did) become truth in subsequent discussions.

She wondered if Julia, with her classes and her theories, her resistance to all her mother's plans, her well-known neuroses (she didn't come home for a year once; she ate nothing but seaweed and yogurt one year; she talked of moving to New Zealand; Muriella knew all this from Marjorie), would want to listen to her too. This was the big question, and one on which, she realized, suddenly queasy, a lot depended. This was what she wanted from Julia Sternberg: someone who would ask her what she thought about things, about books and articles (not that she was reading enough articles, but she wanted to), perhaps even about religions and wars, at least not about good hotels or restaurants or how someone's son was doing at medical school or how the preparations for a wedding were stressing everybody out.

And also what she wanted was to see how Julia did that, how she lived alone with her French artist or whatever he was, how she had avoided the graduation parties and engagements that all of her other friends' daughters had gone through; she wanted the thrill of Julia's insanity, if that's what it was, or just her pretentious bohemianism; whatever it was, it was something that Muriella had never had, at Julia's age or at any age.

Which brought her back to the rack of silk and linen summer clothes in neutral shades and black (lots of black, far too much for summer, in Arthur's view), all of which made her look thin and bony and sagging and would mark her, on any street in the Junction, to any drunken roofer or pretentious little rich girl art history student (not that she was thinking of Julia here; she should not judge her so quickly), as not just pathetic and vulnerable but as actually offensive, as a target for spite.

She pulled out a white linen pantsuit and put it back again.

Why every piece of clothing or smear of makeup was a source of so much agonized indecision was something she did know: it was because she, Muriella, had stepped, a year and a half ago, first from an everyday world in normal colours and lighting—a world in which she had not been happy, certainly, and in which she had been always conscious of slight, of being dismissed, not just by Arthur but by her son, her neighbours, by the world in general; the world had rarely asked her to speak, and when it had, it had jeered at the result—into that dazzling bright overexposure of pain, and that light had gradually and almost imperceptibly faded and now she found herself in a completely new world of opaque surfaces which she did not know how to judge, a world in which it appeared that there was no inside, only outside, that every judgement made by people in the world was made on what things and people looked like (and here she was thinking particularly of television, its cycle of convulsing muscle and breast, its sweat-soaked bikinis, its prismatic vision in which everybody was exactly twenty-three, which she had been watching a lot lately, with horror and fear and a vague regret).

She knew she was thinking in this strange way because, although she was certainly not interested in dating yet, although she had not even been fantasizing about a man to take care of her (she was taking care of herself, just fine), she was at least beginning to be conscious of the fact that no man had come calling, no man had flirted with her, no man had even asked her out for coffee, for a year and a half. She pushed this thought out of her mind like a piece of furniture shrouded in a sheet.

She chose the slimming corduroy pants. If Julia did not appreciate them, that was Julia's problem. Then Muriella called a taxi; she wasn't going to leave the Saab parked on Julia's street.

When Mrs. Pent arrived, walking straight in, Julia Sternberg was standing on her futon, which was the only way to reach the closet. She had just picked a denim skirt and a grey tank top in a sweatshirty sort of material, because it was so hot, hoping that Mrs. Pent would not forget that students' houses were not air-conditioned and dress up too much and sit there in the dank and dim living room growing uncomfortable. Julia did not put on a bra, even though the tank top was tight and thin, and she knew she really should, since she didn't want Mrs. Pent to think she was showing off, but she did, in fact, want to show off, a little; it helped to have some power with her mother's friends; they could be so overpowering. She heard Mrs. Pent opening the front door and calling, "Hello! Hello!" just as Julia's mother would have done, either assuming the doorbell didn't work (which it didn't) or just assuming that Julia was not an adult and could not be expected to be rolling naked on the living-room floor or merely desirous of answering her own door since it was her own door, like an adult, but this only irritated Julia for a second, for when she ran down she saw Mrs. Pent standing on the linoleum that smelled of cat urine and she looked glowing and youthful and hip in her embroidered pants. She looked sexier than Julia would ever be, although her face was long and not beautiful, but she seemed confident about it. Julia wondered why she was still single.

They tried sitting in the garden but the smell of garbage was too strong, so they packed and set up a new camp in the living room, which was dim but at least cool, and they sat on the cushions after trying the straight-backed chairs. Mrs. Pent hesitated only a second before folding her legs under her on the floor.

Julia went into the stained kitchen and took out the cake she had bought at the sad supermarket (the only one, unless you wanted the Jamaican shop where she had very determinedly tried to be pleasant, but would not go into again). It was a yellow coffee cake with nuts stuck to the top with icing that looked like sperm. She put the kettle on for tea. Tea was one thing she had a lot of, in many varieties.

When she brought the tray back in, Mrs. Pent was leaning her back against the kerosene heater. "What is this?" she asked mildly.

"It's a heater, because the heat is really bad here, and it really scares me, because I don't know where Pascal found the stuff to fill it, and also because you're not suppposed to have it in an unventilated room or it will suck all the oxygen out and kill you, so I'm wondering how you're supposed to heat a ventilated room."

"Yes," said Mrs. Pent. "Ventilation rather defeats the purpose of heating, doesn't it?"

So Julia found herself laughing, and talking right away, talking as she hadn't to anyone since Pascal left, indeed even before Pascal left. She told Mrs. Pent that the house next door, which seemed to house at least eight adult Jamaicans, had had a police raid on it one afternoon, which she had watched with some fright but also some pleasure from an upstairs window, kneeling to peer over the sill. Julia had wondered if there would be gunshots.

Mrs. Pent was not as shocked as she could have been by this, so Julia tried another story.

"They're dismantling the factory across the street," she said. "It was just getting emptier and emptier, until I finally realized that's what they were doing. It's the strangest thing, this neighbourhood. It's just dying." Julia wanted Mrs. Pent to find this glamorous, for some reason. Perhaps because she herself did. And perhaps because she had been writing all this in her diary and was proud of what she had written. "There was always the sound of work, you know, machinery, even at night when I slept, and I would have these factory dreams because of the forklifts backing up, and the clanging. I would dream about airports, you know." She laughed a little. "And one night I woke up and there was no banging, no sound like metal, I don't know, caterpillar tracks backing up on concrete. And I realized that was really strange. So I kneeled at the window and I looked down, and the big yard was still a big bright orange square in the lamps, but it was totally empty and the forklifts were all lined up and still, and I realized I'd never seen the factory quiet before, and that they'd emptied out of the yard all of those stacks of drums which I never knew what they contained. It was just a big square of orange concrete in silence." She was talking from her diary. She tried to remember what she had written. "It was like a big landing strip by a railway track. It was really eerie."

Mrs. Pent was listening and munching cake as if she was waiting for the point of the story.

"Anyway," said Julia. "There's no point to the story. It was just eerie."

"I'm sure."

"Because you know I'd never really seen anyone go in or out of that factory. I had no idea even if the forklifts had human drivers. Strange."

"Don't you feel nervous at all? At night?"

"No. Not at all. Well. Sometimes. It gets pretty empty. Just walking from the subway, when you get to the bridge over the tracks. I have to walk over it, and it's pretty empty. It's kind of glamorous, though, too." Julia sipped her tea. "Everything's closing around here. Every day there is one less, I mean one fewer corner store or video store. There used to be a GO train stop, right where the footbridge is. I think it's closed too. I never see anyone there. You know there are streets around here that are still dry, you know, you can't sell any alcohol. There are no liquor stores, and the restaurants aren't licensed. So there are all these little pizza joints and falafel counters and they are so sad, they just die, one after another, and the little two-storey buildings stay empty and get grimier for three months and then another pizza room opens and dies, it's like, it's like amoebas trying to reproduce in a beaker of lye or something." Her diary again.

Mrs. Pent snorted, so that was good, she could keep going.

"I mean it's heroic and futile and they keep being born and dying and being born and dying."

"It is sad. It's very sad. But I do wonder if it's dangerous at all."

Julia realized, as she spoke, that she hadn't really spoken to anyone seriously for a few days. "You know, I was walking along Keele, in the zone that's like blasted, it's this strip north of Dundas that looks like Kabul or something."

Mrs. Pent laughed out loud this time and slopped tea.

"That's rude, I know," said Julia, "and it's not funny because obviously I've never been to Kabul and I'm sure it's quite horrific there and one shouldn't really joke, it's not funny."

"Oh," said Mrs. Pent, "yes it is."

"Okay. It is. Anyway, you know there's one side of the street, I think it's on Keele, that's dry, and the other side is, what do you call it? If it has a licence? Because it's in another ward."

"Wet," said Mrs. Pent decisively.

"Okay, wet, and the side that's wet is much cleaner, and there are people in the restaurants. The other side is like a patch of skin that's become gangrenous and died and it should have been, you know, shaved off long ago. It's like it had turned all black. And of course my house is on the dry side."

"Of course," said Mrs. Pent happily. She helped herself to another slice of the yellow cake with the semen icing.

"But the wet side isn't much better. The other day, in the afternoon, this guy, a man, comes out of this restaurant, on the wet side, which is called like Eritrea or Addis Ababa, which they all are, and he stops and he just throws himself onto the pavement. It seemed like he did it deliberately. Didn't say a word, just threw himself down, face first. And the sound, the sound his head made when it hit, you could have heard it across the street, it was chilling. It was like the sound a watermelon makes when you tap it."

"Oh, don't."

"I know. It was gruesome. And then he just curled up on his side and began vomiting. With his eyes closed."

"Oh, Julia." Mrs. Pent put her plate down.

"Sorry. But I guess that's why they've kept my side of the street dry for so long."

There was a silence after this. Julia poured some more tea.

"So your friend, your ex, I guess, does he visit at all?"

"He might. I'm not sure. He's in Montreal. I haven't heard from him for a while. We're still looking for a third roommate. He's still paying two-thirds of the rent because he knows I couldn't. Which is great."

There was a silence, during which Julia wondered if the vomiting story had not been appropriate. She didn't know why she wanted Mrs. Pent to hear her reflections on the neighbourhood. Perhaps because no one else would. There was really no point to diaries, when it came down to it. "I find it so interesting around here. I write it all down."

"Really? Now that is interesting."

"Mmm. I guess. I'm trying to write something about the breakup. I guess. I don't know what it's about. It was Pascal, actually, who encouraged me to write. He got me writing something every day. But it ends up being a diary. So I try to write about the neighbourhood. The factory, and stuff. Do you know there's a Little Malta in this neighbourhood?"

"What does that mean?"

"I was walking and I saw all these Maltese crosses and Malta Bakery and stuff and sure enough the city had put up street signs that said Maltaville or Rua Malta or something." Julia subsided. Mrs. Pent was only nodding out of politeness. "Only in this city, I mean."

"Yes."

"I mean I like to walk through a place like that and think that tomorrow I'll be downtown in my grown-up costume, skirt and tights and everything, lining up for Second Cup like everybody else, you know, like somebody with a productive role in society who just wants to get a better job. And when I come home, when I come back here, I'll be as far from it as if I were in Hamilton or somewhere, I don't know, in Bracebridge or somewhere. It's not like a city at all here."

"That's so exciting, that you're working in a gallery. It must be stimulating."

Julia put her head back and opened her mouth wide but no sound came out. "*Really* not."

Mrs. Pent looked alarmed. "Why not?"

"Well, I'm just an assistant. I'm like a secretary. Not even. And the art is . . . well, it's mostly photography, not all of it, but a lot of it, and it's all nice photos for . . ." She had been about to say *for the living rooms of divorced women*. "It's not art that I find exciting."

"But still, it's, it's . . . isn't it a good experience?"

Julia thought about this. "There are some things about it that I like. When I get there in the morning I'm usually alone there for a while, and it's a really pretty space. The light comes in in a nice way. And it's all white, and there is a hardwood floor. It's a really beautiful floor. The light comes in this, this one band." Julia made a slicing move-ment with a long, pale arm. "And it angles across the room for about a half an hour. It's like a hand on a clock." She watched her own arm dance in front of her. Her eyes widened for a second. "And for a while I'm answering the phone and imagining I'm the only one who works there and I've actually done something with my life and opened my own fine art gallery and am not just sitting there waiting for something to happen to me, which I am, I guess. I'm wait-ing for Diane to arrive and send me out for coffee." She dropped her arm and looked up at Mrs. Pent and smiled. Here Julia couldn't resist using her diary again, for it was quite good. "Diane arrives at exactly the moment the stripe of light disappears."

Mrs. Pent smiled back. "But you have done something with your life. You're finishing a degree, you're working in an art gallery."

Julia closed her eyes for a second. When she opened them she said, "At first I liked listening to Diane and Angelica talk about the ugly painters." She felt her face heating up. She was going to be inappropriate again now.

Mrs. Pent snorted again.

"I don't know why they're all ugly, but they are, the women, anyway, who are mostly lesbians if they're doing installation stuff, or they're just little mousy good girls if they're doing painting. Which is what I am, I suppose, so I should find it comforting, but I don't." She couldn't believe she was talking like this. It wasn't like her at all. But Mrs. Pent had upset her about the degree. "At first I found the way they looked or the way they didn't care about how they looked a real relief, you know, after Montreal, because everyone cares so much there it gets stressful, and I don't care what I look like. At all. But now I have to admit I just find it ugly and sad and I wish everybody combed their hair after a while."

The windows rattled as a bassmobile passed outside. Then the house was silent again, as if they were in a farmhouse in the country.

"I think," said Mrs. Pent, "that we all get confused about these issues half the time."

Julia felt mean. She said, "Diane and Angelica, they own the gallery, of course they're beautiful still, of course. They wear makeup and long black skirts every day. But now I realize all they're really talking about is money, about who is showing where and how unlikely it is they're going to get a show in New York. It's depressing, to hear them talk. It's just like anything else, like listening to English students at Trinity talking about publishing. All those bright boys ready to kill each other all the time."

Mrs. Pent sighed. "I know the kind you mean. They were in my classes too."

"They're being so very aggressive with each other all the time, you know they're really hurting each other, they're all sore inside, and they can't admit anything."

"They're just insecure."

"I ran into one guy recently, a boy I knew from school, the other day, he was in my post-colonial course, and he was very bright and everything, but the very first thing he asked me was did I finish my degree. Because we all should have finished this year. And he had some kind of idea that he hadn't seen me for a while. He was just dying to tell me he was beginning an M.A. in the fall."

"Wait a minute. You didn't—"

"It's because of boys like that that I quit. I'm not going to miss them rattling off their academic achievements to each other."

"You what?" Mrs. Pent had put her teacup down and was sitting very straight.

Julia folded her legs under her and wrapped herself tight with her arms. "I quit. I quit school."

"No. Really?"

"I didn't finish. And I'm not going back."

"No. I don't believe this. Julia. Really." Mrs. Pent had her hands raised to her face. Julia thought this reaction was a little excessive. She looked as if she was going to cry about it. She said, "But you're so good at it. Aren't you?"

"I don't know," said Julia, who knew that Mrs. Pent was being ridiculous but was nevertheless about to cry herself. "That's just it, I never knew."

"But you did so well, your marks were so good, your mother—"

"My marks were good. But I was too stressed out all the time. I could never get anything in on time, and I was always miserable about, about whether . . . you know, it was very competitive there too. If you spoke out in class, someone would always disagree with you, and it seemed, I don't know, confrontational."

"But you could handle that."

Julia felt her shoulders sagging forward, her head dropping. She pulled her knees up and wrapped her arms around them. "Yes, sure I could. I don't know. I never liked it. I could do the work, but I didn't want to get competitive about it." She knew all of a sudden that this was about all she would be able to say about this. This topic was now over. "That cake isn't all that bad, actually." She leaned forward to stick her finger into the sticky icing and knocked over her teacup, which splashed some inoffensive liquid onto the ancient carpet. She blinked at the spreading stain. Mrs. Pent had already got up to look in the kitchen for a cloth, and Julia called after her that she didn't need to. It was lucky, though, because when they were seated again there was perhaps a chance that they wouldn't have to talk about Julia's education again.

"So," said Julia. "How are you? Are you . . ." She didn't know how to ask about men.

Mrs. Pent said, "You know, really, I can't get over this. I really don't think this is a good idea for you. I can't tell you how much I—"

"Mrs. Pent, you know I really can't—"

"Please, please don't call me that. You make me feel ancient."

"Muriella, I can't talk about myself any more. I don't know why but I can't. I'm more interested in you right now. Are you interested in . . . are you, are you—"

"Am I seeing anyone?"

"It's none of my business."

Mrs. Pent sighed. "No, I'm not. I mean, I would be, but there isn't. Anyone."

"But I mean do you think you're ready? To see someone."

"I don't know. I don't suppose so."

"Because you know I know that feeling. I can't imagine seeing anyone else right now. It's too soon."

Mrs. Pent laughed softly. "Yes. It's not quite the same."

"Oh I know. Of course. Of course it's not. Sorry."

There was no more tea. Julia resisted an urge to stick her fingers into the icing and mush it up on the plate. If she had been alone she would have done this.

Mrs. Pent said, "I am so impressed that you're trying gardening. I wouldn't have . . ." Decisively, she took the last finger of cake. "I'm finding it difficult, myself."

"I tried," said Julia, with relief at finding this even safer topic, "because it seemed like something you're supposed to do."

Mrs. Pent laughed, very deeply and naturally. "That's so funny. That's exactly what I feel. Everyone talks about it all the time and I . . . I suppose I feel left out. So I'm trying it. But—"

"So am I," said Julia, excited by this, "and it's fun when it works, I mean my tomatoes were lovely, when I got them, but it's such hard work, and—"

"It is hard work," said Mrs. Pent, taking a large bite of the semen cake. "And it just doesn't work most of the time. At least I can't make it work."

"So why do we do it?"

"Because everyone seems to enjoy it and care about it so much. And it does look pretty when—"

"When someone else does it."

"Sure. Nothing against gardens per se." Julia felt a little giddy, as if she would chortle hysterically at any minute. This was better than a diary. She said, "It's our parents, I suppose."

"What is?"

"I don't know. Our parents, well my parents, and all my friends' parents, took it very—I mean I guess it was some sort of indicator of order. That if your garden was all squiffy then it was a bad sign of your self, or your own moral order, or something. It wasn't respectable."

"But you're young. You don't have to think like that."

"I know. But I feel guilty. I do. In not doing something about that back garden. It seems so lax. My mother would be shocked."

"Well," said Mrs. Pent, "I'm not shocked. I have no interest in it myself. But here I am, trying too, I don't know why. I suppose it's just a symbol of taking control of your environment generally."

Julia sighed.

"It's a bit like taking care of your appearance. You feel you have to keep it up."

They both laughed at this, for reasons that were unclear to Julia, but she felt like laughing with Mrs. Pent, perhaps in relief that not everybody in the world was quite as stupid as they seemed.

And she had not spoken about Pascal at all, which was a good sign.

VII

"I WANT TO PROPOSE," SAID DEEPAK, "that we end the blind business."

There was a silence filled with sticky chewing. Brian got up to get some more food. He hesitated between the chickpea roti and the chickpea salad.

Jasminka, at the head of the table, and Iris Warshavsky seemed to be struggling with their rotis. The ends of the wrapped bread had grown ragged and were leaking chickpeas in gravy. The conference table was speckled with errant chickpeas. Mrs. Pent was using her plastic fork to pick at a salad on a plate before her. She said, "Do we do things with the blind?"

Deepak's mouth was now full of chickpea, but he shook his head roughly and waggled his index finger at her. His eyes bulged with the urge to speak. He put one hand to his mouth.

Iris Warshavsky swallowed and spoke. "What blind business?" Iris's hair, which she cultivated like a banner of resistance, was particularly wild today, as if she had teased it with a rake before coming. Her reading glasses, which hung from coloured strings, slid up and down her chest as she breathed. She breathed with some difficulty, as a result of asthma. Much of her poetry, when she had written poetry, had been about her asthma.

"He means the adjudication process," said Jasminka.

Brian had filled his plate with chickpea salad and returned to the table. His shirt was sticking to him. There was a rattling little fan near the window which was circulating hot air. The window was nailed shut because an air conditioner was installed in it, and the air conditioner would not have functioned correctly unless the window were sealed. But the air conditioner was switched off, because Jasminka and Deepak both had allergies to air conditioning. Jasminka acquired a headache at the least exposure to artificially treated air, and Deepak had a violent passage-closing reaction that bordered on anaphylactic shock, so he had explained.

The air in the room was thick with roti. Brian sat gingerly, experiencing an expanding of air inside his lower abdomen that he put down to the pervasiveness of chickpeas in his lunch. His plumbing gurgled and hissed.

"I mean," said Deepak, wiping his mouth, "the no names on the applications thing." He held up his hand to indicate a pause while he concentrated on working on something inside his mouth with his tongue. When he had finished, he said, "I don't think we should tolerate blind applications any more."

"I agree," said Iris Warshavsky. And she straightened the drapery of her dress, which had somehow become bunched around her in very large, very stiff cotton folds. It was a very large dress. Brian noticed for the first time that the patterns on it were not just due to fading, as he had first supposed, but were tie-dyed flowers or snowflakes. They had faded so as to look like creases in the fabric, but they were not.

Brian glanced around the table and noticed that Mrs. Pent had looked immediately at him for explanation. He had an idea of the theory behind this, but he did not propose to show his hand until the argument had become clear, and so he stared fixedly at the tabletop. A chickpea rolled slowly before him. An alarming shift of gases inside him was momentarily dangerous, but passed.

"This is something we had better vote on," said Jasminka. "All those in favour—"

"I'm not sure I understand," said Brian. He felt a heat spreading over his face and ears. "Deepak, could you just go over what it is that—"

"Because of the appropriation issue," said Iris Warshavsky.

"Well, look at the trouble it's got us into already," said Deepak. "We funded that fellow writing plays about housing projects and basketball, we thought they were important issues—which they are—and it turns out it's that Gerald Leary fellow."

Iris Warshavsky clicked her tongue.

"And you have a hard time with that," boomed Jasminka. Her voice was rich and round.

"I have a very hard time with that."

Jasminka sighed. "Perhaps we should be clear on what the issues—"

"That guy," said Iris Warshavsky, "that guy lives out in the projects at Jane and Finch for a few years—"

"Ten years, I think it was," said Deepak.

"—and now look at him profit by it, he's made it totally his shtick, and I don't buy it. I just don't buy it."

"Anyone could do it," said Deepak. "Anyone could come along and write about experiences that they . . . that aren't theirs. That aren't their experiences. Experiences that don't belong to them."

"Anyone could come along," said Iris Warshavsky, "and write about anything they wanted."

Brian stared fixedly at the chickpea. He was hoping Mrs. Pent would not say anything. You had to pick your battles here. You had to decide which hillock you wanted to die on. Then he felt guilty in the silence and wanted to say something constructive and so said, "But how would you know, just from the names, if someone was . . . if someone was appropriate for a . . . for a particular subject or not?"

Iris Warshavsky snickered. "We know most of the names."

Deepak smiled. "We know who is who."

"But there might be some names we don't know," said Mrs. Pent. "There might be someone, someone new. You wouldn't be able to recognize someone's—I mean it's someone's race were talking about, isn't it? I mean unless you wanted to have a little box you ticked off for different races. Which would be, well . . ." Mrs. Pent giggled appealingly. "Well, I hate to say it, but it would be racist, wouldn't it?"

There was a pause that rumbled with digestion. Brian noticed that someone besides him was suffering from a surfeit of chickpeas. He put a hand to his face. A cloud of embarrassment passed over the committee. The little fan whined like a nag, aware of its own futility.

Jasminka raised her eyebrows and shuffled some papers on the table. She cleared her throat for a speech. Brian wanted to put his hands over his ears. He wanted to dive under his chair.

He agreed with Jasminka, basically, that Mrs. Pent was not qualified to judge these things, not qualified to judge the suffering and the anger that Jasminka and Deepak had experienced, that this was not a rational argument, it was an argument that it was Jasminka's turn to win, and win it she would, and it was to help her to win it that they were all there, and still he did not want to see Mrs. Pent being destroyed. It may be necessary, but it still was not pleasant.

When her voice came, it was like low notes on a cello. It was as thick as hummus. "You don't need to explain to me," she breathed, "what is racist."

"No," said Muriella. "No no. I don't mean to—"

"Or to Deepak."

"No. No no no. Of course not."

Now came a long silence, the longest yet.

At the end of it, Jasminka muttered, "The question of the blind applications is a difficult one. I think we're all aware of that. As you, Brian, have pointed out, and we're grateful for this dialogue, I'm sure we'd all agree on this, as you've pointed out, Brian, there are advantages to looking at the work, at the work of the artists being submitted, and that there is an argument for trying to be objective about this, about the work and not the artist's qualifications."

"*Objective*," hissed Deepak. "Objective meaning we use Western paradigms of education and formal—"

Jasminka raised a silencing hand. "Yes, I was getting to this, Deepak, there are problems with the concept of objectivity, particularly given that not all of the artists have the same educational background and privilege and sense of their voices being licensed."

Brian patted his pocket for his pen. He had heard Jasminka using this word "license" before and he knew it was now a significant word, one that he should learn to use. He scrawled on a paper napkin, *Licensed voices*. That would be very useful.

Jasminka continued, "One of the mandates of this committee, and of the whole Action Council, from the very beginning, has been to give voices to those who have been or who have felt silenced or not licensed to represent their experiences or their communities."

Brian glanced at Mrs. Pent, who was now looking out the window. It was hard to follow Jasminka closely once she got on about communities; one felt as though one knew the rest. There was often good stuff in it, though.

"And so we don't want to exclude artists from the granting process who . . . whose work alone . . . we want to make sure, to ensure, that things like their work in the community or their status in the community or their relevant life experience is considered here."

"And also to make sure," said Iris Warshavsky in a rather higher voice, "that there aren't people pretending to be who they aren't, and using the experiences of—"

Mrs. Pent spoke sharply. "But isn't writing all about pretending? To be someone you aren't?" She was red, and so was Iris Warshavsky.

Again Jasminka's heavy hand rose to great effect. She was still speaking slowly. "This is an issue that is a little more complex, as well, Muriella. First of all, I don't think that all writing is about pretending. It might be about discussing real issues. But one can also see how it might be a problem, for example, to deal with a writer who created or dealt in a great many stereotypes, say ethnic stereotypes for example, and then claimed that he or she had lived through the reality of a certain situation."

"I'm not sure I follow you," said Mrs. Pent.

"I'm not sure I can explain it any better."

"There was a guy," said Brian, to Mrs. Pent, "who wrote all these native fables, or at least he said they were based on native fables, and it turns out, I'm not sure if they were really native or not but he still offended a lot of native people by making it his thing."

"I see," said Mrs. Pent.

"At least I think that's how it went."

Another silence.

"There was a lot of pain," murmured Jasminka, "about that episode."

Mrs. Pent looked down at her lap.

"I don't mind," said Brian after a while, "the names on the applications because I guess someone's previous career is relevant." No one answered this, so he said, "And as you say, Iris, it's not as if we wouldn't recognize every applicant, or most applicants, by their style, anyway, and what they write about. So it's kind of fake to pretend it's blind, anyway." He sighed and decided to stop talking. He didn't know why he wanted this discussion to just stop, no matter how it ended. Besides, it always ended the same way.

Jasminka said, "Do we need a vote on this issue?"

No one replied. Brian shook his head. Muriella was staring at the window, red-faced. She was fingering her bead necklace.

"I will mark it as unanimous, then," said Jasminka. "There will be no more blind adjudication process for grants."

The next issue was easier. The city had donated some money for a Developing Regions Exchange program, which would enable a foreign writer to visit and be a public writer-in-residence for a period of six months. The writer would be one who could contribute to an understanding of cultural diversity, and so would be from a Developing Region, which meant, as Brian understood it, what they used to call the Third World. A local writer would then be sent in exchange to the Developing Region, which would also contribute to his/her understanding of cultural diversity and global culture. It was clear that the local writer could, in fact, be from any culture, as exposure to Developing Regions was seen to be good in a bracing way for even the most recalcitrant of the elitist establishment, and so the application process would be, as Jasminka delicately put it, "open."

The federal government, through the Department of External Affairs, had miraculously matched the money from the city. The city would provide or renovate a guest apartment for the visiting artist, and External Affairs would provide air travel and a monthly stipend.

This was before the election. The new mayor had cancelled all funding for the program—along with the City Core Development Reading Program, the Community Theatre Front, the Scream in the Park, the Holistic Dance Collective, and the Village Roots School Drumming Project, leaving the Arts Action Council as the only still standing municipal arts organization (the opera and the ballet had long ago been left to fend for themselves, and so were not part of this discussion), albeit with a greatly reduced budget (which explained, in part, why they had not been given their regular catered lunch, but a homemade lunch provided, with much publicity, by Deepak's boyfriend and Jasminka's girlfriend). The mayor had even said on a panel discussion on the rock-video television channel that he thought the various arts organizations were a divisive influence on the community, although he had not explained why before repeating that the arts were clearly a provincial funding responsibility, if not a federal one, and that most residents of the city were hard-working taxpayers who did not feel they were represented by this type of minority-interest group anyway.

"The question," growled Jasminka, "is whether we abandon this initiative altogether or continue to look for an alternate source of funding for the guest residence."

"Couldn't we just find a host apartment for her while she is here?" said Iris.

"You mean someone volunteer an apartment?" said Deepak.

"Probably not mine," said Brian. He smiled hopefully. Nobody even chuckled.

Mrs. Pent looked particularly disconcerted by this discussion. She had turned red again and was staring wide-eyed at the tabletop.

"You mean billet him, or her, with a member of the community?" said Deepak.

"Why not? If the idea is exposure to the issues and problems of the community—"

"Would there be any recompense, any remuneration for the member of the community who volunteered—"

"That's just the problem," boomed Jasminka. "There would not be. We do not have any budget for this. For the residence expenses, anyway. Unless," she said with a slow smile, "unless we can come up with some kind of wealthy patron who wanted to . . ." She paused. "To *donate* an apartment!" (A few chuckles.) "In the current climate, I don't think that's likely. And I don't imagine any of *us* have the resources to take on a free boarder."

"It certainly won't be *my* apartment," said Deepak, and

Jasminka and Iris roared. Deepak beamed, triumphant.

Brian was watching Mrs. Pent, who still had not looked up from the table and was frowning. Occasionally her eyes flickered up at Jasminka and down again. Her mouth was pursed, as if she was preparing to say something.

Brian said, "Mrs.—Muriella, are you . . . are you okay?"

"What?" She jerked her head up. Her face was on fire.

"You look . . . I don't know."

"Oh I'm fine. I'm fine."

"All right," said Jasminka. "I suppose the only option is to approach the provincial level, although frankly I do not entertain great hopes of—"

"I have a possibility," said Mrs. Pent quietly.

"—or to abandon the project altogether, which would be one more example of—"

"I have a suggestion," said Mrs. Pent.

Jasminka raised her eyebrows.

Mrs. Pent spoke very rapidly. "It's just an idea. If no one likes it it's totally fine by me. I just thought I would throw it out as a suggestion. Anyway. I would really, I really feel that I have a responsibility to do as much as I can for the community, and I really would like to get involved more in this sort of, in this sort of process." She swallowed. Deepak began gathering his papers. Jasminka looked at her watch. "And I have a very large house."

Deepak stilled his hand.

"It's a very large and comfortable house. In . . ." She was clasping and unclasping her hands. "And I have a lot of guest rooms. I mean I have a whole separate apartment with its own kitchen and bathroom, which is unoccupied, since I no longer have a . . ." She coughed.

The table was listening very closely. Jasminka had folded her arms, which was an effortful procedure.

"It would be very comfortable, and it wouldn't cost me anything, and I would be delighted to contribute to the artistic—"

"Where is your house?" said Iris Warshavsky, rather sharply, Brian thought.

"It's in Stilwoode Park. It's a little group of houses on a private road just north of—"

"*Stilwoode Park*." Jasminka sat back massively, a down-turned smile fixed on her face. Her turban swayed as she nodded. She seemed grimly satisfied with something. "Stilwoode Park. How lovely."

Brian was trying to picture Stilwoode Park. He had walked through it on an architectural tour once, with a girl who wore khaki shorts and vast sandals, whom he had not been able to seduce nevertheless. He remembered a five-bar gate blocking a road, an entrance overgrown with hanging greenery of archaic description—willows, vines, something he didn't know how to describe but which looked expensive. Even the gate, on a road facing a concrete compound for city buses, looked like something transplanted, being the only man-made wooden object on that street; it had looked like something from a Reynolds painting, something from Mother Goose: Brian pictured a girl in a bonnet opening it.

Brian looked at Mrs. Pent with a new interest. She did not look, with her brassy red hair, like an inhabitant of Stilwoode Park. He had always assumed she was Jewish or Eastern European or at the very least from Montreal. Muriella was not the kind of name one found in Stilwoode

Park. It was the kind of name one found in twin-garaged seventies bunkers past the end of the subway line.

"My husband died a year ago," said Mrs. Pent. "A year and a half. And the house is so . . . I have no need for all the space in the house. And this completely self-contained apartment would be perfect for a writer. It doesn't have a separate entrance, but it's quite—"

"Why," asked Deepak, frowning, "would you have a self-contained apartment in a large house?"

Mrs. Pent looked down at the table.

Jasminka chuckled. "It's for servants, Deepak," she said in her lowest voice. "Well. This might be a possibility." She was nodding and smiling. "This is a real possibility."

"It's kind of a weird introduction to the city," said Iris Warshavsky. "I mean it's kind of not a really representative area."

"How long is the residency for?" asked Brian.

"External Affairs has offered us the living expenses stipend for six months."

"Six months," said Brian. "Mrs.—Muriella, are you sure you want to live with someone, I mean a stranger, for six months?"

Mrs. Pent shrugged, smiled. "I have no idea."

"We're talking about an artist. I don't know if you really know . . . if you've really had any, I mean a lot of experience, you know, forgive me for saying so, with what living with an artist can be like, you know—"

"I," said Mrs. Pent, looking suddenly straight at him, "am an artist myself."

"Right," said Brian. He paused for a second, trying to remember what art Mrs. Pent could possibly be referring to.

As far as he knew she had published a children's book during the Depression or something. He didn't know of any art. "But I mean an artist possibly from a very different background—"

"Definitely from a very different background," said Jasminka.

"Well, that's the idea, isn't it?" said Mrs. Pent, still staring at Brian. "That's why we're *all* here, isn't it Brian?"

"The experience is meant to benefit both the host and the visitor," said Jasminka. "I think it might be very beneficial to . . ." She opened a wet smile. "To the city, and to Stilwoode Park in particular."

Brian nodded. He looked away from Mrs. Pent. "I think it's a terrific idea, don't get me wrong. I'm just wanting to make sure Muriella knows what she's getting into."

"I have no idea what I'm getting into," she said, suddenly standing up. "We'll just have to see, won't we?" She looked at her watch. "I might surprise you, Brian." She began putting her papers into her voluminous bag.

"I will talk to the city about this plan," said Jasminka. "And at the next meeting, we'll decide on an application process, and the eligible countries and so on. And we'll begin the selection process."

"That," said Iris Warshavsky, "will be the fun part."

VIII

BRIAN STEPPED ONTO BATHURST STREET and breathed in the hot air. There was a jackhammer in a pit across the road, a cloud of dust. A streetcar ground the steel rails with its steel wheels; the concrete vibrated. Mrs. Pent emerged from the office in dark glasses, fumbling in a canvas tote bag. She pulled out a flash of car keys and smiled at him.

Brian smiled and opened his mouth and closed it again. He wanted to say something about the meeting, something conciliatory. There was no one around to hear. "Well," he said. "This is very exciting, isn't it? What you're doing."

"Well. It is exciting." She was peering up and down the street. She looked at her watch. The car keys tinkled. They had black rubber handles and some kind of logo. They looked like keys to a jet.

Brian watched her push her coppery hair behind a pale ear. Aside from a web of delicate scoring around her eyes, her skin was smooth, almost translucent. He looked for her green eyes behind her glasses, but the lenses were black. He glanced down at her black linen wrap skirt with its long slit, which exposed a triangle of bare thigh and an entire calf, remarkably clear and unveined, and a strappy sandal with a heel. She did not seem the least bit hot; she seemed to have emerged from an air-conditioned room, and her car keys spoke of the next air-conditioned interior she would enter, one he pictured as black and scented with leather.

He wondered how old she was. At times he thought fifty-five, at times forty-five. Her blouse was open low but revealed only a freckled and rather bony chest, no cleavage.

And her neck was withered.

He looked away, narrowing his eyes in the sun. He wished he was the sort of person who owned a pair of sunglasses, but he never thought of it. "It gets a bit warm in there," he said.

"It was stifling."

"And it can get a bit stressful too. You know, sometimes when we start talking about things like—"

"Brian," she said suddenly, "I think you should come and see the apartment. I mean I think everybody on the committee should, eventually, take a look, just to see that we all agree that it's acceptable."

"Oh. I'd love to. I would be happy to."

"We could go right now."

"Oh. Right now?"

"Well, I'm expecting a friend of mine for tea. You're welcome to join us." She giggled, as if nervous, and controlled herself. "I think you'd love the house," she said.

"Oh, I'm sure I would." Brian felt a rage of heat on his face. He didn't know why it embarrassed him to think of entering Mrs. Pent's house. He did want to see a Stilwoode Park interior. But he did not want to have tea with some blue-haired lady. He made a show of consulting his watch, although he had nothing to do until he was to visit Jason's apartment at eight to play Age of Empires online. "Well, I would love to, but I actually have something—"

"Oh!" Mrs. Pent almost shouted. "There she is." She waved at a figure across the street. She was smiling.

Brian squinted through the dust to see a tall girl in loose jeans waiting to cross. She had a cloud of frizzy hair around her head, and a tiny top with thin straps on her shoulders. He watched her skip into the street and half run towards them. The top was thin as film and tight across her small breasts; her belly was bare and firm. Brian stiffened as he realized with the pain it always gave him that this girl was flawless, beautiful, that she was bringing a cloud of the impossibly feminine over the street to them like an impending storm, and that this would render him ugly and aware of his ugliness, that this would trouble him and silence him, which in turn would would force him to say cutting things, that from now on he would be trying to contain some anger which he never fully could. And then he started and opened his eyes wide, for as she approached he saw it was Julia Sternberg, from his college, from his very own post-colonial class, and he closed his eyes as if the street had cracked beneath him, feeling his stomach sink and his neck go cold, for she was really the worst for him, the worst kind, the kind of girl who knew people he would never know, who would always go out with unshaven boys taller than he, and whom he would always help with assignments and lecture about Joyce to and then mock to Jason Katz, behind her back. There was nothing but humiliation where girls like Julia Sternberg were involved. He smiled at her with the feeling that the effort was splitting his face, and said, "Hello." He laughed shortly.

But she was hugging Mrs. Pent, who was squealing somewhat. Finally, Mrs. Pent said, "This is Brian Silliman, who is on the committee with me."

"Sillwell. Hi Julia. We've met before. I was in your post-colonial—"

"Yes," she said soberly. "Hi Brian." She looked at the cracked pavement, indicating to Brian that she was already rendered miserable by this encounter and wished to be elsewhere.

"You've met?" Mrs. Pent was looking between them with an expression that could have been shock, horror, or physical illness, but which Brian guessed was probably meant to signify surprise.

Brian nodded grimly. "How do you two know each other?" he said.

Julia said, "It's *so* lovely to see you," and she took Mrs. Pent's hands and looked into her black lenses and they both squealed some more. Any sympathy Brian had had for Mrs. Pent had been burned away on this sidewalk. Now he wanted to see inside her house to visually memorize every scintillating detail of it and mentally ravage it, to set it afire with scorn. He would sack Stilwoode Park.

"Well, if I knew you two knew each other, I would have invited you to tea long ago," said Mrs. Pent. "Now you must come with us, Brian. I would love to have you both."

Julia said nothing.

Behind them, Jasminka and Deepak and Iris Warshavsky and Eulalia, the organization's secretary, bustled out of the building and locked it with much heavy breathing, as it took the wind out of Jasminka even to descend stairs, let alone to mount them. They were all whispering angrily. They looked at Brian and Mrs. Pent and Julia and looked away without a word.

Brian did not know what they were whispering about and did not want to know. He was suddenly exhausted. He was so depressed at the sight of them he felt quite self-destructive.

Between that hot boardroom and Mrs. Pent's shallow luxury he would choose the luxury. He would throw himself into Julia's presence as a despairing man leaps off a bridge.

"Sure," said Brian. "Thank you." He did not even bother to pretend to look at his watch.

They walked half a block to find Mrs. Pent's car, with the two women talking about gardening. Mrs. Pent was asking Julia whether she had had any luck with the dahlias and Julia laughed and said she hadn't even attempted dahlias and that Mrs. Pent had seen the little muddy square where she lived and that she was just a beginner, and Brian wondered what kind of person gardened at Julia's age—which must be a year younger than Brian's age, since she would be going into fourth year while he had just gradu-ated, say twenty-three at the most—and thought that you must really have grown up with gardening, with the idea that people gardened, to do it ever, that possibly rich peo-ple gardened from the age of six or nine or something, along with ballet lessons and riding and polo and listening to Bob Marley.

He grinned to himself at the Bob Marley. He would write such a novel of sadness and devastation. He got into Mrs. Pent's black car and sat in the back, on the black leather seats. The dashboard was walnut.

They entered the Park from a hidden northern entrance between two houses on a city street. And then they were crawling down a narrow lane on a hill, engulfed in ancient greenery. A tent of trees blocked out the sky. And between the trees were glimpses of lawn, gables, rosebeds, vaulted windows, leaded panes.

The sound of the city had vanished. There was not even the sound of a lawnmower. They passed a green tennis court, sunk in a sort of pit, thicketed with foliage. It was so overgrown it would have been camouflaged from attack from the air.

All the houses were similarly muffled, with brambles, ivy, swaying poppies, sunk in silence and earth, visible only by their vast sloping roofs. Some of the roofs had little mansard windows in them, the panes open, a square of darkness within. There were no cars (although Brian knew there were cottagey coach houses behind the servants' wings, hiding sleek dormant Jaguars, cached like weapons).

Brian had his face close to the window glass, squinting at every mansion that came in sight. They were mostly in a sort of neo-Gothic neo-Tudor style, some with half-timbering, all with diamond-leaded windows. It was the kind of place a fan of Tolkien would design: houses for rich Hobbits. It was as if you would enter each one of them and find a sleeping princess in an attic, or at least a sleeping nursemaid. There was a glaucous pond with somnolent swans. The whole place made you drowsy. It made you crave cake.

They parked in an earth-smelling garage, and walked the length of a tangled garden, with a pond and a fountain, under pergolas and past stone circles around empty flower beds (even Brian could tell the garden was a little undertended), to get to a tiny rear door. Mrs. Pent asked them to wipe their feet. Then they went through a kitchen and some cool halls, where there were a vast and bloody nineteenth-century oil, a sentimental sunset, and a startling and decadent bunch of flowers drooping in murky water. They passed open French doors that looked into salons filled with armchairs and more rugs, picture frames that weighed as much as Brian did, a dining room with a table so dark and heavy you could make human sacrifices on it, launch rockets from, a table behind which inquisitors could sit, a Star Chamber table. Then into a library with a great stone hearth, a floor of dark-red patterned rugs like moss underfoot, walls of books, and cracked leather sofas. Brian and Julia sank down into them and Mrs. Pent disappeared to make the tea. The library overlooked the garden. There was ivy creeping around the window edges.

Under a glass dome was a baroque clock that could have been made of gold. Possibly looted from some holocausted middle-European dukedom. Brian hoped to see half-unwrapped Pompeian statuary, an oak chest overflowing with doubloons.

Julia sat for a second, then rose and began studying the books, her back to Brian.

Brian looked up over the fireplace at the veneered oil painting of a hawkish man with a lined face, standing beside a grey desk.

He said to Julia, "So. You're in Mrs. Pent's book club?"

"I've been to one meeting so far, yes. I think she wants everyone to call her Muriella."

"Right. Are you enjoying the book club?"

As she turned towards him she was quite literally rolling her eyes. "Well, it's not academic or anything."

"It's more social than academic. I thought so."

"You wouldn't enjoy it. It's not *your* kind of thing at all."

There was something acid about the way she said this that made Brian's digestive system begin recalling the chickpea lunch. He bit his lip, then said, "Well, I think it's great that people are taking an interest in books at all."

"Especially women."

He paused. "What the hell does that mean? If you think I—"

"I think it's such a *scream*," shouted Muriella, as she entered with a tray, "that you two know each other. Were you close, at school? Do you have the same friends, the same circle of friends?"

Julia said nothing.

Brian said, "Not really. Julia was in a different set. You're friends with Suki Northwood, right?"

"We roomed together for a while."

"What I thought."

"And who were your friends, Brian?" said Muriella.

"You wouldn't know them. They're not from here."

"Neither am I."

"Oh," he said. "Where are you from?"

"Montreal, originally."

"Oh. So are you, right, Julia?"

"Mmm." Julia had a leather-bound book open and was frowning into it.

Brian decided he would take about another ten minutes of this. Muriella handed him a cup of tea. She passed a plate of packaged biscuits. He took a deep breath and said to Julia, "You're going into your final year, right?"

"No, actually."

"Oh. I thought you were in third year last year."

"Yes. I was. But I'm thinking I'm just going to leave it there."

"Really? You're dropping out?"

"Well, I guess you could look at it that way. I have a degree now, though, the three-year degree."

"A general degree. Of course. But you didn't want to go on and do just one more year to—"

Julia threw her head backwards onto the back of the sofa, looked up at the ceiling, and blew air out of puffed-up cheeks. The movement extended and exposed her neck, which was smooth and slender and throbbed slightly and caused Brian some pain. She gave a deep sigh. "No, I don't want to." She seemed about to say something defiant but instead looked sad and stopped.

Mrs. Pent was looking at her with crinkled eyes. Brian wondered what this matron, whom he had always found rather silly, although he admitted he didn't know her well, found in this unbearably superior and mysterious girl whose nipples were now, he noted with intestinal consternation, becoming visible in the library's leathery cool.

"You're welcome to join our book club," said Mrs. Pent.

"Thank you." He tried to laugh. "My whole life is a book club, though." He flicked a glance at Julia, but she was not noticeably rolling her eyes. She was back in her book. He wondered what it was. He briefly wished he had written it. "My mother's in a book club. In Barrie. It's weird. I read a lot, but we never come across a single book that we have both read. I think there's a different type of book for book clubs." Julia had not looked up. He spoke louder. "They bake a lot of cakes and bars. And they read a lot of books about slavery in the Deep South and the devastation of Hiroshima."

Mrs. Pent smiled tightly.

"So we haven't read any of the same books."

"That is odd," said Mrs. Pent, "isn't it?"

"Yes it is odd. So," he said, "Julia, where are you living now?"

Slowly, she looked up from her book. She kept a finger on her page. "Oh. In the Junction. Up at Dundas and Keele."

"I've seen it," said Mrs. Pent. "It's not the best neighbourhood, is it?"

"It's all right. I don't mind it."

"Julia's working at the Nady Molochy Gallery."

"Oh," said Brian. He understood the Junction residence idea now. Julia had gone visual-arty. She was working in a gallery and living in some massive industrial loft with an unshaven sculptor. He would never have to see her, then, really; she would pass out of his world and into that one and never argue with him about misogyny in V. S. Naipaul again. He relaxed a little. The world was less threatening when it followed predictable patterns. "You're curating there?"

She shook her head. Her ringlets writhed. "Just working there," she said in a quiet voice. She opened the book again.

Brian wanted to ask her if she was seeing anybody, but it would have been inappropriate here, or anywhere, really, but he did have some vague memory of an artist in her life, for some reason he thought of an Italian or a Frenchman, someone she knew from Montreal. But he couldn't remember the guy's name, and besides, maybe he didn't want to know. The thought that he was too scared to ask a pretty and probably stupid girl if she was seeing someone threw him into a further tremor of self-loathing, and so he could not help saying, "I'm starting an M.A. in the fall."

"That's so impressive," said Mrs. Pent.

Julia said nothing.

After twelve minutes, counted exactly by Brian's watch, of talking about what Brian thought he was going to study ("Theory," he said vaguely, hoping to escape discussion, but Mrs. Pent wanted an explanation, which was not easy, and which seemed to drive Julia further into depression and silence), Brian said, "Well, I really had better be going. Did you want to show me the apartment?"

And Mrs. Pent bounded up and said oh yes, of course, and led them both into the basement apartment which had its own patio on another level of the garden, with sliding-glass doors, under a deck, and a new kitchen with a stainless-steel fridge and a microwave, and a massive washer and dryer; all things Brian was missing from his own basement apartment, which was about half the size of this. He wondered if he could apply for the program next year.

Both he and Julia were enthusiastic about the space, which seemed to please Mrs. Pent. Brian said his goodbyes and Julia actually smiled at him as she shook his hand. Mrs. Pent directed him to the nearest bus stop. As the door closed behind him he thought he heard one of them let out a high-pitched sound, which could have been laughter.

IX

FENNA WILLIAMS BROUGHT IN TWO bottles of Fanta lemon on a tray. She smiled at the Canadian trade envoy, who still seemed too hot, even though there was air conditioning in the deputy minister's office.

"See what you can do for him," said the deputy minister.

"Well," said the Canadian. "I'll ask the culture people at External. They sometimes have these exchange programs or something. Maybe we can get him a teaching job somewhere."

"That would be perfect."

"As I say," said the Canadian, lunging for the Fanta, "we're very grateful for the tariff agreement, which we think is very reasonable, as I said, but anyway, we're very pleased. The beer manufacturers will be very pleased to have access to this market. So anything we can do on the cultural side . . . I'll look into it."

X

APPLICATION FORM

FULL NAME: *Marcus Lavallée Royston*

ADDRESS: *15 Government House Row,*
               Petite Colline, Dunstanton,
               St. Andrew's 17201

WORK ADDRESS (IF DIFFERENT FROM ABOVE):

1. DISCIPLINE (CHECK ONE):
   - ❑ Film
   - ❑ Video
   - ❑ Performance
   - ❑ Music (composition)
   - ❑ Multimedia
   - ❑ Dance (performance)
   - ❑ Dance (choreography)

   - ❑ Non-fiction arts writing
   - ❑ Fiction
   - ❑ Screenwriting
   - ❑ Drama
   - ?❑ Memoir
   - ?❑ Oral Tradition
   - ☒ Poetry

2. PROFESSIONAL HISTORY:

Please give details of your work(s), starting with the most recent, including dates of performance/publication.

I. BOOKS

In No One's Language: A Report on the Feasibility of the Teaching of Creole in State Schools (government report), St. Andrew's Government Press (Dunstanton, 1996).

How the Forest Reads: A Report on Literacy in Impoverished Areas (government report), St. Andrew's Government Press (Dunstanton, 1994).

The Rapture (poetry), Access Books (London, 1982). Winner Commonwealth Writers Prize for Canada and the Caribbean, 1982.

Island Eclogues (poetry), Kilmartin Press (London, 1980). Finalist for Air Scotland Poetry Prize, 1980.

A Hatred of Beauty (essays), Blackwell (London, 1976).

Distant Ships; Barefoot Threnody; The Cloister and the Beach: Three Plays by Marcus Royston (drama), Penguin (London, 1974).

Black Penelope (poetry), Faber and Faber (London, 1970). Finalist for Commonwealth Writers Prize, 1970.

The Tongue that Raised Me, the Tongue I Must Spit Out (poetry), Island Press (Dunstanton, 1968). Finalist for the Booker Prize, 1968.

II. PERIODICALS

Please see attached three sheets.

3. PROFESSIONAL QUALIFICATIONS AND EXPERIENCE:
(You may include here any work with community groups or
outreach programs.)

Education advisor, Ministry of Education, St. Andrew's,
    1995–2001.
Master of English, St. Hilda's School for Girls, St. Andrew's,
    1993–95
Writer-in-residence, University of Wyoming, Fall term, 1976.
Failed D.Phil Oxon., 1972.
B.A. (Hons.), Edinburgh, 1969 (Exhibition Scholarship, 1966).
St. George's Parish School, Havre Morne, St. Andrew's.

4. PLEASE DESCRIBE THE PROJECT YOU WILL BE WORKING
ON DURING TENURE OF THE RESIDENCY: (ATTACH ONE
ADDITIONAL SHEET IF NECESSARY. DO NOT ATTACH A
WRITING SAMPLE.)

A book of poems on themes of memory, sensation, mythology,
rape, loss, and abandonment. Mostly rape.

5. WILL YOU BE WORKING IN AN ORAL TRADITION?
   ☒ YES *
   ❑ NO

If YES, please provide audio tapes and one independent reference
from your community of tradition.

*Note: I see I have misunderstood this question. Poetry is
and has always been an oral tradition. Mine will, however, be
written down.

6. PLEASE NOTE ANY DISABILITIES WHICH YOU THINK
   ARE RELEVANT TO YOUR APPLICATION (YOU MAY INCLUDE HERE
   DISCUSSIONS OF YOUR ETHNICITY OR SEXUAL ORIENTATION):

I am disabled by cacophony, specifically that provided by my housekeeper, who is a black-hearted harpy with a soul of malice towards me. She is a foul sorceress who keeps me in her thrall, a Sycorax of the kitchen, who deliberately cleans the corridor exactly facing my study door as I attempt to do extremely important and stressful business such as filling in grant applications to begin a process of voluntary expulsion and exile—why? why? I ask myself, and I cannot hear the answer, as I cannot hear myself think through the evangelist's radio program in patois (now there is an oral tradition)—to a wealthy and sensible northern country which I imagine to be made up largely of parking lots. This confusion, even this vision, is disabling.

I am disabled by my ethnicity in that I am unable to define my ethnicity exactly and thus unable to feel any confidence about my culture of origin and at a loss in using it as ammunition for any grant applications.

For medical purposes, you may record my ethnicity as follows: my maternal grandfather was ethnically Chinese, of a merchant family originally from Kowloon (I believe); his wife, my grandmother, was as white as English paper. (She was, however, French, a descendant of the first European colonists on this island.) My paternal grandparents—as you seem so interested—were black St. Andreans, which means that they were largely of African and partly of native descent—probably Arawak, but possibly even some Carib, like most descendants of slaves on this island. Both my parents have coffee-coloured skin, as do I, which is certainly a disability in certain quarters of Dunstanton, but a great advantage in others. My elder brother, who died due to injuries accidentally sustained in a government prison cell following a pro-independence demonstration in 1965, was much darker than I. No one has been able to explain this variation, but I am told it is quite common.

I am indeed, perhaps more than in any other way, disabled by my sexual orientation (how prescient of the Arts Action Council!), which is overpoweringly distracting at any times when purely intellectual concentration should be employed.

None of these disabilities is relevant to my application. Have I perhaps got the wrong form?

7. FOR WRITING/PUBLISHING APPLICANTS ONLY:

Please note that support materials in the form of writing samples are no longer a part of the application process. Due to administrative cutbacks, the Literature Committee is no longer able to read writing samples of 20–30 pages as previously required, and this support material is NOT to be included with your application.

XI

"Do you think he's just trying to be funny?"

"Yes, Deepak, he's trying to be funny." This was Jasminka, sounding a little weary. She was being remarkably businesslike about the whole thing, Brian thought.

"Even about the rape part?"

"That I couldn't tell you."

There was a masticatory pause. They just had beef patties today, which were easier to deal with than the roti and left a pretty confetti of flakes, yellow as corn, over sweaters and binders. The fan rattled. Brian had come prepared in a loose T-shirt and shorts today, as if for a workout.

"Well," said Iris Warshavsky, "I don't see any reason for humour in discussing rape."

"Neither do I," said Deepak.

"He sounds a little unbalanced to me," said Iris. "I mean the bit about his housekeeper. He sounds loony-tunes."

"What do you think," said Deepak, "he means about his sexual orientation?"

"I think that's just a joke too, Deepak."

Deepak brushed a constellation of patty flakes off his belly. "Well I think that's in very poor taste."

Jasminka sighed and stacked up some papers. "Well. The problem, though, is not so much this gentleman's application as the other applications."

"I thought there was only one other application."

"This is my point."

"And I thought we threw that one out."

"This is very much my point." Jasminka was good, you had to admit, when it came to this kind of steering.

"Perhaps we should look at it again."

Brian looked at his watch. Mrs. Pent was smiling brightly at one person and then another, with a face that said she was not going to make a judgement on either of these perfectly acceptable candidates in any way that would suggest any sense of apprehension or indeed any entitlement to judge.

"Tom Tupatopunt," read Jasminka. "He claims he is of Fijian origin, but he lives in Baltimore."

"Does Baltimore really meet the criterion for developing region?"

"He stresses the Fijian part."

There were some sighs. Even from Iris Warshavsky.

"He has written some plays."

"And one appears to have been published."

"By something," murmured Brian, "called Empowerment Press."

"Does anyone know any more about St. Andrew's? Is it a developing region?"

"I grew up in Trinidad," said Jasminka, "and on the north end of the island, on a clear day, you could see St. Andrew's. But I never went there. We used to look down on St. Andrew's. It was said there was nothing there to be proud of."

"Why not?"

"I suppose they had no tourism industry. Then they had that terrible hurricane two years ago."

"Oh that was *there*."

"Was there quite a lot of destruction?" This was Iris Warshavsky, suddenly interested.

"Oh yes," said Jasminka, "and there wasn't a lot there to start with."

"So I suppose," said Deepak slowly, "that he does have a lot of familiarity with issues, with serious issues."

"Oh yes," said Jasminka grimly, "he certainly meets that criterion. If that is the purpose of this—"

"I suppose he will have a lot to teach people," said Iris Warshavsky. "People here."

"Listen," said Brian, in a fit of bravery, "Marcus Royston is extremely interesting in himself." He noticed that he had spoken rather more loudly than he intended, and that everyone was looking a little startled, so he coughed and put his fingertips together. "I mean he's incredibly famous. I mean he's very well known. I studied him in school, in university. He had a big influence once. He had some role in government in St. Andrew's just after they got their independence from Britain, would have been in the seventies. He was a minister or something."

"I think I remember that," murmured Jasminka, her eyes narrowed.

"He led a lot of protests and, I think, he was part of the team that negotiated with the British, over independence. I'm not sure. He was really young at the time. His brother died, you know, he mentions that in his thing." Brian sorted his photocopies. "Nineteen sixty-five, his brother died, in police custody, I think that's a joke, by the way, about the accidentally, that's the kind of joke he makes in his writing, anyway, so he would have been in his first year or just about to go to university at that time. I think he didn't finish his doctorate because he was getting really famous already, his first couple of books had already come out, he didn't need to do the doctorate. And then when he was part of the government, that was quite a big deal, in the eighties, maybe, it was a left-wing government, quite a left-wing government. They did all this nationalizing of industry and public health care and free daycare and all this, and they traded with the Cubans and had exchanges, you know, cultural exchanges and everything. There were all kinds of threats of sanctions from the U.S. and everything. I'm not sure what happened to that. No one talks about it any more. Probably they gave up on the Cubans."

Brian paused and saw that everybody, incredibly, was still listening to him, so he drew breath and said, "He was short-listed for the Booker for his very first book. People were saying for a while that he was a good candidate for the Nobel, even. People said he had a shot. This would have been in the eighties some time. Then he faded from view for a while. I think this is an incredible, an incredible opportunity."

"What is a threnody?" said Iris Warshavsky, squinting at her photocopies.

"It sounds as if he's a little overqualified," said Deepak.

"Overqualified?" said Brian.

"I mean in the literary sense. You know, these are all British publishers, all British awards. I mean we might have a problem of perceived elitism here."

"The Nobel Prize," said Brian, "is not a British award."

"What I want to know," said Deepak, "is why we have to do this so fast. I mean why can't we spread the word a little, open it up, and not go with just these applications? I mean it's not really fair to the nations who—"

"Because the money will disappear," said Jasminka. "From External. We have been offered it and we have to use it before the fiscal year ends. And if we don't, I highly doubt we will be offered it next year." She paused, shook her glasses down her nose and tilted her head forward to peer over them, at Iris Warshavsky. "A lamentation," she said, "or dirge."

Brian, breathing rapidly at this opportunity, could not help adding, "From the Greek for wailing song." Then he hung his head and stared at the table.

"External Affairs is, for some reason, very keen on this man," said Jasminka. "Anyway, I suggest we vote now."

XII

Ineluctable modality of the visible.

I find myself wanting to start everything I write with that. Maybe it's because I don't have anything new to write.

But also because if you start with that, the rest is bound to be impressive. Nobody even knows what it means unless they read the Norton anthology notes. And yet the phrase sticks with you, it's the rhythm of it, the mystifyingly intellectual sound of it, all those polysyllables. You find yourself wanting to write it down just to absorb some of the dazzling complexity of it by proximity, by repeating it like a mantra. That's what prayer should be; it's the only way I can imagine prayer, anyway: the repeating of something beautiful and mysterious as a kind of therapy. If you repeat it enough it might impart some of its beauty. It's like listening to music. I should recite, every day on getting up, I wandered lonely as a cloud, or Had we but world enough and time, or The past is a foreign country, until they're drained of all meaning and have become just sound.

I suppose I'm nervous about impressing this visiting poet. Everybody says he's read everything that's ever been written in any language and he's a prick from hell.

And at the same time I want to say, tell me some tricks, tell me how you do it, tell me how you get the words on the *page to sound like oceans and the wind in the trees. Or even just like the words in my head.*

I've been reading his stuff: a lot of it is a little too rhapsodic for me, and the mythological references are hugely dated, he was probably trying to imitate Walcott most of his life, and I don't blame him, but there's a kind of steeliness underneath it which is something like cynicism, or maybe just despair, which makes it intriguing. It's prosy, too, which I hate, but sometimes the rhythm is kind of delicate. It creeps up on you. There is a lot of looking out to sea and metallic heat banging on your head like hammers. St. Andrew's sounds like a god-awful rotting place of flies and garbage. But it sounds as if you can get laid easily there.

One line stuck in my head: A minivan passing sprays/the humid perfume of reggae. It's not bad. Second-rate Walcott. But something almost haiku about it.

I have to go out with Mrs. Pent to the airport to meet him. It makes me strangely nervous. To get to Stilwoode Park from the airport you have to drive into the city from the north, and it's nothing but low-rise sprawl all the way to her house; he won't even see the downtown.

I don't know why I care about this.

I waste my time thinking about how people think of me. I have to stop it. All that counts is trying to write. Trying to write something.

But speaking of people liking me, I ran into Julia Sternberg the other day, one of those girls in the Janie Seagram-Mimi Love-Suki Northwood-Dave Davenport orbit from Trinity, which immediately makes me feel as if I have pustules breaking out all over my face, which I haven't since I was seventeen, but that's the point, I guess. It's odd to see one of those people now. I certainly didn't expect her to be involved with the committee or anything like it. I expect her to be directing rock videos and doing cocaine with guys in black suits, or just married to a guy who runs a publishing house or something. I can't see her sullying herself with all this little squabbling arts council in their corduroy dresses. It turns out she's a friend of Muriella Pent, which is hilarious but predictable (I'm guessing some kind of parental Westmount connection: Julia would be very much at home in Stilwoode Park, I'm sure), and she's in a book club with her, which is dreary and infuriating.

I have always wondered about women like that, if they know what they look like and what it does to us. When she wriggles into a Lycra tank top that clings to her long waist so that you can see the bumps in her spine and the very circles around her nipples, does she look at herself in the mirror and think aha, that'll torture them, that will turn them into drooling idiots, or does she just think, that looks nice? And when she sits in front of you and lifts up her streaming mass of hair so you can see the fuzz curling around the nape of her neck, does she have any idea how painful it is to look at? She can't know. She can't know or she wouldn't do it. She'd dress in a chador or something. Because she doesn't actually want me to touch her, she doesn't want me to be aroused, she doesn't want my lust. She must be totally unconscious of herself. She must be totally unaware of the effect she—they—have on us.

I want to cry every time I look at her. I want to scuttle away and cry.

There seem to be no bounds to my lust these days. Every female form real or imagined, every shape reminiscent of the

swell of breast or buttock, even a curve smudged on paper,
cartoons, the smell of sweat, the outline of nipple covered by
fabric on the crowded bus, the line of panty beneath jeans, the
words themselves, panty, buttock, split, the word or image
that dredges the vaguest buried memory of penetration, all
each individually and together tug at my attention and belly,
distract the eye, the concentration, and the digestive tract. I
dream of penetration and possession, of splitting and bathing,
entering and being swallowed, eating quivering flesh like
fruit and cream, the same escape into sensation that
drunkenness affords.

I myself am full of liquid overflowing in sporadic spurts,
uncontrollably and unpredictably, never ending; I am a leaky
hose, faulty faucet, I am the embarrassing bedsprings
squeaking enthusiastically behind the wall, I am a voracious
digester of pornographic sensation and factory producer of an
eggy stream of concretized lust, my milky sea of reaction.

Christ, listen to me. I sound like Marcus Royston.

XIII

August 12

Dear Desmond,

Thank you once again, my old friend, for agreeing to keep an eye out for Elizabeth in my absence, and particularly for seeing that she cashes the monthly cheques I have left. If she had a bank account it would be easier, as I could have handed them all to the bank and asked them to deposit them automatically, but she doesn't trust banks and has a savings account at the Post, where she must queue each time. Now she avoids the Post because she is embarrassed to admit that she cannot read the statements and brochures that they hand her. (It used to be much simpler: you had a book with handwritten numbers in it. Now it is all computerized.) I am afraid she might think it better if she hoards the cheques instead of cashing them, so please take note if she appears to be lacking for cash. She also needs her spectacles, which I bought for her at great expense, and she refuses to wear them, out of vanity (one would think that vanity would diminish with great age, but I suppose we should not be surprised to find that it does not), so please encourage her to do so if you see her. I am afraid that, without them, she will trip on the back stairs, which are not well lit at night.

I would be very grateful if you would arrive at the house unannounced from time to time to say hello to her and see that she is active, and ask her the last time she was at the Post. The so-called pastor at the barely Christian church she attends, a little Barbadian rat with a gold tooth called Evans, can be counted on to get her out of the house if she is broody. The church is the little open-air one on the Longue Anse road just out of town, on the way to Lafleury, with the garish green mural and the faded words New Messianic Brotherhood or some such. (It's the kind of sign that would have been a political slogan—with very similar semantic content—twenty years ago. Now the old signs would look more ridiculous than the Pentecostals do. Where are the messianic signs for Halliday and his crew? I suppose they are the ones that say Coke and Fanta.)

It was a cruel joke of God to allow the hurricane to so blithely tear the roof off the cathedral of Sainte Geneviève in Alexis Square and leave that roadside voodoo stall standing, untouched. Perhaps there was a message in it.

As there was in the election itself.

I will be sending her any extra money I can save, to your care. And of course I will also ask you to read to her the enclosed letter, and all the future letters I will send her.

The residency is to last until the middle of February, although I'm not sure if I will. I'm not sure if I'm going to stay there the whole time. I don't know where I would go next, but I feel I cannot stay here.

I just found the trunk containing the old winter coat I have not worn since my last trip to London, ten years ago. It is stiff with the stink of mothballs, a coat of vinegar, it seems, but holeless and serviceable. I have no idea if it will be warm enough. I found my Magdalen scarf with its primary stripes, so strangely Deco or Bauhausian for a place built some time

in the *1400s*, and an absurd black beret that I wore in
Edinburgh. The band fell out of the beret as I picked it up,
and it gave off a cloud of dust like a halo, but I think I shall
take it as I venture into the unknown. In many ways it feels
like stepping into the past. I shall attempt to be an
undergraduate, or at least a beginning graduate student,
while I am there. I have no idea what I shall find there.

I am thinking, as I'm sure you have guessed, Desi, that
this trip will provide me with the necessary quiet time to think
about my future. I am not sure if the island holds any future
for me now, given the current climate and how I seem to be
seen. I feel no bitterness about this (nor do I reproach you for
attempting to work in partnership with the new minister, to do
what you can from the inside): the people chose what they
wanted in a democratic election. The fact of having lost a
battle makes the battle no less great.

But I must admit instead of bitterness I feel simple
despair. I tried so hard, as you know, to leave the island in
the sixties and seventies, to find the European brilliance my
poor old father, trained in an English religion, so believed in.
I wanted to be free of our miserable past, and to find my fame
as an international man, and as you know I found that
impossible. I have tried to live among my own people for the
last twenty years and was beginning to feel, to understand,
how I could come to say that and mean it, my own people.
And now I feel the same old sense of difference, the same
irritation at the provincialism of thought, of aesthetic, of
politic, the rut of defeat we live in, the same sense that I have
never been truly a part of my own island. I know that this
sounds nineteenth century, like the melancholy of some
coddled German poet, and I do not mean to sound self-

aggrandizing and melodramatic when I say that there is perhaps no place where I will ever feel I am truly at home.

I am curious about this place I am going to, where everybody, I would guess, feels the same way. I am curious to see how people live in a place they are not from. I suspect they do it differently.

The only thing holding me back now from leaving for good is, of course, Elizabeth, and this is why I am so grateful for your protection of her. As you know, I have no real need of a housemaid, and she is more of a hindrance to me than a help, but we are so much a part of the other's life that I cannot imagine telling her to go. Furthermore, she is too old now to find work elsewhere. She has been frail, too (though no less fierce), since she lost her infant grandson (Suzanne's youngest) in the flood following the hurricane. She is the only family I have left now, my one remaining link to my parents, indeed as much a parent to me as they were (she was, you will recall, their maid Hannah's daughter, who often fed me and met me at school when Hannah was too busy and, later, too old). Take care of her.

Affectionately,
Marcus

August 12

Dear Witch,

I have told Desmond DuPré to keep a close eye on you to see that you do not destroy my house in my absence. Remember to cash the cheques at the Post on the first of every month. I have told Julian Bernardine at the corner café not to sell you any lottery tickets, and Desmond will be watching you like a hawk on this too. Remember to wear your spectacles. Do not be vain about this; you are too old for vanity. What would Pastor Evans say about your vanity? I will return in the middle of February, and if I find you have even ENTERED my study, even ONCE, or TOUCHED one of the books in stacks on the desk or floor, I will drink rum punch for a week and you will have to take me to hospital again.

If you need anything, go to Desmond.

Marcus

XIV

JULIA'S VOICE WAS SLEEPY.

"Darling did I wake you up?"

Julia made a humming noise. Perhaps she was clearing her throat.

"It's noon, darling. You weren't sleeping?"

"Ham," said Julia.

"What?"

"Hi."

"It's Muriella."

"I know. Hi."

"Are you all right?"

"Oh yes. Fine." There was a pause in which Julia yawned. "It's Sunday. I like to sleep in a little on Sunday."

Muriella pictured her curled in a rumpled duvet with her long hair in her eyes and sleep on her face. Her eyes puffy. She wondered if she was wearing anything or if her shoulders were bare. Her tummy lurched, bewilderingly. "I'm calling all in a rush because I'm off to the airport to pick up our new writer."

"Oh yes."

"And I just thought of you, I thought how much I would like you to meet him because he's so brilliant and you, you would probably love him."

"Have you met him?"

"No, no, but everyone says he's brilliant. He must be. Darling, is this not a good time?"

"No no, it's, yes."

"What I mean is you're alone? I mean I don't mean to pry, but if you aren't, I won't talk."

Julia laughed a sleepy laugh. "I'm alone. I'm not with anyone these days, Muriella. I've just been sleeping a lot lately. I don't know why. It's very—"

"It's not that I, it's nothing to me one way or the other. I'm not your mother. I just don't know if you and your friend are still together or if he comes back from time to time or what."

"Which friend."

"The painter fellow. Your Montreal friend."

"Pascal."

"That's it."

"I don't think he's coming back."

"Oh, thank God," said Muriella. "I don't think he was good for you."

Julia was silent for a second. "It does mean I think I'm going to have to find a roommate, which is sad."

"Why?"

"Why is it sad?"

"No," said Muriella. "Why do you have to find a roommate?"

Julia giggled. "Because, Muriella, Pascal has been paying part of the rent in this big house. I can't afford it on my own."

"Oh. Oh I see. It's money?"

"Yes, Muriella. It's money."

"But why don't you move in with me?"

"With you?"

"You know how enormous this house is. You can have your pick of bedrooms. And it would be absolutely free."

"Oh Muriella. That's very nice of you. That's very generous. But I couldn't move in with you."

"Why not?"

"I just couldn't depend on you like that. I would be a pain to live with. Thank you, anyway. I'll tell my mother you offered."

"I didn't offer for your mother, I offered for you. Listen, lovey, think about it."

"Okay."

"Now, listen, I must rush, so would you like to come with me? To meet Mr. Royston? Or is it too early for you?"

"Well . . . I don't, I'm not even on the committee."

"Well you should be. That's another thing. I would really love to have you on—I would love you to join."

"Why?"

"Why? Because. Because you're so clever and you love literature, and you have so much you could contribute. And you'd learn so much. I mean I'm learning so much."

"You think it would be good for me."

"Well, yes, it would. Of course it would. It would take you out of—it would be stimulating for you. I worry about you working in that gallery, and where you live."

Julia laughed again.

"And this sleeping all the time." Muriella twisted the phone cord around her fingers. She looked at her watch. "And to tell you the truth the committee needs another . . . needs someone like you. I think you would be a great asset."

"I don't have the experience."

"Of course you do! You have your degree, which is more than I—"

"I don't have a degree."

"Julia, don't start that. You know what I mean."

"I'm just saying it's not true to say that I have a degree. Besides, isn't there some sort of selection process?"

"Yes, there is, but everyone gets on who wants to because it means doing work and the more people who can make the phone calls and read the manuscripts and what have you the better, so the more the merrier. That's how it works."

"Oh. Muriella, I don't think I would be right for it. I don't have the—I would be intimidated."

"Is it that Silliman boy?"

"Brian? Sillwell. No. It's not him. Partly it's him. I feel uncomfortable around—"

"But I would be there!"

Muriella heard her sighing alone in her bedroom. She pictured a futon on the floor, the blind drawn and the air close. "All right, lovey. You think about it. I would love you to give it a try. It's exciting. You'll see."

"I'll think about it."

"I'm going to keep pressurizing you until you do."

"Okay." Julia's voice was faint.

"That Brian Sillwell is just a nervous boy, Julia. He's all right, really. He wants to be nice."

"He doesn't do a good job of it."

"Was he nasty to you? In school?"

"His friends were always—"

"Him, though. Him personally."

"Him personally . . . not directly. I don't remember. No. But they always managed to make me feel uncomfortable. They're so smug, and so aggressive, and so—"

"Brian Sillwell? Aggressive? I don't think so. He's shy."

"Well," said Julia weakly, "you weren't there."

"I've got to rush, lovey."

Julia exhaled loudly. "O-*kay*."

"I'm sorry to wake you. I want you to come to one meeting. Just one. Promise me you'll come."

"I'll think about it."

Muriella hung up the phone and clacked into the hall on her new shoes. She had wanted to be a little taller to meet a famous poet.

He probably would not recognize the shoes for what they were. He might not know what Prada meant. Then again he might.

She felt guilty thinking of this, for she knew, she told herself, it was of no value or interest to anyone how much her shoes had cost. It was certainly no indication of her worth to the world. She knew that. But the fact that she knew what they were made her feel more confident. She took a deep breath. She didn't know why she was nervous.

She was a little unsteady on the bare concrete in the dimness of the garage. Her toes were already pinched. She pushed the switch to open the garage door and it began its clanking and squeaking upward ratchet, as if lifting an enormous weight.

"Come on," she said. The bar of outside light grew into a wide glaring screen. She blinked into it; for a second the outside world was all white, and her guts dropped as if through the floor of her belly, and there was the pain again, the pain of the past year, the feeling of utter nakedness and rawness, as if all her skin had been peeled away in the light. Heat rushed in.

The rising pane of aluminum stopped moaning and the

soft black driveway and the green-and-yellow garden became clear and shimmering. She slid into the black leather of the Saab and switched on the engine, feeling the hyperperception she had not felt for some time, since the last time this had happened, the same sensitivity in her fingertips, in the way her teeth touched, her vision outlined in diamond edges. Shaking a little, she put on her square Chanel sunglasses and rolled slowly forward, into the day. Once the car was in motion it began to subside.

At the end of the drive she saw David Rodney walking slowly up the road towards her. He carried a newspaper and a string bag, full of apples, and his red tennis hat, and he looked old and slow and sad. She rolled down the window and waved to him. His eyes on the road and his head nodding slightly, he approached.

"Muriella," he wheezed, at her window. "Lovely day."

She took off her glasses so as not to frighten him, her hands still trembling a little, and smiled as warmly as she could. "I'm off to pick up my writer."

"Oh yes." He squinted over the roof of the car, as if witnessing an approaching army.

"The residency is beginning."

"Oh yes." He paused, frowned, and said, "What's this, now?"

"I mentioned it to you once before. In the garden? The visiting international writer. From the Caribbean. Will be staying with me. For six months."

"Staying with you?"

"Yes. In the basement apartment."

"In the maid's room?"

"It's a whole self-contained apartment. Yes."

"Oh."

"He's a very famous writer," said Muriella. The air conditioning was seeping out of the vents now, a faint breeze eddying around her linen jacket, battling with the heavy block of day at the window. The light was still hard; she wanted to put her sunglasses back on.

"From the Caribbean."

"Yes. From St. Andrew's. I mentioned this to you once, in the garden. He'll be a great presence to have in the Park. I'll have a party, once he's settled in, and you can come and meet him."

David Rodney compressed his eyelids in the glare. "That will be nice."

"I imagine he might liven things up around here," said Muriella in what she thought was a gay tone.

David Rodney sighed. "You think things need livening up? You should have been at the residents' meeting, Muriella. We missed you. Things were pretty lively, let me tell you. You should have heard Ralph Poziarski's little wife get up and go after me like I was someone she—"

"I'm sorry, David, I couldn't make it. I'd better rush now, I'm late. I have to pick up—"

"And things are going to get a whole lot livelier, by my count."

"One can only hope." He didn't seem to hear this. Rapidly, she said, "I'd love to hear more about—"

"Six months?" He was staring at her with open eyes.

"Sorry?"

"Six months he's going to stay?"

"Yes."

"Are you sure that's wise?"

Muriella took a deep breath. She had an urge to roll up the window. But she said, "Why would it not be wise?"

"Well, I mean a stranger in your house. For that long. You don't know . . ." He stopped talking there, looking at his bag full of apples with wide eyes as if he had just realized they were at the end of his arm.

"No. There are all sorts of things I don't know. I'll call you about the party."

She hit the power button and the window hissed upwards. The air conditioning took over. The car slid down the hill towards the gate.

Jasminka's house was actually not far away. Once outside the Park, the landscape changed to blocks of boxy brick houses with rusting metal awnings, in fading stripes of green and white, over each doorway. The commercial streets were lined with roti counters and electronics repair shops. Jasminka's house was grander than most on her street: it had a half-timbered second floor and a 1920s look: it was a cheap copy, Muriella could not help thinking for an instant, of Stilwoode Park. She also wondered what else Jasminka did for money, as the books of poems she had written in the 1970s surely did not provide downpayments for detached houses north of Bloor.

Jasminka was waiting outside, gleaming in African robes and a turban shot with gold thread. She glittered in the sun.

She heaved herself into the car with surprising ease. From somewhere in her folds she pulled out a hand-lettered sign that read, "MARCUS ROYSTON." The last *N* was crushed by the edge of the cardboard. Muriella found this endearing.

The traffic was bad. They stopped and started on the

401. Jasminka did not speak. It was only by the shine on her forehead that Muriella realized that Jasminka was just as nervous as she was.

They did not need the sign. Once they had parked and weaved through the crowds of Somali families—there must have been three or four planes from Somalia or maybe Ethiopia all leaving or arriving at the same time, because every square inch of both levels of the terminal was Somali at the moment they arrived, maybe five hundred Somalis on each level, with pushcarts piled high with bags—once they had pushed and weaved through these and found the zone where passengers from Marcus Royston's plane had arrived, the Caribbeans were long gone; a thick and pulsating crowd of Eastern Europeans lined the crowd barriers around the sliding-glass doors, many carrying bunches of flowers in cellophane wrapping, some singing. As Muriella stood on her toes and peered towards the glass doors, she was distracted by two small girls in dresses and white tights and shiny shoes and headscarves, dancing while their parents clapped, swinging each other around by the hands. She felt dizzy.

"There," said Jasminka, and pushed her way into the crowd.

Muriella followed and quickly lost her. When she emerged into an open space she saw them: Jasminka quivering and talking, her hands clasped high and in front of her, beaming and perspiring as she talked to the tall and slightly stooped black man in the raincoat. His face looked strained. He was not smiling.

Muriella stood and watched them for a moment. She

knew this was Jasminka's moment, so she would not intrude right away. The man had pale brown skin, paler than Muriella had imagined. He was much paler than Jasminka. He wore wire-rimmed glasses, and had the barest fuzzy moustache. His hair was half grey. She watched him strip off his raincoat and fold it over one arm, nodding and listening to Jasminka. His hands were long. Under the long grey raincoat, he wore a soft grey suit and a shirt with no tie. It was the kind of suit Arthur would have worn. He had two bags: a nylon sports bag that said AEROSPORT TEAM STAR, stuffed to bursting, and a massive blue vinyl suitcase wrapped in a blue vinyl strap. The vinyl was cracking and peeling. He had a black nylon briefcase hanging from a shoulder.

Muriella approached, smiling. He tipped his head to look at her over his glasses with wide black eyes. She held out her hand. "Hello," she said. "Welcome to—"

"This is Muriella Pent," said Jasminka. "It's her house."

"How do you do." He bowed slightly as he shook her hand. The whites of his eyes were cracked with red. His eyes passed slowly downwards, over her body. She wondered if he was noticing her shoes.

"Welcome to Canada. It's an honour to have you here. How was your flight? You're going to be awfully hot in that suit." She was hating herself even as she spoke. But she could not stop. "The house is very cool, though, even though I've never had air conditioning. I don't see the point. And so many people—"

"I was just telling Mr. Royston," said Jasminka, "that the committee has no problem with any—"

A roar erupted from the crowd around them. Waves of

cheers passed up and down the lines of waiting people. Two tall men were jumping up and down next to Muriella; one bumped her into Marcus Royston, who steadied her. A sea of Slavic families was bursting through the sliding doors in variegated colour. They shouted and cried; they carried babies and boxes and pushed carts stacked like caravans. There were ancient women in headscarves, carrying bottles of spirits. There were skinhead men in dark glasses and leather coats, and wives in stilettos and fur jackets. Each family was stopped by a rush of embracing relatives, plugging the flow; people were tripping over spilled sports bags.

"What is this?" said Marcus Royston over the noise, his eyebrows high.

"It's just a plane arriving," shouted Jasminka. "Let's get outside."

A song had begun around them, like a stadium anthem.

"It's always like this," said Muriella. "A minute ago it was Somalis." But he had turned to follow the bobbing turban.

Muriella fought with two women and a four-foot man in a pinstripe suit over baggage carts. She paid the four-foot man four dollars for his cart. He looked disdainfully at the money, said nothing, and waddled away.

The three of them got the cart loaded and pushed it to a dank concrete tunnel that roared with noise. It seemed to be full of smoke and upturned luggage carts and honking taxis and crying women. There were men in peaked caps standing in the traffic, waving their hands and shouting the echoing fragments of words in an apparently foreign language.

Muriella stood still. She was afraid to step into traffic or children.

"Go get the car," Jasminka shouted. "Bring it back here."

Muriella had seen Jasminka like this before: her tone was not actually as offensive as you first thought it was; it was Jasminka taking charge. Muriella had seen her like this in committee meetings, and had been grateful for it then, as she was now.

There was a hand on her elbow. She looked up at the tall black man's lined face. "Shall I come with you?"

"No no. Thank you." She stepped off the curb into a squealing of brakes.

The airport was under construction. The Saab idled in a column of cars in another tunnel lined with metal barriers and orange signs. The steel girders and reinforcing rods of the tunnel were exposed. A bus was trying to nudge ahead of her. The bus was full of men in Sikh turbans. Someone was honking behind.

Beside her, Marcus Royston had taken out a notebook and pen. Even Jasminka had stopped talking. The interior of the car had taken on the distinct scent of alcohol.

Muriella tried to relax her grip on the wheel. "It's been like this for as long as I can remember," she said. "It's been under construction for four years, and it's supposed to be under construction for the next four years. Can you believe it?"

"It is like hell," said Marcus Royston gravely. His voice was soft.

Muriella giggled. "Yes. I suppose it is." She pulled on her wrap skirt to minimize the slit. His eyes were on her legs.

"There was a Royston in Trinidad," said Jasminka, "who was mayor of San Fernando. He was a close friend of my father's. Might he be related to you?"

There was a very long silence. Marcus Royston's head

was tilted upwards, as if he was thinking very hard. The car jerked forward. They emerged into daylight, but the traffic was still stuck.

Finally he spoke. "When do you think you might have my first cheque ready?"

"Cheque?"

"I understand there is a monthly stipend or honorarium. I shall need it right away." His accent was rippling and fluid; almost Indian, a sort of watery high-English with strange long vowels and valleys; it was almost Irish and almost New England and not at all the harsh Jamaican that Muriella had, she supposed, expected. It sounded like the past, like a place Muriella had never been.

"Oh yes. We have it. I have it with me. Would you like it just now?"

"Why not?" He looked at Muriella and smiled. He had nice teeth.

"Oh, let me. Here." In the back, Jasminka was fumbling with her bag. This bag was so large Muriella sometimes thought of it as the Heavy Bag. There was much breathing while this took place.

When Jasminka found the cheque they were moving quickly on a feeder lane, about to merge into the main highway. Muriella was stuck between two trucks and couldn't see the lane she was about to enter. Her hands were white on the wheel.

"Here it is." Jasminka leaned forward, blocking her rear-view mirror and waving an envelope close to her face.

"Jesus," said Muriella. She was into her lane without accident. "Sorry."

"This reminds me," said Marcus Royston. "I have something for you, too, Mrs. Pent." The accent clearer there: *somethin*.

"Muriella, please."

"Certainly. Now, is it in this bag?" He lifted his nylon briefcase onto his lap and began his own rummaging.

The Saab was doing 120 with five feet between it and the cars in front and behind. Muriella swallowed.

"It must be in a suitcase behind. It's just a little gift. For your house. Since you will be putting up with me."

"That's very sweet of you," she said. "You didn't need to at all."

Jasminka cleared her throat. "Tell us about the political situation in St. Andrew's now, Mr. Royston."

Muriella accelerated into a free lane. She felt the car pulse forward like a snake under her foot as she pushed. There was nothing but flat and hurtling highway lanes on either side of them, as if to the horizon. In the far distance were overpasses. The vast sky was brown and yellow.

It took an hour to get downtown. The Allen Expressway was jammed and immobile; Eglinton was a glacier of fuming cars. On Oakwood the Saab vibrated with the beats of the black-tinted Hondas waiting on either side of them at every light. People seemed to be standing still on every sidewalk, pale and grey or dusty, too exhausted to walk. A black man in a woollen toque and a black overcoat and bare feet walked into the traffic and spat on the side of the car. Then he walked away again. He seemed completely sober. Marcus Royston had stopped answering Jasminka's questions and was scribbling in his notebook again. He seemed to take a great interest in the corner of St. Clair and Oakwood.

Muriella entered the Park from the north gate. She had to get out to open it, and then close it again once they were through. Jasminka and Marcus Royston were silent about this procedure. Muriella was beginning to feel less grateful about Jasminka's command.

She breathed deeply once they were inside. The day went quiet.

The lawns were deep green. Gaye Northwood's ivy was looking lush. Muriella was saying, "That one is an original too, Gaye Northwood's, that's the cookie Northwoods, they make cookies, I mean, her grandfather, anyway." She knew she was describing the things she would describe to one of Arthur's friends, but she couldn't help it; she didn't know this man, she didn't know what tone to take. She decided on architecture. "Now that timbered one is *not* original, that was built to look just like the others some time in the forties. That belongs to Frank and Olivia Daurio now, they're new, they've only been there ten years or so. That brick one with the pointed windows is actually older, that's about eighteen ninety, it was a priory when this was just countryside. That's just Victorian, I find it a little mournful. There's a single man I don't know anything about in there now, he drives a little red sportscar which is usually there but it's not today. Now on your left you're going to see really the biggest house in the Park, which is authentic, it was the first one built as a Park house, about nineteen twenty-four, when the Park was first laid out, and that was built for Adam Dimmock-Hall, who was the railway man who became city planner, but his money was from England, originally, and that's now the Poziarskis, he's the developer." Muriella drew a breath.

"When you say authentic," said Marcus Royston in his gentle voice, "what do you mean?"

"Oh, I mean authentic Stilwoode. Nathaniel Stilwoode, who was the architect who designed the whole place. The original buildings, I mean. That's why it's called—didn't you get the information sheets I sent you?" Muriella looked in the rear-view mirror at Jasminka, who was staring out the window. "Jasminka? Did you include in Mr. Royston's package the information about the history—"

"I don't recall," said Jasminka very quietly.

Muriella wondered what battle Jasminka was fighting here. In committee meetings Jasminka had a hard role to play, she knew, between so many conflicting opinions, and she listened, she really did listen, Muriella thought, to what Muriella had to say, but as soon as they were alone she became forbidding again, a walking pamphlet for the Black Socialist Worker or something; Muriella felt that everything she, Muriella, said in Jasminka's presence came out of her mouth as a kind of perfumed mush, as something like cream, that was it: as a rich and cloying stream of pure white cream.

It was always petrifying to see Jasminka's steely side (and it did seem to always come out in the direction of Muriella, it was a side that was turned to her and to Brian Sillwell and to no one else), but at the same time it was encouraging to realize that it was probably Marcus Royston who was making Jasminka nervous. Jasminka didn't want to ally herself with an embarrassing white woman right away; she didn't know how a revolutionary poet would take to her. But then she didn't know the poet at all. It occurred to Muriella that Jasminka didn't know what she was doing, which was a happy thought. It was encouraging merely to see Jasminka nervous, at all. It was something Muriella would have to remember, to store away.

"Oh," said Muriella. "I sent pictures and everything. Of the house. I thought you would have been so interested." She wondered how long he would go on letting them call him Mr. Royston. She had already told him to call her Muriella, and he had merely nodded.

"I'm not sure if——"

"I am interested," said Marcus Royston. "Tell me, who was this architect?" No hard *r* in the word: *ah-chitect*; he was suddenly more Caribbean. It was as if he had a different accent for every word.

"Here we are. Let me just——let's get out here and we can go in the front door, and then I'll park it later."

They stepped out into the dazzle and all shaded their eyes as they surveyed the facade. The air was heavy and humid. Butterflies hovered.

"Nathaniel Stilwoode, he was English, and he was a disciple of William Morris, who was the Arts and Crafts man? It's all about being organic to the English landscape and English artisanal tradition, and it has these medieval references, it was a movement that led to Art Nouveau and——"

"Yes," said Marcus Royston. "I know about Arts and Crafts. But was Morris not eighteen sixties or eighties? Didn't you say that this was nineteen twenty-four?"

"It's a little later, yes," said Muriella.

"A little later." Marcus Royston had a wide smile.

Muriella felt herself blushing. "Well, this is Canada," she said apologetically. "Apparently he hadn't had a great deal of success in England, but when he came here it was still a new thing."

"I like the turret," he said. "It's very romantic. If a little kitsch. And that great sloping roof. It's almost Swiss. And the leaded windows, and the half-timbering. It's all rather Walter Scott, isn't it?"

"Muriella," said Jasminka, "if you'll open the trunk I can, we can all get Mr. Royston's bags out."

Marcus Royston made no move. "It's wonderful that this is a Canadian, if you don't mind my saying colonial, copy of a movement that was long dead in Britain and which was itself a copy of some mythical medieval past." He chuckled some more. "So when you say authentic you mean an authentic copy of a copy."

"Well," said Muriella, her face very hot, "it is actually highly regarded. It is seen as a perfect example of Arts and Crafts. It's one of the few developments of houses in a group that are all the same style. I had an English professor here two years ago, who was writing a book about Arts and Crafts. He seemed to think it was very important."

"Did you read the book? When it came out?"

"Yes. Unfortunately he cut everything out about the Park, but there was an interesting footnote." Muriella hesitated, then said, "*He* was very condescending about it too."

"Oh, my dear, I don't mean to dismiss it at all," said Marcus. "I find it lovely, I find it endearing. I find it interesting how we look at things. That rather forbidding priory you pointed out to me"——he waved up the hill——"that's clearly Victorian medievalist, and in being authentic Victorian it is a copy of the Gothic. And being built in Canada, it is a copy of what was being built in England, so I suppose you could call it a kind of colonial Victorian

Gothic, but at any rate the idea of the authentic scarcely seems to apply." He sighed. "Anywhere."

"Canada's not a colony," said Muriella.

He hesitated, then said, "Not any more. No."

She went to the trunk to pull out his bags.

In the cool entrance hall she had prepared a great bunch of hollyhocks and lobelias which had already started to moult organic clusters and strands onto the rug. Marcus Royston stopped in front of the big MacDonald. "That's a very . . . that's a very big sunset," he said.

"That," said Muriella, delighted, "is a Group of Seven."

"Ah."

"Are you familiar with—"

"No."

"They are our most important artists. The country's. They were radicals. For their time."

"Which is?"

"That one was nineteen twenty-four. That's J. E. H. MacDonald. He was one of them."

"Nineteen twenty-four." Marcus Royston was angling his head.

Jasminka tapped her foot.

"Radicals."

"Yes," said Muriella. "They were scorned at the time. They were too avant-garde for public taste."

"I see." He stepped closer to the canvas and squinted. He stepped back again. "And what exactly is avant-gardist about this one?"

"Well," she said with a little laugh. She held both palms upwards. "Well." She looked at the painting for the first time in ten years and saw a bloody orange sunset. There was a group of walking people in the foreground. Their clothes were painted very carefully. She tried to remember everything she knew about the Group of Seven. "It's quite valuable."

"Would you like to see the apartment?" said Jasminka

"It's through the kitchen and down," said Muriella. "Would you like some tea first? Did you eat on the plane?"

"Perhaps," said Marcus, still engrossed by the painting, "we might all have a glass of wine together."

"Oh," said Muriella. She put down the big black sports bag she had lifted. "All right."

When they were settled in a corner of the big drawing room, with Jasminka distant, across a swirling sea of pale blue silk Tehran carpet, on a low and armless Queen Anne chair that seemed too small for her, and Marcus Royston crossing his long legs in the capsule of a deep floral loveseat, with a tray and a bottle of cheap Chilean white on a leather ottoman between them, Muriella had already told Marcus about the young-adult book she was working on, and the new novel about the immigration of the Jews, and the children's book she had published in 1981. Jasminka kept interrupting to ask the visiting writer what he was working on and what he thought of colonialist studies of his work, and Marcus Royston kept smiling and turning back to Muriella and asking her to go on. He didn't seem at all tired after his journey; in fact, he seemed quite relaxed. Jasminka and Muriella had a glass of wine each and he finished the bottle. "And do you enjoy the theatre?" he asked Muriella.

"Oh *yes*." Muriella was feeling a little cooler, leaning

back against the padded arm of the biggest sofa, a floral bed, deep as a tanker, still holding her empty glass. "We have a great deal of theatre here. I go all the time. We have—" She crossed her legs and stuck one foot out, dangling her new backless shoe on her toe. She watched Marcus Royston's eyes follow the line of her leg. She dropped her foot to the floor.

Jasminka was also watching Muriella's legs. "We have a very vibrant theatre *community*."

Muriella felt the declaration of war as a cold front from across the room; Jasminka's face was dark. Muriella decided, with much more experience of conversations with men, no matter how intellectual, in this room, that if Jasminka was going to play deadly serious then she would be all froth and flippancy. They would see who would win. "It's too bad you weren't here a few weeks ago, or you would have been able to see *Joseph and the Amazing Technicolour Dreamcoat*, which I'm sure you must have seen before, but it was a really good production, and it's just closed. But it was really terrifically well reviewed, and it was the longest run, I think, for any of the big shows, at least for the past few years. I saw it here, and I had seen it in New York *and* in London, and I have to say—"

"I was thinking more of the small theatre," called Jasminka across the expanse of carpet. She shifted on her low chair. Her knees were spread wide under her robe. "We have a great deal of community-based theatre here, and some of it is very brave. Very brave indeed."

Marcus was looking towards Jasminka with a smile on his face that might have been described as bemused. It occurred to Muriella that he was not listening to anything either of them said. He may have been mildly drunk. "Oh!" said Muriella. "I forgot! The baseball."

"Oh yes," said Jasminka, nodding sadly. "The baseball."

"We have to go to the baseball."

"I would be delighted to," said Marcus Royston. "May I suggest we open—"

"No no," said Muriella, "we have to, we really have to go to a game. We don't have a choice. It's in a few weeks, isn't it? It's the first game of the season for the Blue Jays, the baseball team, and we have to go because the mayor gave us tickets. He said to welcome you. There's a little note for you in the envelope. There's four tickets."

"It was his contribution to the program," said Jasminka darkly. "Four baseball tickets."

"Have you seen a baseball game before?" said Muriella.

"Yes. Oh yes. I lived in Wyoming for a time, many years ago, when I was writer-in-residence there. I was taken to a baseball game." He paused, staring towards the dim dining room. "I don't remember much about it."

"I've never been," said Muriella. "So you can explain it to me."

"I've never been either," said Jasminka, "and I don't think I'll be coming." She took a deep breath and began the process of standing up. She gritted her teeth and heaved forward, sticking an arm out to grab a Regency side table that tottered alarmingly. With her other hand she took a fistful of upholstery from a nearby sofa. There was a moment of uncertainty before she achieved maximum torque, as she began to tilt backwards, her thighs half off the chair and her face puffy and bursting; Muriella half stood, for a second, in case she would be needed to help out (and was not without pleasure at the advantage that would give her), but the crisis passed and Jasminka rose, solid and panting. "Well," she said, "you will want to settle in and rest, and we'll be seeing each other very soon."

"Yes," said Muriella. "I'll show you your apartment, and I have a key for you, don't let me forget, and I'll let you get unpacked, and you'll probably want the evening to yourself, and tomorrow I can show you around, where the grocery store is and so on, and I can give you a tour of the city if you like, we'll—"

"Oh," said Marcus Royston, standing suddenly, "I almost forgot myself. My present." He strode out into the entrance hall where his bags were still stacked.

They heard him shuffling and grunting for a few minutes. At one point Muriella looked over at Jasminka, who was still standing and looking down at the carpet. Jasminka looked distinctly lost. Muriella shook back her hair and smiled her nicest smile at Jasminka.

Marcus came back in with a box wrapped in a plastic bag. He kneeled beside the coffee table and took off the plastic bag, which he shoved off onto the floor. He pulled the box apart and a small brown sculpture emerged. He handed it to Muriella with an embarrassed look. "It's some local art from the island."

It was a small horse, made from woven brown straw or wicker. It had thick legs, stuck to a flat board with wheels on it, and a string you could pull it along with. "It's a horse," said Muriella. "It's lovely."

"It's a mule," said Marcus Royston. "We have some on the island. They are still used on farms, in the interior."

"What's it made of?"

"Banana leaves. They weave them when they're green."
Marcus Royston took it from her gently and stroked it for a
moment. "And then they turn brown."

"It's beautiful," said Jasminka.

"It's quite lovely. I'll put it up here on the mantelpiece."

"It's just a small thing. I thought something from the
island, to show you . . ." He trailed off. He handed it back
to Muriella almost glumly.

She hefted it in both hands. It rattled. "Is it hollow?
There seems to be something in it."

"I have no idea." He seemed to have suddenly turned sad.

"I'll be off," said Jasminka.

"Yes," said Muriella. She looked at the sad dried brown
thing and was momentarily horrified at herself for wondering, really only for a second, if it was the kind of thing they
used to stick pins in for magic. She put it on the mantelpiece, where it was at least quaint if not really to her taste.

XV

MARCUS TRIED NOT TO LOOK OVER THE railing which was at the level of his knees. The seats below him dropped off as steeply as a cliff. He felt suspended in the girders and struts and scaffolds of the great dome ceiling. He wondered why they had to sit so high up when there were so many empty seats throughout the stadium. To their left and right and just below them there were patches of blue plastic seats. There were people scattered throughout the vast space, a space at once outdoors and in, open and enclosed, mountaintop and gymnasium, obediently sitting in sober clusters in their assigned seats, separated by expanses of plastic and concrete. Muriella and the two young men had been very serious, endearingly serious, about finding their seats and sticking to them.

The colours everywhere were artificially bright. The field, far below, was bright green with crisp white lines; it couldn't have been real turf. The seats were so blue they were almost fluorescent, and the video screen, as big as a cathedral roof, showed the players' faces as metallic orange and pink, outlined in black. Sometimes the pixels on the screen dissolved and then quickly realigned themselves in jumpy lines. The very air under the web of steel trusswork overhead seemed charged with an unnatural light. Perhaps the air, like the turf and the seats and the clammy hot dogs and the players' faces, was synthetic, a cheaper version than the stuff outside, and everyone knew about it and accepted it.

Marcus opened his little notebook. Under his last note, *Children on cellphones, policemen with bullet vests*, he wrote, *Blue plastic chairs. Very comfortable.*

There was a distant rustle of applause from another part of the stadium, and the taller young man, sitting on the other side of Muriella, shouted, "That's it, Fernando. You hit it with the wooden thing. Base hit. *Rriba, rriba.* Extra tacos *por senhor.*" There seemed to be no movement down on the field. The players were still standing around, although perhaps their positions had changed slightly. The other young man was explaining to Muriella—"He made it to first base"—and Muriella then turned and explained the same thing to Marcus.

It was she who had found the two young men, presumably to use the extra tickets. One was the nervous Brian, whom Marcus had met at the rather depressing meeting of the committee that had brought him here. He seemed eager to please, if a little intense. The loud and tall one was his friend with a biblical name, possibly Joseph or Nathan. He was being amusing. "Gonzalez becalmed on first base. He ruminates. The cosmos waits."

The speakers erupted again with crashes of electric music. Marcus wrote, *Each player: blast of pop music coming up to bat, else wouldn't recognize players (too far away). Music bits each have cultural reference, audience laughs. Sign language.*

"Op," said Brian's friend, "the Robobabes approach."

There was a team of young women in tight little dresses working their way up the stands, separated by banks of seats. They each carried a bag of prizes, which they were throwing into the audience. They smiled and tossed their long hair; they wore plenty of makeup.

"What is it they are throwing?" said Marcus.

"Miniature replicas of their own breasts," said Brian's friend. "Pornographic videos. Opiates of various kinds. What you have to do is avert your eyes, or fill your ears with wax. Tie me to the mast." He stood and waved his arms. "Hey! Fembots! Lara Croft! I await!"

There was a kind of hysteria as the objects began raining on their own section. The teenage boys in front of them wrestled and swore over them. Marcus was sure one was going to topple over the railing and cascade into the bright air.

One of the girls was level with their row and smiled at Marcus. Her dress seemed to be made of a kind of filmy rubber: it was white and emblazoned with the Budweiser logo. Marcus could see her nipples, the lines of her bra as it squeezed her sides. As she turned and bent to rummage in her sack, her saw the line of her thong underpants between her buttocks, the triangle at the bottom of her back. The men around were screaming quite unbelievable obscenities at them.

Marcus wrote, *A thin strand wraps the pubis, snakes between the thighs, tickles the tailbone. It is too intimate to see. I would be the hand that grasps that mound.*

"Sirens!" yelled Brian's friend. "Stepford wives! I have wept and fasted, fasted and prayed—" He leapt up and caught the thing that was hurtling overhead. The catch was quite impressive. He sat down and unwrapped the bundle. It was a black Budweiser T-shirt. "Hey!" he shouted. "I wanted a cap! Does the cap come with a backhoe? You get the cap and you get to drive a forklift home. Throw me a cap!"

"Ladies and gentlemen," announced the massive invisible speakers all around them, the voice of God. "We have good news. The rain outside has stopped, and we are about to open the roof."

A feeble cheer went up. Marcus looked up to watch the fantastically complicated underpinning of the roof, like the underside of a railway bridge. Nothing happened.

He waved at a beer-selling teenager.

Muriella didn't offer to pay for this one. She was smiling tightly.

Brian's friend was watching the field through tiny binoculars. "Double play," he squeaked. "Of course, and so we fizzle out, as usual, a feeble, premature fizz, a perfunctory effort to play the game having been made. Look at them shuffle off. They look relieved. Resigned, is what we are. This is an existentialist baseball team, they don't know why they're there. *Les Etrangers.*"

Marcus swallowed the buzzing warm beer and stared at the domed roof, which was moving, with no sound, slowly sliding. He had expected a great rumbling, as if of thunder, but it slid on oiled wheels. A crack of light appeared, then a sharp yellow ray came down and lit a corner of the field. There was a murmur from the crowd as the sky began to appear.

Marcus was reminded of Muriella's garage door, with its noisy ascent, its miraculous glimpse of the day.

Muriella put her dark glasses on. She had dropped her smile.

The roof was peeling back and uncovering a sky vaster, it seemed, than it had been when they were merely outside. Humid air filled the stadium. There were still clouds blowing quickly across the opened bowl, and the sky between them was a dark blue. One half of the stadium, their half, was flooded with a dewy golden light. There was a great majesty to the space, the sheer hugeness of it.

Marcus burped happily. He wrote, *Strange beauty of contrast of natural light with white, the earthy warm on the eerie cool.*

Another wooden crack from the floor of the bowl, the sound of a twig snapping, brought a flash, to Marcus, of somewhere else: dusk, a dusty field, evening cricket. Boys in green and yellow running, and the smell of burning in the air. There was often smoke in the air. Watching from the roadside. There were no bleachers, but sometimes a crowd would gather. There was a stand for cold drinks and johnnycakes, sometimes a minivan parked to play reggae from its speakers. Marcus avoided the drink stand so as to avoid the fellows with the minivan. Most people knew who he was; he did not know other people. So he stood alone. He did not always know how to talk, anyway, to people from the country.

Always a stranger, even when relaxing.

Nutmeg bitter in the grenadine.

He watched the sun fall on the nape of the neck of the teenaged girl sitting two rows down. She reached behind her and pulled her hair from its knot and it fell down her back, yellow in the light. Then she stood and turned to look up at the opening sky, and in doing so stretched and arched her back, so that her little belly pushed forward between T-shirt and jeans and the light caught on her navel ring. Marcus, sorry for himself, found this sight stirringly beautiful.

He glanced across at Muriella, his hostess, and considered her narrow thighs in their black casing. She wore a lot of

RUSSELL SMITH

black, it seemed; it was for drama, he guessed, not mourning. It flattered her. He wondered about her brittleness. She would have softness somewhere. He looked away, then looked back to look down her blouse. Nothing much there.

He considered his chances with her. His skin was to his advantage there, he judged. It was likely something she had never tried before.

He could lay a hand on her taut thigh just then, right there, and see what she did. She could leave it there or she could politely push it off. Either way, she was too polite to make a thing of it. It would be a way of seeing.

But it was the thought of what would follow that fatigued him. He could do it or he could not do it; he could have her or he could not. It wouldn't make much difference. What he didn't want was a great deal of effort.

"Hideo Kurami," said Brian's friend, in what was meant to be a Japanese accent. "Samurai pitcher. Pray Stayshon."

Muriella murmured, "I hope you're not offended by Jason."

"Not at all, not at all."

"He doesn't really mean, I mean he's not really . . ."

Marcus waited. "Not really what."

"Well, the racial humour . . ."

Marcus barked. "I am well used to racial humour. It's one of our specialities, where I come from."

"I see."

"I write about race, quite a bit, you know."

"Yes, of course."

"I see no point in avoiding its discussion."

"Yes, well, this isn't really a discussion, is it?"

"What, jokes? Oh yes they are. Oh yes they are."

Muriella paused. Then she said, "Are you enjoying yourself?"

"Very much, yes. But I don't understand why they stopped playing just then. One man was running for home, and another man was caught out, and he just stopped running. Why did he not score? I seem to recall that happening in the earlier innings."

Muriella giggled and said, "I have no idea."

Brian shook his head with some amusement, as if the question was ridiculous, and said, "I couldn't tell you. I've never watched this game in my life."

His friend downed the rest of what must have been his fourth beer and said, "Oh, don't ask. Do not even ask. That is only for the inner circle to know, the initiates. The ones with the hoods and capes. They resent people like you coming and poking around for that kind of information. Don't ask. You don't want to get involved."

Marcus laughed.

"In fact, we should get out of here. Right now."

Everybody laughed. Briefly, and without thinking about it, Marcus let his hand rest on Muriella's thigh.

"Well," she said brightly, "only four more innings." She stood up. "I'm off to the powder room."

So that was that.

"Another beer, Marcus?" said Brian's friend.

"Why not? Why not?"

"Marcus, I want you to have my prize. This Budweiser T-shirt will be your first indigenous costume."

Marcus turned to watch Muriella working her way up the narrow concrete steps to the hangar-like door to the next level, where the hamburgers and the washrooms were. It was a long walk up, and there were people filtering up with her in a slow stream. She walked carefully. Her hips were narrow. She was very fine-boned, very dainty.

So that was that. If she was not interested, it was probably because she was all dried up inside, and that was her problem. It was not something personal, nothing to feel hurt about. It was something to forget about.

A disembodied cheer rose from somewhere in the bowl. Nothing seemed to have happened on the field. A thunderclap: fireworks burst from the roof.

XVI

August 20

My Dear Witch,

I am living in a very large house in a beautiful park. I have my own apartment in the basement, with two small windows that look onto the garden (just above ground level) and one window that looks onto a small pathway that runs alongside the house. You will be amused to know that this apartment was built for a maid. There is no longer a maid. Perhaps I am the maid.

I do not know what I mean by that. I have been treated very well.

I hope Desmond is reading this aloud to you. (How are you, Desmond? I shall write to you soon.)

The house is quite old and is covered in ivy. There is a garden with some flowers, although it is untended. There are many wide beds, and good soil, which would make a lovely vegetable garden if you could get your hands on it. You would be disappointed that no one has planted any sweet potatoes or christophine or even tomatoes, although it is hot and sunny all the time. (The weather is the same here as it is at home, although the dusk comes later in the day. They say it will grow cold soon. I cannot imagine this.) You could make a beautiful garden of it.

The house is in the middle of a very large and ugly city,

*but it is hidden in a park that's full of trees and other
lovely houses, built just for rich people. The city stretches
for miles and miles, but it is mostly blocks of houses.
At its centre there are blocks of very vast and very tall
skyscrapers, but no one lives there, and the area is deserted
after dark. The city is on a massive lake, a lake so big you
cannot see the other side of it. You would think it was the
sea, but it has no smell. It is a sort of sterile sea. (It is
not really sterile; you cannot swim in it, because it is
polluted.) I rarely see this lake, for it is separated from the
city by a huge highway and so is difficult to walk to. And
the buildings are so tall you cannot see around them. It
feels as if we are in the middle of a vast concrete plain.
I miss the sea.*

*If I walk out of the park and to the north, I come across a
strip of small shops on a wide street. If the street were
narrower, it would look a little bit like Dunstanton. There
are West Indians there from all the islands. There is a café
called Castries. You can buy johnnycakes from a shop called
Dunstanton.*

*There was a large sign on the highway, as I approached
the city in a fast car, that said simply, WRONG WAY. I
had never seen a sign like this before. I tried not to take it as
an omen.*

*I do not know what the people here want me to do while I
am here. I have been taken to a great many meetings of
people who say they are writers but who do not seem very
interested in writing. They seem to want me to petition the
mayor of the city to give them more money. I do not know
why I should do this. I have seen some of their writing and it
is very poor.*

The mayor gave me a ticket to a baseball game, which was confusing. (Both his giving me the ticket and the game were confusing.)

Then the people who brought me here took me to see a performance of some African drumming by people who were obviously Jamaican. It was very pleasant and competent drumming, but it was not very complicated and seemed somehow desperate. Then I met some of the white writers, who are some of the country's most famous writers, and they were all women who were very quiet and pale. Two of them seemed to be Ph.D. students (Desmond please explain this). We ate in a restaurant, but few of them could eat from the menu because they are vegetarians. They drank very little and talked a great deal about money. They all do a great deal of business with foreign publishers and film companies and they talk about this. They have agents who represent them and they asked each other several times if they thought they should move to a better agent, who could obtain more business deals for them. They are quite wealthy: they buy houses and travel to Europe and talk about this a great deal as well. One of them had to leave early because of the cigarette smoke.

I fear you will not be interested in all this, dear Witch. I am trying to think of what you will find interesting.

It is difficult to find grenadine syrup or nutmeg syrup. Most people drink beer. I do not have any problem in drinking beer as well. You would be very surprised by the food, which is very light: they eat many salads. You would probably disapprove, you would wonder how a nation could keep its strength up without eating stews and dumplings and christophine with cheese sauces, which you would no doubt feed them, dear Elizabeth.

Are you wearing your spectacles? Remember that Desmond is keeping an eye on you and that you are not to buy any lottery tickets.

Yours,
Marcus

XVII

"WELL, SHE SLAPPED HIM. I CALL THAT asking for it."

"She slapped her own husband."

"But that's as a result of the abuse that she suffered."

"When was that?"

"I don't have such a big problem with slapping a husband."

A gust of laughter. Coffee slopped from shaking cups.

"One shouldn't joke."

"No."

"I think she's trying to say that violence breeds violence."

"Who," interrupted Marcus, "is trying to say this?"

He noted that the very fat one had her eyes closed. Her coffee cup slowly rising and falling on her belly.

"Well," said Muriella tremulously, "the author. Rosemary Wellington."

"I see," said Marcus. "Well, I haven't read this novel, as I've said, and I apologize for not being so prepared. But I'm not sure we can say the author is saying anything."

There was a long silence before Muriella said, "Why not?"

"Because that's not how novels work. It's not really about saying something. It's about telling a story. A story of fictitious people. People she made up." Marcus sipped from his coffee cup, which contained brandy dyed brown with an ounce of coffee, now cold. He had found the liquor cabinet in the library and knew that Muriella probably knew by now that he was regularly serving himself from it; she kept it restocked anyway.

He felt some guilt at dashing the conversation into pieces like this. But he was growing bored. He knew it was not his role to discourage. Marcus had been to book clubs before. One, anyway, in Wyoming in 1976, which had been made up of faculty wives and had a professor visit them each time and lecture them in a stern and paternal way. This one had no lecturer, no male presence but his own, but the procedural rules had not changed. There was no alcohol served, but a table loaded with cookies and squares and bars, which the ladies had brought, and which, it was understood, no one was to touch until after the discussion was over. The cookies were a reward.

He had been invited as a kind of spiritual presence, he knew, a benign presence, to bless. To inspire and encourage, not to condescend. He knew this.

There was a large group here, seven ladies and the nymph, the girl Marcus could only think of as the nymph, who sat tightly on the edge of a wooden chair without saying anything and occasionally wrote things down in a notebook and seemed very serious and afraid. The ladies had short hair, mostly, and spectacles with wide plastic frames, and there was the one enormous one who expanded over half a sofa (they were in the sprawling living room, where furniture was scattered like defences in concentric rings, where one could choose whole areas to retreat to or claim as occupied) and who had now wisely settled into sleep. There was one sexy one in high heels and some cleavage and much gold jewellery. But even this one, who would normally have been Marcus's sole reason for speaking or even staying awake at such a gathering, was eclipsed by the nymph, even though the nymph's body was completely covered from wrist to neck in mud-coloured cotton, in corduroy trousers and a jumper made for sleeping or camping in, she could not hide her hair or her face. She had tried to hide how tall and slim she was, and was keeping silent with the practised wisdom of the fatefully beautiful girl among other women, and Marcus knew that she knew that Marcus had seen her and recognized her instantly and would never stop looking at her, and Marcus knew that this would make her sad, and had even noticed that she refused to look at him even when he smiled pointedly at her, and still he could not stop watching every movement she made, every time she lifted her face in the lamplight or dropped her head so the ringlets of her hair fell forward and were pushed back again by her long hand. He watched her knees shaking slightly as she wrote in her notebook, and her narrow forearms tensing as she wrote (what did she write? was she writing anything about him?). He could watch her doing nothing in this way with absorption, for a very long evening, he imagined, as one can watch the languorous pans of a French film. He felt sorry for her, for he knew that there was nothing she could do to stop him looking at her, or to stop the other women from hating her as soon as she spoke.

"But that's saying something," said the sexy woman with the cleavage. "Telling a story, in a certain way, is saying something. It's saying something about the world."

"This is true. In a way, it's saying something. But in a very indirect way. This is a very complicated question. It's not saying . . ." Marcus took another swig of brandy and cold coffee. It had been a long time since he had had a conversation like this. "It's not saying all people are like this, or I the author am like this. It's saying these two people, these people I have made up, are like this."

"What do you think she's saying, Mr. Royston?"

Marcus sighed. "I'm trying to say—"

"I think she has very important things to say," said Muriella, "about poverty, and the effects of poverty on—"

"She has a lot to say about slapping husbands," said a loud woman. "I wonder if she made that up?"

"I wonder about the lesbian affair."

"She hasn't admitted to anything, in interviews. In *Vanity Fair* they pressed her pretty hard about it."

"I didn't like that part, I must say."

"I could hardly read it."

"You don't have to sleep with another woman just because you don't like your husband."

"It's one thing to say that poverty is hard and life in Mississippi is hard, or wherever—"

"It's Tennessee, I think."

"—and another thing to say that same-sex relationships are just fine, they're just the same as any other relationship. I have a hard time with that."

"Well, I think she's trying to say they are," said Muriella, "and what's wrong with that?"

"Muriella!" There was frantic giggling.

"I just felt she didn't come across well."

"That's not the way to solve things."

"If she was abused as a child—"

"Who was?" said Marcus in the commotion. "The author or the character?"

"It's still not a great message to send."

"You don't solve violence with violence. That's the thing—"

"That's the thing she doesn't understand."

"But it's not the *author*," said Marcus very loudly, "who doesn't understand. It's the *character*. You're confusing them."

"Marcus," said Muriella, "who cares? You can't say there's no connection between the two? The character is someone we're supposed to admire, someone we're supposed to identify with—"

"Do you admire Hamlet?"

Muriella swallowed. "Yes. I don't remember Hamlet very well, but I think I do. I think you're supposed to sympathize with him."

"You're not *supposed* to do anything." He realized he was shouting now. He put his coffee cup down on a table and shouted. "What you're *supposed* to do doesn't matter. It's what you *feel* that matters."

The doorbell chimed. "That will be Howard," said the sexy woman.

"I think Hamlet is a self-absorbed little prick. And I don't approve of slaughtering your enemies in duels. If William Shakespeare didn't want me to feel that, that's too bad. Then William Shakespeare has not done his job well enough. What he wants *doesn't matter*."

There was male laughter in the entrance hall, the stamping of a big man. The sexy woman's voice tinkling in response.

"All right," said Muriella, "I don't know where you're going with that. All I'm trying to say is—"

"What time is it?" said a lady.

"—is that books, novels, have a responsibility."

"Oh, do they?"

"Well, they have a wide influence. They influence how people behave, and—"

"How they *behave*? How do they—"

"How people think, anyway. People, young people, can read them, and if they're not shown positive influences—"

"A literature of positive influences. How familiar, my dear, I am with that idea. You and the government of St. Andrew's, my island, would—"

He stopped, unsure of who he was arguing with. He noticed that the nymph was watching him. She had closed her notebook and was staring at him, her eyes darting between him and Muriella, wide. He straightened his back and said, "If this woman, this character, is confused, or unlikeable, that's what literature is about. It is not about providing positive influence, or solving the problems of poverty. It's about all the things, all dark things that . . ." He drained his cup. "All the dark things that motivate us." He stared straight in the eyes of the beautiful young girl and said, "Sex. It's about sex. Largely. And corruption and decadence. And all the terrible, terrible things we think." She looked away. But her eyes had been bright.

Marcus turned back to Muriella and saw that she too was watching the girl. Then she looked back at him, and her eyes were cold.

"Hello everyone," boomed a man standing in the door. He was six foot five and balding and fat. He wore a linen jacket and khaki trousers.

"Hello Howard," echoed the ladies. Several of them stood up, placing coffee cups on side tables, stretching on their stocking toes. They went and kissed Howard.

"Howard, this is Marcus Royston."

The big man loped towards him, hand extended. With a vague sense of disappointment, and some effort, Marcus hauled himself out of the deep chair.

"Howard Van Biesbrouck, pleasure, welcome to the country, heard a lot about you, great that you want to help out the ladies with their club, it's a great idea, I say, great thing."

"Pleasure," said Marcus. The man loomed over him, blocking his sight of the nymph.

"Ready to go, sweetie? Part of the deal, Marcus, is I get the house to myself for a couple of hours and I have to pick her up when it's over."

"Marjorie, I'll catch a ride with you."

"So what do you think of the group, Marcus?" said Howard Van Biesbrouck. "Standards high enough for you? They're pretty bright girls, aren't they? I couldn't make my way through some of the stuff they bring home, pretty serious stuff, I have to say. I'm in the manufacturing business myself, just a dumb businessman, don't get a lot of time to read, let the wife do that for me." He barked a laugh and all the women around him laughed too. "No, it's pretty impressive, seriously. Its a great group, really, great idea, no harm in it, anyway, keeps them busy, doesn't it, ladies? Keeps them happy, I guess."

"Muriella," said the sexy woman, a raincoat over her arm, "thanks so much. I'll call you, I'm sorry I have to—"

"Before everyone leaves," said the loud woman, standing, "why don't we relax a little and have some goodies? They're just sitting here and there's no point in letting them . . ."

There was more flustered rising and stretching and clattering of cups and saucers as the ladies moved through to the dining room and kitchen. With dignity, the enormous one opened her eyes and heaved herself off the sofa. She made no acknowledgement of having been asleep. Briefly, Marcus admired her.

"All right, chauffeur is leaving," shouted Howard Van Biesbrouck. "Do what I'm told, Marcus." He winked heavily and shook Marcus's hand again. "Don't let 'em order you around. They can be tough." He kissed two more women and ushered his little metallic wife towards the hall as she blew goodbyes and laughed.

Marcus followed the ladies into the kitchen, but the nymph was gone. He found her in the hall, putting on a denim jacket. "How do you do," he said, sticking out his hand. Through the open door, he could see the big man and the blonde wife manoeuvring down the curved path to the waiting cream car.

"Hi." She giggled. "I'm new here. I enjoyed—"

"Your name." Her hand was cool. He wouldn't give it back to her.

"Oh. Julia. Sternberg."

"How do you do, Julia Sternberg. A great pleasure." He relinquished her hand.

"I wanted to say I enjoyed what you had to say. Very much. I agree with you. Totally. It's ridiculous to, to say . . . I don't know. Anyway." She pushed her hair behind her ear and stepped towards the door.

"Go on."

"Oh. I mean they, it's a common mistake to confuse the character with the author. And to think you can see the author through the fiction."

"Or that that's important."

"Exactly. In school we used to talk about this a lot, about intentionality, and the critique of intentionality, it's just so . . ."

"You studied literature in school."

"A little. Not really." She seemed to be concentrating on buttoning her jacket. "I'd better go."

Marcus stuck his hand out again. "I would be delighted to talk more with you about this."

"Me too." Her face was red as she shook his hand. "And I liked what you had to say about darkness. About art being about darkness. I think it is too. I *really* do."

"We should talk about that too."

"Okay. Bye." She almost flew to the door.

Marcus went back into the kitchen to face the ladies with a tingling in his hand, as if he could feel the imprint of her white palm on his.

XVIII

"Well, he's just arrogant, is what he is. He lectures."

"He lectures where."

"You're not listening, lovey. He lectures everyone, me, everyone. He's condescending. He doesn't seem to be interested in anything that goes on here, except history, he—"

"What do you mean, history."

"He goes to the archives, I don't know what he's looking up there, and he keeps walking around Casa Loma, you know, the castle, and asking—"

"It's not a castle, Mom, it's a house, it was built by a millionaire, it just looks like a—"

"I know what it *is*, Johnny, I know all about it, and I told him it was a private house and I know it's supposed to be ugly, because everything Gothic is supposed to be ugly all of a sudden, but I don't find it ugly, I find it romantic, anyway, he keeps asking me all sorts of questions about when it was built, I don't know when it was built, and he asks them all with this sort of smile, as if he thinks it's all very funny and he's going to make fun of it."

"Weird. Very weird. This is what I worry about."

"He's obsessed with Fort York now, you know the old fort down by the waterfront, it's all done up for tourists now, where they have the students in uniform and changing of the guard and what have you. He takes the subway down there to watch."

"More than once?"

"Oh, twice a week. He's fascinated."

"Scary. It's scary is what it is." There was a clatter down the line, as if her son was rearranging plastic objects on his desk. He murmured something to someone in his room.

"Are you listening?" said Muriella. "You're distracted by something."

"No. I have to leave the office though, Deborah's not coming home at six and Estelle leaves at six."

"What is—why isn't Deborah coming home?"

"She has Pilates. It's her stress-relief thing. So I have to go in a minute. But you're okay, anyway, Mom, you're not worried about him?"

"Worried about him? What do you mean?"

"I mean you feel safe and everything? He doesn't frighten you in any way?"

"Frighten me?" Muriella squealed. "No, he doesn't frighten me. No, I'm not . . . he's not insane, if that's what you mean."

"Well, you said yourself he drinks too much, and he gets aggressive all the—"

"He controls it very well. You'd never know unless you knew."

"I just don't like the idea very much. I never have. Of you alone there with someone, someone like, someone you don't know staying in the house."

"Oh now you're being silly. I'm perfectly—"

"What's this about bringing people over? Does he bring people into the house?"

"Well, I told him he could, of course. So it's my fault. But he's bringing people over all the time now. Students, mostly, who want to talk to him and ask him questions, and they end up drinking and smoking in the library and they leave it a mess. It stinks in the morning."

"Terrible. Terrible. You don't think there's any, any funny stuff?"

"Sex? No, there are not a lot of women in that group. He would love it if there were, I'm sure. He flirts with everyone. Absolutely everyone. Absoutely anything that moves."

"This is what I mean, Mom. Is he coming on to you? Tell me honestly. Does he come on to you?"

"To me, no." Muriella was staring at a card that showed a woman's naked buttocks, half in shadow. She folded it in half, and then again. She folded it into a tiny square. "He doesn't come on to me."

"You can't allow these people to—listen, are you sure they're students? What kind of people are they he's bringing over? Are they . . ."

"Are they white people? Is that what you're asking? They're white and black and everything. Arabs, everything. That I don't mind, that has nothing to do with it."

"Mom, listen to me. Listen to me now. You have to put your foot down. You have to get tough with these people. If you don't want them in your—"

"No, lovey, it's not that that I mind. I think it's important for him to have a place he can teach from, that he can call his—"

John snorted. "*Teach?* Is that what you call staying up all—"

"Listen, lovey, it's not that, it's really not that."

Her son sighed. "I have to go now, Mom."

"It's more that . . . it's embarrassing to say, I shouldn't say it, but it's upsetting to me that he doesn't show more, more gratitude, I suppose."

"Of course. You've given him everything. He's living off you, Mom."

"Well, not really. I just donate the house. His expenses are paid by—"

"Whatever. Whatever. Mom, I have to go."

"But that apartment is comfortable, really, it's very comfortable, it's nothing to be ashamed of. I don't understand what he wants. He's just so arrogant. He's the one who isn't doing any work, from what I can see, and I'm the one he thinks is unimportant." Muriella felt her voice getting high, and could not stop it. "He's just unimpressed by everything, by the house, by my position, my fundraising, my role in the Arts Council, I'm not no one, you know, am I, am I no one?"

"Of course not, Mom. I really, really, truly have to go now."

After she hung up she was glad she didn't tell him about the pornography exhibition. That would have really upset him. She unfolded the invitation. She didn't know why she had been staring at it throughout the conversation. She had found it discarded in the library, after Marcus had asked her to come with her. All the boys went, the students Jason Katz had brought over to meet him, and Julia Sternberg too, to her alarm. She had found the card curiously gross. The image was grainy black and white, a woman's buttocks as she bent. One knee must have been raised high, the other leg planted on the ground. The contrast was so high that the bright curve of one cheek shone white, and the cave between her legs was black. But that dark crevice caught your eye, caught your eye and held it, for a tuft of dark hair stuck out there, wiry hair that hung downwards in silhouette. It seemed to be matted, as if wet. Those few curling black strands were the centre of the image. Muriella disliked the hair; it was too long; it looked dirty. Without the hair, it would have been a pretty art nude. That wet creeping hair was what made the image pornographic, and was why—she couldn't explain this to Marcus at the time—she had been afraid to go to the show, and she hadn't wanted Julia to go either. She had an image of Julia's pale skin somehow stained by wet hair.

The words under the photo read, "Velvet Salon IV," and underneath, "Fourth Annual Festival of Art and the Body."

The young people had all gathered at her house, all excited and laughing, to take Marcus with them. Julia would not meet her eye, and came and left without speaking. She stared at the hardwood floor while waiting for Marcus to finish his drink. Muriella stared at her little halter top, her bare belly, her slim shoulders with the dark and light ringlets falling loose on them.

He had come back sullen and tired, dropping leaflets on the hall table that were discount coupons for sex-toy stores, invitations for submissions to journals of erotica, advertisements for "boudoir photography."

She had found more of them in the pockets of his linen jacket, when he left it on the coat rack.

Marcus had, in fact, come on to her, she supposed, once, she could have told her son this, when he asked: at the baseball game, when he had touched her thigh; she was sure she had not misinterpreted that. But he was drunk then, not that it made a difference. And she had been shocked and alarmed and didn't know what to think. But she had thought about it afterwards. And now she had given him the message, without even thinking about it, once and forever, that she didn't want to be touched. Which of course she didn't.

Muriella crumpled the card, but could not throw it away. She slid it under the cigarette box, on which stood the straw mule that Marcus had brought on the day of his arrival, still perched there, still stiff and cocky and curiously unexplained.

While Muriella was having this conversation with her son, Marcus Royston was at a French restaurant downtown called the Select, being interviewed by a young white woman with the extraordinary name of Candace Bundle. She had short hair and spectacles and apparently massive breasts which shifted beneath a loose green T-shirt, obviously unconstrained under there, like a heaving sea as she moved. Candace Bundle worked for a magazine called *Next*, which was going to put him on their cover. Marcus had looked at *Next* and found it to be almost entirely about rock music. She was asking him questions about his childhood and his upbringing and then about his political activism and why he had abandoned the struggle in St. Andrew's. She knew a great deal about his political background. "I'm not really into poetry," she said, "I'm kind of on the politics side of things, but I would love to read yours, it seems so relevant. I would really love to. Which one should I start with?"

The restaurant's windows were closed and there was not enough air conditioning. Marcus wanted water. Around them, waiters were talking too loudly, laughing, clattering as they cleared tables. Marcus thought of Elizabeth. But there were no black people in the restaurant; there had not been all through lunch.

The waiters were setting tables for dinner in the mid-afternoon lull. Marcus was feeling the despair of being in an empty restaurant on a bright day. The last lunch eaters had gone. The foam inside his coffee cup had dried into ridges. His brandy glass was empty and he didn't want any more. He was sleepy from brandy and jumpy from coffee.

Outside, the light was harsh. Girls in tiny skirts and stacked shoes passed, laughing behind glass. He felt his blackness in this restaurant.

And he did not know how to impress a woman he could not seduce.

The jazz on the stereo was turned up too loud. He shifted in his seat and said, "I didn't abandon any struggle. We had won our struggle. In nineteen sixty-six. Nineteen sixty-six was when we won independence. I was only . . . I was eighteen. And we have had a democratic parliament ever since."

"Yes, but there has been a political struggle, I mean, since then, right?"

"As in any country. There was a left-wing party and a right-wing party. The right-wing party is now in power. I was employed in the government under the other party."

"The party that fought for independence."

"Yes."

"And since then you've spent a lot of time away, I mean out of the country."

"Well, I, not really. I studied abroad, at—"

"Would you call yourself, consider yourself, an exile?"

Marcus took a deep breath. "An exile." He looked out at the street vendors. "An exile. An exile from what?"

"From your homeland. Your country."

Marcus laughed.

"Would you not consider St. Andrew's to be your country?"

"Oh yes. Yes I would. My passport says it is."

"But it's not your home?"

"Well. This is an interesting question. I am not sure I feel at home anywhere. My education makes it difficult for me, in St. Andrew's, to . . . I have met people here, here in this country, who make me feel at home."

"Really? What kind of people?"

"The man who runs the roti shop near where I live. Where I am staying. Not because he is from a similar culture. We have very great cultural differences, he and I. But because he is also a foreigner here. Wherever he goes, in fact. He will always feel that he has no home. This makes me feel at home."

"Homelessness."

"I suppose."

Candace Bundle brightened. "Homelessness is something we could talk about. You know there is a huge, *huge* homeless problem in this city."

Marcus peered again at the sidewalk vendors, the bright T-shirts, and then at his watch. "Have you been to Fort York?"

"Sorry?"

"There is a restored nineteenth-century fortress down by the waterfront. It's quite well done. They have soldiers in uniform, and they do certain drills, like—"

"Oh, Fort York, right. Yeah. No, I haven't been there. Why?"

"Oh, you should. It's your heritage."

She smiled. "Military things don't turn me on that much."

"Ah."

She looked back at her notes. "Would you say that there is an institutionalized racism in the literary culture of this country?"

"I'm afraid I don't know very much about the literary culture of this country. But there is racism everywhere else, so I suppose there must be here as well."

"Have you encountered racism here?"

He hesitated. "Yes. Yes I have." He was thinking of the man who had come to pick up his wife at the book club. *Great that you want to help out the ladies.* "There is more unconscious racism than there is . . . than there is open hostility, but all the same."

"Can you tell me what happened?"

Marcus thought about this. *Don't let 'em order you around.* That poor idiot was not a threat, really. "A wealthy man was condescending to me. It may have been because I was an artist, not because I was . . ."

"A person of colour."

Marcus sighed. "I think he probably would have spoken like that to any artist, anybody who was not wealthy. I don't know if it was racism. I really don't."

"Of course it was racism!" Candace Bundle placed her pen flat on her pad. Her eyes were wide.

"You don't know what I'm talking about," said Marcus gently. Something about this conversation was tiring him. "The reason I asked about Fort York was that you should really go there. It's delightful. It really takes you back in time. I find it very comforting."

"Comforting?" She laughed shortly. "Why?"

"This is what's interesting. It's the architecture. There is a system of British forts in the Caribbean, most of them are older than that, and made of stone rather than brick, but there are certain architectural constants. The arches, for example. Lovely brick arches. And the drainage systems. I find I am fascinated by gutters. There are forts, high in the hills surrounding the port of Dunstanton, which is the capital city, which is where I live, which collected rainwater in a system of stone grooves, which drained into barrels. And there are holes at the base of the walls, with what do you call them, drain holes, for water to run out, and the incredible thing is there are little stone arches over every outlet, little arches six inches high. They would have required a stone-mason to cut every one. It's exquisite. In these jungles. They built these forts in the late seventeen hundreds early eighteen, so, much earlier than your Fort York, and yet—"

"It's the same colonial mentality that built both of them."

"Oh, exactly. Exactly. When they sent sailors to build the forts in Saint Andrew's, they were conscripts, usually, they were often pressed into service, so they were a form of prisoners. And they used slaves, of course, to build, but they hadn't brought many slaves over yet, that really happened in the nineties or even—"

"There were slaves long before the eighteen nineties!" Candace Bundle's face was red.

"The seventeen nineties." Marcus watched her scan her notes, drum her fingers on the table, and look out the window. He decided to keep talking. "The first forts were built by British sailors, in the most appalling conditions. They hoisted cannons up through ravines, using the most ingenious pulleys and bridges, quite incredible, in that heat, you can just imagine how crushing the heat and the humidity must have been for them, particularly since they had no choice but to wear their full uniforms, the great red serge, you know, red wool jackets, and full leggings and under-clothes, it was all mandatory. We have a little museum set up where you can learn these things. There wasn't quite enough information about uniforms at Fort York. I was wondering how they dealt with the cold. At any rate." Marcus took a sip of water, watched Candace Bundle look at her watch. "I have a great deal more to say on this."

"That's okay, but I still have a few more questions I want to ask you and I have to be out of here by—"

"The enemy was the French, of course, same as here. And there was dreadful fanaticism. Imagine these officers, ship captains, noblemen usually, aristocrats, arriving in a ship and getting a force organized to find stone, quarry it, build a camp to house labourers, feed them, find water sources, and get this stone up these jungly hills, and dig foundations, and build these fortresses, and then haul their cannons up. There was disease, of course, and men dying of God knows what, heat like hammers on their heads, heat unlike anything they had ever imagined, the horizon gone all blurry from heat, the taste of metal in the mouth. The roar of hot wind on the mountaintop. Think about it. Imagine the kind of madman who must have been in charge of getting those things done. So far from any other authority. The king of slaves. It must have made him feel like God. There is a kind of madness that took those Englishmen in the tropics. I wonder if it took them here too."

Candace Bundle was rereading her previous notes.

He said, "I suppose there is a madness in making monu-ments of these places. The way we make museums with cheery diagrams of battles and gun emplacements. And we pay students to dress as soldiers, and put them in pretty uniforms. In my country, they are monuments to slavery. Tourist sites, informative. Monuments to cruelty, unbearable cruelty. Hunger, degradation, torture, starvation. I suppose it's like the gas chambers in Germany, you can tour them. But it's presented in a different way. Monuments to madness."

Candace Bundle looked at her watch again and said, "Are you planning to get involved in the writing, activist community here?"

"Is that the same thing?"

She didn't answer.

"In either case, I think not." Marcus waved for the waiter. "I am really only interested in the past."

The headline, when the article appeared, read: "Caribbean's father of revolutionary conscience scorns artist's responsibility for social change."

The text mentioned his "well-calculated air of fatigue," and that he obviously dismissed the literary community here, from an obviously Anglocentric point of view.

Candace Bundle had interviewed an American "writer /activist" called Tom Tupatopunt, about Marcus Royston's reputation, and this man said that Marcus Royston was well known to be an anglophile and who had been marked by a private-school education and then spent too much time being admired and cosseted by a white establishment.

Marcus counted the word *community* nine times in the article.

He thought he would have no trouble remembering the name Candace Bundle.

XIX

"A LIBRARY," SAID THE CHIEF OPERATIONAL officer, reading carefully, "is more than a collection of books. It's a community of users."

Brian was at the back, standing. He had a plastic glass of wine. So had the man with the sleeping bag. The man with the sleeping bag always seemed to be next to him, however Brian moved around the room. The sleeping bag was tightly rolled and sat on top of a vinyl bag with two handles that the man carefully placed at his feet every time he stood next to Brian. The man had a raincoat which was still largely coherent and on his feet were the remnants of shoes. He had one hand cupped full of cubes of cheese that he had taken from the table with the wine. He was concentrating fully on the cheese and the wine. He did not smell, as far as Brian could tell. But his presence kept Brian from concentrating on the Mission Statement.

"In the wired world," read the chief operating officer, "and an age of diminishing support from municipal and provincial sources, the role of the library must become more flexible, more proactive."

If Brian stood on his toes and looked over the back of the man with the television camera in front of him, he could see Marcus in the front row. Marcus had his legs crossed and his head deeply bowed. The only way you could tell he wasn't asleep was by his foot waggling in its polished leather shoe. It kicked forward every time the chief operating officer said "interactive." Beside Marcus was Jasminka, in a glittering turban, looking majestic and territorial. There were television cameras cruising and flashbulbs. The audience was mostly librarians, Brian guessed. They wore a variety of perfumes. The media women, at the front, held the heavy blue folders which held all the details of the Mission Statement.

The chief operating officer had a grey suit, a grey shirt, a grey tie, and a tie clip which appeared to be made of pewter or possibly lead. "The virtual library has no physical centre. But there is still a role for physical libraries as centres for interactivity, for community outreach . . ."

They had already heard from the chief publicist and the representative from city council (the mayor had been regretfully unavailable). No librarian had spoken nor, apparently, was going to speak. The librarians sat absolutely still in rows.

"And a way of uniting the community."

Marcus's foot jerked.

"Seniors' reading and exercise groups, preschool access days on Tuesdays and Wednesdays, the Mothercare program which provides excellent access every morning for mothers in the community . . ."

The foot fluttered like a flag. Marcus's head did not move.

"It is now my great pleasure," read the chief operating officer, "to introduce our guest speaker, who has kindly offered to say a few words about the Mission Plan, a writer and an artist with an international stature, the author of several books of poetry and plays, who happens to be our honoured guest here as guest artist in the City Arts Board Action Council's Residency Program, I on behalf of the Metro Library and Information Access Network am pleased to present Mr. Marcus Royston."

Marcus stood very slowly in the applause. It seemed, from where Brian was standing, that his eyes were still closed. He stood still for a moment, still hunched, before straightening and stepping towards the podium. There was only one bad lurch before he got there.

Marcus gripped the podium and stared down at it. He wore a dark suit, a white shirt, a dark tie, and a burgundy pocket square like a wound. His forehead gleamed, wrinkled. His eyes were not visible behind his glasses. He did not seem about to say anything. The television cameras hummed. The man with the sleeping bag had finished his cheese and was now licking the palm of his hand.

Marcus looked up at the ceiling. There was some coughing. He opened his mouth and with great deliberation said, "I'm not sure." He looked down again. "I'm not sure why I'm here, really. I am not sure why I was asked."

The chief operating officer, standing to one side, smiled firmly. His hands were clasped behind his back. The librarians shifted, fanned themselves with the Mission Statement.

"I grew up in a very small town, which was really, genuinely, as you say, a community." Marcus reached for the glass on the podium, grasped it, and carefully brought it to his lips. This operation held the attention of the audience for a minute. He replaced the glass without spilling. "This town is called Havre Morne, and it is, as far as I know, still there, although I am glad I have left it. I was at a church school there which was not, like your church schools here, Catholic, it was a Methodist school, and my father was a master there, for he was a Methodist minister. There were not many books in my school, and I quickly read through those in my house. I would read in the garden on Sundays, beside the chicken coop." He straightened, put his hands in his pockets, and went on more quickly. "There was a library in the central square of Havre Morne. Next to the Catholic cathedral. The Cathedral was French built. The library was British built. At any rate, I have a hard time seeing a library as a centre of community. The library, for me, was a place of solitude and quiet. It still is."

The chief operating officer was still smiling, although he had folded his arms across his chest. He was shifting his weight from one foot to the other. The chief publicist was smiling too, but kept looking at the chief operating officer. The librarians had begun to whisper.

"There were places I could get to in my reading which I wanted to visit, which I thought I would never visit. There were people, in my reading, more sophisticated than those around me. The library, to me, was an escape from my community."

The librarians stopped whispering at this. And the chief operating officer stopped smiling.

"Later, when I left that place and went to university, and then came to live in the capital city of St. Andrew's, and then lived in London and in the United States, there were other libraries which were always, to me, a place of work. I did my research there. I did my writing there. It was not a place of community, except perhaps if you're thinking of that invisible community of people who have written the books that are in the library. But I fear that's not what you're thinking of."

Marcus took some more water. His voice grew stronger. "And I am sure that there are many, many people who use this library and all the other libraries in your system or network, I see you call it, for work, for serious work, and I'm sure that they would be displeased by the Mothercare days and the children's hours and the seniors' social clubs that are going to displace them, because of course they will displace them. And if I were a senior citizen, which I one day, soon, will be, I would be offended, honestly, I think, offended, by the idea that what I need is a social club with bridge and bingo and what have you, who can imagine these things, and not a library where I can read and work." He pulled his hands from the pockets, gripped the podium and drew breath. "I am sorry to denounce your Mission Plan. But I think it will destroy your libraries. I am sorry. As I say, I am surprised I was asked to speak on this plan. My views on this should have been somewhat predictable. I am not sure why I was asked. I am sorry. Thank you."

As Marcus sat, carefully holding on to a chair-back to prevent swaying, the applause from the librarians grew until many of them were standing. The women at the back, in front of Brian, lifted their hands into the air to clap. Brian did too.

The chief publicist was at the microphone. He tried to speak above the clapping. "Well," he said, smiling furiously in the light, "I'd like to thank Mr. Royston for his provocative comments, which are always, believe me, welcome, in this dialogue, because that's what we like to think of this as, a dialogue."

The applause began to die. The librarians began to pick up bags and move.

"I think perhaps we won't have a question period now, as planned," the chief publicist shouted into the microphone, "but if you'd like to stay and enjoy the refreshments—"

The television cameras closed around Marcus. The media women were holding microphones up to his face. Brian looked for the chief operating officer but could not see him. The man with the sleeping bag had disappeared.

XX

October 17

*This afternoon I walked from the house down through the
bundled houses of the Portuguese, their gardens bristling with
sticks. They gather sticks and poles and rusted rods and make
scaffolding of them, for their grapevines, so their gardens look
like shantytowns whose walls have blown off in the wind. It
looks like home. The Portuguese are all old, I'm not sure
why. They bustle about in their gardens in old cotton dresses
and heavy jerseys, red-faced and heaving. The alleys between
the streets, for garages, are running with grape juice. The
garage doors are open and the empty grape boxes are stacked
inside, and in front of the houses, on the curb. The air is thick
with a sweet and rotting smell.*

*I kept walking down hills until I was where the real white
people live, in the old Jewish quarter. I walked down a street
full of dark mansions which are now divided into warrens, for
students in art history or poetry. No engineering student would
live here; it is too decadent. The houses on this street are
sensuous and secretive, elaborately curlicued and verandahed
towers of Victorian brick and peeling wooden balustrades,
some squat and rambling, some narrow, most at least three
storeys high, with pointy roofs and attic balconies, all
crammed together in two competitive rows, all muffled with
ivy. They seem top-heavy with additions, turrets and
balconies that threaten to topple. Cooing pigeons under the*

*eaves. The pavements are thick with wet yellow leaves that
wash right up to the carved doors.*

*It had grown dark—quite suddenly dark—as I began
shuffling down it, and then it began to rain, but the trees tent
the black street so completely I was protected. The street
whispered with water. City of secrets. I could see into some
windows, and see that rich people had renovated some of the
houses, restored their mouldings and stained glass, painted the
living rooms dark poppy and the bedrooms steely teal. The
studies, book-lined, hunter green. There were no people
visible. Outside these houses were prams and tricycles; wired to
the more sombre buildings were bicycles, racks of bicycles,
some locked together three deep. In these houses, harsher lights
shone, and windows hung with flags and blankets. These were
the students, the decadent poor.*

*Rotting apples in the piles of leaves; the smell an earthier
one than the grapes, too much, overpowering, too fruity, a
smell of declining empire. In many ways a mood reminiscent
of Edinburgh. I liked it. I felt at home there.*

*A brick synagogue, with stained glass glowing azure and
rose. A swastika spray-painted on the door.*

October 21

*Hard rain. It hammers. It is a sheet, a wall of cold spikes,
waves of cold. It rakes the storefronts and cars and cracks and
holes and boards and streetcar tracks, it sweeps the wrinkled
men in the doorway of the community-aid shelter. It is cold,
grimly cold, determined and relentless, massive vengeance.
Surfaces swell and slosh, the pavement dances with splash.*

In the women's-aid office, dirty girls take refuge from the fury and stand dripping in the lobby, bewildered by their sudden disarray. They look out the blurry window as if trapped inside.

The house is dark and musty, my boots and trousers dripping. The rain drums on the roof. My basement room is dim and silent. The hum of heating. The window is grey, liquid, the sky a sea. I sit at my typewriter and in the comforting rattle all I can write is a list of women's names.

October 22

The fall: low clouds like an aluminum lid. Inside, a hissing warmth, a house of two strangers, circling. Everything is inside here, interior. Then sudden bright days of high winds, the air in the mornings like a slap to the face. How can it be so bright and so cold, as if the air has been sucked from the day, as if one enters a vacuum? One feels that the spaces of life have been reversed: it is outside that is temporary, inside that is real. We scuttle indoors to live.

She is moving in here, as her house is too cold. I will not be here for the arrival of the moving van, the sadness of her boxes, her parents' cast-off furniture, the skis she no doubt no longer uses. It will make me feel old.

Mermaids and angels have the same terrible hold on dream and rib cage, abdominal panic. Both are eternally young, beautiful, glowing, capricious, forbidding, distant, cold, will bring you redemption. Both do not exist, but I confuse women with them, women I have met at cocktail party, lecture, seen on streetcar, women whose corner of fabric, line of dress, falls in architecture over knee or ankle, heartrending, woman who becomes artifice, cathedral.

Angels soothe without flesh. Mermaids dance with the devil, and with firm white breasts and the shrivelling caress of fish dance you into the deep.

If she knew I mythologized her in this way she would be irritated that I didn't know her neuroses first, she would be resentful of angelhood, imagehood, the deep fictional sea, she would be rightly afraid of the gelid non-life of mermaids.

October 23

Fall: roaring skies, wet streets, brown leaves. The students talk always of apartments, of nothing but apartments, rents, ways of sharing, of diminishing expenses, then of transport, of bus routes, borrowed bicycles. The young writers talk of films, of documentaries, of writing children's television programs, of Web sites, of marketing product lines, they want to sell T-shirts with their names on them, they are always planning businesses, foreign sales on comic books not yet written, they must think, always and all the time, about translating something written into something that is more easily bought. They stay up late at night and listen to each other's plans, wide-eyed, numbers and names and who owns what company, they can talk money forever.

Narrative poem: the striving, the selling. The young desperate for careers, the striving of even the wealthy to stay so, the grasping, the sense of imminent yawning failure. Make parallel with the culture of the taxi drivers in the market in Dunstanton, the borrowing and negotiating, the turns as proud driver and begging sycophant, the chattering under the awnings.

It will be hard to interweave. I do not think I will ever write this poem. Or perhaps any other.

October 24

Fall: a turbulent grey sky, gravid clouds, the rustling of leaves. A pitter of rain.

I have turned from rum to scotch, like a white man. Poem about Scotch. Play on warmth/colour/poison.

a mouthful of scotch, a ball of bright copper in the mouth.
I hold a ball of copper in my mouth.
A mouth of burning copper.

Play on paradox of looking warm and cold with ice at the same time.

A sudden memory of childhood: wooden desks, no glass in the windows, a breeze from the sea carrying the smell of earth, bare feet, hungry for lunch, chanting lines of poetry: The highwayman came riding, came riding.

October 25

Fall: a brilliant blue day, cold-bright and windy. A blond day.

She lives here now and I pass her quietly in the hall or in the passage beside the house, if we think Muriella is watching. I think Muriella knows.

I want to cup this sisterly woman's full breasts in my hand, have her weep against my cheek.

October 26

Sunday again, still fall, grey and blustery, falling yellow leaves. City of secrets. Baths are drawn, doors are closed. This house is like Apollinaire's hotel:

Fermons nos portes
A double tour
Chacun apporte
Son seul amour

XXI

JASMINKA HEAVED SUDDENLY, INTER-
rupting Iris Warshavsky, whose voice was growing high.
"There is absolutely nothing we can do about what he is
saying in the press. Absolutely nothing."

"We could do something." Iris Warshavsky was twisting
a paper clip, weakening it so it would snap.

"What?"

"We could cancel the program." She would not look at
Jasminka. The paper clip came in two. She held the two
pieces.

"That would be a little bit extreme, I think."

Brian and Muriella were silent. Brian watched her staring
at the tabletop, her arms folded. She did not look embarrassed, for once. She looked serene.

"He is entitled," breathed Jasminka, "to say what he
thinks."

"Is he?" bleated Deepak. "Is he really? To say whatever
he thinks, no matter how offensive? Did you read what he
said in the *Next* thing? He said that racism doesn't exist in
this country."

Iris snorted. The pieces of wire shot across the table.

Brian leaned forward. "That's not exactly what he said."

"Then he gave that speech in the library," said Iris
Warshavsky, "where he was rude, just plain rude, with his
sarcastic jokes about communities."

"I'm not sure it was sarcastic," said Brian.

There was a silence, in which he could hear a swishing of rain. The room smelled of damp clothes.

"He was drunk," murmured Brian, as an excuse.

"Then he told *The Globe and Mail* that he didn't believe in government support for the arts."

"It was the *National Post*," said Brian. "And, again, that's not exactly what he—"

"It is how the editorialists took it," said Jasminka quietly. "And now they're holding him up as a model. I suppose you all saw the editorial."

"Great," said Deepak. "That's just great. Now we're on the side of the *National Post*. Terrific. And then there was that English guy, that obscene Englishman who has the call-in show on TV, and he was talking about him too, how wonderful, how fantastic we now have a black man saying there's no racism in this country, we just handed this to him, he was delighted, just delighted, he was gleeful, it was like he'd finally found a good nigger and wanted to show all the other niggers how good he could be."

"Deepak," said Jasminka.

"That's what he was saying."

"It really does not make us look good," said Iris Warshavsky. "It's not good for all the arts. I think we have to put a stop to it."

"By cancelling the program?" said Brian.

"Yes. By cancelling the program."

Brian sank in his chair. He looked at Muriella, who was looking at the rainy window. She was twisting her red hair into strands. She wore a black top of something clingy and he glanced at the outline of her breasts, shallow and low on her torso, rising and falling. Her skin was pale, and for the first time he noticed she had green eyes. Her neck was long. In the green light from the ceiling she was almost beautiful. On realizing this, Brian looked away, feeling a little sick and guilty, as if he had been lusting for his own mother.

There was a bumping outside as someone tried to open the door to this room. This door was always broken or stuck, and locked, for some reason, from the inside. Jasminka looked offended. Brian got up to open it but it opened on its own, and Marcus Royston's head popped out from behind it, peering, as if he was just checking to see if the room was occupied. His glasses were splashed with rain and had slid down his nose. "Ah," he said, and pushed his way in, in a heavy raincoat and an umbrella he had not managed to completely collapse.

And behind him was Julia Sternberg, in a rain suit made up of shiny trousers and a shiny top. It looked like something you would go fly-fishing in.

They came in with much shaking of wet objects and the moving of chairs, and then the rustling of Julia's rain suit being removed (under which she was still impenetrably clad, in turtleneck and corduroys), and the finding of a closet to hang the rain suit and the umbrella in, and then the finding of the backs of chairs, in the absence of a closet, on which to hang the wet things.

When Marcus sat he was relaxed. He took off his glasses and polished them with a white handkerchief. "I just wanted to come," he said, "and say hello, because it is odd, don't you find, that I have never truly met you all, and I wanted to let you know how grateful I am for all the work you have done for me." He put the glasses back on his face and blew his nose with the white handkerchief. Then he smiled at each committee member in turn.

There was a silence before Deepak said, "It's a pleasure to finally meet you."

"Yes," said Iris Warshavsky. She looked miserable.

Jasminka said, "I've been meaning to invite you. I am so glad you're finally here. And Julia Sternberg, our new member, who, you may not have met everyone yet?"

Julia shook hands with Iris Warshavsky and Deepak, and said how honoured she was to be a part of the program and how she was looking forward to working with everyone. She added quickly that she already knew Brian Sillwell. She did not look at him.

Brian then had a long opportunity to look at her. He noticed that she turned to look at Marcus Royston whenever he spoke, and canted her head to one side as if admiring a particularly complex and intriguing structure.

Marcus was saying, "I have to say, I should say, that I am sorry for causing trouble for everyone so far. I hope that . . ." He trailed off and threw his hands upwards, shaking his head and smiling, as if he was speaking of the importunity of the rain, and everyone around the table smiled, smiled because they could not help it, because Marcus, in his English tweed jacket and his grey coffee skin and his odour of damp and wine, in his apparent helplessness, was sympathetic, charming, his mere presence was charming. "I understand," he said, "that my remarks at the library caused some objections here, and I would be happy to, well, if it interests you at all, I'm not sure if it's my role to . . ." Here he took his glasses off again and held them at arm's length, frowning, to analyze them, as if he had perhaps picked up someone else's glasses and was debating whether to keep them.

There was some coughing around the table.

"The library," said Jasminka finally, in her voice of doom, "is not connected to the Action Council in any way."

"Oh I know, I know." Marcus was still squinting at his glasses. "Which is why I didn't understand why, what I heard was that there had been some consternation. This is what I didn't understand."

"Well," said Deepak, leaning forward, "it wasn't us who was consternated. It was the library people. They were a little upset that they invited you to come and promote the program and then you went and trashed it."

"No, they never asked me to promote it. They asked me to give a talk on what I thought of it. Which I duly did. There was no mention of promotin'. I will never understand why they didn't ask me what I thought on the issue before they asked me to speak. There seems to be an understandin' here, I gather this only from the short time I've been here, so please correct me if I'm wrong, please, seriously, please do, but it seems that there is an understandin' here, among all people, that we will only have positive and supportive things to say, that we will agree with everything and support each other. It did not occur to the library that I might disagree with them. This is very different from what I am used to, from where I come from, where the expectation is that we will disagree." He said this with a wide smile. His glasses were carefully reinstated on his nose, then adjusted. "But why were you upset, Mr.—"

"Deepak," said Deepak.

"Why were you upset, in particular?"

"I didn't say I was."

"Ah. My mistake. I understood that you were."

"No."

"I see. No problems then."

There was more coughing after this.

Jasminka said gently, "Well, let's admit that we, as individuals, and again there is no connection whatever between us and the library, supported efforts to make the city library a little bit more welcoming, a more open and pluralistic place, and that would have involved making it more community-based, more community-centred. But this is neither here nor there."

"I see." Marcus nodded happily, then blew his nose again. "And you think that being community-based would mean making it a little more ethnically conscious, as well?"

"Well," said Jasminka.

"Yes," said Deepak and Iris Warshavsky together.

"A little more race-based," said Marcus.

"Well," said Jasminka, "that's not how anyone would—"

"It doesn't matter," said Marcus, "as you said, it's neither here nor there. Anyway. Don't let me interrupt. What were you discussing before my intrusion?"

This time there was not even any coughing. Brian shifted on his chair. He knew that if he or Muriella didn't mention the possibility of Marcus being sent home, nobody would. But he didn't. He didn't know why he couldn't, but it was just too much trouble at that moment.

Muriella did speak. "There was some discussion, Marcus, over what you said to the interviewers, at *Next* and at the *National Post*, about racism in the country?"

Marcus closed his eyes as if tired. "What did I say?"

"That it was something of an overrated issue," said Deepak. "Racism."

"Oh. Did I? Did that worry you? Why?"

"Simply because we disagree with you," said Jasminka. "But we don't have to discuss this. It's not our business."

"Yes," said Marcus, "this is the question, isn't it? How much of your business is it? I take it that it has become so much your business that you are wondering if I still have a right to be here? Or am I guessing too much?"

A streetcar rumbled past outside so loudly that the silence was not so uncomfortable this time. To Brian, it sounded as if the rain was intensifying outside, a concert of engines and splash.

"I assure you," said Marcus, still smiling, "that it is all immaterial to me. I am merely curious."

"But that's just it," said Deepak quickly. "Immaterial. To you. You don't care. And you make it clear that you don't care. There are people here who worked for you. We all worked for you. And you keep saying you don't care and it all doesn't matter. Of course our feelings can be hurt by that."

Marcus blinked and dropped his smile. "Yes," he said softly. "Yes. I am sorry. I am sorry." Again he looked deeply tired.

"And when you say that race doesn't matter, that it isn't an issue anywhere, it sounds as if you, I don't know, it sounds to me as if you just don't want to talk about it."

Marcus spoke slowly. "I have spent a great deal of my life. Talking about it. Perhaps I am tired of it now. But I also do honestly feel that in this place it isn't . . . that it isn't quite as limiting as . . . I don't know." He looked down. His glasses had fogged up again.

The next voice was so clear and high Brian jumped, as if a stranger had walked into the room. Which she had: it was Julia, speaking for the first time. "Marcus," she said, "of course it is. Of course it's an issue. It's an issue for you as much as it is for Deepak or for Iris or for Jasminka or for me, for that matter." She was sitting very straight, her cheeks flushed. She was looking straight and high, at no one in particular. "I know you're conscious of your race, of your colour anyway, whenever you walk into a restaurant or a cocktail party or whatever, even if people do know who you are. I know I'm conscious of it, if I go into a roti shop or something. And also . . . also there's just how it affects your background. How you had to learn everything from a foreign power, and how you had to learn to do everything in a white way when you went away to—"

"I wouldn't call it a white way," said Marcus tightly, "I'd call it a British way, which is partly what I am."

"But you're not. You're not. You know you're not. You've told me you're not."

Marcus sighed. He wrapped his arms around himself and closed his eyes. It occurred to Brian that he was probably craving a drink. It was already afternoon.

But people weren't waiting for what Marcus would say. They were waiting for what Julia would say next. She was calm now. Deepak's face was astonished. Even Iris Warshavsky was attentive. Jasminka seemed to be smiling, though it was hard to tell.

"And maybe if you don't feel it, Marcus," said Julia, "the people in this room do, I'm sure, having had different experiences in this country, where they are more in a minority than you were in your country, if you see what I mean. And we didn't all win scholarships to go away to Edinburgh or wherever. So it's unfair to say that race doesn't matter. Of course race is culture and culture determines where you go to school and what kind of advantages you've had, and if we judge everything, particularly works of art, by the standards of say, I don't know, say Edinburgh, then we're using a race-based standard, and people's . . . different kinds of expression aren't rewarded. And I do think there's a kind of politics operating there to keep things kind of the same. Anyway." Now she looked down, and for the first time she reddened, as if suddenly aware that she had said so much. "Anyway," she said in a quieter voice. "I know these issues are complicated. I'm just trying to contribute to this debate."

"Hear hear," murmured Jasminka.

Marcus looked up at Julia, but not with bitternes. He smiled and wrinkled his eyes. It seemed to Brian that he was proud of her for saying all this, which irritated Brian, not because he disagreed with what she said (and he didn't agree with all of it, either), but because he was impressed at how she had put it. He did not recall her speaking like this in classes at school. He was proud of her too. He hoped that Marcus had not had anything to do with it.

Julia spoke again. "You know, just speaking personally, I'll always be from my childhood, which is Jewish, and from Montreal, which is a very specific thing. What writer was it, I forget, some English writer, said one is from one's childhood as one is from a country. Something like that."

Marcus breathed, hunched over, "Forster, I think."

"That's so interesting." Another bright voice, this time Muriella. She sat at the far end of the table and had to speak up. "I have always felt that, you know, Julia. One is from one's childhood. It's exactly like that. It's as if you're speaking another language now, but you can always speak the language you come from."

"What?" said Brian.

"I understand you exactly," said Julia.

"In other words it's more a question of culture than race," said Brian.

As they argued this, and as Deepak calmed down and talked about it too, and as even Iris began to talk about who she was and where she came from, Brian watched Marcus growing more sleepy and saying less.

XXII

"*Air Liquide*," said Jason Katz in a French accent. "Deejay Air Liquide. You would have to be gay." He was wearing a straw cowboy hat which he probably hoped made him look like a guy who worked in film or at least rock videos, but it didn't. They were in a roti shop, listening to reggae and drinking Ting, and they were playing their favourite game.

"It depends," said Brian, "on what my genre would be at that moment. My techno name would be Roomtone. Deejay Roomtone. And then—"

"Death," said Jason, "for hard techno. Deejay Death. Or Hardhat. Deejay Hardhat."

"That's good. Why are you wearing that hat?"

"What's wrong with my hat?" Jason touched it front and back with both hands as if straightening it in a mirror. He looked very serious and Brian laughed.

"Does it come with spurs and chaps, or a little badge? Is it Halloween?"

"What's your ambient name?"

"I have other hats, you know, you could wear, like a medieval helmet, with a visor, it comes with a whole suit of armour, and a shield, you could walk around like that if you liked. Or how about a hobo costume, with overalls and the stick and the little bundle in a red handkerchief?"

"Shut up," said Jason. "Chicks like hats like this."

"Aha. Why is that?"

"It makes them think you listen to folk singers and blues and stuff, guys who have gravelly voices and sing about jumping freight cars. Don't laugh about the hobo thing. It would work."

"But you don't. Listen to that."

"Well, now, you have me there. But if they think you do, they love you. They love that. It makes them think you have a huge cock."

Brian said, "Oh. I see. And then for ambient, or ambient techno, I'd be Deejay Ativan."

"That's good. Deejay Xanax."

"Better. And then for funky house and breaks I'd be Bag. Deejay Bag."

"I would have a really mellow funky set," said Jason, "almost deep house. And I would be . . ." Jason hiccuped and grinned. "Deejay Doctor Lovewaggler."

Brian looked at Jason's extremely pale face and his spiky hair and his very long neck and his blue-and-brown plaid shirt and the cowboy hat and he began to laugh. "Lovewaggler."

"Like a late-night-radio guy. The Doctor."

They were both laughing hard now. "That's you, man. That's you. The Lovewaggler."

"I am *the* waggler."

"You are such a waggler."

"You're listening to the smooth fruity sounds," said Jason in a deep black voice, "of Deejay Doctor Lovewaggler, coming to you from deep inside my cranial cavity."

"And from plenty of other bodily cavities besides."

"You got to keep yoh bitches in *line*, man."

"*Beeyatch.*"

The man behind the counter was frowning at them, so they tried to stop hooting. When they had subsided, Brian became aware again of how sad it was that he was spending his Saturday afternoon in a shop that smelled of curry with Jason, which was not sad in itself, but it was a reminder that there were no girls laughing with them.

Jason was apparently reminded of the same thing, because he said, "When was the last time we went to a funky party?"

"We don't go to funky parties."

"We could pay to see a deejay."

"There's nothing good. No one good ever comes to this town any more."

"That's because this town sucks."

"Why don't people have parties?"

"Maybe they do," said Jason, "and they don't invite us."

"I don't think they do. Nobody has a place big enough."

They both contemplated the advantages and disadvantages of parties. At parties there were girls, but you couldn't speak to them because you were a loser, and if you did speak to them, they usually didn't stick around very long, so you were even more of a loser. But at least there were girls there. Brian knew they were both thinking about this without speaking it.

Brian said, "Marcus Royston meets lots of people. He meets smart people and writers and profs and women. All kinds of women. How does he do that?"

"He's famous."

"He's not that good-looking. And he's black. Is that it?"

"He's not at all good-looking. He's famous. That's all it is. He's famous. We have to get famous and the same thing will happen."

Brian thought about this. He said, "No one has had a welcoming party for Marcus Royston."

Jason frowned. "Why would we? I thought you—"

"Because all the people come for him. We host it."

"Where? In your basement?"

"Where do you think?"

Jason blinked. "Ah. I see. The good widow."

"The good widow. Big house, big party."

"We do all the inviting."

"And Royston. We let him do it as well."

"Would he be into this?"

Brian got up and went to the payphone by the video game. Then he had to go back to get a quarter from Jason. He called Muriella's and got her and she told him she had installed a private line for Marcus in his apartment, so he had to find another quarter. When Marcus answered it sounded as if he had been sleeping. He said he thought a party was a wonderful idea, as if he did not care if there was a party or no party or anything else in the world that he had to decide. "Something to do," said Marcus.

"A jump up," said Brian.

Marcus laughed at this. "A jump up. All right. I was wondering if you people had parties at all."

"Excellent," said Brian. "Excellent. Lots of people." He hesitated, then said, "Lots of young women."

Marcus laughed again. "Good for you."

"Good for all of us."

Marcus paused. "Yes."

"Yes." Brian pumped his fist towards Jason. Jason made a wanking motion at his crotch. "Yes. Now we just have to convince Muriella."

"I think I can help you there."

When Brian sat down, Jason was writing on a napkin. "First, all those chicks who came to the reading he did at the department."

"They were in fine art, I think."

"He can find them."

"Then the deejay guys who were at that Black Cultural Centre thing he did."

"They were good," said Jason. "And the guys in the market who run the bike collective, get them to bring all the anarchist girls."

"In boots," said Brian, "and dreadlocks. And tattoos." He drank deeply from his Ting.

"Excellent," said Jason, writing. "Excellent."

XXIII

A TUESDAY. THE HOUSE WAS DIM AND quiet. Muriella shook her umbrella in the hall. She left her wet raincoat on the bench. She unzipped her boots and walked in her stockings to the kitchen. The tiles were cold underfoot. She could hear the fridge buzzing. Soon the heat would be coming on. She unrolled the newspaper. She read the editorial in the kitchen, wondering if she should hide it from Marcus. He had seemed so down lately. But he had expressed no interest in reading it.

She sat as still as she could, listening. It was impossible to tell if Julia was in her room. She was often up there, quiet for hours at a time. Perhaps she was sleeping. And then often she wasn't; she was out for days at a time. She wondered if Julia was lonely.

She had stopped wondering that about Marcus. That's what she told herself. It was pointless to wonder about Marcus. If he wanted to be quiet, she would be quiet too. She didn't know why all this quiet should bother her.

It was possible that he was at home now, sleeping in the basement apartment. She stood up, shuffled into the dim entrance hall. She wondered if she should go up and find Julia, offer her some tea, ask if she had read the editorial. Muriella was sure she hadn't. She could show it to her. She could show her, in a rare moment of power, something she didn't already know.

But she stopped with her hand on the banister. There was something about the dark staircase that made her belly tighten. There was really no reason, no reason at all, not to go up and just check on Julia. Just to see if she was in or not. Muriella stood still, listening.

There was a rushing of water from the broken gutters outside the front door. It came from a constant spout like a waterfall, like a sheet in front of you, when you opened the door. The flagstones at the doorstep were cracking, slowly heaving. Arthur would have had them fixed, coming home from work early to point out to her what time it was and the fact that the contractors had not yet arrived.

It was moments like this, moments of standing still in a cold house and remembering something, that she knew she should avoid. They presaged an onslaught of grief that would be paralyzing. They were the brief few minutes of clarity before she sank. She imagined it was like the aura that epileptics felt before a seizure: a feeling that everything was crystal before it cracked.

This was exactly the kind of day it would come on her, although it had happened less in the preceding months, and when it came there was nothing to do: tears gushed up like broken pipes in the basement. Once it began there was nothing to do but splash about in the puddles, let the heaves shudder through you, fade and heave again, until they stopped. It may take all morning. It may take all day. You may have to go to bed, exhausted as if ill, purging images (a car drive with Arthur, the kids in the back, singing together, was one that came a lot). You knew that it would pass; you just had to wait.

This moment—the fear of the attack—was sometimes as bad as the grief itself, as it led to panic. There were ways of dealing with it: you had to do things with your hands, walk, anything but sit still; she should be turning on lights, a radio, telephoning, she should put her boots back on and head back outside where at least she could walk away from the house. (But she was cold and couldn't face the rain again.)

And the sighing sound again. Muriella listened, her hand on the banister to keep her still. It could have been a creak in the wood of the house, the boards underfoot, or a bird, a chirp from outside. But the birds didn't sing much in the rain. Perhaps she had not heard it. It was more like a sound a dog would make when shifting in sleep, a whimper.

She took two steps towards the living room and stopped again. It was a snuffle, a sniff, the sound of soft motion. It was not coming from upstairs. Her heart was beating in her chest.

She walked into the empty living room. No lights were on. The daylight through the leaded panes was grey. There was a whimper from the library.

She knew she should turn and walk straight into her bedroom and shut the door. There was no reason at all for her to know whatever was going on in the library. She felt tears rising in her throat for no reason, no reason at all. She would take a nap.

She stood and listened for voices. The sound had stopped.

She coughed as loudly as she could and switched on a light with a snap. Then she walked slowly and deliberately to the library.

She stood in the doorway and at first thought the room was empty. And then she saw a dark bundle of tweed heaped over the chair and writing table against the window, and this bundle was Marcus. He was sitting with his head down on the table and his hands covering his ears. His back was quivering. There was a newspaper and an empty brandy snifter on the table beside his head. There was no one else in the room.

She called his name.

He sat straight up but did not turn around. He was wiping his eyes. He cleared his throat but did not speak.

She gave him a moment—and a distant part of her brain was calmly aware that the moment of her own grief had passed—and stepped across the carpet to him in her nylon feet and put a hand on his shoulder.

Harshly, without turning, he said, "I'm all right. I'm all right."

She said, "Can I bring you another drink?"

He patted her hand on his shoulder. He gave a broken laugh. "That would be very kind." He put his hands on the table in front of him and put his head down on them.

When Muriella returned with the bottle, he was sitting on one of the leather sofas with his legs crossed and his arm stretched out along the back. He did not look as if he had been crying. He was looking at the carpet. There was a spot on his trouser leg, and his shirt collar was frayed. Marcus's shirts were always fresh; he would have hated that Muriella had noted the stain. He was not aware of it. A wife would not have let him wear those pants. This filled her with tendernesss.

She always wanted to clean his glasses too; she didn't know how he could see through them.

She poured him a drink and sat at the other end of the sofa. She curled her legs under herself. She watched him and tried not to reach out and stroke his arm. She wanted him to put his head on her shoulder and cry. She wished she could have been there for the crying. She felt full of something fragile and soft, something that was no longer just relief. She felt so full of something she thought she would cry as well. She stroked her shins through her shiny nylons.

"I suppose," said Marcus after a silence, "that I was missing Elizabeth."

Muriella went still. The warmth drained from her. Her stomach tightened again. She sat in silence for a moment as Marcus sipped gently from his snifter. She looked at the garden, thick with the ropy branches of leafless shrubs, all red and brown and dark with wet. The rain had stopped. There were streams of water still falling from the ragged remnants of leaves. She did not trust herself to speak. She shivered.

But since he did not say anything, she asked what she truly did not want to know, which was, "Who is Elizabeth?"

He raised his eyebrows, and Muriella tensed, waiting. She knew it was important for her to know, even though she didn't want to know. "Yes. Tell me. I want to know."

"An old woman. My family's maid. She raised me. I see her . . . I am used to seeing her every day." His voice was very quiet.

Muriella exhaled sharply. "A maid? Your maid?"

"Since childhood, yes. A nanny, I suppose you could say. She is the daughter of my father's maid. She knew my father. My father was a minister. She is older than me. Very old now. And she is unwell. I support her, really, but we pretend that she is my maid. I was just thinking about her. I don't know how she . . ."

Muriella wasn't listening. She was smiling. She wiped a tear from one eye. She wanted to laugh. She breathed deeply. "Well, that's all right."

"Yes, I'm sure she's all right. My old friend Desmond—"

"Were you upset by the editorial? In the paper?"

Marcus hesitated. "Yes. Yes I was. I don't want to be on their side."

"No. I thought not."

"I don't want to be on anyone's side."

Muriella did not answer. She was feeling nothing but joy again, relief like a liquid inside her. There was sun breaking onto the wet garden.

"I suppose I became upset," said Marcus, speaking slowly, "because I reread an old poem. A poem that had been very important to me. About the Caribbean."

She slid along the sofa towards him. "Tell me about it."

"There's nothing here weird enough for me. This is not alternative. Look, they have like *Caro Diario* here, and that cute Holocaust comedy and stuff. It's for girls, this place. They might as well have Julia Roberts movies. This is like the Hallmark cards of alternative video stores."

"There's *Faces Of Death*."

"What volumes? Only four and six are good. And they're not really as hard-core as that German series, came out in the eighties, *Death Around the World* or something. It was nuts. It was psycho. It might be illegal here. We should look for that one."

"We should look for that *Chosen* thing. Is that what it was called? *Chosen* or *Eternal* or something kind of mythical. *Begotten*, or *Misbegotten*. It was this grainy black-and-white thing with all these naked writhing bodies—"

"With the blood sex? Is that the one?"

"Yeah, blood, like an immaculate conception using blood. Alternafix used to show a label on it saying, 'Weirdest movie ever made.'"

"*Weird*," spat Jason. "What do they know about weird. That is for people who find *Eraserhead* weird. *Eraserhead* is only the beginning of weird. Weird is like drugs, you need harder stuff after a while. What about this *Latex Hotel* one?"

Brian considered. It was German and had a rubber mask on the cover, with tubes coming out of the nose and a bulb attached to the mouth. The woman whose face was behind the mask was strapped into an arrangement of tubes and pipes and steel rods that looked like the interior of a cockpit or an assembly line. There were tubes coming from her crotch, filled with a white liquid. Brian sighed, "It looks a little dull, actually."

"Okay. Operators are standing by." Jason pulled down a Japanese animated film about aliens and schoolgirls in white panties. "Dude," he said, "your call is important to us." He leaned towards the rack of New Arrivals and said to a gap between tapes, "Tea. Earl Grey. Hot."

That was when Brian spotted Julia Sternberg over in France by Director. "Shit."

"What? Oh. Oopy. Smells like teen spirit."

"Hi Julia."

She at first looked at him squinting, as if she didn't recognize him. "Oh, hi," she said. Her bicycle helmet was still on her head, which made her very tall and bulbous.

"You remember Jason?"

"Hey," said Jason. "Operators are standing by."

"How are you doing?" said Brian. "Now."

"Now? Fine. How are you doing."

"You still working at the gallery?"

"Yes."

"Cool. Cool."

"It's all right," she said. "What are you doing? You decided not to go back, right?"

"Oh, I went back." Brian sighed. "I went back all right."

"He caved," said Jason. "He went waggling back. Making a sort of high whining whingeing noise. Slobbering for the academic nest. Like the zombies who go back to the mall. He knows where his home is."

"So you're both in school again?"

"Yes," said Jason. "For the time being."

"Are you enjoying it?"

Brian shrugged. "Yeah. Sure. It's easy. It's less work than undergrad was. They leave you alone more."

Julia was looking at the floor. "What are you doing your thesis on?"

"Oh, they don't have theses any more. You just do a lot of course work. It's super easy. It's just what you do when you want to put off doing anything else. You should do it." He tried a laugh but it went high and twisted.

Julia looked at her watch. It may have been Brian's imagination, but he thought she was blushing.

"You looking for a movie?" said Brian.

"Oh." She looked down at the tape in her hand and then held it behind her back. "Nothing."

"I'll tell you one thing," said Jason, "you're looking in the wrong section. France. *France* has forgotten how to make movies. They only make movies with cute kids in them now. What have you got there?"

"I wasn't going to get it."

"Hey, nice. Period drama, lots of white dresses. You don't need to get that, I'll tell you what it's all about, it's about how rural people are good and the rest of us are bad. Bad, bad. And beautiful girls are pure and noble. And they have to be able to marry who they want, even the poor guy, because he's nicer than the rich guy. There. You don't have to see it now. Hey, why don't you just read the Bible instead? Or go to Sunday school, or, I don't know, an AA meeting or—"

"What are *you* getting?"

Brian glanced at the box in his hand. He was still holding *Latex Hotel*. If he put it back on the shelf it would just draw more attention to it. So he turned the cover inward. "We're looking for this German thing, at least we think it's German, there's no dialogue in it, it's called *Begotten* or something." His face was hot.

"Hey, there's a whole Richard Kern section," said Jason. "I wonder if Eric Kroll's ever made a movie?"

Julia was staring at the box in Brian's hand. She reached over and took it from him. "Nice," she said. Her expression was hard to read.

"That's just nothing."

"Right. Have you seen *Man Facing Southeast*? I've always wanted to see it."

"Yeah, no," said Brian. "That's one of the ones you always see on the racks and you think you should see it but there's something about it that sounds a little, I don't know, squirmy. Like messagey. Plus no one's seen it, either, no one you know. It's one of those."

"It's supposed to be beautiful."

"Beautiful kind of turns me off," said Brian shortly.

"Right." She flicked her eyes at the ceiling, then she turned from them and put her French film back on the shelf. She looked a little silly in her bicycle helmet. "Oh, you should see *City of Lost Children*. It's—"

"I don't do any movie with children in the title," said Jason. "Or snow. Don't do children, don't do families, don't do Tom Hanks, don't do talking fucking pigs."

"Have you seen *Cube*?" said Brian. "It's gruesome. Scariest movie you'll ever see. And smart. It's like my worst psychic nightmare." She was looking at *The Last Metro*. Brian blew out his cheeks. He couldn't help saying, "Don't get that. What do you want to get that for? The violins on the soundtrack?"

"I like Catherine Deneuve," she said softly.

"Why?" said Jason.

"Why? I don't know. Why do you like any actors?"

"Well, usually when we like things," said Jason a little too loudly, "we are able to articulate some reason for our reaction using this sophisticated system called language, with words and things, it's really a very fine instrument, very delicate, you can express—"

"Jason," said Brian, "shut up."

Julia's mouth was closed tight and her eyes were bright. She swung her knapsack on her shoulder and put the video back on the shelf.

Brian followed her into American Directors. "Hey, I'm really glad you're joining the Action Council. It was really good, what you said in there. You know, we could really use you, a new voice, it gets a little silly in there sometimes."

"I'm not sure I'm really joining. I was just kind of sitting in."

"Why not?" said Brian. "Why not?"

"I'm not smart enough, Brian. For you guys."

"Sure you are. I mean, that's not what I mean, I don't think I'm so smart. Jason's just trying to be funny." She said nothing, so he said, "Anyway, it would be fun. You should come back. Please come back."

"Maybe."

"Yeah. Maybe I'll see you at Muriella's some time."

"Yeah." She was reading a box cover closely.

"Okay."

"Well," said Jason, at the cash, "that went well, wouldn't you say?"

"Shut up."

Jason handed the Velcro stickers they had chosen to the guy with studs in his face behind the counter. "Open the pod bay doors, Hal."

Dolefully, without looking up, the studded guy said, "I'm sorry Dave, I can't do that," and punched numbers into his keyboard.

In Muriella's library, Marcus was reading to her from a book of French poetry. It was a library book he had brought up from his room. He had lit a thin cigar which stank in the damp room. He was reading poems about rain and autumn, and translating as he did. "He sort of hates nature more than he loves it. Here—'Oh autumns, winters, springs soaked in mud, seasons to put you to sleep' . . . see." Marcus turned some more pages. Muriella wasn't sure if he was still speaking to her. She listened. "See. Obsessions. Here. 'Great woods, you terrify me like cathedrals. As cathedrals do.'" He was tracing the lines with his fingertip. "'I hate you, oceans! How I would like you, oh night, without these stars that speak a language I know!' You see how unpredictable he is. He never says a nice thing. And he gets offensive, really offensive. There is a sort of S and M fantasy about lesbians. He writes a love poem to his mistress that says that her eyes flow with a poison that drugs him, and her spit, her saliva, is numbing and sends his soul towards '*les rives de la mort*, the banks of death.' In another one he compares her to a rotting corpse. It is described in great detail, the corpse. In very vivid, one might say very luxurious detail. This is eighteen fifty-seven. And this is taught to French schoolchildren. Taxi drivers can recite these poems to you in Paris. There is one about sleeping with a whore . . ." He flipped pages, scattering ash. "Whose body is also described as a corpse. Really. Here. '*Une nuit près d'une affreuse Juive.*' It's a Jewish whore. Misogyny and racism too. 'One night next to a frightful Jewess.'" He barked a coarse laugh. "Tell that to the Arts Action Council. If they only knew. Unfortunately it's quite arousing." He took a long drag on the foul cigar.

"How do you know French?"

"School. English school. They teach you French."

"In . . . on the island?"

He snorted. "Yes, on the island. We had an old Englishman who taught us French. I never learned how to speak it, really. His accent was appalling. But they thought reading was important."

"That's funny," said Muriella very softly. "They teach them French here for years at a time and they can't—" She stopped herself. She didn't want to stop him lecturing. She held herself very still. The rain had stopped. A watery sun was washing the garden.

"This is the thing," Marcus said after a silence, "that people don't understand about poetry. It's very upsetting. It's very dangerous. It was Cyril Connolly, I think—that prick! Don't you think he must have been a prig? You don't know him? You're not missing much, some amusing things, anyway, he wrote once in a memoir, or an introduction, that his masters at school forced them all to translate Latin poetry, Horace in particular, without noting that the poetry they were reading was chiefly advice to drink and make love and be sort of generally irreligious. He said that his morality was irrevocably damaged when he began to read the poems."

Marcus drank and smoked. The room was beginning to feel hot.

Muriella asked, "Who was the French poet?"

"Baudelaire."

"Baudelaire. It's lovely."

"Yes."

"I wish I could read it in French."

"I wish you could too."

"Could you read me some more in French? I like hearing you speak it."

"Not now." Marcus was silent for a while. Then he said, "I hate my education."

"Why."

"Why. Because I am only articulate in the language of slavery."

Then Marcus got up and walked to a pair of leaded windowpanes and tried to open them. It was getting stuffy in the library. He struggled for a few moments with the windows. Muriella would have got up and helped him but didn't want to change the subject, didn't want to stop him talking. And when he did yank the windows open and strangely warm late-season air, air like summer air, humid from the recent rain, seeped in like a perfume, Marcus went on talking. He stood by the window, he paced around, he smoked cigars and drank brandy, and Muriella sat with her feet folded up under her, feeling damp and rosy in her library, and listened to him talk.

She watched the skin on his forearms, where his sleeves were rolled up. It was darker on his arms, it seemed, than on his face. She wondered how it changed over his body. If it was darker on his belly, in his groin. She had never touched black skin before, not while naked, anyway. She wondered if it felt different.

"Do you know," he said, "that when I first went to Edinburgh I could not afford even a drink in a pub. I ate in college, or in my room. I could not afford a meal even in a pub. My scholarship was in pounds, of course, not in my currency, but it still wasn't enough, and my currency was worthless."

"You were very poor, growing up?"

"Not at all. By the standards of St. Andrew's. Not at all."

"But by our standards."

Marcus laughed. "Yes. Very poor. My father's church had no glass in the windows."

"So you were very isolated, when you first went away."

"Let me tell you about my childhood."

Which he did: he talked about the sleepy Sunday afternoons, his father's sermons. He talked about reading Greek myth and English legends, the Trojan War and Robin Hood, the fair Maid Marion, sitting on a concrete verandah shaded by a nutmeg tree, in the acid smell of the chicken coop in the yard, the rotting fruit smell of dogshit. "It was very strange, when you think about it, that I did not think that she was white, that they were all white, and I was not, or only partly, which means I was not, and everyone I read about was white. I thought that's what the world was."

He talked about scrambling up and down the dusty hills of Dunstanton, where there were crumbling fortresses built by first the English and then the French. "British military architecture is the backdrop to my education," he said, "to every important phase in my life. The architecture of your forts, the one, I have been looking at downtown, is the same as my home. It is my home." He paused. "People say I should go to Quebec City. And to Halifax. I would like to see this Halifax. And this castle. This castle that you can see out your window."

"Casa Loma. It's not really a castle, it's a house."

"I know what it is. A Canadian millionaire's house that is meant to look like some fantasy of medieval Scotland. Everybody wants these roots, these roots in particular. All false, all false."

"It's not false," said Muriella. "He may really have been Scottish. I don't know."

"It's a country without a style. This is like my country."

"Do your parents look black?"

He looked at her with his eyebrows raised.

"I mean, did they. Have darker skin than you."

"No, not really. My mother was half white and half Chinese, so she was quite pale. My father was quite black, yes. Blacker than me. But more British. He could recite Gray's *Elegy Written in a Country Churchyard* when he was a child and did so all his life, frequently. It was a kind of warning to us, when he would do it, that we weren't working hard enough at our lessons. It was a nostalgia for a better time. When people weren't trying to change things, and getting arrested for it. He didn't like that."

"Do you miss home?"

He puffed out his cheeks. "Do you miss your home?"

She said, "This is my home."

"You answer so certainly."

"Well, it is."

"Then it is."

"Yes." She hesitated. "My son and daughter are not here. I miss them. Sometimes. But not a lot."

"You miss your husband."

"Sometimes. I miss having a husband."

"But you don't miss him in particular."

Muriella shifted. She felt very hot. "Yes, of course him in particular. He was a good man. I still feel rather numb about it." They couldn't talk about this much more or she would cry. "My son is in Edmonton, and we don't speak enough, perhaps because he is in Edmonton, or perhaps because I don't . . . admire his wife very much, or perhaps because he doesn't understand why I would waste my time with this Action Council business and my own writing. There is a gap there, or a barrier. I think he wishes I were more as I was, when Arthur was alive, when I was very concerned about, I don't know, about the other people in the Park, and my fundraising, and the house and having people in it."

"You still have people in it."

She smiled. "A different kind of people."

He laughed.

She drew in a breath and said, "And were you married?"

"Oh yes. Oh yes. Once."

Muriella waited. Then she said, "Was it long ago?"

"Yes."

"Was she . . ."

"Was she white?" he said, smiling.

"Yes."

"No, she was not white. In those days I would have scorned a man, a man like me who married a white woman. She was from St. Andrew's. She was active, as well, in forming the new government after independence."

"But it didn't work out."

"Obviously not." Marcus yawned.

"Why not?"

"Well, at first because it just didn't work out. I am not well formed for . . . for—"

"For monogamy," said Muriella.

"Yes," said Marcus. "So at first it didn't work out because of that. And then it didn't work out because she died."

"Oh, Marcus."

"I don't mean to be flippant. But I do. How else can I be?"

"Did she die in the revolution?"

"Oh no, no. Not many people did, really. It wasn't really a revolution. It was just a change of government. It was before the change that people died. In jail cells and so on."

"Like your brother."

"Yes. But she and I were already separated when she died. Cancer."

"She must have been very young."

"Yes."

"So you have no children."

"No."

"Did you ever want children?"

Marcus sighed. "This interrogation is not like you."

"All right. Never mind. It's strange that you don't want to talk about yourself. Most writers . . ."

"That's all they do talk about."

They both stared at the lozenges of sun on the carpet.

Marcus said, "Of course at some times I wanted children. Most of the time I didn't, because I was writing, writing a book, and they were like offspring, in a way. At least I thought they would be."

"And now?"

"Now I am not writing so much."

"Oh, but you—"

"You asked me if I miss home. Let me tell you. I have been receiving letters from a friend of mine. Jackie Mornay. A taxi driver. He sits in the square, in a main square in town, near the marketplace where the cruise ship passengers get off and buy small bundles of nutmeg or sarongs or woven straw, like that silly mule I gave you." He nodded at the straw mule on the mantelpiece. "He sits in the square beside his taxi, asking tourists if they want a lift. He does not get many fares, because the tourists are afraid of him. The atmosphere in that square. I wish I could describe it to you. Everybody wants to do a deal with you, a deal of some sort. It is only men who spend their days in the square. There is a man who will trade you one hundred bottles of motor oil for a room in your house, and so on. If you are a tourist you will be offered guides, or herb, or homemade reggae tapes which often have nothing on them at all but a rough recordin' from the radio. You know." He laughed a little, then stopped. "There is a café there. With women in it." He took a gulp of brandy. "You know, I have thought that the people I have met here, many of them, remind me of the men in that marketplace. The way the writers do business." He shook his head. "It is very . . . I can't say. Grasping. Everybody here doing business. Struggling for deals. The sense of failure around the corner, always, I feel it when I take the subway, the desperation for money. It is a kind of frenzy."

"I can't say I feel that, said Muriella quietly. "Even around me. I guess I've never known anything else."

"You don't have it, my dear. You don't have the frenzy. You don't have to. Anyway, my friend is in trouble, because his taxi has been confiscated. He had an expired licence, and so on, who knows what he did wrong, safety violation, I don't know." He sighed. "He needs a new taxi and a new licence. If he doesn't get it, he . . . he will not know what to do."

Muriella did not know what to say to this.

Marcus said, "Are you very rich?"

Muriella laughed high and clear. "Don't be ridiculous. I'm not at all rich. I have no—"

"This house doesn't make you rich?"

"Not at all. The taxes on the house are enormous. They are cruel, really, cruel. There are some investments, Arthur left them, but they're totally tied up—"

"Investments." Marcus laughed tightly. "I would say you are wealthy."

Muriella said, "You don't understand, Marcus." There was a firmness to her voice that made him look at her.

"You don't understand what wealth is. This is not wealth. There is wealth in the Park that you don't . . . that you can't imagine it."

"I can imagine it."

"Oh, I'm not sure you can. It is not the same as having money."

"It is not." He smiled at her. He leaned back into the sofa.

"No. It is not. It has a lot to do with where you come from. It's when you live in the Park because your grandfather and great-grandfather did and they each married someone who lived next door. It's not when you come here from Montreal, it's not when you marry an insurance broker, it's not when you have a funny long last name, which people will find out, I assure you."

Marcus was still staring at her, his eyes wide. "You don't have a funny long last name."

"Oh yes I do. My father's name was Giannakopoulos. It's a Greek name?"

"You're Greek?"

"Greek Italian. Yes. I like to say Canadian, though," she said drily. "Some wouldn't. You don't understand. I'm not the same."

Marcus thought about this. He said, "I understand."

Muriella sighed. "I suppose you do."

Quietly, Marcus said, "You own the home outright?"

"Thankfully, yes. But the house is not worth as much as you think. The taxes, the upkeep, the repairs, this house is more of a liability than anything. The taxes alone—"

"This house," said Marcus, "is worth the entire year's budget of a school in Dunstanton. Perhaps three schools.

Perhaps an entire school board. You, my dear, could buy my friend a new taxi and not even notice it."

"No, I couldn't, Marcus. Money is different here. It doesn't go as far."

He sighed. "I know. I know."

Muriella rose and opened more windows. The air that entered was steamy. "It's getting hot. Indian summer. Turn your back for a moment."

"What?"

"I want to take my pantyhose off."

She waited till he had shifted, uncomfortably, on the leather, and she hiked her skirt up. She wriggled them down, peeled the sticky film off her legs, and kicked them into a pile in a corner. She didn't care if Marcus saw them there. The new air on her legs, she walked back to the sofa. The leather was cool on her skin.

His eyes darted to her legs and away.

She took a deep breath and said, "What do you think of what they're saying. On the Action Council. Of sending you home."

Marcus laughed deep and loud.

"You don't care."

"Not really," he said. "I think you care more than I do."

"Well yes, I do. I do. I've been trying, I've been trying so hard to, to do my best to . . . I don't know, belong, I love art, I really do, I was always interested, and they don't seem to—I don't know, nothing I do seems good enough."

"It never will be. If you love art, you shouldn't be on that committee."

Muriella crossed her legs. "So what do you suggest I do? Become an artist myself. It's a little late for that." She had stopped saying, she realized, that she was an artist. She wondered when that had happened.

"No, you can be involved. You can always be involved. But in art. In the real thing. Not these committees."

"How."

He waved his hands, splashing a little brandy. "Have a party. Have a big party. Show them." He was smiling to himself at a private joke.

"That's it. A party."

"A big drunken party. A jump up. That's what it's all about."

"I will have a little of that." She stood, straightened her skirt, and went to find a glass. Passing the stained-glass window beside the front door, she saw a blur of moving colour outside. David Rodney's red hat. He was always pruning her brambles without her permission. Gathering evidence of her gardening ineptitude. Sometimes he was a little too helpful.

She sat with Marcus and poured some brandy. The bottle was half gone. It burned her lips and throat. She coughed a little, then had some more. She stood and went to the window to look for David Rodney, hiding among the branches like a ferret. She leant against the writing desk with the telephone, against the window, now occupied with a vase of chemical-smelling lilies. She didn't know what a ferret was exactly. "A big party," she murmured. She ran her fingers over the furry lily leaves.

"With lots of artists." His voice was close to her ear. He was standing behind her. Lightly, he put his hands on her hips.

She held still. A warmth passed up her, from her waist to her neck.

"And terrible people." His moustache was tickling her ear. His lips were gentle on her neck.

She turned and lifted her face up to his, and he kissed her on the lips. She let her arms hang as he unbuttoned her blouse and kissed her chest, the tops of her breasts. Roughly, he hiked her skirt up around her hips, and she felt his knee pressing against her crotch. She shivered. He put his hands in her armpits and lifted her suddenly onto the little desk, where she sat with a gasp, and almost fell over backwards. She flailed with one arm, knocking over the vase with the lilies. She did not hear it smash on the hardwood floor, because he was pulling her skirt down over her hips, and she had to grab his head to steady herself, gasping.

XXIV

"PEOPLE PEOPLE GIVE IT UP GIVE IT UP GIVE IT UP, GONNA MAKE SOME NOISE, GONNA MAKE SOME NOISE FOR THE MAN YOU ALL BIN WAITING ON, FROM - TOE-RONTO CANADA, GIVE IT UP FOR DEEJAY FURR-RY DEEEE!"

Muriella could hear this, and a subsequent hoarse roaring and what sounded like breaking ceramics, from the garden, where she had been trying to get some of the young black men to put out a fire someone had started in a garbage can. The fire was out, a pall of burning rubber in the cold air, the lights in all the neighbouring houses on, and the young men, she did not know which young men—the giddy group she had met before, on the front lawn, or a later, colder cluster who had been in the kitchen, turning their backs to her, or a new bunch altogether, she didn't know; it was dark—had moved to the darkness at the bottom of the garden and become a pretty painting of moving points of light, smoky fireflies. Her shoes were sinking into the earth, and she shivered in her clingy dress. She had taken a long drag from a joint one of them had offered her, taken it without thinking about it, the third or fourth puff she had had tonight (the first having been, however, the first she had had since about 1978), and now she wrapped her arms around her chest, so exposed by the deep V-neck of the dress, and looked up in wonder at the lights coming from all her windows, the throbbing and shrieking spilling over the whole Park. The DJ had been set up in the front living room in an effort to contain the sound, precisely to avoid the windows on the rest of the Park, on David Rodney's garden, and still from here it was the loudest thing she had ever heard.

There were people dancing in the living room and smoking in her bedroom. There were dreadlocked turn-tablists and frat boys in plaid shirts who had shaken her hand and been very polite, but all stared at her chest. She had talked to some Arab diplomats, from a consulate, who had all had little moustaches and had been very sombre. How had Marcus come to know Arab diplomats? Who had invited them?

She thought about this with a sense of surprise, but not with fright. She was surprised at her own wonder at the event. She felt a strange lightness which frightened her. She told herself to try to be less detached. She tried to take a sip from her martini glass and found it was empty, and went into the house looking for Marcus or the sculptor. Perhaps the sculptor, for confidence, before Marcus. She would not think about where Marcus was.

The DJ had some kind of rapper screaming in Jamaican over the music. The windows rattled.

She found Brian Sillwell and his friend Jason in the kitchen with more men in black who looked the same but slightly older and three young women who all looked to be seventeen and drunk and half-naked.

"Kind of a post-whatever thing," said one of the men.

"More like neo," said Jason Katz, who wore a red bow tie that glowed with little red lights. "Neo whatever."

"Neo whatever. Exactly."

Muriella said, "Have you seen the sculptor?"

"Hey," barked Jason Katz, "hey, hostess." He held out his hand. "I'm Peter Jennings." His voice went deep and Germanic. "*Have you seen John Connoh?*"

"YOU WANNIT ROUGH," screamed the rapper in the living room.

Jason shouted at the refrigerator, "Tea. Earl Grey. Hot."

"Muriella," said Brian, "I want you to meet some journalists. This is James Willing, and this is Dominic—"

"Filmmaker," said Dominic. "Not journalist. Pleasure."

"Lionel Baratelli, he's a writer too. And this is Krista, and, I'm sorry, Ashley? Amber, and Angelique."

"It's a very great pleasure to be here, Mrs. Pent," said the one with the sideburns who said he was a filmmaker, stepping between her and the girls. "I've been meaning to talk to you, to ask you, when you have a moment, about applying for the program, for the residency, because I have some projects that—"

"IN A RAGAMUFFIN STYLE."

Muriella smiled and threw her hair a little, her mouth opened slightly, staring at each man right in the eyes. She was still cold from being outside and her dress felt very thin. She stood before them with the feeling that she was completely naked, and she smiled and held out her hand to each of them. They each stared at her breasts. She laughed with each of them, and the oldest one, the natty one with the salt-and-pepper beard called something Italian, kissed her hand, looking mournful. Brian was laughing in a high rattle beside her. She put a hand on his back and rubbed it. She felt his thin shoulder blades. "Brian," she said, "will you find me another martini? And where is Mr. Royston?"

"I'm not sure," said Brian quickly, taking her glass.

She almost tripped on two people sitting cross-legged in the hall, and squeezed between all the people talking and smoking on the stairs. On the middle landing she found the sculptor. He had short black hair and dark stubble and a black T-shirt and grime under his fingernails and a whiff of underarm wherever he was, and she had had a long talk with him at the beginning, and then lost him again. And when she stepped between him and the girl he was talking to, some fantastic dreadlocked redhead in a tiny tank top with piercings all over her face, she smelt his sweat again. He smiled at her and told her the girl's name was Nicola. Muriella smiled at the girl and then closed her eyes, just for a second, and put her hand on his bare bicep. When she opened her eyes again the girl was gone and he had turned to face her, there on the stairs, and was still smiling at her.

"You were telling me about your work," she said, gripping his arm. She breathed in his smell.

"Yeah. Polyethylene, mostly. I burn it, a lot, and then it melts, it's very malleable."

She said, "What's your name again?"

He leaned forward, but his voice was lost in a shriek from further down the staircase and a wave of drumming from the living room.

"I'm Muriella."

"I know. Muriella, I've been meaning to ask you, I've been looking for a space, I need a lot of space, to do the burning in, and I do some welding—"

"You need a space." She sighed, now bored. "There are plenty of rooms here."

"Here?"

"You can have the upper bedroom." Muriella was looking around for Marcus. At the foot of the stairs were three lesbians in jeans and bandanas. They had been reading poetry aloud, earlier in the evening. How had he met all these people?

"For welding?"

"Sure." She couldn't see Julia Sternberg, either. "I have to find another drink."

And at that moment Julia was coming down the stairs, tall and bare-shouldered, with her hair like a briar wood in a fairy tale and her skin flushed and raw, and her mouth open and swollen, and Marcus behind her, in a white shirt with the sleeves rolled up, and his hands in his pockets, smiling, and Muriella's insides seized up, cold. She looked Julia in the eyes and Julia looked away and kept walking. Marcus stopped and leaned forward to kiss Muriella on the forehead, his hand on her shoulder. Muriella looked up at him, and then he kissed her wetly on the mouth, right in front of the sculptor, and she let him.

Marcus pulled her down the stairs past the entwined people and into the library, where they sat on the leather couch and he recited lines of French poetry to her. "'*Mon enfant, ma soeur,*'" he said, "'*Songe à la douceur.*' Parking is never free." He pulled her hair loose from its scrunchy and kissed her shoulders. "Do you know that today, on my travels, I saw a poster for a lecture being given by a llama. I would like to see that. A lecturing llama." He was now kissing the tops of her breasts.

She pretended to ignore this and squeezed out, "I think it must have been Buddhist. A Buddhist lama."

"Oh, I know. It was about dharma. Dharma enlightenment." Marcus giggled. His face seemed congested. "You know, you know what I think about that? I think." He began to giggle.

Muriella sighed. She wanted him to keep kissing.

"I think lama lectures are a dharma dozen."

"Christ."

Marcus was braying to himself, wiping his eyes. He kissed her gluttonously. People were passing into the room and out again. She could smell the girl's shampoo on him, from his face and the top of his head, and she could do nothing but lie there and whimper. After a while he just got up and wandered out.

Julia was in the kitchen, leaning against the marble-topped island and being talked to by Brian Sillwell. He was asking her what part of town she lived in and whether she liked it and what she was doing for a living and she was looking around for Marcus and feeling that some part of her was dying, although she didn't know why.

"So," he said, "where do you go to drink?"

"To drink?"

"Or hang out or whatever. I need to know new places to go." His face was red and he was leaning too close to her, his hand on the counter beside her hip.

She clasped her hands behind her back and leaned against them, against the island, and said, "I don't really go out."

"I see," said Brian, blowing air out of his cheeks. "Okay."

Julia did not know why her not going out seemed to irritate Brian so. She didn't listen to the next thing he said, and there was a blast of yelling from the DJ anyway. She saw Marcus come into the kitchen all smiles and start talking to the journalists, who gathered around him like dogs at feeding.

"Or is that just ridiculous. Do you find that ridiculous too."

She turned to him with an expression she hoped was attentive. "Sorry?"

"Would you. Like to go out with me. Some time."

"Oh."

"For a drink or something."

"Oh. Sure. Okay. I don't really . . . I don't really go out much." She stared at him. She didn't understand how any-one could ask her out at that moment. She didn't know what he wanted.

"Of course," he said, and laughed. "Okay. Maybe it's not a good idea."

"No, sure. I would. I would go out for a drink."

"Don't trouble yourself," he said, and Jason Katz was suddenly with them, carrying beer bottles, pressing their cold against her bare arms, chattering like a chimpanzee.

Brian turned his back to her and moved to join the clus-ter around Marcus. Soon Jason was gone, and Julia was aware of standing there alone, and only then was able to think of how she might appear, how she must have appeared to Brian, and she wondered if she really was cold, cold as perhaps Marcus thought of her too.

She tried to catch Marcus's eye but he was fixed on a girl with a see-through top who looked like a stripper. There was such focus in his eyes, such concentration, she felt like weeping.

She had seen him look at her own self like that and didn't know if she enjoyed it or not. She had seen Muriella look-ing at her like that. She had seen Muriella earlier that evening in her bare dress and even she, Julia, had felt a shiver of something, a cold spark in her spine, a tightening of the skin on her neck, not lust, not desire for Muriella, but a recognition of what Muriella felt, a jealousy perhaps of wearing the dress, of feeling her own nipples against the sheen. Sometimes, dressing in the morning (she didn't know why this came to her now), Julia would look at herself in the mirror, at her long torso, and she would picture herself on a stage, stripping away her clothes, and this would cause excitement that would often end in shame, and she felt both now. Her back arched.

She wondered if Marcus knew that about her. He didn't, because she was just a mousy unhappy woman to him, and this thought tightened her muscles, made her tilt her head back and look at the ceiling and puff out her cheeks.

But Brian and his friends weren't watching.

Brian certainly didn't know this about her, these currents that Muriella's dress sent into her chest and groin, and she wouldn't want him to. Brian probably found Muriella disgusting. Perhaps Julia was disgusting.

Her mother would certainly find her disgusting.

This thought made her angry.

She sucked on her beer. It swelled inside her, foamy. She realized she was not really there, not really in that room, but watching it from afar, the girls and the men and the geometry of stainless-steel appliances and the funny shards of light reflected on them (the halogen lamps, their tiny tinniness and the metallic rays they provided), and she found that interesting. Perhaps it meant she could do anything she liked in it. Perhaps this was freedom.

Marcus was laughing, wet-lipped. It was as if the sound was turned down. He looked at her and looked away again. He was not seeing her. He—and this was the problem, this was always the problem—he had no idea what was in her, and what was that? What exactly was in her?

Marcus was all abandon. (He was leaning back, letting the stripper girl move closer to him, narrowing his eyes; he would be with her in a bed in two hours if nothing intervened. This thought occurred to Julia rationally and distantly.) And Julia was not abandon; she could not let herself go, not like the girl in the clear top, she was her own mother, she would never be enough for him, unless he knew (and he didn't know) what was running through her, what heat the idea of Muriella's dress (and perhaps even Muriella's breasts themselves, yes, why not) forced into her, a hot air duct opening.

How would he know that she was just like that girl, or wanted to be just like that girl, or could be, anyway?

Julia was clenching her teeth. No one was talking to her and she knew she would show them something. They thought that she was standing there alone because she was uptight, or cold, or hysterical like her mother, and she would show them that they had no idea what she could do. What could she do? She had no idea. But she knew that she really wasn't her mother, and they didn't know that she saw herself standing on the counter, swaying, peeling off her top. All of them watching.

She could rip her clothes off right there, and the people would close around her like teeth. (She was hot between the legs. Why not?) Her naked body, and the hands of people covering her like fleshy leaves, scurrying over her body, closing over her. She would be devoured.

She liked this word, *devoured*, and said it several times to herself, and it made her more excited each time.

Her beer was empty; she wanted more. Then she would do something.

On the other side of the island, against the fridge, Marcus was talking to the journalists. They were smiling and nodding almost hysterically as he talked. "Well, you know who she is, don't you?" Marcus was saying. "That woman who interviewed me. Candace Bundle. You know that that's not her real name, don't you? No. No no. It's not. That." He took a long pull on a joint that someone had handed him. "Is a stage name." He handed the joint off. "Exotic dancing. Stripping. It was in . . ." He exhaled. "Moncton. Or Saint John. A well-known exotic dancer in Saint John. I assure you." He turned on the tall blond one, James Willing, with burning eyes. "Because she told me. And that's not the only stage name she has used. She was known in, in Prince George British Columbia as, as Candy Mountains. Candy Mountains." He had to repeat this because the young men were all laughing and shaking their heads. All except the dark ferrety one with sideburns called Dominic, who was not laughing, but who had extracted a small notebook from his jacket, and a pen.

Marcus saw the girl standing alone with her jaw clenched and he approached. He took Julia by the hand and led her away, up the stairs.

Brian watched them go, and then he put his beer bottle down on the marble with a snap and walked to the journalists. "Hey," he said to the one with the sideburns and the notebook, "had a chance to interview Mr. Royston?"

"Oh yes," said Dominic. "Oh yes. Why? You got anything else?"

"I was on the committee that brought him here."

"Oh yeah." Dominic was closing his notebook.

"Yeah. He was the only candidate. Did you know that? He was the only candidate."

Dominic turned his narrow face slowly towards him and clicked his ballpoint pen. He did not put the notebook in his pocket. "Say that again?"

XXV

THE UPSTAIRS HALLWAY WAS EMPTY, AND her bedroom door was ajar. Muriella moved silently towards it, steadying herself on side tables and picture frames.

She stood in her doorway and looked at the two of them on her bed. They were only sitting, she cross-legged, he on the side of the bed, holding her hand and murmuring. He was smoking a cigarette, in her bedroom.

"Hello," she said gaily, and Julia looked over quickly. "It's all right. You look lovely." She closed the door and walked carefully towards them and sat on the edge of the bed.

There was not much else to do, at this point. Muriella had stopped wondering about why she was doing what she was doing.

Marcus smiled, did not stop stroking Julia's arm. She tried to pull it away, but Muriella saw him hold it tight. With his other hand he flicked ash onto the carpet. Muriella could smell his body and her perfume, something fruity, and smoke, the sweet vegetal smell of dope from downstairs. It was as if the whole house was burning.

She reached over and took Julia's other hand. She began to stroke the inside of the girl's arm.

Julia looked at her coolly, her lips slightly parted. Muriella guessed that she was drunk, or stoned, or both. She wore a tight green top, and her bony chest was bare. Muriella watched her slow breathing, her flickering lids. She wanted to touch her, to feel whatever power Marcus felt when he touched her. Julia was clearly there to be touched.

There was a throbbing of drums through the floor.

"Are you having a lovely time?" said Marcus breathily.

"Yes, darling. Are you?"

"Lovely." He looked around for an ashtray, laid his burning cigarette gently on a book (*The Artist's Way*) on Muriella's bedside. Muriella writhed across the bedspread to be closer to Julia, who stiffened a little as Muriella pressed against her. Muriella could feel Marcus's eyes on her now, on her falling shoulder straps, on her long legs, her black skirt riding up, alongside the girl's legs in jeans, and she felt her breathing quicken. She kissed Julia's ear and looked back at Marcus.

Julia was looking at Marcus too, with wide eyes, and Marcus was smiling at her, nodding, leaning forward to stroke higher on her arm. Muriella was smoothing her thick hair, tangling her fingers in it, saying, "What beautiful hair, what beautiful skin, I have always found you, I have such a crush on you, young Julia." She was trying to sound like Marcus; it wasn't working. But Julia was relaxing, letting her head drop back, breathing slower.

Marcus stretched himself on the other side of her, and their hands ran all over the girl while she breathed and fluttered. She did not try to leave.

"He hasn't actually published anything," Brian was saying, "since nineteen eighty-two."

"Nineteen eighty-two," said the journalist called Dominic. He was writing in his book.

"It was a political choice."

"Not to write anything."

"No no, to bring him. Listen to me."

"I'm trying."

"He was a political choice. He's not a writer. He's all washed up," said Brian carefully, with distinctness, because he was having difficulty speaking. And he was trying not to think about what he was doing. Then he clutched at the countertop because he thought for a second that he might fall over. It passed. "I shouldn't be telling you this."

"No one," said Dominic quietly, "should tell me anything." He looked at his watch, took a long pull of beer from a bottle. "But they do."

Julia Sternberg's top had come off and Muriella was cupping her breasts with amazement. The skin was as smooth and taut as any photograph, the nipples small and hard, and the girl's breaths and little gasps, the quivering heart just under the skin, were thrilling; they reminded Muriella of her own body, once. She thought briefly about taking her own dress off, to touch the little breasts with her own, but knew that Marcus would be watching them both.

He was nuzzling Julia's neck, one of his long hands flat and brown on her belly. Muriella had strands of her frizzy hair in her teeth and eyes. The two of them worked their hands over the girl, pulled her tight jeans down (Muriella did not touch her between the legs; she watched Marcus do it), they took one nipple in each mouth.

Marcus switched the lamp off and they writhed together in silence.

Julia turned to Muriella and kissed her on the mouth. Muriella felt Marcus's hand tugging at her dress, then her breasts coming free and touching the girl's skin. It was like swimming, swimming in a dream, in something warm and poisonous. She slid her finger between the girl's legs and felt Julia push up against the pressure, grunting a little, her back arched and firm.

Muriella watched herself do this with the same feeling you have when you realize you are eating half a tube of raw cookie dough. The dough is stiff and sweet and warm and filling and sickening, and you can't believe you're eating it. You see yourself in a mirror with your mouth full. Appalled, you eat more.

When they were all unclothed and touching, with hairy parts rough against smooth, and Marcus hard against them all, and salty smelling, Muriella took his long penis in one hand and rubbed it. His skin was darker there, black in the fuzzy groin. She wanted to lick it, to see if it tasted different from white skin. It was rough in parts. Perhaps that was his age.

He rolled over Julia so he was between the two women and let himself be rubbed, and then he rolled heavily onto Muriella and forced her legs apart and pushed himself into her, where she was already wet, and she gasped and felt him familiar inside her, for they had done this several times, in the afternoons and nights, in this same bed, but never with Julia Sternberg beside her in the darkness, holding her hand and breathing quickly, the girl's nose at her ear.

When Marcus finished his pumping and pulled out and spurted his stuff on her belly as he always did, he rolled over, gasping, and reached for his cigarette on the side table, and then, clumsily and breathing hard, found his lighter and lit it in the darkness.

Muriella and Julia lay side by side without touching each other. Muriella was then afraid that Julia was disgusted by her body and hating her, and she hoped no one would switch the light on.

Julia sat up and sat there in silence, then reached over the side of the bed for her top.

Marcus was breathing deeply and slowly. Muriella knew that they would have to get up and leave him there.

Julia did it first, without saying anything or looking behind her, and Muriella followed, giving her a second to clear the hallway and the staircase. She dressed in the darkness and closed the door on Marcus, who was asleep.

She put on some makeup in the upstairs bathroom and went down into the carnage.

Brian Sillwell was alone in the kitchen. The journalists had left in a hurry. He had seen Julia Sternberg come downstairs with her hair all wild, an hour after Marcus had taken her away—she had come into the kitchen and taken a ginger ale from the fridge and left again—and then he had taken a full bottle of vodka from a cupboard and opened it. He was drinking it as fast as he could from a plastic cup.

Muriella came in and it looked as if she had been with someone too. Her hair was loose and her lips were red and her thin dress showed even more of her breasts, which Brian had tried not to look at before, but which he looked at closely now. He had to admit they were not bad, and her waist was slim and her nipples clear through the black dress, which was cut so low you could see the beginning of a fold under each breast. It irritated him that even Muriella Pent was attractive, and more sexual than he was, but then again it was not unusual or surprising, really, for everyone but him at a party to be having sex or at least know how to, to have secret relationships or secret possibilities, previous flirtations, already in place, easily activated by a loud party, or even to be able to initiate these relationships by some complicated code normal people have, perhaps a special secret handshake; all this was not unusual or surprising because it was not unusual or surprising that everyone, even Muriella Pent who was probably close to fifty, was more attractive and more sexual than he was.

"Hello lovey," she said, close to him, her hand on his arm. "May I have some of that? Are you having a lovely time?"

"No," said Brian.

"Why not." She took the cupful of clear liquor that he had poured her, squinting. "It's too bright in here, isn't it?"

"I think I'm a bad person," said Brian.

"No, you're not. Should we move into the, into outside, or the library or something?"

"We shouldn't act," said Brian with difficulty, because she was pulling him and trying to get him to move, "out of jealousy, or things, bad things. We shouldn't."

"You don't do that," said Muriella, tugging, "do you?"

"I don't know," said Brian. "I think I'm bad."

The sculptor came in in a gust of sweat, with Jason Katz and the ferrety journalist with the sideburns called Dominic, and the two older guys looked at Muriella and then looked at each other and smiled as they went to the fridge, and Muriella dropped Brian's arm and said, "Who isn't? Who isn't bad? You think you're bad?"

"You think yoh *bad*?" echoed Jason Katz, doing some kind of dance.

"Almost everybody in here is an idiot," said Muriella loudly.

"No kidding," said Brian. He looked at Muriella, smiling. He had never seen her like this. "Cheers."

"Calumny!" said Jason Katz. "I'm bad, I mean I'm *bad*, I'm a bad motherfucker, but I'm not an idiot."

"Oh, you're an idiot all right," said Brian grimly.

"Mrs. Pent," said the ferrety journalist called Dominic, "may I ask you something about the committee, the arts committee, you know the Action Council, that's in charge of the program, you know the visiting-artist program? I'm really interested in the program."

"They're all idiots," said Muriella. She downed the vodka in her plastic cup.

Brian felt his eyes widen as he looked at her. Her eyes were red and narrowed, as if the light was hurting her eyes. Her skin was pale and blotchy, her hair tangled, and she looked suddenly angry, and her nipples were larger than ever in that thin black dress. He wanted to put a hand on her waist, but didn't.

"Sorry? Weren't you on that committee with . . ." Dominic pulled out his little notebook and flipped pages. "With some well-known local artists, like Deepak Chaudry and—"

"Deepak Chaudry is the biggest idiot of them all," said Muriella, and Brian let out a furious laugh like a bark. He felt a new glee descending on him, like the arrival of paramedics with sirens.

"Deepak Chaudry writes little moral tales for children," said Muriella casually, crossing her ankles and leaning on the dishwasher.

"Yeah," said Dominic, giggling. "Yeah, I guess he does." He was writing in his notebook.

Muriella said, "Excuse me, it's too bright in here."

When she was in the dim hallway, in the roar of the drums and the DJ's screaming, Muriella stopped and leaned against the big painting of the burning sunset in the darkness as people passed her without looking, or at least without speaking to her, which was fine with her, as she was breathing hard and gulping. She was not thinking about what had just happened upstairs with Marcus and the beautiful girl, but about what she had just said, which was unlike anything she had said before, and not even anything Marcus had told her to say, and exactly what she thought, and the journalist had written it down in his book. But she really didn't think Deepak Chaudry was a good artist, even if she wondered at what had given her the authority to say so or even think so, as she was not even an artist herself. At this precise moment she realized that she was in love with Marcus.

Brian had watched her move somewhat shakily into the hall and followed her there in the hopes of being able to touch her as he steadied her or at least have her pull on his arm again, which had been pleasant in a troubling way. The hall was very dim and hazy and the noise and the crowd had not abated, and at first he did not see her leaning against the big ugly Group of Seven. He noticed that the house smelled pleasant, like winter, like Christmas, as if someone had lit a fire in the fireplace.

He saw Muriella and moved to her. He was just standing by her side, smiling, when people first began coming down the stairs shouting about the smoke. Some people were even shouting that there was a fire somewhere, and then Brian could see that the stairwell was full of smoke, and it was coming from upstairs, in clouds, and then he felt that his eyes and throat were burning, and he said abruptly to Muriella, "Fire. There's a fire."

Her eyes were big and confused, and so he took her cool hand and yanked her out from against the wall and they followed the crowd which was coming out of the living room, sweaty and dazed, and cramming the entrance hall. He tried to get through them, but there was too much pushing, so he pulled Muriella back through the hall and the kitchen, which was now also smoky, and the smoke smelled bitter now, not pleasant, and he struggled through the sliding-glass door onto the first patio and pulled her into the outside air. He made her run down the stone steps to the next patio and even onto the grass before they turned around and looked up at the house. There were people piling out of the kitchen now and the library, and even out of the library windows. There was a smashing of glass from somewhere, and a lot of shouting. He saw Julia Sternberg run towards them and then stop and turn around before she reached them. Brian put his arm around Muriella, who was shaking, but he didn't know what to say. He scanned the upstairs windows; there was no glow, no sign of flame, but in the darkness you could see movement like the shaking of branches in wind, which was trails of smoke seeping from the frame of one window, a mansard right in the middle of the long sloping roof, and he pointed at it and Muriella said, very faintly, "My bedroom."

Brian wondered if anyone had phoned. There were ten people on the lawn and the patios and more outside and they were all just standing looking at the little ribbons of smoke flying from the upstairs window, streamers on an ocean liner at night.

Muriella was murmuring something, her voice scratchy. Brian leaned his head towards her. "Marcus," she said. "Marcus."

"Where is he?"

"In my bedroom." Her voice went high and wavery. Her hands went to her face.

"I'm sure he got out."

She pulled away from him with sudden strength and scrambled up the stone steps to the patio. Brain ran after her and pulled her back from the kitchen door. He was shouting, "You can't go in."

She was shrieking, "He was asleep. He was sleeping. And he's drunk. And he was smoking. He started it. It started in there."

Brian pushed her away from the kitchen door and yelled, "You stay here." He made her stand on the lower patio, and he ran back into the house.

The kitchen was only hazy but the hall was quite thick. The music had stopped and the rooms seemed empty. He looked in the big drawing room, where the dancing had been, and the library, and the conservatory with the piano, and saw no one, and trod over the plastic plates and crushed pieces of broccoli and dip on the blood-red Persian rugs towards the stairwell, which was dim with smoke. He held his breath and ran upstairs and looked in every bedroom with his hand over his mouth.

The end of the hall was black. The smoke was thickest around the last door, which was closed.

He ran at it with his shoulder, which hurt, and then he stepped back and grabbed the handle. The door opened easily. He began coughing as he stepped into the room, because he was laughing a little at the fact that he had tried to break the door down before he had thought to open it, and then laughing about the fact that he was laughing, there, which was absurd, and then he stopped laughing when he saw the form on the bed, lying still.

There were no flames, but billowing smoke from something on the floor on the other side of the bed.

Brian shook him and slapped him, and Marcus moaned. He had wrapped a sheet over his face and was breathing through it, swearing faintly. The rest of him was naked.

The smoking mess beside the bed was bedclothes, a down pillow with a black hole burned in it, reeking, and a hardcover book in the middle of it, smouldering. There was an upturned ashtray among the sheets. Brian went around the bed and kicked at the pile, and it burst into little flames as high as his ankles. He yelped and jumped back, and then ran at it again, stomping it.

The curtains were also blackened and smoking.

When the flames were out he was coughing again. He pulled Marcus off the bed by his legs, and the tall man landed on the floor with a bump, his head propped at the bottom of the bed. Brian was shouting at him, he didn't know what.

He pulled him upwards by his arms, and Marcus responded a little, rising to his knees and sitting down again. Brian got him sitting up against the bed and then looked around. There was a blanket or quilt folded on some sort of bench against the window, which he grabbed and threw at

Marcus. He pulled him up again until he was almost standing, and wrapped the blanket around him. Then he bent at the waist, pushed his shoulder into Marcus's belly, as he had seen paramedics do in TV shows, and grabbed him around the thighs. Marcus flopped over his shoulder as if he knew what to do, and Brian tried to lift him.

He staggered and rose, and fell against the bed and tried again. Marcus was moving, but not trying to help, as if he were too drunk or simply uninterested.

He was muttering something like, "Not worth it."

"Get on my back," Brian shouted. He turned his back to Marcus and stooped. "Get on my back. Piggyback."

With his eyes closed, the older man wrapped his arms around Brian's neck, and Brian grabbed his long thighs to his own hips and stood. He shook and staggered to the door, and walked, jerky, a bundle of bones on his back, down the smoky hall.

He made it down the stairs by leaning as heavily as he could on the banister and sliding Marcus's weight down it. Marcus groaned.

As he heaved though the kitchen, puffing and coughing, to the open sliding doors, he heard sirens from outside. Marcus's mouth was wet against his neck. He was drooling.

Brian ran with his bundle down the patio steps and onto the lawn, and dumped it at Muriella's feet. Marcus sprawled and coughed, displaying his thin nakedness, his long sex, and wrapped the blanket around himself and curled up in a ball.

Brian was breathing hard. He put his hands on his knees and bent over, dizzy. His legs were shaking. Muriella was kneeling at Marcus's side, taking his hand, whispering to him.

Brian stood up and looked around him. Julia Sternberg was standing there too, right next to him, silent and watching. There were people all over the lawn, in a strangely bright light; all the lights in the house were now on, and sirens in the air. There were smashes and shouts from inside, and two firemen dressed like giant insects came out of the kitchen, from where he had just emerged, bristling with axes and breathing apparatus, goggled and faceless and huge.

The air was cold and Brian couldn't stop shaking. No one was saying anything to him. Five or six people he didn't recognize were just standing around watching. Julia Sternberg was looking at him, white in the stark light, with her mouth twisted. It looked as if she was disgusted by something. Brian didn't know what she thought and didn't care. Julia Sternberg could think anything she liked. He sank to his knees on the earth, which was cold. He felt absurdly cold, and sleepy for some reason. He wished someone would bring him a blanket.

Then firemen were all over him in a furious noise, a cackle of radio static and shouting, wrapping him up in a blanket and carrying Marcus away. He let himself be put on a stretcher, because he couldn't stop shaking, although he was aware that he would look ridiculous being carried away like a child in front of Julia. He wanted to walk away from her.

As he was carried down the path to the front he glimpsed Muriella's old neighbour, the guy with the red hat, in a raincoat over a bathrobe, watching through a gap in the hedge.

Julia Sternberg, he thought again, could think anything she fucking liked.

XXVI

"I GET THEM AT MOUE, OVER IN ROSEDALE, on Yonge Street, you know Moue? They have excellent croissants as well. Is that too strong for you? I have hot water."

"Yes." David Rodney nibbled. He was sitting deep in the padded chair, looking very spindly, and Muriella worried idly that he might have trouble rising out of it again. "Very nice."

Muriella was listening, listening hard for sounds from downstairs or upstairs. Both Julia and Marcus were home, but she didn't know where they were. The heat had come on and made whining noises in the pipes, under the floors, distant wailing noises that you could mistake for something, for someone in distress, walled in a room somewhere. It was interfering with her listening.

David Rodney sighed and tried again. "Muriella, the thing is, you understand as well as I do that residency in the Park is a membership. Your *husband*, Arthur, was voted in as a member by the residents' association. Now membership is a, is a—"

"I know who Arthur is, David. Was."

"I'm sorry?"

"You don't need to put such a stress on husband. *Husband*. I'm sorry. Go on." Muriella sat back in her chair. She stretched her legs out in front of her, in her new jeans, and David Rodney would not look at them. She closed her eyes and listened. The heat was swishing.

He cleared his throat, the sound of a dishwasher finishing its cycle. "See, membership is, is a, well, I hate to say it like this, I don't mean to be blunt, but it's a privilege. It's not just money that gets you in here, Muriella. Gets one in, I mean."

She opened her eyes. He was red-faced, staring into his tea. She looked at her watch. Jasminka was coming at four and then she would be alone again, which was fine.

"You're not helping me at all, Muriella," said David Rodney deeply.

"Say what you want to say, David. I have no idea what it is."

"Oh, I have an idea you do. I have an idea you do."

She sighed. "Oh please. I have someone else coming at four."

"All right," he said. "All right. The point is very simple. Membership is a privilege which can be revoked at any minute. It's up to the residents' association." His voice was high and grainy, the voice of an old man. "If the residents' association decides that someone, a resident, is no longer, is no longer conducive, ah, or I mean is not a *beneficial* influence in the Park, if that resident is creating disorder or being, even, destructive to the, to the unity or the well-being of the Park, then that resident—"

"The *unity*? The unity of the *Park*?" Muriella laughed sincerely.

"Then that resident can have his or her privileges revoked." David Rodney had gone hoarse. He slurped his tea.

"You would try to have me expelled?" She laughed again.

"It has happened. In the past."

"Not in the twentieth century, David. It's a funny idea, though. It's very romantic." She couldn't stop laughing.

"You would have me expelled from my house for being immoral? That's wonderful. Is there a badge or a letter I have to wear?"

"Now listen. It's nothing to do with moral or immoral. Although I must say I wouldn't want any children passing—anyway, never mind. There's nothing we can do about what you do in your private time. And that is not our interest."

"Oh no."

"No. It is not. It's a safety issue."

"I'm not *safe*?"

"The burning of noxious gases in the Park is not permitted, according to the terms—"

"Oh, it's *Vincent*. I see. David, Vincent is a sculptor. He is an artist."

"It doesn't matter what he calls himself, Muriella, if he's burning toxic chemicals up there—"

"Oh, it's polyethylene, David. It's a standard building material. I'm sure he knows what he's doing."

"Mrs. Poziarski can smell the fumes in her bedroom, and that's almost a hundred yards—"

"Well, you get your court orders or whatever you need, David. Go for it. Go crazy. Go nuts," she said, and giggled, for she knew she only said that because Jason Katz said it. She stood up. "Is that all you wanted to tell me?"

"If you find it a joke," he said, standing shakily, "I would warn you that the association won't. Nobody is happy, Muriella. Nobody. You'd be surprised. If you don't want to take this seriously—"

"I'm glad to have united you all," said Muriella gaily. She stretched. "All your differences forgotten. Wonderful. So best wishes to you. Best wishes to you all."

David Rodney swept up his hat from the arm of the chair. It was his winter hat, not the red one, it was a plaid tweed hat with earflaps. Muriella knew every year when to switch the heat on when David Rodney began wearing his tweed hat. "Is that what you'd like me to report to the residents' association?"

"Report whatever you like."

"You're not going to present any defence. You have the right, you know, to explain what you think—"

"Defence for what?"

David Rodney was shaking his head. He slapped the limp hat against his hand as if dusting it.

"My message to the association is to knock yourselves out. Come and get me. Would you like to take one of those mille feuilles with you? The stripy ones? I'll never eat them all."

When he was gone she stood still and listened again, but could hear nothing but the whistling of the strange old heating system, which could have been a creaking, could have been a moaning. The house still smelled of wet smoke, of sodden burned wood. It smelled like a beach in the morning.

Jasminka was the next visitor. This was also a brief visit. Getting Jasminka in and out of her coat and boots and the placing and lifting of the Heavy Bag took more time than the interview, in which Jasminka wanted simply to say that the Action Council was considering terminating Marcus's residency prematurely, because it was harming the reputation of the program, which was desperate, to start with, in the current political climate, for funding from the municipal government. Muriella did not listen closely, but promised to explain the situation to Marcus as best she could.

Jasminka consumed the rest of the pastries.

After she had gone, Muriella tiptoed up the stairs and stood at the doorway of Julia's room, which was open. The bed was unmade, the room empty. There was a flimsy flesh-coloured bra on the floor. Muriella felt a quick rush of anger that Julia's underwear was so ugly. It irritated her that Julia didn't care. That she didn't need to care. That Julia didn't need pretty underwear.

And then she heard a heavy step in the hall and the cough that Marcus had had since the fire, Marcus, coming up from his apartment in the basement, and she tripped down to look at him from a landing. She called his name and he looked up.

"Hello," he called, and smiled up at her. He was pulling on his raincoat, his scarf.

"Hello." She wanted to ask him if he was alone, but she could see he was. She wanted to ask anyway. "Going out."

"As you see."

"Yes."

He buttoned his raincoat. He wore bulky sweaters underneath. He hadn't brought a winter coat.

She asked, "Will you be seeing Julia?"

He hesitated, then said, "Yes. I will be."

"Yes."

He said, "Is there anything you would like me to tell her?"

"No." There was another silence. "Nothing."

"Yes. Well then. See you later."

She watched him leave and then sat on the stair. The light was going so early in the day the house was already dark.

Marcus had spent the last several days with Julia. She didn't know where they were going in the evenings and they were coming back separately, and late, but she knew they had been together. She had not spoken with Julia about the sex on the night of the fire. They were both pretending it hadn't happened. The fire had seemed more important, in the week that followed, the sleepless week of repairmen and hammering, of hauling Marcus back from the hospital, of calls from the newspapers. Marcus chatty and giggling. He had apologized once, sincerely, and not mentioned it again. The repairs to her bedroom, the upstairs hall, the corner of the library under the bedroom that had been soaked as well, the corner of roof, and the mansard window were going to cost twelve and a half thousand dollars. Muriella had not thought about this much, but she thought about it now.

It was in this moment that she thought, for some reason, of Brian Sillwell, perhaps because it was so obvious that he was in love with Julia too, and Julia didn't even seem to know it. She was more afraid of him than ever since his performance during the fire. And Brian was probably lonely, in fact she knew he was lonely, and he was a nice boy, really.

He was the only person she thought of calling in that moment.

So she walked into the kitchen and picked up the phone and did, and she said, "Would you like to get together some time, to talk about maybe what we should do, what the committee should do?"

Brian seemed surprised by this. He said, "Get together?"

"Yes. To form a strategy. Or something. I don't know what to think."

"All right. Sure, Muriella. I'd love to."

"What are you doing this evening? I could make you a

meal, if you like."

There was a long silence before Brian replied, "This evening would be fine."

XXVII

A N D   S O   B R I A N   C A M E   T O   B E   L E A N I N G
against Muriella's fridge with a glass of white wine in his
hand and watching her sliding a tray of baked salmon fillets
out of an oven set high in the wall. He had walked through
her house, which still smelled of wet char, of burnt rubber
and rot and fresh paint, noticing with a little tenderness the
empty rooms, still covered in tarpaulins, where painters had
been working, the blackened top sections of wall around the
staircase. It was a little chilly; perhaps the window in the
upstairs bedroom had still not been repaired. There was
plastic sheeting instead of glass doors to the patio. The
house smelled of a campsite after rain.

And of course he had still taken in with gluttony, as he
had walked through, the Krieghoff winter scene like a
chocolate box, in a gold frame as heavy as a sleigh, lit by a
discreet little frame lamp that probably cost about as much
as a new bicycle, no point in wondering what the Krieghoff
had cost at auction ("Nicky and I had a friendly little tussle
over that one, but Thor was reining her in from over the
telephone, and Muriella had her heart set on it, being from
Montreal . . ."), and the five-thousand-dollar rugs and the
ten-thousand-dollar sideboard and the dark shelving in the
library built by aged craftsmen from, where, Sussex, of
aged wood soaked in cognac, champagne, infant deer
blood, wood from an enchanted forest, only available from
a single boutique in Geneva, by appointment, as long as the

owner knew your family tree—and lamps as heavy as how-itzers and vases made apparently of solid diamond and bowls, *bowls* so dark and patterned they looked as if they had belonged to hemophiliac Russians in an age of slave labour, bowls that you could buy a *car* with . . . He had thought, at first, that he would refuse all food but Iranian caviar, demand an eau-de-vie scented with crushed wood-cock beak. Make a stand, show her what he was made of.

Now he was watching her thin arms flex and the freckles on the backs of her shoulders, where her dress was cut away. It was strange that she was wearing a dress at all, for a din-ner in the kitchen on a weeknight, but it was definitely a dress, a party dress even, perhaps even the same clingy black dress she had worn at the party with the fire. It showed her shoulders, her bony chest, her thin legs. She wore running shoes instead of heels, though: she looked like a club girl.

The girls Brian knew from university did not wear dresses, even to clubs (they didn't go to clubs); Julia Sternberg, for example, would have been wearing elabo-rately pocketed combat fatigues had she invited someone to dinner in her kitchen, although Brian could not imagine her doing even that. He imagined Julia Sternberg lived on take-out sushi and the occasional bowl of popcorn. He imagined she found entertaining, with cooking and everything, to be uptight and small-town. He didn't know. He was trying not to think about Julia Sternberg, especially about Julia Sternberg and that old slack fuckfart Marcus Royston, that sex-smelling boozy prick.

Brian took a deep gulp of wine and tried to listen to Muriella. She was asking him, in fact, about Julia and whether they had had any contact since the fire, since,

Muriella was saying, looking at him with a twisted grin, Brian knew that Julia was so terribly impressed with his behaviour that night.

Brian snorted.

"Oh yes she was," said Muriella. "Ouch." She flapped her hand, threw oven mitts into the sink. The fish crackled. It smelled of burning wood and garlic. "Now if you could hand me that bowl of salsa. It's the mixed-up greeny things. Thank you. Yes she was. She thinks you're a hero. She couldn't believe she was standing there, and we were all just standing there, everybody was just standing there and not doing anything. You were the only one. Now she's even more afraid to talk to you."

"Sure she is."

"Look, I know you're not happy about her being with Marcus. Who is?" She gave a little burst of laughter like a girl.

"Where is Marcus? Tonight?"

"I don't know. He is out a lot." She hesitated over the fish. She held the bowl of salsa in one hand. "I don't know where Julia is, either." She gave that tight laugh again, and Brian saw the cords stand out on her neck, white and thin, and he didn't like to look at it. But he couldn't help looking at her waist, so taut, and the flat breasts so visible behind the black. He felt a little dizzy in the smoky kitchen, in the smell of wine and fish. She was wearing a soapy perfume, or perhaps a body powder or hand lotion, something that smelled like shampoo, and Brian couldn't decide if it made him excited or ill. He didn't know what he felt about lusting after Muriella (for he had come to the point of accepting that that was what it was); he shouldn't feel guilty about it, he knew, but he did wonder if it made him some kind of fetishist. Could he touch that waist if it turned out to be wrinkled? And what if the breasts sagged when released from the shiny black fabric?

That image made his belly tighten and his heart accelerate.

So he had his answer.

He drank his wine.

When they sat and ate, and she was so attentive and giggly and red-faced, it occurred to Brian, like a faint radio signal received by accident, that he was being seduced. He chewed his fish and cilantro salsa, which was fabulous, and decided that he didn't feel very much about that, except a certain sexual excitement. If she slept with him, then at least she wasn't sleeping with Marcus Royston, which was one thing in its favour, but then he couldn't pre-emptively sleep with every woman, every night, that Marcus Royston was likely to sleep with, although it might be worth trying. Even that didn't excite him. He sighed. He hadn't felt much about the world lately.

After dinner they sat on the cracked leather couches in the library that came from some film set about tycoons and she poured him a brandy in a glass the size of a cabbage and offered him a cigar. He laughed and said he would try a cigar, although he had never smoked one, and she brought him a box with brown lozenges of various sizes in it. She encouraged him, gently, to take a small one, although there were pale coffee-stained cylinders the size of Polish sausages in the case. "You have to have a very big cock to smoke the massive ones, I suppose," he said, and she laughed and said,

"Actually, I can assure you that is not the case," and he laughed and coughed and turned red. He brushed his hand against her knee as he took a cigarillo as dark and stinky and wrinkled as animal stool, and she lit him with some heavy silver paperweight thing that spouted flame. She curled her legs up beside her, and he saw her bony knees. He felt tender towards them.

The smoke burned his mouth and throat and nasal passages and he coughed. "Jesus Christ," he hacked, "what are you supposed to enjoy?"

"Don't inhale. Just take it in your mouth and blow it out."

"I didn't. I did that." He tried to breathe deeply and pull again on the cigar. It was like a mouthful of flint. He was finding it funny that he was drinking brandy and smoking a cigar on a cracked leather couch in a library filled with dark shelves and dark rugs and vast ugly frames holding vast ugly landscapes which all seemed to be painted with palette knives the size of spatulas; it was like a cartoon from *Punch*. This is probably what Julia Sternberg suspected he was like all along. He coughed happily. "I've never really pictured myself as a gentleman's club kind of guy. We need a fire going, and I should be in a bathrobe, a silk bathrobe, paisley."

"A smoking jacket."

"That's the thing looks like a bathrobe?" He took a sip of brandy and that burned too, and made his eyes water, and he laughed and coughed. "These things are supposed to go together?" he wheezed. "They go together because they both taste like burning tires."

Muriella laughed and slapped his knee. Brian felt filled with a certain destructive glee. Quickly, so he didn't have to think about it, he leaned forward and tried to kiss her on her mouth. He swayed and she lurched, so he missed, but she understood and held the back of his head. She guided his hot face to hers.

Her mouth tasted of wine. He ran his hands over her shoulders, her sides and waist. She was kissing him rather frantically, sucking on his lower lip in a way that wasn't entirely comfortable. Her eyes were closed. Carefully, ready to withdraw like a rabbit if burned, he moved his hand to her upper side, just under her arm, where it could slip around to the front if such time came as he found enough confidence to do so. The warm skin under the shiny thin fabric was making him excited. The thought of the breasts hanging down under there, unrestrained by the cottony sports bras of his previous successes, of indeed his only experiences, made him excited before touching them, too excited, in fact, and he tried to think about multiplication tables, as he had once been told to do. Perhaps it would not come to that. But before he knew it he had slipped his hand around (a new confidence took him with Muriella, he didn't know why; perhaps it was that it was clear to everyone, for the first time in his sexual life, that he was not expecting to enter into a relationship with her, or perhaps it was because he simply did not find her as attractive as girls of his own age, and so did not feel so desperate, which was a sad thought, at any rate, it did wonders for his confidence and not coincidentally his body) and grasped a yielding breast, surprisingly firm and full, with a point as hard and thick as any he had touched. She whimpered a little as both his hands explored her front. She shifted so the front of the dress opened and he could see, excited beyond reason, at least one hardened nipple, extraordinarily long and red, something much used, overripe, and on the verge of corruption. She leaned back, pushing it upwards. Conscious of his ridiculousness, he dropped his head and sucked it like a glutton.

"Well," said Muriella, "that happened."

Brian covered himself with a blue sheet. He wanted her to cover herself too, but he couldn't ask her that. He glanced at her breasts, pale against the blue, the nipples downturned, the skin slack. He looked away. The room was dim and close, and smelled of their bodies and that sweetness, that talcum-powder smell which was too strong. He knew that now was the moment to stroke her hair, kiss her or caress her or something. He could still taste her saltiness in his mouth. He reached for his brandy snifter, on the bedside table. It was sticky and empty. "I'm going to get some water."

"Me too please," she said softly. She seemed sad.

In the flowery bathroom, Brian washed his hands with soap. He splashed his face. He hated the wallpaper.

When he returned he got quickly into bed and covered them both up with the blue sheet and put his arm around her shoulder and said, "I'd better go."

"Yes."

He kissed her ear. She put his hand on his chest and, incredibly, his body began to rouse itself again, and his chest tightened as he remembered his frenzy of a few minutes before. Her wetness. The smell surprisingly strong. He kissed her on the lips and it passed.

"Well that helped, for a while, didn't it?" she said faintly.

"What?"

"We both had our revenge."

"Oh," said Brian. The hair on his neck had curled. "No. That's not . . . ." But he had nothing else to say.

"No," said Muriella. "I don't mean I don't like you. I like you very much. You're sweet."

"Sweet," said Brian sharply. He reached for his watch.

"And strong." She was smiling.

"Oh."

"You can stay here if you want."

The soapy scent of sheets and shampoo and whatever it was made him feel ill. "I'd better go."

"All right. Don't be bitter, darling."

"I'm not bitter." He got out of bed and looked around. He remembered that all their clothes were downstairs, on the library floor. He stood there naked, with his hands on his hips. She was up on one elbow, looking at his crotch. "It sounds as if you're bitter."

"No," she said, and looked at his face and smiled. "No." She giggled and fell back onto the bed.

Before he left she said distinctly, "Call her. Try asking her out. You've never tried that, have you?"

He pretended not to hear.

In the library, which smelled of ancient debauch, he switched on a lamp. He began picking up his clothes. There was a notebook on a coffee table, a black bound student's notebook, not a scribbler or a steno pad for taking notes, more like a sketchpad, the kind of notebook you buy if you are writing down Thoughts, so Brian, barefoot and without a shirt, picked it up and opened it. The writing in it was tight and small and feminine and blue, not Marcus's (he had seen Marcus's yellow notepads all over the house, with their black felt-pen scrawlings), not Muriella's (he had seen her fridge-door notes to herself, their looping frenzy). He put the book down as if it were hot.

He found his shirt and began buttoning it and then picked up the book again. He sat on the arm of a leather chair, feeling vaguely that if he were to sit in the seat, the front door would swing open and Julia would come at him in tears.

He decided that if he read anything concerning sex with Marcus, or any scorn or hostility directed at himself, he would put it down in instant self-preservation. But it all seemed to be descriptions of things.

The entries were not dated.

It's still freezing cold, although I keep the kerosene heater roaring all day, and write in the living room right in front of it, even though it has warnings all over it saying that if you use it in an unventilated room it's going to suck all the oxygen out of the room and you are going to pass out and die, which makes little sense for a heater, right, I mean if you are trying to heat a freezing cold room the last thing you want is ventilation, right? What are you supposed to do, open the window?

There was one sheet which was loose, a page from another notebook, and had what appeared to be poetry on it.

Late August light

*The steel-bellied clouds are etched in gold,
a concern in the sky, premonition
of terrible joy*

He stood up, dizzy, drunk on something, he didn't know what, hot and cold. He closed the book and buttoned his shirt. When he was fully dressed, he opened the book and found the sheet again, removed it. He folded it as if to put it in his pocket. Then he unfolded it and flattened it on the table to try to remove evidence of its having been folded.

He slipped into the kitchen in his socks. It was blue-white from the neon bar over the stove. There were pens in a holder and a notepad stuck to the fridge. In the glow, he tore off a square of paper. He slid back into the library, hoping Muriella wouldn't wonder what he was doing wandering around. He heard nothing from upstairs.

He copied the lines onto the square. He folded it in four, and put it first in one pocket and then in another. He didn't know why he felt he had to hide it. He wasn't going to be searched for it.

On closing the heavy front door behind him—it always closed with a thump that sounded like bank vaults, cathedrals, thick carpeting—Brian felt a mist on his face. The Park was dripping. He walked under the drooping trees in the darkness. A naked woman was in there, inside the big house, all shuttered up, in bed, completely naked, and he had been in there.

And he had Julia's words in his pocket:

>   ... *premonition*
> *of terrible joy*

He began to run.

XXVIII

MURIELLA WAS SITTING ALONE, AS USUAL, and trying to sum things up. She was having a cup of tea in the kitchen and trying to take stock. The word that had immediately presented itself on beginning this process was *wreckage*, and now she was repeating this word to herself, even though another voice was saying that this was probably an exaggerated thought. But wreckage was attractive in its drama. The wreckage, she thought, of: (1) my home, particuarly the bedroom where Vincent, the sculptor, was now burning polyethylene; (2) my standing in the Park; (3) my relationship with the arts community, in other words with all the artists of this city and by extension of the country; (4) my relationship with Marcus; (5) my relationship with Julia; and (6) my life.

She paused here and counted them up again. The only one that could possibly be questioned was the last one. But there was great pleasure to be had in considering it this way. *Wreckage!*

At least she hadn't slept with Vincent, which amazed her really, but she hadn't really wanted to, which was evidence of something. Some sense or order remaining in the universe.

She realized that she had forgotten to add her relationship with Brian Sillwell to the list, but strangely didn't feel too wrecked about it, unless the desire for more sex with him could be counted on as more wreckage. She didn't know what was wreckage any more.

She wondered if it was too early for a glass of white wine.

She wondered lately, a great deal, if she was simply growing nasty. She should feel much more guilty about Brian—and about David Rodney and the poor Poziarskis and the toxic fumes, which really were unpleasant, although the Poziarskis were far too far away to really appreciate how unpleasant; if they only knew!—and she didn't, somehow. Feel guilty. What she did feel strange about—not guilty, but strange, a sense of wonder—was what she had said about Deepak Chaudry to Brian and that journalist and everyone at the party. Because it was really not nice, but also because it was the first negative thing she had said, since being on that Action Council, about any work of art, and she wondered if this was Marcus's influence, since he had showed her so much poetry and she had met so many writers through him (not all good ones, she could now say with confidence—but how?), but partly because she had heard him dismissing so many of them. Was this what it was all about? Knowing so much that you hated everything?

But she really couldn't read Deepak Chaudry's stories about racism and she realized that she had never liked them, and now that she knew she didn't, there was no going back.

This made her exhale sharply and feel, perversely, a kind of happiness.

She stood up with a sense of glee and decided to phone the photographer who was a friend of Vincent's who needed a studio. She had a feeling he did mostly nudes. That was something.

Muriella was alone at this time because Julia and Marcus were in the roti shop five blocks away, having the talk which they did not want to have in her house. It was a talk that neither one actually wanted to have or thought they needed to have, but they were having it anyway.

He looked sleepy and distracted. His white shirt was bright in the fluorescence. It was a shirt that needed cuff-links, but the cuffs were rolled up instead, revealing his long narrow forearms with their perfect coffee skin, which Julia no longer wanted to touch.

He said, "I am very sorry that you felt that way. I have already said this."

"I know," she said. "It's okay. You don't need to go on saying it. It's not your fault. Nothing is your fault. I'm a . . . I'm a big girl."

"By no stretch of the imagination could you be described as a big girl." He said this so dolefully that it made Julia relax a little and she let herself smile. "But I know what you mean."

"I knew what I was doing. So did Muriella."

"Perhaps I was the only one who didn't."

"Yes. Maybe. Anyway, I just thought we should talk about it. And I had to tell you why I was sorry, why I'm sorry, about not seeing each other any more, but I just thought we should make it clear."

They both had coffee in Styrofoam cups which they were not drinking.

Marcus said, "I have never understood that."

"What? Not seeing each other?"

"No no. That is quite clear. The talking about it. It is not something I have ever understood. Why we must make everything clear."

"You would prefer it if I just avoided you for a while and you would get the message?"

"Yes, actually. I would much prefer that."

"No you wouldn't. It would be childish. Of me."

There were four black men waiting for rotis and talking and laughing with Errol, who was behind the counter. The shop was loud with reggae, and damp, with streaks of brown water on the floor, and the smell of frying and curry. No one was paying attention to Marcus and Julia; she had come there enough that for once she felt invisible there, and could talk almost in a normal voice.

Marcus said, "I find it actually more hurtful that you would tell me. I do not want, I suppose . . ." He smiled. He attempted a sip of his coffee which was grey. "I would rather not be confronted with it. With the coldness of it."

"I haven't been cold," said Julia quickly. "If anything, the way you treated—"

"I know, I know." Marcus had a hand on her arm. "Of course you are not being cold. That's not what I mean. You are anything but cold to me. Besides, I deserve everything."

She said more gently, "No, you don't. I deserve everything. You didn't force me into—"

"What I meant was that it is still a rejection."

Julia frowned. "I didn't think you would be worried about rejection. You seem not to—" She was going to say *care* but stopped herself. "To worry about . . . about what people think. About anything."

"No, I don't. I worry about what I can have and, increasingly, what I can't have."

She laughed. "Well, if you're worried about women, I'm sure you won't have any problems. There are plenty more . . ." Something about his face made her stop.

"There aren't plenty more. There are not plenty more like you."

Julia felt a quick warmth spreading through her. It was terrible to see him sad, sad as he had seemed so often lately, but a great pleasure to make him vulnerable, for once. And she knew he was right about this, really. He would be too old soon. He was already too old. "Marcus," she said, "I think you're depressed."

"I'm fine."

"What are you working on?"

Marcus narrowed his eyes. "Yes, there will always be women."

"You see, you're depressed."

"What is depressing about that?"

Julia looked away. His eyes were too bloodshot to look at. One of the young men at the counter caught her eye and smiled at her, so she looked back at Marcus. He hadn't noticed the young guy's stare, which was good, because she had found he could get puffy-chested about things like that, was liable to amble over and introduce himself to the guy, let him know who he was. She said, "You know what is depressing about that."

"You mean that is not enough?"

"No. It's not."

"Ah."

Julia could tell he was already bored with this conversation. But suddenly, and quite loudly, he said, "You mean what will I have when they dry up?"

"You will have your writing."

Marcus was still for a moment. Then he looked at his watch.

Julia decided not to talk about him any more, or everyone would be in tears in a minute. "I feel, I guess, I know you don't want to talk about this any more, and forgive me, but I feel that I have to explain . . ."

He sighed, folded his arms across his chest.

"I feel I have to explain why I acted so out of character that night, at the party, because that's what it was, it was really out of character for me, and I really want you to know that."

"Why do I have to know that? Why can't you say it was indeed in character, a very important part of your—"

"No. Listen. It's not. And I know you're not interested in this and I don't care. I'm just talking for me now. And I want you to listen. All right? Because I've listened to you. A lot."

Marcus's eyes were wide. "All right."

"All right." Julia tried to slow her breathing, then went on. "You know, you can't really imagine where I come from."

"And you can't imagine where I come from."

"No, I can't. Don't be angry now, Marcus." She reached across and put a hand on his stiff forearm. The skin was cool. "I didn't mean . . . I just want to tell you this story. All right?"

"All right." His shoulders were tight.

"I grew up . . . my mother, and her sisters and her friends, were very keen on me getting married very young."

"Everyone's mother is like that," said Marcus.

"Yes. Well, anyway, my mother is very conservative, like everyone's, I guess, and she always irritated me, not because she's a bad person or anything, in fact she's a really sweet person who means well, but she just doesn't understand anything that isn't, I don't know, money, I guess, anything that isn't money."

"Ah."

"And so she always bothered me, with her expensive drapes and carpets and clothes and jewellery, and none of them, even my friends, when I was back there, in Montreal, had any taste, really, I always felt it was rather crass, and so I felt very relieved when I came here and got away from that, and tried really hard to live a simple life, and I ended up living with an artist who turned out to be a, well, not very nice." She breathed.

"Would you like another coffee?" said Marcus.

"No thank you. Anyway, I couldn't go on living in that empty house, so I ended up living with Muriella, who is very different from my mother in that she really does like art, I think, or at least she's learning that she does, she doesn't always know why she likes anything, but she's changing in some big way which is fascinating and exciting, and anyway, I don't think my mother would get it at all. And by the way, I think you've had a lot to do with that. You completely opened her up to think the way she wants to think, to be more . . . you know that party would never have happened, she would never have come up with all those people even a year ago, even six months ago. It was so totally unlike her."

"She didn't come up with those people."

"Sorry?"

"She didn't come up with all those people. It was the boys, those boys. Brian and his friend."

"Jason."

"Yes. They did all the inviting. It was because of all those people, whom they hardly knew, that it grew so out of hand."

"Oh. I didn't know. Anyway, even though Muriella has changed a lot, and I think she'll go on changing, there is still a part of her that's holding on, that's holding on to her old Stilwoode Park self, that's like . . ."

"That's like your mother," said Marcus.

Julia bit her lower lip. She shivered: the door opening and closing, the damp on the floor. "A bit like my mother. Yes."

"And then at this party," said Marcus patiently.

"At the party. I had a bit too much to drink. And I was very stressed and tense and angry, at you, because I knew you were with Muriella and whoever."

Marcus rolled his eyes and looked away.

"Anyway, I'm not blaming you. But I got all crazy and I just thought I'll show you, I'll show you all how wild I was. I guess I wanted to prove how not like my mother I was. And I wanted, in some sick way, I suppose, to come between you and Muriella. I didn't really know what I was doing."

Marcus turned to greet some new guy who was clapping him on the back. The reggae seemed even louder now. Julia pulled her raincoat up over her shoulders. The guy had a young woman with him, a black woman with her hair in cornrows that looked painful. The guy did not introduce Marcus to the woman, but Marcus smiled at her and she smiled back and he watched her plumpness in her tight jeans and stacked soles all the way to the counter. When he turned back to Julia, he said casually, looking down at his coffee, "So you didn't enjoy it at all."

Julia thought about this. In a very small voice she said, "Parts of it. Yes, I did. Very much. I remember the naked bodies." Her face felt hot. "All the skin looked very beautiful in the dim light. It was all blue."

"You had never done that before."

She shook her head. "I suppose you have."

Marcus shrugged.

"Yeah. Anyway, I don't remember all that much else. And I feel awkward about it, with Muriella, now, although she doesn't seem to feel it. She seems fine. But I also realized that you didn't . . . that I wasn't everything to you."

Marcus was silent. At his silence Julia felt a cold which was part pain and part relief. She knew there was not much more to say now. She pulled her raincoat on. She said, "I think that's going to be the end of my craziness for a while."

"Good." He looked back towards the counter, the incredibly high and round rump of the girl in the jeans.

Julia said, "Do you want to walk back to Muriella's with me?"

"Ah. No. Thank you. I will stay here and have another coffee."

Julia smiled. She wanted to get outside. As she buttoned her coat she said, "But I also wanted to, just one more thing, I wanted to say that I owe a lot to you. You gave me a lot."

He said softly, "And you gave me a lot. What did I give you?"

"A confidence. And you made me realize I didn't . . ."

He wasn't listening. The girl at the cash had turned around and was smiling at him.

Julia said goodbye and kissed him on the cheek and he hardly noticed.

In the perpetual rain, the desolation of St. Clair Avenue was cleansing. Julia walked slowly, getting wet. What she had wanted to say to him was that she had also known, from doing that thing with him and Muriella, and just from hanging out with him all the time too, that she didn't want to be an artist.

She would walk down the steep wide empty street back to Muriella's now, although she couldn't live there for much longer. This caused a gust of panic, on the hill in the rain: where would she live? In a tiny box like everyone who was too fucked up to live with people? The thing was, she wasn't that fucked up. She really wasn't. She knew she wasn't any more. Perhaps being alone was not the best thing for her, on balance.

So she went down the steep hill to Muriella's potpourri-and-polyethylene-scented house.

XXIX

SATYRICAL POET SETS SLEEPY STILWOODE AFIRE
BY DISH

Special to Buzzer
Photo collage by the Jester

More drunken and hysterical hijinks from my sources in the sober and intellectual world of Literature: it seems that world-calibre (yet strangely unproductive) St. Andrean poet **Marcus Royston** is in still more trouble. The perennially relaxed middle-aged import, always a dab hand with the ladies—any ladies, any ladies at all—is at the centre of some literary shrieking, ever since I revealed (see *Buzzer* 38) that his nomination to the plush and expensive post of City Arts Council writer-in-residence was by no means a unanimous decision, nor was the competition fairly held. The fanatically politically correct Action Council (literature committee) wasn't quite so obsessed with fair representation from all corners of the globe on this one: they jammed through the $30,000 appointment of the moistened poetaster without considering any other candidates at all.

Why? Turns out some éminences grises hidden deep in the bowels of External Affairs (otherwise known as the Ministry of Pleasing Banana Republic Dictators) had their own reasons for inviting to the post this non-prolific, sentimental writer of mythological romances and (*That's enough about poetry!—Ed.*). Owing to impending trade deals with the newly capitalistic (and barely democratic) government of St. Andrew's, Minibananas had to offer up some pro-forma cultural agreement, and help get the lubricated troublemaker out of the range of local St. Andrew's media. (Turns out he's not such a big fan of St. Andrew's new tinpot, Prime Minister **Jojo Halliday**, who made a name for himself by quickly eliminating most social programs in the hurricane-wracked island, and purging (*That's enough obscure reggae politics!—Ed.*) The strong-armers at External, never too big on effeminate subjects such as poetry in the first place, threatened to withdraw all funding for the program unless the politically strategic Royston was installed. The Action Council forgot about their every-man-to-the-barricades rhetoric for a moment and caved in to the demands from the Big House.

Anyway, now more news surfaces about the antics of the privileged prick: Remember that strange house fire in Stilwoode Park last week, during a party that was well-attended by an enthusiastic, multi-ethnic and wide-eyed crowd? Yes, it was at the same embarrassingly large neo-Arts-and-Crafts pile where the libidinous scribbler is holed up. The mansion belongs to society dame and artistic dilettante **Muriella Pent**, grateful widow of insurance exec **Arthur Pent**, she who has spent the long days since the old man's demise attending fashion shows and lunching at Holt's and calling herself an Ahtist; seems she contributed the maid's quarters in the basement to the Action Council's political scheme, and that's where Royston cooks up his influential works, between rum punches. Muriella has turned the venerable old house—designed, as she likes to boast, by Nathaniel Stilwoode in 1916—into quite the bohemian salon, installing nubile young students and unshaven performance artists in all the spare rooms, much to the displeasure of the respectable neighbours. There is, of course, no truth to the scandalous and outrageous rumours that the spry Royston, who must be pushing sixty, has managed to bag all the ladies on the Action Council, and a few more besides. It pains me particularly to hear that some have been spreading vile gossip about the leg-over king, suggesting that he has been having simultaneous horizontal mambo sessions with both his wizened hostess and with an underaged student who is also living in this house. I am sure that this gossip is mere fancy, as the great man's artistic sensibilities are far too sensitive for such shenanigans.

But about that fire. After the smoke cleared and the doobies were hidden away, the source of the flames was traced to an upstairs bedroom where Royston, fatigued after some heavy philosophical conversation and a drink or two, had been having a little mid-party snooze and a cigarette. Seems he forgot to butt that cigarette out, and snapcracklepop, one menopausal mansion on fire. It's unlikely that Muriella will sue him for damages, of course, as she knows that one pays a high price for artistic creativity as monumental as Royston's. (The lubricious limericker has produced a grand total of zero books since 1986, despite having been supported by one government or another his entire life.) Some unprincipled tongue-waggers have even suggested, totally without evidence, that Muriella was in the room at the time of the fire, along with—get this—a third party, engaged in some frisky frolics in the altogether. (*Shurely not the young student?—Ed.*) I will not be party, of course, to such malicious speculation.

Oh, and another thing: Juicy background on one of Royston's sworn enemies, oddly named *Next* magazine writer **Candace Bundle.** The well-nourished hack was, you will recall, the fierce feminist who demolished Royston's chances of ever winning the Ignatius Barnaby Sensitivity Award by a stinging profile last

October, in which Royston was made out to be a bit of a self-obsessed prick. Seems the sometime poet of Island Liberation wasn't keen enough on being the poster boy for ethnic representation, etc., for Bundle's tastes, and she got a few other failed poets (no doubt jealous of his cushy digs in Stilwoode Park) to slam him in the piece. Ever wonder why Bundle's so big (so to speak) on respect for women and the marginalized? And ever wonder if that's her real name? Turns out it's a stage name, from a previous life: Bundle was a professional peeler in Las Vegas before she packed on the pounds—guess that's when she decided that the exploitation of women's appearances was all wrong. The silly name wasn't the worst of her monikers: I hear she also went by the egregiously adolescent name of **Candy Mountains**, during a stint in the luxurious hotel bars of Prince Rupert, B.C. How the mountainous have fallen!

Does Dish know? Send tidbits in confidence to
dish@buzzer.com.

XXX

Writing in the Castries cafe, smell of frying, reggae on the radio. Weak coffee. Rain outside. Homesick for heat.

The girl has slipped away (the nymphs are departed, ha) and I don't know if I am bereft or relieved or bitter. I have been left before and can close myself like a corpse to loss. She will join the ranks of women who did not want me (despite what she thought), and she will be happy and I will forget.

Still, I dream of pale flesh that bruises. Her long legs (always bruised). Her skin always cool. Her rib cage sharp and fragile under the palm. Her body so resistant, never on fire. The shame and thrill of possessing a body, something not entirely yielding.

The barbed penis: Japanese prints portray it as toothed, violent, a weapon. One feels that one does damage as one causes pleasure: as if the pleasure itself were damaging. Perhaps this is just residual guilt over the act itself.

It is in this endless self-analysis that one's desires become fears. Through guilt over those desires.

Always, this sense of defiling. Perhaps it was her age. (But I feel it with M. too.)

A loss of something I never really had. Still, I feel it: the bruised thighs no longer mine. Fumbled over by nervous boys.

Perhaps she can give herself to them.

I have begun several letters.

Dear Julia,
I am sorry I was cold in the café when we had our talk. I felt
more than I revealed. Perhaps I was cold because I was
indignant at being so dismissed. I was surprised at my
dismissal. You have more power than

My dearest Julia,
You have more power over me than you ever knew. Or perhaps
you did. But you and I are not

My love,
Were we ever

My gentle
It may seem to you that I was
You were never as passionate with me as
unless your passion is unlike

What is the point? To let her know that it was she, in fact,
she who simply did not love? Why disabuse her of her
delicious victimhood?

XXXI

To: jsthenosjones@planetview.com
From: deepakc@onepeople.net
Message sent: 0945 on Monday, November 17

jasminka—i never talked to that guy at buzzer in nfact i have
no idea who it is who writes that stuff. I did talk to the guy at
the star, as i have every right too do, and told him what i feel
about the situation what do you expect me to do? what do you
want me to say—things i don't beleiev in that make everyone
feel comfy? i do believe, as i told him, that it is typical ofthe
way things work in this country that the work of a dedicated
and pluralistic group of arts workers has been hijacked once
again by the interests of the homogenious elite, and i think you
know whom i am referring to. it saddens me that muriella
pents house and her circle of friends, which have nothing to do
with the action council, is now seen as the centre of our
activities and representative of our viewpoints when it is not
the case at all. and royston seems to be totally under her spell,
which is not how we wanted this city to be represented when
he goes back to saint lucia. And if you want to point the finger
of resposnibility for the source of the information that got into
that magazine, i would strongly suggest you suspect her and
not me, as i don't even know such people as write for
magazines of that type or nature. once again it is a white
woman who has come to dominate an organization which was
supposed to stand for the voices of the voiceless and the

underrepresented in this society, and her power in this runs totally contrary to the whole point of this committee, which was to be fairly represented by ALL the voices in this culture, powerful or not, and i ask you how fair is that?

Deepak Chaudry

November 21

Dear Muriella,

This is to inform you, and the other members of the Arts Action Council (Literature Committee), that as of Wednesday, November 19, City Council, further to a motion by Mayor Campbell himself, has suspended further funding of the Literature Committee, pending an internal inquiry by the Action Council into the methods and records of the Literature Committee, particularly in the matter of the selection of Marcus Royston as the first Writer-In-Residence. The Mayor has claimed that the Committee is "in disarray," that there is so much disagreement among members of the Committee that it is no longer functional. The Mayor seems to be basing his evaluation of the Committee on what he has read in the media, particularly in the non-mainstream media, including the satirical press. It is also possible that he has been struck by the discordance of opinions which various members of the Committee have expressed to the media in various interviews on this subject. We certainly have not presented a united front.

The Mayor is also insisting that the Committee be "opened up," as he says, to new members of his own choosing, who will be parachuted in to the next meeting to express the views of the Mayor and, apparently, some of the residents of Stilwoode Park, who are now claiming an interest in the outcome of the Residency.

This is of course unreasonable political interference in the operations of the City Arts Board and in the artistic process, and runs directly contrary to the principle of arm's-length arts funding which has always governed our artistic community.

Of course, I intend to keep the Committee functioning, as far as possible without the interference of any new, partisan members from outside the artistic community. The withdrawal of the few monies that the City contributed to the Action Council will not greatly affect our meetings, which will take place henceforth in the residences of Committee members as volunteered by them on a rotating basis. (The meeting places will exclude Muriella Pent's residence in Stilwoode Park, as it seems to be the site of some tension, and the meetings might interfere with the privacy of the Writer-In-Residence.) The funding for the travel expenses of the Writer-In-Residence was of course contributed by the federal government, and remains, so far, unchanged.

I have begun a vigorous protest to City Council, and to the Mayor in particular, about this unreasonable and uninformed decision, and about the slander that the Mayor has himself perpetuated about the commitment and hard work of the volunteer members of the Committee. I am also taking legal advice about the possibility of a legal action against the Mayor; of course a major fundraising drive would have to take place before such an action could be undertaken, for which I would ask the strenuous help of the Committee.

From now on, press releases regarding the actions of the Committee will be drafted and released only by the Committee as a whole, with full approval of all members. Members of the Committee should NOT speak to the press or any other media without prior consultation with the Chair.

Suggestions for the time and place of our next meeting should be sent to me immediately via e-mail.

Yours sincerely,
Jasminka Sthenos-Jones
Chair

P.S. Muriella—I would ask in particular for your cooperation in the matter of speaking to the press. Your comments regarding the work and talents of the other Committee members were not helpful to the public perception of the work that we do. In general, holding a party to which the media were invited (without, I note, inviting the other members of the Committee or even consulting with them), and then provoking a public discussion of the Committee's decisions was, to my eyes, an act deliberately calculated to undermine the respectability of the Committee and the authority of the Chair. It is in large part owing to this arrogance that the Committee is now facing the number of problems it does. I would remind you that, although we are grateful for the use of your mansion for the Residency, the position of Host does not confer any special privileges. I remain Chair of the Committee and decisions taken by the Committee will be taken through consensus, as supervised by me. Thank you for your cooperation in this matter. J. S.-J.

November 21

Dear Jasminka,

I assure you that I never spoke to any press or even knowingly invited them to my party, but this is of no importance. I am not terribly worried about the press. I am sorry I didn't invite the members of the committee to the party, but I didn't think they would enjoy it. Marcus seemed keen on a party which had nothing to do with committee business. You missed an alarming fire which destroyed several rooms in my house, and some valuable heirlooms which I suppose I should be embarrassed to own.

Anyway, the point of my note is to invite you to another event in my house: a screening of some short films by Vincent Michalofski and one by Dominic Snow, and perhaps a dance performance (if I can clear the remains of the burnt carpets from the living room in time, and if the choreographer comes through) by some young friends of Marcus, who have just returned from Prague with a new piece called "Catachresis." There will also be some photographs on display in the front hall and kitchen by Tammy Lo. And dancing afterwards with music by—I hope!—a DJ whom Dominic has recommended to me, but who has not confirmed yet. The performance will begin at 8 p.m. next Friday, November 28. I hope you can come.

Yours,
Muriella

P.S. I still have no e-mail—sorry!

XXXII

"AND NOW THIS SO-CALLED PHOTOGRA-pher," said Olivia Daurio, "who has the girls coming and going, honestly, some of them look as tough as nails. Wouldn't want to meet some of them in a dark alley, no, honestly, I really don't feel comfortable, I wouldn't feel comfortable at night, getting out of my car, it's awfully dark under the big willow, you know, next to Shirley's house, and I honestly don't feel comfortable with who knows who coming and going at all hours from that house."

"That's another thing we need to talk about," said Shirley Melnyk, "is lighting."

"Some of them just look like they need a square meal," said Ralph Poziarski in his deep voice. He was sunk into his chair and all squished up like a gnome. All the chairs at Shirley Melnyk's were leather and sunk too deep. "I wouldn't be afraid of that. You just blow hard and they'd fall over."

"I think it's more than food they need. Some of them could use a shower too, and one of them doesn't even have a winter coat, you see her getting out of a taxi and freezing at the front door, shivering, in this little plastic raincoat. And bare legs."

"Some of them wouldn't be out of place in a trailer park."

"I haven't seen any of these girls," said Frank Daurio. "Haven't spent enough time studying Mrs. Pent's front door, I guess. Sounds like I've been missing something. Love to see one." He rose and went to the bar trolley to pour another Scotch and soda, which his wife didn't watch.

"What she doesn't seem to remember, or want to remember," said Linda Poziarski, who had a chickpea samosa on a black plate balanced on her nyloned knee, "is that this is not a public park. This is not a public thorough-fare." The plate jiggled. She touched the pastry with the end of an extended little finger and then put the finger to her tongue, as if to check an electric current. Samosas were Shirley's little fetish since she had been experimenting with vegetarianism. Everything Shirley Melnyk ordered these days seemed to have chickpeas in it. Linda Poziarski put the plate on a side table.

"Well, actually," rumbled Eric Cuthbertson, "it is." He was sitting slightly outside the group, at one end of a leather sofa with his long legs crossed. He wore a green tweed suit with argyle socks and leather shoes with heavy leather soles, and a check shirt and a silk tie. His hair, which was partly brown and partly silver, would have been too long had it not been, always, swept back cleanly like this. It never came loose, never drooped over his high forehead. He also wore a silk pocket square. This was the first thing he had said all evening, and he said it very quietly, which made everyone listen very closely, for he was a lawyer. So was Ralph Poziarski, or had been, anyway, before he got into develop-ment, but Eric Cuthbertson was a different kind of lawyer. He was a Scottish lawyer. "We cannot bar access to the Park. And we certainly cannot restrict residents from having visi-tors. Has anyone been actually harassed by any of these vis-itors, or had any incidents or run-ins or anything of that nature." He spoke very slowly and clearly. He did not have a drink or a cup of any kind.

The fireplace hissed and cracked.

"No," said Olivia Daurio, "but—"

"I only wish," said Frank Daurio.

"But there's the problem of the fumes, from that sculptor."

"That is a problem," said Eric Cuthbertson, "if it's an actual safety or health issue."

"Well the fire was an actual safety issue, wasn't it?"

"Who knows what he's getting up to with those girls," growled David Rodney.

"Would you like some more hot water in that, David?" said Shirley Melnyk.

Eric Cuthbertson cleared his throat. "And we do not actually have a chance, a legal chance, of evicting a resident simply because we do not like her guests. Or for any reason, for that matter. The last time it was done was nineteen thirty-five, and it made the papers even then. In not a positive light, I must tell you. The laws regarding evictions have grown significantly more sympathetic to evictees since then, as we all know."

Both Frank Daurio and Ralph Poziarski grunted sympathetically at this.

"Let alone to evictees who happen to be influential women who *own their own houses*."

There was a silence as the assembled company waited for David Rodney to begin reminiscing about Arthur.

"Her husband was a good man," came the wrinkled voice. "I remember when he came back from Montreal with *her*, I remember asking what her family name was, and she wouldn't even—"

"Hello, hello everyone, don't get up, hello Eric," said a clear voice, and then there was much rustling and dropping of napkins and almost everyone did get up, as Gaye Northwood had breezed in, all blondeness and cream wool. "Don't get up, Linda, sorry I'm late."

Several of the men had vacated their chairs for her, and Olivia and Linda had glanced at each other twice, first with raised eyebrows and then with smiles that were not entirely false.

"Nice to see you here, Gaye," rasped David Rodney. "Must be something important on your mind to get you here."

"Can I get you a glass of wine?"

"How was London?"

"Henry says he's so sorry he couldn't be here," said Gaye Northwood, folding herself into a very upright chair and taking a glass of white wine without appearing to look at where it came from. "He's in Lucerne." She shook her hair back and crossed her legs. Certainly, her hair was dyed, but restrained in such a girlish hairband that no one could resist being charmed. Her smile was very confident. "Don't let me interrupt."

Now, there were several people here who had never even met Gaye Northwood (including Ralph and Linda Poziarski, who were relative newcomers), although they had grown up eating cookies with her husband's name stamped on the package, and now fed their children these same cookies, and indeed had moved to the Park on the understanding that one of its charms was to be her neighbour, so this was a moment of some tension and excitement both for them and for Shirley Melnyk, who probably wanted to underline the event somehow. But the conversation moved so quickly to the question of Muriella Pent that introductions would have acknowledged that tension and spoiled this magic, this almost unimaginable moment of neighbourly companionship. It was as if polite people, everyone was aware, simply assumed that one knew all the best people, and that to introduce one to them would be faintly gauche.

"It's not that I think it's in itself a bad thing," Gaye Northwood was saying, with her wineglass at the end of her fingers, "and Henry agrees with me on this, to have these programs, and that the Park should be involved, I think it's a wonderful thing, and we're all art lovers here, I know we all take a very active interest in the arts, and in fact—"

"Art is one thing," said David Rodney, "loud music in the middle of the night is another."

"But rather than attacking, David, rather than trying to demolish this program, which, let's face it, would not be very good for the public image of the Park, why not try to get involved, ourselves?" Gaye Northwood's voice was very smooth and dry, with that aroma of Englishness in the round vowels which made her seem possibly foreign, which was odd, because it was well known that she was from Regina, but it did remind one that she and Henry spent so much of their year abroad. It was very difficult to argue with that voice, unless one had Eric Cuthbertson on one's side, and Eric Cuthbertson was being silent.

"Get *involved*," said Frank Daurio.

"I mean it's our community," said Gaye Northwood. "Instead of being negative, we could get involved, and change things from the inside, and get this thing under control."

Eric Cuthbertson leaned forward and spoke. "You are all aware that the Mayor has invited members of the business community to volunteer for service on this arts council, which is I believe called the Action Council for the Arts. He is particularly interested in having residents of the Park join the committee."

This time Frank Daurio's sigh was audible.

"I would love to get involved," said Olivia Daurio in a tiny voice.

"So would I," said Gaye Northwood. "I mean it's not as if we have nothing to offer. Many of us spend a great deal in supporting the arts every year. I know that Shirley, you yourself have a great deal to offer, with your expertise in the Southwestern style, I know you've collected a lot of native artworks."

"It's all Plains Indians," said Shirley Melnyk, smiling very wide. "All the furniture in the east wing, and all the handicrafts."

"Is that what it is?" said Linda Poziarski. "I always wondered. It's lovely."

"And the family room is done in that style too, the wall treatment is exactly—"

"They go to Santa Fe," said her husband, "every spring, I love it too, but the desert always gets me down a little."

"Do you do the opera there too?"

"This is my point," said Gaye Northwood, holding up one hand. "It's not as if we have nothing to offer. And if we get involved, as this is a perfect opportunity to do so, since there's practically an open invitation right now, this is an opportunity to contribute something back to the community, including our own community, and perhaps ensure that the next artist-in-residence is someone a little bit more—"

"A little bit more of an artist," said Ralph Poziarski.

"A little bit more productive, perhaps, yes."

"More real art, you mean, more genuine art and a little less video and photography and whatnot."

"Well, we could ensure," said Gaye Northwood, "for example, that the criteria for entrance are a little bit more strict, and more carefully upheld. Now, no one is going to suggest that Muriella, who has been very generous in the first place to, to contribute—and I'm sorry to see that Muriella isn't here, as I'm sure she would have positive input on this, but—"

"Muriella has never attended meetings of the residents' association," barked David Rodney, "she can't be bothered."

"I think," said Linda Poziarski, "she's a little bit on her high horse at the moment about everything that's been going on. Above it all. She wouldn't grace us with her presence tonight."

"Well," said Gaye Northwood, "that's unfortunate, but, that's a choice that she has made, which means, I'm sure she would welcome—the point is, without her input here she can hardly complain about whatever decisions we take, which is unfortunate, but that's the way it works."

"This is a choice that she has made," said Shirley Melnyk.

"Exactly."

"This point about the next artist in the program," said Eric Cuthbertson.

"The *next* artist," whistled Frank Daurio, and shook the ice in his glass.

"Is very interesting, to my mind." Eric's voice was measured, like Gaye's, and slow. "If we had a presence on this committee, it would not be inappropriate to suggest some changes in the criteria for selecting the writers who are invited." He hesitated here, and put his fingertips together in a gesture which may have seemed affected in a man dressed otherwise. "I mean, surely there are a great many deserving and decent artists out there who actually have something to contribute to the community."

"What I want to know," said Shirley Melnyk, "is why it has to be a foreign artist at all, since this is a Canadian program. I mean it is Canadian tax dollars we're talking about here, isn't it?"

"Careful, Shirley," said Ralph Poziarski, "they'll be accusing you of racism next." This did not draw a laugh.

"Well, this is an issue that could be raised," said Eric Cuthbertson very slowly. "It is a federally funded program, with some municipal money involved as well. It would not be unreasonable to raise the possibility that this money should be going to Canadian artists."

"Hear hear," said David Rodney.

"This is a very valuable program," said Gaye Northwood, "that Muriella has begun here."

"Or it could be," said Olivia Daurio.

"Or it could be, exactly, and I don't propose we destroy it at all. Just get involved. I will be the first to try."

"Shall I open another bottle of wine?" said Shirley Melnyk, springing up, and she was so excited she knocked over a glass, which for some reason unleashed a round of boisterous laughter. Olivia Daurio clapped her hands, as if suddenly very, very happy.

XXXIII

CORRECTION AND APOLOGY

In *Buzzer* 39 it was erroneously reported that writer Candace Bundle has worked as an exotic dancer in British Columbia and other places. Ms. Bundle has, in fact, spent her entire life in Toronto and never worked in that profession. Ms. Bundle has been a respected journalist in the field of culture and gender politics for over three years. She has also never used a pseudonym. *Buzzer* retracts the statements that were made about her, and apologizes unreservedly to her and to her lawyers for any harm or inconvenience these inaccuracies may have caused.

XXXIV

Static. A hissing like a passing train.

"Hello?" she said again.

Then two electronic pips, as if a warning of failed communication. Muriella was about to hang up when a voice chirped, very distant. "Hallo. Hallo."

"Yes? Hello! Hello!" She was watching Marcus's back as he ate the salmon salad she had prepared for him. Through the leaded window onto the side alley she could see snow falling. The first snow. She wanted to show Marcus. "Look, lovey," she said. There was a hammering from upstairs that had been bothering them all morning; Vincent working with old computer parts now, which he took apart with a cute small sledgehammer Muriella had bought for him one entrancing afternoon at Canadian Tire, and bought with some pleasure, because she could imagine using it in some way herself one day. And there was also the drone of beats from the front living room, where Christoph the photographer had set up some lights and huge paper backdrops and was shooting something that involved two girls and a lot of old bicycle parts, and he always had some techno going to relax them. He was using the turntables and amplifier that were now permanently left there, since it didn't seem as if that room would ever get cleaned up (they were still working on the library), and it ended up cheaper to just buy the system than to rent it for every event. But none of this irritated her quite as much as Marcus's bent back at this moment, his yellowed and stained cricket sweater. It wasn't quite jealousy any more—she had not been sleeping with Marcus, or anyone in fact, and, as far as she knew, he had not been sleeping with Julia—but a lack of something, a lack of feeling. Not his; hers. She trilled "*Hello*" one more time into the phone and then, "Is this on? Hello Cleveland! Are you feeling all right!" and was about to try to say something funny that she had invented herself, when a voice came back, distant as a cricket at night.

"Hallo," came the voice, muffled, British-sounding and oddly formal, as though a voice from a history book. "I am looking," it said, "for Mister Marcus Royston."

"One moooment please," she said in what she thought was a British accent, and said to Marcus, "It's Lord Prendergast from Mauritius. He wants you to sleep with his daughter. Or it's the guy from the video store. Look out the window."

He took the cordless handset without laughing. She crossed her eyes at him.

"Desmond," he said. "Desmond, old man. What's wrong?"

He began to pace around the kitchen. He refused to look out the window, although Muriella kept gesturing. He waved her away.

"When?" he said. He listened for a long while.

"Don't forget you're helping me shop at five," she called to him.

"And where is she now."

Something about his voice made Muriella go quiet. She sat down.

"Yes," he said. "Is she conscious?"

Muriella clasped her hands together and went very still.

"So she's stable at least. Yes. Is she speaking at all?"

He listened again. "Christ," he said. He took his glasses off and rubbed his eyes. "I see. Yes. Yes. Good God, Desmond. Yes, I know. Thank you. Thank you for taking her there. I don't know what to say, except that I will . . ." His voice wavered a little. He cleared his throat and went on. "I will be back at once, of course. Thank you for everything. I know you do. I know. Yes, I, of course. I don't know, I'll have to check flights, I don't know if there's one every day. If there's one today I'll be on it. I may have to go through New York. It may be tomorrow, tomorrow evening, that I arrive. I'll let you know. Oh, I'm well, I'm fine, as always. Yes. I'll let you know. Thanks."

He hung up and stood still for a minute, staring at the fridge. He put his glasses on and they slipped down his nose. Muriella did not move. Finally, he said, "I have to leave."

"Yes," she said. "It's Elizabeth."

He nodded, and she saw that his hands, hanging at his side, were shaking. She opened a kitchen cupboard and took down a bottle of brandy she used for cooking. She poured some into a teacup and handed it to him. "I'll call about the flights," she said. "How is she?"

"A stroke," he said, and his voice cracked again, as if his throat was dry. "A stroke. Desmond found her, we don't know how long she had been there. She has woken up but is not speaking." He was breathing rapidly.

"Marcus, I'm so sorry. I'm very sorry. I'm going to help you."

"She can move one arm," he said in a high voice. He turned to stare at her and his eyes were wide and bloodshot. "Desmond doesn't know if she recognizes him or not."

"Marcus," she said firmly, "it's going to be okay. We'll get you back there. I'm calling about flights now." She pulled out the heavy phone book from under the kitchen island. He had turned his back to her and was trembling. "They can do wonders with strokes now, you know," she said firmly. "They have rehab, and physio, even if she's not speaking now, often it takes a few weeks, or even months, and if she's in a good hospital, they can, they can . . ." She trailed off, as he had looked at her with his eyebrows raised. It was not a look she liked.

They were silent as she looked for her travel agent's number. "It's either World or Planet something," she said. "It's a gay fellow, he's brilliant. I think it's Jeff."

He sat heavily at the kitchen table. "I'm very sorry, Muriella. About the program."

"I understand. Don't worry about anything. You're going home now." And as Muriella picked up the phone and hauled out the phone book from under the kitchen island with a sense of power for some reason, a sense that she was doing something important for once, a strange rushing wind of relief began to fill her as well, a soaring feeling.

"I must go home," he said, and he began to cry.

There was a clatter as someone came in the front door. They heard Julia singing in the hall, dropping boots on the tiles.

"She's usually so quiet," said Muriella, flipping pages.

"Hello," called Julia. "It's snowing." She slid into the kitchen on stocking feet. Muriella glanced up at her. She wore her work clothes: her black skirt, her fitted jacket. Her hair was tied back and her cheeks were red. She looked like a girl.

Marcus was staring stiffly away, his back to her.

Julia went to the fridge. "It's like a postcard out there, it's like a snow globe, you know, that you turn upside down, it's like it's not even cold, it's kind of fantasy snow. You feel you could roll around in it in a party dress. Can I have a yogurt?" She closed the fridge door. "What's wrong?"

"Marcus has had an emergency at home," said Muriella. "He has to leave."

Marcus hunched his shoulders and put his hands to his face. Julia did not go to him. She stood staring at his back as it shuddered, her mouth open. And Muriella saw the same things pass across her face: a shadow flitting, then passing. Her features relaxed, and she breathed deeply. It was a lightening, a cleansing. Then her eyes burst with tears.

And as Muriella thought of the two of them living alone in the house, she felt the soaring feeling again. Like a rising force from below. A light under her feet. She picked up the telephone.

XXXV

THROUGH THE GREAT SCREEN OF GLASS, three women were talking in lamplight, like characters in a silent film. Brian stood on the sidewalk. The gallery had high white walls, a glossy wood floor. There was a coffee table with huge magazines on it, magazines printed on vast sheets like posters. One woman leaned against a counter. One woman paced in and out. Julia nodded, standing in the centre of the floor with her arms folded. The woman at the counter was holding her hands out as if cradling an invisible melon. It looked as if Julia was being scolded for something.

Several people walking fast on the street, their collars turned up, slowed and stared in as they passed. It was as if the women were performing in this set for the street. Brian knew they were used to being watched in this frame, and so would never look out and notice him.

They were all dressed in long black skirts and grey jackets. One had a tight grey tank top and large flat breasts that absorbed him for a while, because she didn't appear to be wearing a bra. But he was more interested in Julia, her hair back, her flat shoes, her black tights, dressed like a grown-up. He wondered if she enjoyed dressing like that, if she was more comfortable like that than in her combat pants. He wondered if he could ask her a question like that and not offend her. He wondered if he could ask her any question and not offend her. He almost walked away from the window.

But there was something about the way she was running her hands over her skull now, smoothing her hair, that looked tired, just plain tired, in a way that did not involve him, and this was reassuring.

The clouds edged in gold.

He pushed open the glass door of the gallery and called her name.

She turned to him and smiled and said she would be ready in a few minutes, that Diane had just asked her to do something, and she introduced him to Diane and to Angelica, who did not smile or look at him. He said he would wait outside, and she said he didn't have to, he could sit on the leather sofa, which he did, growing hot in his duffle coat. She and Diane stood in front of a computer and talked about invoices. Julia apologized several times. Then Diane left them alone and Julia did not talk to him, she just typed in the computer.

There were black-and-white photographs on the walls which were mostly of the shadows made by ferns on white walls. They seemed to have been taken in a desert, or somewhere where people went on holiday. One of them was selling for fifteen hundred dollars.

After a while Brian said he would wait outside, because he was getting too hot. Julia apologized, said she was really sorry, but she would really only be one more minute, and he said not to worry, and he went onto the street and looked at the traffic and the people in their coats who were so tired and eager to get home.

When she came out she had shadows under her eyes, and her hair was coming loose.

He said, "I'd thought we'd go to Crimson, since it's close."

She said, "Am I dressed right?"

"What do you mean?"

"For there. I'm just wearing my work clothes."

"Sure." Brian honestly didn't know what she was talking about. He said, "You look great," but she didn't answer. He said, "I don't think there's any right clothes. For there."

"Okay. I've never been there."

"Really? It's right around the corner. I would have thought you go there all the time."

"I don't go out much."

"Me neither," said Brian quickly. And this ended that conversation.

The bar was painted in black lacquer, and crowded. They sat in a row of tables down the centre of the room, and people against the bar bumped them. There were people wearing cowboy hats whom Brian had seen on television. They were laughing very loudly, and there was country music playing. Brian read the menu by holding it up to catch light reflected off the mirror behind the bar. It was all small dishes, meat on skewers. "The tandoori chicken pieces sounds good," he shouted, and then, "but you're a vegetarian."

She shook her head, looking surprised.

Brian said, "Sorry."

A waitress in a T-shirt that said "Pussy" took their drink orders. Julia ordered a mint tea, which made Brian's stomach sink a little. He asked for a Canadian and she said they didn't have Canadian, or Export or Blue, and she listed all the beers they had, which were all European or were named after villages with streams and mills. Brian ordered something called Harrietville Cream, at random.

Julia said something to him and he said, "Sorry?" and she said it again and still he shook his head and so she leaned forward and he leaned forward and she shouted, "Sorry about the wait. When you came to get me."

He said, "No trouble." There was a silence and then he said, "Those women weren't very friendly."

She shook her head. "They don't like me."

"Why not?"

"I don't know. I don't care enough."

"About what they do?"

She nodded. "I don't care about the art for divorced ladies' condos."

He laughed at this, but it was a dangerous conversation, for he was bound to betray ignorance sooner or later. Julia leaned forward and to one side to reach for her bag, and her white blouse came away from her chest and he saw a strap and edge of smooth stretchy white bra. His head was buzzing with the noise.

She pulled her hair loose and shook it. Then she put an elastic ring in her mouth and began pulling her hair back and smoothing it into a ponytail. This involved lifting her elbows high and frowning. It seemed like a lot of work. Then she took the elastic from her mouth and worked the hair into it. "Hah," she said, as if relieved. "Now. How have you been. How are your burns?"

"Oh, I really didn't have any burns. I didn't even stay in the hospital overnight. I was coughing a lot, and dizzy and stuff, because of the smoke, but I didn't have any damage. I was just a little dizzy. I'm still coughing a little more than usual, it's a little troubling, but they say I didn't have any real damage. They say that will go away."

He immediately began coughing, and Julia looked pained, so he tried to stop, and coughed with his mouth closed, which hurt.

"I couldn't hear all of that," she shouted, leaning forward again. "But I really hope you're okay."

"Thanks," he said, coughing. He was trying not to look down her shirt. The waitress in the Pussy T-shirt flashed past him, and he followed her belly, the little silver stud. The waitress was not wearing a bra. There was another one in a short black skirt who kept bending over tables, and the skirt rose up the backs of her thighs. Brian looked back at Julia and saw that she had followed his gaze to the black skirt. She began to search her bag again.

He wished they were outside, walking in the cold. The smoke was making him cough. He said, "I kind of like this time of year, you know. Very turbulent. Very dramatic skies." He took a breath and said, "I love it when the skies are all mixed up. You know, when it's part dark and threatening and then there are streaks of light behind it, you know. Like a kind of promise."

He waited, but she just looked down. She almost looked sad. She said, "You know, I really wanted to tell you. How impressed I was, we all were, and."

The waitress arrrived with the beer and the tea. Her breasts were level with Brian's eyes.

"Grateful, I guess," said Julia. "That you took that big risk and went into the fire, I mean I really couldn't—" She stopped talking.

"Sorry?"

"Never mind."

Brian watched the waitress swing away into the crowd and looked back at Julia, who was also watching her. "Sorry," he said.

Julia picked up her bag again. "I usually have lipstick."

"What?"

"I can't find my lipstick. In my bag. I must have left it."

"Oh." Brian laughed. And only then did the thought unveil itself to him, like a headache that has been in the background, that she was irritated by him watching the waitress, which was ridiculous, and bad, because even though he could hardly help it, as she was practically naked, he should at least have been more aware of it, but it was also encouraging, in fact exciting. The music had changed to a roaring kind of rockabilly and the television people started whooping and he realized, a toothache added to the headache, that he hated this place, and that she hated it too, and that he had only chosen it because it was fashionable enough for Julia Sternberg, and that he had got that completely wrong too, and that he in fact knew nothing about what she liked or didn't like and couldn't even guess. He coughed. "Why don't we leave," he shouted. "After these beers. Go somewhere quieter."

She nodded firmly and smiled, so he had got that right.

"All right then."

Once the door had closed behind them, they breathed in the hard air of the street. There was a grinding streetcar, lines of cars with stereos, but it was quieter. "Phew," he said, and she laughed. "Now where."

"How about Sake."

"I don't know it."

"It's a little Korean place just down Queen."

"Take me there."

They had to walk through the crowd of skinheads and goths gathered outside Icon, and then cross the street and through the beggars outside the community centre on the corner, the pools of urine. There was a woman lying on the steps without a jacket on, with a cardboard box of french fries and gravy spilled over her. A guy with a pigtail and a face like a compost heap blocked their way, swaying, and Julia grabbed Brian's arm as they walked around him. Once they got to the other side of the intersection, she did not let go of his arm. He felt her hand through his coat for two blocks.

Sake was grey concrete, with a sound of running water. There was a table of designers in black, and another table with a couple in sweaters who looked like graduate students. "This is great," said Brian.

"It's a little expensive," said Julia.

"Oh."

"Hello," said a waitress who carried menus. She was small and Asian and had hair dyed yellow and white lipstick and white eyeliner, and she wore a red gingham dress with puffy sleeves like a rag doll's, and running shoes and white knee socks. They followed her to a low table by the bar, where the bartender smiled at them and said, "Hi guys." He was an Asian kid dressed entirely like a cowboy, with a satin embroidered shirt.

Brian looked at the menu and said, "Yow. It is expensive."

"I know. Don't worry, I'll pay."

"No, don't be silly. I asked you."

"No, I'd like to. I'd love to. I have a job."

"I'm not that hungry anyway," said Brian.

"It's good," said Julia. "It's really good."

"You eat. I'll have another beer."

"No, you eat too."

Brian giggled. "No."

"All right. We'll drink and see how we feel."

"You want another herb tea?"

"No." She looked around. The bartender was rattling a silver shaker. "I'm ready for a drink. I'll have a glass of wine."

"Excellent," said Brian. He had stopped coughing.

Once they had their drinks (Julia's wine came in a little ceramic tube thing; Brian ordered a beer whose label was in Japanese, which he found cool), she said, "So. How's school?"

"Good. All right. Busy."

"I thought you said it wasn't as much work as—"

"That changed. I have essays due. I'm a little stressed out about it, actually."

"Still. Nice to be stressed out."

"Yeah?"

She said, "What else are you working on?"

"What do you mean."

"Aren't you writing something?"

"Oh. Yeah, I guess. A little. How's your wine?"

"Funny. I think it's Korean."

Brian whinnied and then got it under control. "That's funny. A funny idea."

"No, I think it is Korean. Taste it. It's a little sweet. And kind of chemical."

"Nice. Nice. How did you know I was writing something?"

"Well, you always were. In school. I thought that's what you would do when you graduated."

"Oh. Well, I try things from time to time. But they suck." He giggled again. "I try not to talk about it. I'm insecure about it."

"You're insecure? I have a hard time believing that."

He whinnied again. "Oh boy. Believe it. Believe it."

"You always seem so confident."

"*Me?*"

"About that. About thinking and writing. I'm sure I have a much harder time with it than you do."

"I bet you don't. You write—" He stopped.

"Oh, I don't write anything."

He stared at her. "You don't."

"Nope."

"You should."

"Listen," said Julia, "I really hope you are working on something, because you have a lot of talent."

"Really?" Brian looked around the restaurant. "I wonder why that other place is so crowded and this place is nicer and it's empty."

"I mean it," said Julia. "I remember that play you and Jason wrote for that Varsity fundraiser thing, and—"

"You *liked* that?"

"I thought it was funny, yes, and I remember the presentations you did in school, the books you read, I was so impressed all the time it made me actually scared."

"Of what? Of me?"

"No, not of you, exactly, although I have been scared of you, but just that I couldn't do it. Of stuff that I couldn't do."

"But of course you—"

"But I didn't have any background. I never thought I could—I never thought I should be there."

"Ah yes," said Brian. He sipped his beer. "Fraud syndrome. Everyone else knows what they're doing but I shouldn't be here. I'm only here because they made a mistake at the registrar's office."

"Exactly. And someone was going to find out any minute, and I would be exposed."

"Two policemen would come to your door one day," said Brian, "and say, I'm sorry, I'm very sorry—"

"There's been a terrible mistake, it wasn't you we meant to accept, it was this other girl who's smart, now—"

"Now would you mind packing up all your stuff, here's a box. I know. I know." Brian shook his head. "Only women think that, you know. Only women have that."

"I know. I know they do. And it's your fault."

Brian whinnied. "My fault? You wouldn't even talk to me. How would I have known what I was doing to you?"

"I wouldn't talk to you because I was scared. That you would make fun of me. And you did."

"When did I make fun of you? Name one time. Name one single time I made fun of you."

"When you and Jason were together you were rude every single time I saw you."

"Ah," said Brian, "with Jason, that's different, we were rude to everyone. That's a different set of rules."

"I see."

"Sorry about that."

"You know, said Julia, pulling her hair out again, "when I first walked into that post-colonial class, with—"

"Twenty thirty? With Martell? That was wicked."

"Yeah, except I walked in that first day and I saw you and Jason Katz sitting there, and you were sitting right at the front—"

"Like geeks."

"—and chattering away with John Cresswell, who was editing, you remember, the thing—"

"Yes, yes, old Cresswell, he was never very serious, though, really, he—"

"And you had all these books already, and I had this actual feeling of sickness when I walked into the class, I honestly just about puked, I went cold and I thought, oh God, no way."

"Really."

"Really. I almost turned around and walked out and went straight to the department office to look for another course. It took a lot of will just to walk to the back of the class and sit down. I just thought I would keep my mouth shut the whole time."

"Why? Why?"

"Because I was scared you would make me look like an idiot."

"That's ridiculous," said Brian, shaking his head. "That's ridiculous." He downed the rest of his beer. It had gone too fast. "You know what? I was scared when you walked in. I had almost exactly the same feeling."

"Me? Why?"

"I hated that you were there, actually, because I knew it would make me all self-conscious and tongue-tied."

"Tongue-tied?" She laughed a bright peal. "You acted so superior all the time. You knew I didn't . . . Why?"

Brian shrugged. A wave of heat rushed his face.

"No, really. By me? Why?"

His face was burning. "Are you finished your wine?" And as he said it he realized that for a few minutes, quite a few minutes, he had not been thinking about impressing her or not offending her or controlling something about himself which would not be one of the attributes he thought she might find attractive; he had merely been talking, talking to her as if it was a completely normal activity, as if she was just a person. And although that brief vision of how confident people talk to each other all the time had now faded with the onset of his searing face, and he was back in himself again, it had been like a blind briefly opening on a starry night. He said, "So what made you change your mind?"

"About what?" She looked away.

"About me. About talking to me."

Now she was turning red. She twisted a strand of hair in her fingers. Brian saw that she wore no nail polish and her nails were blunt. "Well," she said, not looking at him, "I guess it was the night of the fire."

"What did I say?"

She laughed. "Nothing you said. What you did. When you went and rescued Marcus."

"Oh that." Brian looked around. He needed another beer. "I didn't rescue anybody. He would . . . the firemen were coming anyway. They would have rescued him. I was just stupid."

"They told Muriella that he would have been dead of smoke inhalation in fifteen minutes."

"Yeah." Brian didn't know what to say to this and so giggled. He tried to stop and snorted instead.

"And I thought you were . . ." Her voice went very low. Her eyes were on the table.

"What? Sorry?"

"I thought it was brave. Which is cool."

"Oh. Okay." He was going to vomit from embarrassment if the waitress didn't come over at that very second. "Hello!"

"How are you guys doing?" said the waitress doll.

"We need you," said Brian. "Are you going to order food?"

"Not if you're not."

"I can't afford it, and I don't want you to pay for me. I'm embarrassed," said Brian. "But you order something. I had a late lunch."

"Where do you live?" said Julia.

"Where do I live?"

"Yes."

"I guess we're okay for now," said Brian to the waitress, and she danced away. "Oh, where I live sucks. It's at Ossington and Davenport, which is a kind of badlands. And I live in a basement."

"A basement bachelor?"

"No, it's a one-bedroom, actually. I lucked out with rent."

"So two people could sit on a sofa and eat a pizza."

"There isn't a sofa, actually."

"Is there a floor?"

Brian smiled. "Yes, There are floors in all the rooms."

"So lots of places to eat pizza on. Why don't we go there—no, really, don't be silly, I've lived in all kinds of dives, and it's just that I don't want to go back to Muriella's right now—"

"No," said Brian, reddening again. "No."

"So take me there and we'll order pizza."

Brian stared at her for a second, her grey eyes and the traces of freckles across her nose, and the sea of hair from her forehead, and her mouth set and determined but a little upturned, her eyebrows raised, waiting for him, and he was so stunned that this was happening to him he laughed. "Okay," he said, raising his hands in surrender. "Okay. Sure."

"What?"

"That would be fun." He had to stop laughing because it would turn to tears in a minute. He looked at her and he felt like bursting, dissolving somehow. Her face was open to him, and through it was sunlight, a garden. The universe was opening its doors to him, perhaps allowing him to become a different person altogether.

XXXVI

WHILE THEY ATE THEIR PIZZA THEY talked about Martell's post-colonial course and what Julia thought of Homi Bhabha, which was less than what Brian thought of him, which made Brian think some more about him, although they more or less agreed about Edward Said, which was pleasant. It was pleasant when they agreed and pleasant, for Brian, when they disagreed, so eager was he to show that he was interested in what she said, which he actually was.

Julia sat cross-legged on the one armchair that Brian had brought in a van from Barrie when he had moved here, an armchair that had been in his parents' basement, and Brian sat on the floor against a bookshelf and occasionally darted glances at her feet and toes in their opaque stockings, mar-velling at the womanliness of women's things, the way women knew about them, about things like stockings. She kept her long skirt demurely tucked between her legs, so there was no other glancing to be done, which was fine by Brian at this point. He was happy to talk; indeed he had convinced himself that he would be happy if talking to Julia Sternberg was all he was ever allowed to do.

After the pizza she persuaded him to show her Age of Empires on the computer and did not laugh; she giggled when the elephants swayed slowly across the battlefields, but it was a giggle of pleasure, not of mockery. Brian showed her the scenario he was working on, Hittites and

Babylonians, and she loved the shiny armoured horses, the way they pranced, and he was pleased that she appreciated such things as graphics, which he did. She asked him to burn a copy of it for her, which he said he could do on Jason's burner, as well as any CDs that she wanted, or a mixed CD, which he would love to mix for her, if she was interested in any of the ambient stuff that he had, which she was, as she was sick of all her music and Muriella didn't have any, didn't even like her playing music in the house, because she wasn't used to it, which was probably just a generational thing. They were both surprised that Muriella had the best of everything but the shittiest little Eaton's stereo system from 1975, which wasn't even in the main living room.

The conversation died for a few seconds after that because they were both wondering if they should talk now about Muriella, and about Julia and Marcus, and possibly about Brian and Muriella, which Brian didn't know if Julia knew about and wasn't going to tell her if she didn't. Brian decided he didn't want to know about where things stood with Julia and Marcus at that moment; that she had not brought up his name all evening was enough for him. And Julia seemed to feel this, for she left it alone too, and Brian knew somehow that she knew that this was something they would have to talk about some time, possibly even the next time they met, but not now, just as they both understood (he thought) that he would not try to kiss her tonight, that neither of them were ready for that but that it was actually, unbelievably, a possibility for the future, which was too frightening a thought to contemplate at that moment. Brian was content to call her a taxi and put her in it and not even touch her, not even shake her hand at the door, but smile a lot, which she did too, and wave her all the way down the street, until the red tail lights were pinpoints.

He cleaned up the pizza box and the dishes and saw that it was past midnight and he knew that he would not be able to sleep, so he turned on the computer and in the somewhat hysterical blue light of the screen he began to type and type away.

XXXVII

HIS FLIGHT WAS LATE GETTING OUT OF Pearson. Once on the plane, they waited on the tarmac while the air in the cabin grew hot. A half-hour passed, by which time Marcus had wriggled out of his jacket, now crumpled at his feet. The little white loudspeakers in the ceiling were repeating the same fifteen minutes of anemic jazz, all treble. Marcus tried to concentrate on his breathing, on keeping it steady, and he tried to concentrate on not concentrating on the breathing of the other passengers, on the air they were breathing out. He tried not to concentrate on the fact that he was breathing in all the air they were breathing out. He had a middle seat; on either side of him were short-haired women in trousers. The trousers had pleats and they were brown or beige. The women looked exactly like all the men.

By the time they began rolling, almost imperceptibly, down the runway, the light outside Marcus's oval porthole had faded to a kind of fluorescent blue. And then they kept making lumbering turns and making off down further runways, thrumming along with cushioned bumps, like a giant bus, towards some apparently more perfect runway that seemed impossibly distant. They rolled along like this for twenty more minutes, Marcus counted, turning and turning, and travelling and turning, and slowing and speeding again, until it seemed that they were just going to drive to San Juan, or at least keep wandering around these miles of asphalt until the urge to travel had passed, or until the passengers had fallen asleep, or died.

Then they stopped. The jazz continued to whine.

He stayed calm because of the drinks he had had in the terminal, and because of the drinks he had had all afternoon at Muriella's. The thought came to him, as if from a great distance, that he was barely conscious. His head buzzed. There was a strange contained quiet everywhere in the plane, the quiet of drowsy people after a day's work, a collective waiting for alcohol, like cows waiting for the arrival of feed.

When the engines finally began to roar and the speed of takeoff pushed his head against his seat, Marcus was hardly excited. As they banked over the airport, now suddenly small, he saw the sunset, yellow over grey. And then the flat roofs of flat factories, square tiles on a board, and the crude calligraphy of highways, the wide loops, the grim underscorings. There was a golf course like an open sore.

The tin jazz had finally stopped. The lights went low and Marcus felt a fear of the dark, possibly a loneliness, so he switched on his private overhead light and fished for the magazine in the seat pocket. He had not brought a book because he knew he could not read it. He had not read a book for some time. The magazine was filled with articles about companies and their successes, and had photographs of white men in casual clothing standing in front of office buildings which all seemed to be in suburbs. Marcus was actually momentarily distracted by what could only be described as the fanatical blandness of this magazine, the blandness of death. He looked around at the white people in their casual clothes, many of whom were reading the magazine, and he was emptied out, and wished he had not thought of death.

After a delay of what seemed like many hours or even days, during which he had possibly been briefly asleep or unconscious or dead, he heard the tinkle of a cart, and he watched behind him, his neck stretched, to see the lugubrious progress up the aisle of the cart which he knew would eventually, if he brought to bear superhuman patience, reveal itself in front of him and be laden with beer and wine and possibly even spirits in tiny bottles.

He looked out on the electric dusk. The night was darker now and he could see lakes beneath him, metallic plates in darkness. There were no more factories, but sometimes a forlorn line of highway. They were too high to see cars.

After the drinks trolley, and all the suffering of waiting it caused him, all the angst of wondering about its supplies, about how much they would allow him to have, he experienced another buzzing calm. He watched the black floor of lakes and forest beneath him with a growing interest.

No one had taken him into the countryside, into the famous wilderness of this country, and he wondered why. He certainly had not felt any curiosity about it himself, while in the city. Nobody there had evinced any, either. Perhaps they had never gone there. This was strange, considering all the romance you heard about it.

He stared at the darkening floor of forest and wondered where he had been. He felt the floor of his stomach opening up and dropping away as he thought that he didn't really know, that he didn't really know where he had been or where he was.

He was a little cold. He gulped whisky and soda and tried to dissect the despair that he now felt creeping over him. This was more than loss, it was horror, the sort of horror that comes from knowing that the world is a place with no centre, a senseless place. Afloat in the sky, with a choice of beef or chicken, which would taste the same.

Vast lakes were slipping away underneath him, the flat land a stained tablecloth after a meal. A queasy tessellation of lakes. He supposed he should have paid the landscape a little more attention.

He couldn't look at the emptiness. His stomach was disgruntled.

A queasy tessellation of lakes.

He closed his eyes and images of the country came to him: grimy shops on streetcorners, parking lots. The great colonial mansions, as false as painted facades in a desert.

And who was he to complain of falseness?

The carpeted hotel bars, the ubiquitous jazz played by black men. The same pieces of music in every hotel bar.

The bag-carrying West Indians shuffling along St. Clair West. The blue air of the sports stadium like something synthetic. The highways to the airport in their continuous angry construction, the machines constantly picking at a giant sore, the rumbling and hissing of insects.

The land below had vanished; it had turned black.

The tasteless chicken came. It had no smell except the smell of heat.

No: this was not a place, not a real place. That land below was not treated, by anyone, as a place. And it had no smell, for one thing. A place was a beach with the remains of a fire, a smell of fruit, of car exhaust, of human skin and waste. That was a place he knew and could define. He could describe that place. And it was where there were people—the cold waved up and down his body. People that defined him.

So he thought of Muriella, alone in the big house, perhaps sleeping with the beautiful girl: they had become skeins of pale fabric waving before him now.

Muriella waiting for what traveller to return home.

He took out his notebook and wrote:

Penelope, her feet cold on the dusty rugs, bought by a
wealthy man from dusty merchants now long dead, but not
brought by Odysseus himself who may not ever have existed

He finished his whisky and looked around for more. Stewardesses were walking the aisles with bottles of wine, offering more. He should have ordered wine.

Penelope waits in a cold northern house behind the walls
of a great city, floating on a muddy darkness of leaves,
of invisible water, and dark frozen earth. A queasy
tessellation of lakes.

He was unsure of the spelling. But confident that he should attempt the description of a country he was seeing for the first time, as it slipped away.

The lights went off and the movie began.

XXXVIII

THEY WERE WALKING IN AN UNSPECIFIC direction away from the Bakery, which was one of those non-sexual places in which they had been meeting for almost a month, to talk about Brian's professors and his essays, at non-sexual times like breakfast, where they ate bacon and eggs and there would be no pressure to embrace or kiss sociably at the end of it. They were walking down Bloor Street when Julia squealed and ran towards a tall guy in a leather coat. Brian hung back as she hugged the guy, who had longish hair and hadn't shaved for a few days. The guy stepped back to look at Julia and said, "Look at you, babe, Miss Academic," and hugged her again. While enduring this procedure, Brian noticed that the guy's neck and cheek-bones were shaved, which meant that he was either growing a beard or was keeping this shadow at this perfectly ugly nascent bristly Italian state, like some kind of pop singer of the 1980s, perhaps shaving it daily with a special razor that kept it as bristles. This was the kind of thing that irritated Brian. Perhaps he was just irritated by the fact that the guy was the kind of guy he had always imagined Julia going out with. Also, he had those Australian slip-on little boots that people who worked in film wore to make it look as if they camped in the outback or wrestled alligators or something, and Brian hated him for that as well.

Julia introduced the guy as Paolo, and Paolo shook Brian's hand with that ridiculous rock-boy holding on to your thumb thing, which Brian always flubbed, as he did now. Paolo had a silver chain around his wrist. Paolo turned back to Julia and smiled. He told her he was directing commercials, for money, but he was working on a short, and that he was back at painting, which was going really great, he had a studio space on Sorauren, even. He said he'd seen Pascal, just last week, in Montreal, and that he was doing great. Julia just nodded at this.

Paolo took out a pack of cigarettes and began the elaborate process of tapping and cupping and lighting one, flashing the silver chain, as if he was settling in for a long conversation on this snowy street corner, or at least posing for a really cool shot of a guy lighting a cigarette on a snowy street corner, and he shook back his curly black hair and said, "So, how *are* you?"

Brian resisted the urge to call over Julia's shoulder, *I'm very fine, thank you, Paolo*. She answered hesitantly, about the gallery, about working on a piece of writing. Brian felt a pang at this, as it was something she would never admit to him, and here she was doing it to this guy who, if he could read at all, probably thought that writing was interesting insofar as it was a blueprint for a really cool shot.

Paolo smiled and shook his head all the way through Julia's answer, as if he was amused by something only she and he knew about, and finally said, "So. Looks like things are very different. For you." He glanced quickly over at Brian and back at Julia and, Brian thought, very quickly, almost imperceptibly, raised his eyebrows. He smiled what may have been intended to be a friendly smile but which had a clearly legible subtitle which read: *Your little friend is another one of your odd and amusing pastimes which are endear-*

ing since they show your intriguingly capricious nature, but non-threatening since we all know that you will drop them and re-enter the normal world of larger-penised men eventually.

Brian made a face like a baby and said, "Oh, the humanity."

"I'm actually great," said Julia. "Listen, we have to get going, but I'll, I guess I'll see you around."

Then there were several more minutes of uninterrupted embracing and expressions of infinite support and love and promises of imminent contact, and finally Brian and Julia walked away. He was relieved that she had not, at least, jumped into a muddy Range Rover or a rusted Alfa Romeo with the guy and driven off.

They walked up Bathurst, past the grunting streetcars making a loop out of the subway station and stopping traffic, and the crowd waiting in the cold under the concrete awning. They sky had turned grey. Finally, at the next lights, she said, "He's someone who I didn't really hang out with myself, a lot, but he was part of a crowd I used to hang around with."

"Ah." Brian was waiting for her to say, *He's really talented*.

"He's a friend of my ex."

"Oh."

They walked for a while in silence. Brian said, "Is he really talented?"

"What?"

"Is he really *talented*."

"No. Not really. I don't know. I've never seen his stuff. What's so funny?"

"Nothing." He whinnied. "Nothing. I'm an idiot. Why, tell me, I'm curious about that crowd, tell me, why don't you hang around people like that any more?"

"People like what?"

"Like that guy."

"What is that like?"

Brian sighed and trudged. His boot had snow in it.

She said, "I don't have anything against them."

"No. Of course not."

"Do you?"

"Well," said Brian, "they're a little hairy for me. That guy is."

Julia laughed and in the thin air her laugh was bright. "I think it's so cute that you're jealous of that guy." She took his arm. "I have so little interest in that guy." They had come to the lights and stopped. He could feel that she was looking at him. He wouldn't look at her so she put her hands on his shoulders and turned him to face her. She was smiling and her cheeks were red. She put her woollen mitts over his ears, pulled his head towards hers and kissed him on the lips. Her lips were cold, and he imagined that his were as well, but still she tasted like living skin. She kissed him for a long time and wouldn't let go. He squeezed her to him but could feel no body through her padded coat. When they drew apart her nose was running. He said, "Well. We're going to my place, right?" and she laughed and ran ahead.

They came down the basement stairs stamping snow off their boots. They sat together in the one armchair but did not turn on the lamp with the orange shade. The snowy light from the high window was grey. Julia ran her hands over his neck and shoulders and unbuttoned his shirt. She also wore a shirt with buttons which he undid. He began breathing faster when her shoulders emerged, bare and bony, and white bra straps and the smooth white swelling of her breasts. He kissed her collarbone and she whimpered a little, which was a great reward, the whimper, something he didn't deserve, and he laughed and kissed her neck and her ears and pulled her hair out of its ponytail and ran his hands through it.

When their shirts were off, they stood and moved together, touching, towards the bedroom. He stopped her in the narrow corridor and pressed himself against her so she could feel his hardness, and she held his hipbones and pulled him against her. They stood there kissing in their socks. The furnace kicked to life behind the drywall.

When they were in bed and naked, they were quiet and gentle. Brian trembled and giggled too much. He could not stop kissing her everywhere he could; he kissed her belly and thighs and turned her over and kissed the backs of her thighs; he lifted up her arm so he could kiss her armpit, which made her squeal. He kept returning to her neck and shoulders.

He was particularly nervous about the condom, which he had only ever used successfully a few times in his life, and which Muriella had not cared about much. Julia helped him with it, and it relieved him to find that she did not seem much more confident about its manipulation than he did.

And when he slipped inside her she was very quiet, breathing hard. It did not last long, but as he shuddered and tried not to, she made little noises which were half whimper and half gasp, and which Brian remembered for many hours afterwards, in the stuffy room next to the roaring furnace.

XXXIX

PARTITION

A story by Muriella Pent

*A girl waits in a café. There is calypso music playing
on an old radio. A smell of fried fish. Outside, it is raining.
She is cupping a coffee in Styrofoam. Although the coffee is
too hot, the Styrofoam burning the tips of her fingers, she is
holding it to capture the sensation. Or perhaps because she
thinks she deserves it, deserves to experience the discomfort.
She is like that.*

*Outside, it is raining. The girl watches a phone booth
across the street, in front of a shop that sells Italian
cappuccino makers to restaurants. This shop has greasy
windows and is never open.*

*She knows that occasionally he has used this same phone
booth to call her, when he cannot call her from his house. Now
she has not seen him for some days and she is wondering if he
is calling anybody else from the same place. She came here
yesterday as well, and watched for half an hour. She knows
this is silly.*

But she cannot call him at home.

*She is wearing a ski jacket that was her older brother's,
and her hair is tied back and she wears no makeup. Still the
man with dreadlocks behind the counter tries to talk to her.
Even when she doesn't reply.*

Smiling at her with a gold tooth.

Her eyes sweep the street. At any second he will appear, a tall man with dark skin in a grey raincoat. It is as if she is willing him to appear.

The girl grimaces as the Styrofoam stings her fingers. She lets go for a second and the pain subsides. She grips it again. She holds on to it. There are tears in her eyes. She holds on to it.

XL

MURIELLA VOLUNTEERED TO GO TO MEET Dr. Winthrup. He was arriving in the middle of the afternoon, on a weekday, and the other Action Council literature committee members were busy: half of them (the Stilwoode Park half) were in the final, flower-arranging stages of the planning of the Crohn's Disease Ball, the other half still refusing to do any work that rich white women should be doing. Jasminka had bravely remained the chair, but she firmly refused to do any carrying and fetching, particularly any fetching in regard to a choice she had strenuously opposed. Jasminka, in fact, was boycotting all action other than strictly controlling every meeting.

The voting on applicants to the residency was one thing she could not control.

So Muriella was floating on a slow stream of traffic in sunshine, in the construction zone surrounding the airport. The construction did not seem to have advanced since the last time she had driven there, in mid-winter, to abandon Marcus forever to wherever he now was. Somewhere hot. It was warm on this day, in the Saab with the windows closed, cool and bright outside, on one of the undecided days of spring, and the lanes advanced circuitously through the plains of scaffolding without interruption, with pleasant intervals between cars; it was not stressful, so far. It was like being in a Dali. She even found the parking lot and a place on the sixth level and an elevator down, and was at the

Arrivals gate with minutes to spare. She bought a frothy cappucino-ice-cream thing from a clean counter. The whole place was like a dream of cool, clean, airy blandness; it was like a holiday from beautiful things, which had its own charm. Muriella wondered if Dr. Winthrup was the kind of person who would find a comment like that amusing or self-indulgent. She would try him.

And the whole terminal was strangely quiet that day; there were no floods of Slovakians or Saudis or Newfoundlanders with lobsters in cardboard carrying cases. Perhaps people had stopped coming, since Marcus had left. Perhaps the whole city, the whole country, was calmer since Marcus had left. Perhaps it was time for Muriella to admit her calmness to herself and think about what having a normal life was going to mean. Perhaps Dr. Winthrup would prove instructive in that regard.

This thought made her aware of the time that had not passed (ten minutes before the flight arrived, and then there would be a delay for baggage), and she was no longer happy with the sterile corridor and the sturdy families waiting in their sweatshirts and jeans. It was likely that these people were waiting for friends or relatives from Edmonton, since that was where Dr. Winthrup's flight was arriving from, which meant that they were probably themselves from Edmonton or thereabouts, which meant that they were in all likelihood representative of what people from Edmonton or thereabouts tended to look like, and since Dr. Winthrup was himself from Regina, which was thereabouts, he might reasonably be expected to look something like this too. This realization made the time slow and then stall completely.

Muriella wandered upstairs to Departures, where there were more magazine stands and people who might have been going to Europe, which did seem to make them a little more careful about what they wore, and even about what they ate. She paged through *Vogue* while glancing hopefully at a queue which seemed predominantly Italian and contained some nice leather shoes and a couple of leather suitcases and even a dress and a skirt. Then she had a white wine spritzer at a sports bar while looking at a hockey game on the big screen. It must have been a final of some kind, because people were very talkative about it, and the bartender was sweet.

By the time she got back down to the Arrivals level, and found the right set of doors again, the Edmontonian crowd had dissipated. There was a smallish man in green tweed standing alone in the middle of the concourse. He looked so panicked and hopeless that she knew right away it was Dr. Winthrup. He was young, much younger than she had expected; a man in his early thirties, clean shaven, with arty spectacles and receding black hair. His face was pink and smooth. She loosened the shawl around her shoulders so that it would flow behind her as she moved forward, and called, "Dr. Winthrup." She took wide strides towards him, making as much noise as she could with her heels. She took off her sunglasses as she approached and shook her hair loose. "I'm so sorry to have kept you waiting."

He recoiled a little, as if she was about to embrace him (and she would have, if he hadn't recoiled), and seemed both relieved and angry. He didn't smile. "I was beginning to think—"

"Have you got a cart?"

"A cart?"

"For your bag. There are some over there. It will cost you a loonie. Do you have a loonie?"

"Oh." His face turned red as he searched his pockets. He kept looking around him as if he were being jostled by a great crowd, but there was no one in the concourse but a Sikh security guard who was watching Muriella sadly.

"I have one," said Muriella.

He scurried towards the carts with backward glances at his bags. Muriella wondered if he was afraid she would steal them.

His trousers were not bad, but his shoes were pointy.

He really was very young. He probably wore the tweed to pretend he was older. Muriella smiled at him and wrinkled her eyes, the way she did when she ran into Brian and Julia, as he hauled his cart behind her clicking heels.

In the car he had a little trouble with his seat belt. "Can't seem to make it—"

"Don't worry about it," said Muriella.

He ignored this and buckled himself tightly. It was a good thing, because he seemed frightened by the speed at which the Saab could take corners; he grabbed the base of his seat.

"Don't worry," said Muriella, "it's a very good car."

He laughed shortly and said, "I'm not very used to speed, I'm afraid."

Muriella accelerated out of a tunnel and into a lane bordered by concrete crash barriers like a canyon; you could see nothing on either side but scaffolding and girders. The lane was winding and the Saab handled it very well. Dr. Winthrup was silent until they hit a real road.

"So," said Muriella, "you're from Edmonton."

"Oh no. I just had to fly to Edmonton. From Regina. I'm from Regina. That's where I teach. Actually I'm from Winnipeg. But I teach in Regina."

"Oh yes. I knew that."

They merged into the vast angry highway. Now they were going truly fast, and Dr. Winthrup had tightened his grip.

"Why did you have to fly to Edmonton?"

"Oh, I don't know. You know how the airlines are all in a mess. You can't seem to go anywhere easily. It was the cheapest way, I suppose. My travel agent did it."

"Well. You survived."

"Yes."

The flow slowed. Teams of cars lined up, idling. A shadow filled the sky: a jet passing low.

Muriella said, "So you've heard all about the house? And your part of it, the guest apartment, and everything?"

"Oh it's your house I'm staying in?"

"Yes."

"Oh, goodness, I'm sorry. I didn't know."

"That's all right."

The traffic started and stopped. They weren't even on the 401 yet.

She said, "I think you'll like it."

"Oh, I'm sure. It sounds lovely."

"There's one problem, well not a problem but a little complication, which is that I have a choreographer using the front salon as a studio. We've cleared all the furniture out and taken the rugs out and put a barre in and some mirrors, and the furniture's cluttering up the other rooms a little, but it's lovely, actually. And she's there a great deal of the time, with some of the dancers she's working with."

"You mean they have music playing and everything?"

"Oh, the music's not the problem. It's very soft music, and they're not above where you'll be living, it's at the other end of the house."

"Well," he said, flattening himself into his seat as they accelerated again, "that doesn't sound like a problem at all."

"No. The only thing you have to get used to is the dancers. Part of what she's working with is nudity, a nude dance thing, so they often practise naked, and you might run into one or two of them, or pass by from the hallway."

He laughed. "Men and women?"

"No, just women." She glanced at him and saw that he was red again. It made her giggle. She said, "They don't mind. In fact I rather think they're showing off a little bit. Anyway, you get used to it."

He laughed again, bright red.

The traffic heaved forward. "Would you mind some music?"

"Not at all."

The radio was on the jazz station. She left it there: the aimless saxophones matched the abstract landscape. "Saxophones always sound white to me," she said.

He laughed again, a tight sound like what Brian Sillwell made.

"So," she said, "the book you're working on."

"Yes," he said, straightening. "It's on Canadian literature. When it was at its peak." His voice went higher, and he spoke faster. "Beginning with some early settler novels, you know, Moodie and Grove and people like that, and it goes right up to very modern names, Munro and so on."

"I see. Anything contemporary?"

"Well, yes, Munro, as I said, Atwood and so on."

"I mean anyone younger than that."

"I said *at its peak*."

"I see. Well. It sounds fascinating."

"Yes," he said. He drummed fingers on his knee. "I hope to show, what I hope to show is a certain amount of subversion in the discourse, I mean subversion of dominant modes, you know, dominant discourses, American ones and so on. And of course a reaction to this new kind of urban crap that's so dominant now, you know, the Torontocentrism that's just so commercial and so dominates the publishing world. Since the whole industry seems to be based here now, I mean no offence, but the regional voices that so really define this literature have been silenced, or are being silenced, you could say, and this represents a real . . . a real loss, I think."

Muriella sighed.

"What I'm looking for is any kind of reappropriation, or transgressive—"

"Are you married?"

"Sorry?"

Muriella took her sunglasses off. She looked at him.

He shook his head. "No, no." He giggled a little, and turned red. He did that very easily.

She took him into the house through the garage. He took his shoes off and left them at the door, and she told him that he didn't have to and he hesitated but left them there.

"Yes," she said, "for the ersatz. It's beautiful ersatz, I suppose. That can happen."

He was staring out a diamond-leaded window from the dining room onto the bare garden. The black flower beds still bore muddy traces of snow. He said, "Ersatz? In what way is it ersatz?"

"This is new," she said, "in the hall." She led him back out to the hall, where the big Group of Seven sunset had been. She had just purchased a large abstract oil in shades of grey and black, with chalk markings and photographs on it. It was so large it had become one wall. "It's based entirely on photo collage," she said. "And then the successive layers of oil and newspaper were based on successive manipulations—"

"Interesting." He was looking at his watch.

"In the library," she said, pointing, "there's a Group of Seven."

She followed him in. The afternoon light was slanting in, already warmer than it had been a week ago. The shadows of early buds danced on the rug. He stood in his sock feet with his hands in his pockets, slightly shorter than her in her heels. "Extraordinary," he said. "Now that is beautiful."

She stood behind him in her heels, feeling tall. "It's very sensual, isn't it." His neck was freshly barbered and clean. She put a hand on his shoulder. "This reddish orange here."

"Yes." He was blushing again. "I suppose so."

"May I call you David?"

"Of course." He turned towards her, his face tilted upwards, his glasses slipping on his nose.

"David. You're going to have to learn not to blush like that if you're going to spend any time with me."

"Aha." He nodded and tried to laugh and whinnied just as Brian Sillwell would have done.

"I generally have a sherry at this time of day. Would you like one?"

"No thanks."

"Anything?"

"Well, a cup of tea would be nice. If you're . . ."

"No problem."

She clicked out, and when she was in the kitchen, he called, "You know, a beer might not be a bad idea. What the hell."

She checked her messages while she poured the drinks. Her son: again: "Hey, Mom, just wanting to check everything was okay. Hope you're doing better. The new guy you have coming in sounds a whole lot better, I must say. I was really relieved to hear about him. He sounds a lot more like your type. Maybe things will settle down a little now in your life, you can get some peace and quiet for a change. Anyway, Deborah sends her love."

Muriella deleted the message.

She brought the drinks through on a silver tray. David Winthrup had taken off his tweed jacket. He had a short-sleeved blue cotton shirt underneath.

"I took my jacket off," he said.

"Yes," she said.

"It was a little warm."

She set the tray down and sank into the leather sofa. He seemed unsure of where to sit. She unstrapped her shoes and kicked them off. She sighed and wiggled her toes in their nylons. She undid a button of her black blouse. The blouse was silk. She brought her feet up onto the sofa and folded her legs under her. His eyes were on her thighs. She looked him in the eyes and said, "Well. I have to say I think you are going to meet a great many writers and artists here. Perhaps different from those you are used to."

"Looking forward to it," he said stiffly. His eyes darted across her chest, the loose silk. She was not wearing a bra.

The room was very quiet. The sun had moved so low as to throw rays right onto the silver tray.

"Yes," she said, "I think you are going to learn a great deal from this residency." She poured his beer carefully into a tall glass.

"I certainly hope so." He put his hands in his pockets.

"Come and sit down. Here." She held the cold glass up into the ray of sun and stroked the warm leather beside her.

David Winthrup took the beer from her and gulped. His eyes were wide, a little unfocused. He was a little out of breath, and his mouth hung open, his lips shiny in the sparkling light.

XLI

May 28

My dear Muriella,

Many apologies for my long silence. I received your letter.
Elizabeth was buried last week. Here in penitence is a poem
for you.

Love,
Marcus

IN A COLD COUNTRY, FIRE

On the beach the hammering light
is a promise of ships to come.
The beach is the stage for the serial drama
of sea, the theatre that cups
the chrome crowns of waves, shattered
by the mallet of day. And in this haze,
the curtain is raised on what we could see: we could be ships
and leave. We could stay here and walk
along the sand, watching the prospect of sea.
Or we could float towards the end
of the line of blue and blue
and furious dancing white,

where the lines disappear and the air
is too hot to breathe.
Even the sound of sea is muffled, on a beach,
it wheels and flutters as gulls, a vast roaring conch, an echo
of your ear.

Even these lines are scratched in sand, and will fade.

Here is my beach: the end of island, portal
to the blurry blue globe, proscenium lit
for what visions will dance
and grimace and shimmer across.

I am come home, having crossed the seas and doggedly drunk
on other islands and crossed forests from the air, and seen mirrors
of water like plates in the blackness below, and having slept
with the salty women of my ports, and come home to find Elizabeth
dead. And my palms a map of forests, of fire
in Northern towns.

In dim and dripping mansions—there was always
water running outside—and vines wrapping the sills
like arms—there are carpets like pools of wine,
and a grey winter day outside.

Lightburst through winter cloud is golder,
colder, distanter than sun, a memory of day,
a streak of recollection like fragrance in a closet,
a taste that one has in a dream.
Flashes of paint near the lines of the roofs,
with wires where birds wheel and sit,

a flicker of flame in a film.
This is representation, this is an echo of heat.

In heated rooms we light candles,
and paint the walls in red
and ochre and fawn.
We lay our rugs on the floor,
and lie on the patterns of wine
and saffron and henna and rust
and the windows rattle with wind.

In candlelight you fling your hair
across my chest, a flurry of sparks.
You crackle like fire in a tent.
The touch of motley skins and our pallid
whispers while the furnace is labouring,
roaring and grunting in the ducts.
The hiss of dry air.

I am drinking amber heat that tastes of smoke
and has an edge of cold, the sharp blade of ice.
It drifts in my veins like snow
and carries the pictures of places I've been,
of sunsets and people in rooms with smoke
and a sense of the wood outside.
It looks like the light in the sky.

We make these worlds for ourselves,
and wait for the light to come back.

On that cold island I left
a woman who waits and weaves,
and I see her now in this sea,
slipping away with the flash of scales
She is hard and soft, a long river twisting.

I am come home, now, and will not leave again.
I am happy to wrestle this beach into symbols,
these scratches. I could not describe it
so easily then.

And perhaps that coupling, the resigned
opening and exchange of entrails
that coupling wrenches from the body
burned something open in her
as well. The blood was flecked in gold.

That lozenge of distant light through a rent in the cloud
a hole in the season,
brighter than memory of sun,
was a promise like the flames
that you unfurled over me in the dark,
a banner and babble of shouts,
a ripple of streamers proclaiming
some festival, some joy of our own making, triumph.

THANKS

Maya Mavjee
Anne McDermid
Martha Kanya-Forstner
Bernice Eisenstein
Jowita Bydlowska
Christa Conway
Ceri Marsh
Stephane Beauroy

The Canada Council
The Ontario Arts Council
The Globe and Mail

Marcus's comments to the librarians are based on things that Jane
Jacobs said in a similar situation in Toronto in 2000.

Russell Smith is the author of the illustrated adult fable *The Princess and the Whiskheads*, the short story collection *Young Men*, nominated for the Toronto Book Award, and the novels *Noise* and *How Insensitive*; the latter was nominated for the Governor General's Award. He writes the weekly "Virtual Culture" column in *The Globe and Mail*. Smith lives in Toronto.

Pierre Simon Fournier *le jeune*, who designed the type used in *Muriella Pent*, was both an originator and a collector of types. His services to the art of print communication were his design of letters, his creation of ornaments and initials, and his standardization of type sizes. His types are old style in character and sharply cut. In 1764 and 1766 he published his *Manuel typographique*, a treatise on the history of French types and printing, on typefounding in all its details, and on what many consider his most important contribution to the printed word—the measurement of type by the point system.